Advance Praise for *Auraria*

"*Auraria* is like nothing I've ever read before except maybe *Through the Looking-Glass*. Envision Lewis Carroll on a romp through the mountains of Georgia, discovering a land of shimmery mystery and spirits, humble monsters, quirky characters, singing trees and vengeful fish. This whole world has sprung from Tim Westover's brain yet remains firmly and lovingly the real thing, the actual Georgia landscape echoing with folk traditions of the southern Appalachians. The best part is that Tim Westover can really write. I'd give an Aurarian pot of gold to do what he's done with language in the service of imagination."

Josephine Humphreys, Hemingway/PEN Award Winner, author of *Dreams of Sleep* and *Rich in Love*.

"Mr. Westover brings my beloved Georgia to life, complete with spells, haints, and moon maidens. Not since Wendell Berry has an author woven such a beautifully intricate southern community."

Ann Hite, author of *Ghost On Black Mountain*.

"The legends, myths and history of the North Georgia mountains (along with some very inventive additions) are woven into a wonderfully entertaining story."

Victoria Logue, author of *Touring the Back Roads of North and South Georgia*.

Auraria

A Novel

Tim Westover

QW Publishers

2012

This is a work of fiction. All of the characters, organizations, and events portrayed in this novel are either products of the author's imagination or are used fictitiously.

AURARIA

QW Publishers
Grayson, GA USA
www.QWPublishers.com

ISBN: 978-0-9849748-0-1

First edition published in 2012 by Q W Publishers

Printed in the United States of America

TO CHLOË

Book I

Holtzclaw hadn't heard of Auraria until his employer sent him to destroy it. The tiny town, nestled into the curve of an unimportant mountain river, had no reputation among capitalists or tourists, but even insignificant places can be expensive to acquire. Holtzclaw rechecked his traveling bag—all the money was still there. The thousands of dollars in federal notes were just ordinary paper, but the gold coins were the strangest he had ever seen. Instead of eagles and shields, the coins were stamped with images of bumblebees, terrapins, chestnut trees, and indistinct figures by a stream. The figures might have been bathing or even panning for gold; they were too small to tell. Shadburn had said the coins were minted in Auraria from local metal. The gold was returning to its source.

Opening the traveling bag was reassuring, but unnecessary. If any of the gold had gone missing, Holtzclaw would have felt by the heft of the bag. Besides, who could have taken it? He was the only passenger in the stagecoach. His other supplies, too, were present: pen, ink, linen paper, his notary stamp. The weight was a sign that all his work lay before him. If he met his employer's expectations, Holtzclaw would be gone from Auraria in a few days, and his traveling bag would be much lighter. The worth of land deeds is not measured by their weight.

Even past noon, blue mist filled the Lost Creek Valley. The stagecoach descended from the ridge, fording a stream that cascaded from a moss-painted cliff. The air was heavy with water. Holtzclaw tried not to breathe in the mists, thinking they could imbue his unacclimated lungs with sickly airs. He already felt ill from the jolting and jostling of the iron-bound wheels over the road.

Beside the road, a boy was fishing from a fallen log that balanced from a precipice, giving him a clear cast into the emptiness of the valley. His feet swung in space above the fog. Holtzclaw saw that the boy's fishing pole was just a gnarled branch, still covered in bark. The poor should take better care of their possessions, thought Holtzclaw, since they have so few to look after. He leaned out of the window and called for the driver to stop.

"There's no water below you, young sir," Holtzclaw said to the boy.

"Doesn't matter," said the boy. He snapped his fishing pole back, and a fish flew up from the mist. Holtzclaw recoiled from the sudden projectile, which the boy caught with practiced hands. Neither the crudeness of the fishing equipment or the lack of a body of water had hampered the boy's ability to land a catch.

"I'll sell it to you," the boy said, pushing the head of the fish through the open window. "They're good eating."

The fish's ruby body and barb-like fins were dusted with a golden residue. Its eyes were like two gold coins. Holtzclaw doubted that it made for good eating. The boy must be judging by rural standards.

"First, you must tell me how you caught it," said Holtzclaw.

"You don't have boys that go fishing where you come from?"

"They fish in sensible places. Creeks and ponds. Wet places, not empty ones."

"Mist is wet, isn't it?"

"But it is an entirely different state of matter. Water sustains life, but mist is a vapory nothing."

"Not if it's thick enough," said the boy, "I just throw out my line, and the fish latch on."

This spilled the secret of the boy's scheme. He must have hooked some local trout to the end of his line, then spooled it out so that the fish disappeared into the fog. When a stagecoach like Holtzclaw's came down the Great Hogback Ridge Road, he hauled up his supposed catch and sold it to the naive traveler, who thought he was buying into some wondrous phenomenon.

"Here," said Holtzclaw, pleased that he had not be hoodwinked. "I'm going to give you a few coins—not for the fish, but for the effort. From now on, you should be more honest in your business. Set up a little booth in the square and sell what you catch in the streams. It's hard work, but you'll find it more rewarding than these transparent tricks."

"It's no trick, sir," said the boy. "I won't take your money if you don't want this fellow. I'll throw it back." The boy grasped the fish by the tail and flung it sidearm. It whirled into the mist below.

"For lies, I'll give you nothing." Holtzclaw hollered to the driver and the stagecoach rattled on, crashing over every rut and rock.

The mist lifted as the stagecoach continued downwards, and the view from the ridgeline became clearer. Breaks in the trees afforded glimpses of the Lost Creek Valley, rolled out just as on Holtzclaw's map. The Lost Creek entered at the head of the valley and meandered for five miles before it exited through a gorge, white with the foam of waterfalls. The town of Auraria—thirty houses and a squat commercial square—clung to the river. Scars marred the valley walls where trees had been stripped away for pasture, ridges cultivated into narrow rows of crops, and smears of mud left behind after mining.

A chickadee and a titmouse called out from overhead; a terrible warbling from the woods answered them.

"Turkeys," said the driver of the stagecoach, breaking his silence, "or a singing tree that's out of tune. No, has to be turkeys."

The driver had introduced himself as X.T.—a name simple enough for even an illiterate to draw. He pointed to brown shapes that waddled through the underbrush. "Folk drive them into town to sell, but some of the birds get lost and go up in the hollows. Now if it were a singing tree, that would be a real sight. It belts out old mountain tunes when it's had too much sweet water to drink."

Holtzclaw took out his notebook to record the details of this pastime. Evidently, the locals, after some stout local brew, climbed the boughs of a tree to sing ballads and folk lyrics—and they sang poorly enough to be mistaken for warbling turkeys. Perhaps Holtzclaw could employ it as a distraction.

The jostling of the stagecoach troubled his handwriting. A wheel bounced off a stone, and his head was thrown against the window glass. "Is it much farther into Auraria?" he asked, rubbing his injury.

"Still a fair piece, Mr. Holtzclaw," said X.T.

The stagecoach had left its station in Dahlonega at dawn that day. Holtzclaw had planned for the journey to take no more than five hours. Through the settled acres around the county seat, the stagecoach had kept an excellent pace. A private turnpike had provided the best stretch; Holtzclaw would have gladly kept paying the toll if the road had stayed so comfortable. But the smooth traveling was too short. On the Lost Creek side of the Great Hogback Ridge, the road was only a cart path. Farmers' wagons, turkey drivers' nibbling herds, and rainwater flowing from the heights both made and unmade the road by turns. It was clear now that the primitive suspension of the stagecoach was inadequate for the mountain road and for Holtzclaw's sensibilities.

"I'll walk from here," he said to X.T.

"Still a fair piece, Mr. Holtzclaw."

"I will be in a fair number of pieces if I keep on with you."

X.T. shrugged. "If you still want the old Smith place, then, it's over the Saddlehorn two miles, then you'll take the Post Trace down into the valley. I'll haul your boxes to McTavish's."

"Is there any other inn in Auraria?" Scottish hospitality and cuisine had not impressed Holtzclaw in the past.

"Well, there's the Old Rock Falls Inn and the Grayson House. We don't like to put up guests at the Old Rock Falls. The whispering walls make strangers nervous. The Grayson House has a rough crowd. They bring out the chuck-luck wheel every night, and sometimes folks lose a finger."

Were his deadlines less pressing, if the land was not pining to be purchased, Holtzclaw would have questioned X.T. further about these superstitions. But it was already later in the afternoon than he would have liked, and he had important visits to make. "Take my things to the McTavish's then."

"Want me to wait for you on the road?" asked X.T.

"Not necessary," said Holtzclaw. "I'll enjoy the constitutional. Fine day for a walk."

He climbed down from the stagecoach and stretched his journey-stiffened limbs. He was clean-shaven but with admirable sideburns—a young man's fashion, and Holtzclaw could still, with some truthfulness, call himself a young man. His hairline had retreated only a short distance up his forehead. He removed a bit of fluff from his bowler; it was black, matching his wool suit. Beneath his double-breasted coat, which was studded with monogrammed gold buttons, was a crisp silk shirt. In his breast pocket, he displayed a folded handkerchief.

"You'll get your fancy getup all muddy if you head off by yourself," said X.T.

"I assume you have laundry tubs and soap, somewhere in your town?"

"Sure we do, if you get there."

"Are there robbers out here? Thieves?" Holtzclaw pressed a hand over his satchel and the gold it contained. Maybe he should stay with stagecoach, despite its discomforts.

"Nothing like that," said X.T. "We're honest folk—and so's the singing tree."

Before Holtzclaw could protest, X.T. cracked his whip. An explosion split the air. The horse leapt forward, and the stagecoach bounded over the terrain like a jackrabbit. Holtzclaw watched his remaining possessions disappear down the rocky road. By the time they got to Auraria, they would be shards and splinters.

Two days prior to his arrival in the Lost Creek Valley, Holtzclaw was spending the evening working in the Milledgeville offices of his employer, H.E. Shadburn, Land Acquisitions, when Shadburn himself entered the office and opened a bottle of claret.

Shadburn, sixty-four years old, was twice Holtzclaw's age. He was a head taller as well, which was evident even when he was sitting down. His knees jutted above the level of his hips; he could not relax even in the overstuffed chairs of his offices. His chin sported a deep cleft, and Shadburn, when worried or pensive, worked his thumb in this space. Several of his shirt buttons were fastened into the wrong holes. His appearance was not inspiring; great businessmen should wear great suits. But appearances don't figure into balance sheets and, to judge by his balance sheet, Shadburn was a spectacular success.

Gas lights glinted off Shadburn's balding head as he poured a glass of claret. Drinking was not Shadburn's personal custom. While his sideboard held full shelves of every clear and colored liquor imaginable, he kept them for the tastes of his clients and agents, rather than his own.

But Holtzclaw loved claret. It was a weakness, though he did not yet call it a flaw. The sight of the wine eased his annoyance at being disturbed. "I'd thought you'd gone home," said Holtzclaw. "I was tidying the books on the Franklin deal. The final tallies are coming out quite nicely. A handsome profit."

"You flatter me," said Shadburn.

"It's the opposite of flattery. It's income minus expenses. And then the magistrate came through with the rights-of-way just in time. It's impossible, how you manage such things."

"It isn't perfect. Franklin still wants to keep those ridiculous furnaces and plow around them. Blasted fool idea. If I'd bought that land for myself, the first thing I'd do is knock them down. What does a modern plantation need with old iron smelters?"

"Maybe he wants to try smelting some iron," said Holtzclaw. "Hammer out a nail or horseshoe."

"He'll end up with slag and waste. He should stick to his talents. Cotton. Corn. Peanuts. Turn the crops into money and then buy proper nails and horseshoes from a man who knows what he's doing. That would be better use of his land. I hate to see him waste it."

"He did pay us," said Holtzclaw.

"Paid us, did he?" Shadburn wriggled in his clothes. Holtzclaw didn't remember them being so ill-fitting. "Well, yes, that's worth something."

"Did you come to talk about Franklin?" said Holtzclaw. "Are we buying some other properties for him?"

"No. Franklin's small potatoes," said Shadburn, working his thumb into the cleft of his hard chin. "I have information on a far more useful project. A hundred lots, a hundred owners. The whole town."

Holtzclaw began to emit two contrary expressions of astonishment—a rising grunt and a low whistle. They collided somewhere near his lips and tripped over each other. "Who's the client?" he asked. "Piedmont Mills? Amalgamated Bitumen? Cotton speculators? Coke miners?"

"I am," said Shadburn. "Or rather, the town itself. Auraria and its valley."

"Auraria? Which Latinism are they aspiring to?"

"'Aurum,' as in gold," said Shadburn. "It is more a hope than an industry. A few companies tried to sink tunnels into the mountain, but ended up sinking their investors instead. Most of the townsfolk left for California in the '40s. The remainder are reluctant farmers, always looking under their plowshares for nuggets. Sometimes, someone still finds one, and it's enough to keep the creaky wheel turning for another few years."

"And you think there's promise in abandoned mines and a ghost town?"

"Every land has a higher and better use." Shadburn stood up. "We can take the railroad as far as Dahlonega. We'll set up an office there, and you'll go on to Auraria by stagecoach."

"You're not going?"

"I have a thousand other tasks in Dahlonega that must come first."

Shadburn handed him a burlap potato sack. Inside, among roots and clumps of earth, were hundreds of gleaming gold coins. Holtzclaw withdrew a handful, noting the decorations that marked them as products of a peculiar mint.

"You'll have plenty of ordinary money, too," said Shadburn. "But this gold is our special weapon, which must be treated with as much care as dynamite. It's what the people are chasing, and it will move them when federal notes fail. What are federal notes but promises and paperwork?"

"That's poppycock," said Holtzclaw. "Notes spend just as well as gold."

"Some highlanders feel otherwise."

Holtzclaw shut the bag, but found no way to tie it closed. "What are you going to do with this land, once we've bought it?"

"Why, improve it!"

"How?"

"Go and see, Holtzclaw."

Thus Holtzclaw found himself walking alone through the mists of the Lost Creek Valley. X.T.'s allusions to robbers and thieves soon faded from his mind, and then Holtzclaw was sure that he'd done right to leave the stagecoach—there'd be one less local oaf stalking his movements. Financial gossip is the fastest news, and he would only have a short time to buy the most essential properties before prices jumped.

Holtzclaw followed the road that X.T. had called the Saddlehorn. Rhododendrons encroached on the path, the crowns meeting overhead. Out of a mass of vegetation rose two narrow, straight columns. As Holtzclaw neared, he saw that one was a tree, blackened by a lightning blast. The other was a metal chimney. At the top, ravens had made a nest. What kind of creature would place its fragile young in such a perilous place? There were safer, natural trees not twenty feet away. Perhaps the ravens were drawn by some residual smell from the top of the chimney. Vegetation obscured any trace of what kind of structure had once belonged to the chimney. An iron forge would not be likely so far from a primary line of transport. The chimney was wrong for a pottery or kiln.

As Holtzclaw stood pondering, the chimney belched. Steam, not smoke, issued from the top. The nest held firm and the ravens were unperturbed. Holtzclaw hoped that the people of Auraria would be more easily moved than the birds.

The path to the Smith homestead cut off from the main road, tumbling into the darkness of a valley grove. Mud and loose stones compounded the precariousness of the slope. He placed his weight on a rock covered with slick moss, and Holtzclaw's incorrect shoes slipped. His right foot slid forward while his left leg tilted back. He fell in a hump into a leaf-filled hole.

"Blasted fool rocks! Blasted fool hills!" he shouted.

"Can't blame the rocks if they're trod upon by a fool," said a voice from below. Rounding a bend in the path was a mule. Behind the mule was a canvas-covered cart, and behind the cart, a man.

The mule put its face in front of Holtzclaw's and yawned. An aroma of oats and turnips washed over him, and a moist pink tongue played between the beast's enormous teeth. Then, licking its lips, the mule backed away.

"Help you?" said the mule's master to Holtzclaw.

"I'm looking for the lands of Mr. Smith," said Holtzclaw, struggling to his feet and brushing off leaves and dust.

"Well, then, you've arrived. You're covered in them right now," said the man. "Well, not exactly. They belong to his widow, Octavia. And Smith's not even the most recently deceased. She's had another husband since then, and he died, too. Call her the widow Smith Patterson. And I don't even know how long that will hold."

"Are you a relation of the lady, or an employee?" asked Holtzclaw.

"Some of both, I guess, or on my way from one to the other." The man blushed, turning his leathery skin burgundy. "The widow Smith Patterson wouldn't like some stranger stalking around here. I think I'd best take you on down to the house."

"That would be kind of you," said Holtzclaw. "But weren't you on your way to sell your turnips?"

"Turnips keep," said the man. "Guests don't."

Again the mule flashed its teeth, but this time Holtzclaw dodged its breath. At the man's invitation, Holtzclaw climbed on top of the canvas-covered wagonload. This new method of transportation was even less comfortable than X.T.'s carriage. He felt like he was sitting on a mixture of rocks and mashed potatoes. The cart tipped and rocked on the steep path, threatening to spill both Holtzclaw and turnips, and Holtzclaw grabbed for the sides of the cart. But the wheels were better suited to the land than Holtzclaw's shoes, and the journey was short.

The path widened into fields of corn, with pole beans growing between the stalks. A dogtrot cabin stood inside a neat, swept yard. A row of cows lined up against a straight-rail fence, and a woman stood framed by one of the cabin's doorways.

"Strange load you got there, Clyde. You find him growing in the fields, or are they paying for turnips in city folk now?" said the woman.

"Someone I picked up on the road, Ms. Octavia. Said he wanted to see you."

"How pleasant," said the widow Smith Patterson. She could have been forty or four hundred years old; Holtzclaw did not know how the air and sun worked on the skin of mountain-folk. She wore a straw hat and simple clothing—a long checkered dress, turned-up sleeves, and a high collar.

"You have a name?" she said.

"James Holtzclaw, of Milledgeville. I have a business transaction to discuss with you, on behalf of the Standard Company." Shadburn had wisely given his company a vague name. Other developers, without the benefit of Shadburn's insight, picked clumsy names pleasing to investors, like the Red Top Mountain Hotel and Recreation Development Company, or the Oconee Ridge Timbering and Sawmill Authority. Besides being too revealing, they prolonged already lengthy business conversations.

"The Standard Company? Not a big company, is it?" said the widow Smith Patterson.

"A small but industrious operation, like yours," said Holtzclaw. He smiled.

"A big company would have sent a herd of men, not just one muddy fellow with a satchel."

"Precisely." He persisted with a smile.

"Well, what's your offer?" The widow stood on the porch, two feet above Holtzclaw, and looked down her long nose at him.

"May I come inside?" asked Holtzclaw. "Perhaps you'd prefer to conduct business in more accommodating and private circumstances." Haggling from the stoop was not advantageous. He had to look up at his adversary.

"Anything you want to say, you can say in front of the mule. And Clyde."

"I must say that you have a very beautiful farm here." Holtzclaw tried his best, but his words came out with too much flattery and not enough superiority.

"It's a lot of work," said the widow Smith Patterson. "It took a lot of work to put it together, and it takes even more to keep it going every day."

"Now that you've built this all into a very respectable enterprise, don't you think you deserve a reward?"

"Such as?"

Holtzclaw found it difficult to condescend to a woman standing several feet above him.

"Such as a life of leisure," said Holtzclaw. "The freedom not to run your life by the cycle of crops and weather. A little money for city luxuries. With the lifetime of hard work that you have already spent, you could buy another of peace."

"I hadn't planned on retiring," said the widow Smith Patterson.

Holtzclaw found this puzzling. He thought she would have been glad to get off the land, away from the shovel and hoe. "You can't mean to work this farm into your old age."

"Even past it. I'll be buried right under the cornfields. Still have a hand in raising the crops. Push up the stalks from below."

"Are your husbands buried there, too?"

"I buried my husbands down in the graveyard, where I don't have to look at them but twice a month. Everything that you see here, I made it. Before me, there was nothing. Weeds. Rocks. Springs. I turned it into corn, sorghum, sweet potatoes, fat cows, big smoked turkeys. Now where are you trying to get, Holtzclaw, with your beat-around-the-bush words? You better get there quickly. I have hams to cure that are bigger than you."

Holtzclaw scratched at a small bug that had made its way behind the flap of his right ear. He felt incompetent, and it was not a feeling to which he was accustomed.

"What I meant, ma'am, by my introductions, was that I wanted to buy your land. The Standard Company wants to buy your land. I'm prepared to offer you a fair value, which you can put towards your comfort. If you are parsimonious with it, it may last you to the end of your life, and you needn't work another day. Leave the cornfields just as they are. Here, I have ready money. Think what it can buy."

Sensing he was losing control of the conversation, Holtzclaw employed a favorite gambit. He withdrew a wrapped bundle of bills from his traveling satchel. The sight of money was meant to create a visceral feeling of happiness in the landowner. If the owner would hold the bills, so much the better. The smell and feel of the crisp notes were more persuasive than the sight.

"Money's a bad guest," said the widow Smith Patterson, keeping her arms crossed. "It doesn't stay long enough, and it makes an awful mess as it leaves."

Whoever invented this silly proverb was trying to sell more almanacs. "I can assure you that, for your forty acres, this is an excellent price," said Holtzclaw. "We can make considerations for your timber, crops, livestock, and improvements as well. They need closer inspection; I cannot appraise them from a plat."

"It's a mess more than forty acres."

Holtzclaw cursed himself that he had not realized it. Her land was more than forty acres, if it encompassed the whole muddy path from the road down to the homestead, as well as the cleared pasture where the cows were arranged, the corn and pole-beans, and the other fields that Holtzclaw could glimpse between the halves of the cabin.

"Forty acres are registered under the name of your late husband—your earlier late husband—at the land office in the county seat," he said in his defense.

"That's what Samuel Smith, my first husband, got in the land lottery. Land's changed hands since then. We just haven't been up to Dahlonega to file it." The widow Smith Patterson considered for a moment. "The lottery land is just the first forty. Then Bertold over the hill died and his son didn't want the land; he was out in California trying to make it. So I bought it. The piece in between belonged to the twins, and they moved to North Carolina. Bought that, too, so eighty more. That left old Butterbean surrounded; he couldn't get his cart to market without rolling over my land, and I didn't much care for old Butterbean, so I didn't make it easy for him. Well, he moved off without telling anyone—just vanished one day, and I bought up his farm for a song from his son, who wanted to drink more than dig. My second husband, Odum Patterson, came with forty acres of his own; it was a happy chance that his land was right next to mine. Poor Odum, though, he didn't live long. Sickly man. His estate had enough in it to buy the James place. Then just a few months ago Clyde over there and I started courting; he still lives out on his place but we're working his farm like it's part of mine, and if there's any selling, I'll be the one to speak of it."

"Yes ma'am," said Clyde, from atop the turnips.

That was four hundred acres in all, the whole hillside. Five fewer trips for Holtzclaw, five fewer negotiations. It was the first lucky stroke of the trip, but it would be a fivefold catastrophe if he couldn't persuade her to sell.

Holtzclaw was prepared to fight. In cases of refusal, the land purchaser has many options. If coercive talk and emotional arguments fail, he can appeal to neighbors and family. A confederate can be found who has both a connection to the owner and a personal motive, even if the motive is no more than a finder's fee. Failing that, a host of legal remedies can be applied. A judge will often see reason before an owner, or a mayor will think of the greater good. And below that are a host of clever tricks. Once, Shadburn cleared several acres upwind of a stubborn homesteader and introduced a breed of malodorous swine. And there are many silver-tongued and colorfully named maneuvers known to the profession: the Charleston Chomp, the Cincinnati Slip-off, the Asheville Attitude, the Fitzgerald Flip. But Holtzclaw trusted none of them in his present situation. Instead, he made a surefire move, one that had particular power in Auraria.

"While I'm sure you have an excellent value in yellow corn here," said Holtzclaw, "I can pay you in yellow gold." He made a flourish with his hand; he wished he'd worn white gloves, like a magician's. From his traveling bag, he withdrew a handful of the local coins. He tilted his hand, as though he were going to let the coins fall, and the widow reached out against her will.

Her eyes became radiant as the coins tumbled into her palms. "Well, now, that's some pumpkins." She held the gold coins as if they were fragile living things.

It was remarkable how quickly her attitude changed. Shadburn had told him about the local mania for gold, but it was quite another matter for Holtzclaw to see it for himself. It was foolishness, of course—one kind of money is just as good as another. But these people of Auraria had sought so hard for gold that it addled their brains when they came in contact with it. Still, Holtzclaw did not feel dishonest in his dealing. He would pay the widow in hard currency. It was her own flaw that she surrendered to the coins.

"Shall we continue our discussion inside?" said Holtzclaw. The look in the widow's eye was her agreement to sell. The rest would be paperwork.

"No, right here is just fine for me." She plopped down on the porch stoop. "You wanted to buy the whole lot, fields and buildings and all? Knock 'em down?"

"Yes, the four hundred acres. I imagine they will be cleared for my employer's purposes."

"What purposes are those?"

"They are my employer's purposes. I'm just an agent."

"There's the house here, the barn, smokehouse, root cellar, the springhouse." She was distracted, staring at the coins. "Clyde's cabin, which isn't much of anything. He's got an iron shop out the back, all rusted out. We've got a hundred acres in corn, twenty for sorghum, ten in oats, and twenty acres for pasture."

As she spoke, Holtzclaw noted each item in a ledger, requesting dimensions for the structures and providing a value. The widow Smith Patterson pressed hard only on the smokehouse, which she claimed had a supernatural ability to preserve a ham against all corruption, and for which Holtzclaw let her win a price that was double his estimate. He tallied up the numbers, double-checking for mathematical mistakes. He had not made any, either accidentally or on purpose. For some speculators, the common man's unfamiliarity with numbers and figures represented a source of profit, but Holtzclaw could not abide an error with his name signed to it.

The final contracted amount was substantial. The widow Smith Patterson and her helpers could not hope to earn its equal in five years of hardscrabble on the mountainside. Holtzclaw counted out the sum into towers of gold coins on the swept porch. The last tower was crowned with two federal quarter-dollars, a denomination not available in gold coins.

Holtzclaw gave the contract over to the widow Smith Patterson for her mark. Instead of an illiterate's scrawl, though, she executed a florid signature that shamed Holtzclaw's.

"When does your employer arrive to evict us?" asked the widow Smith Patterson. "Or did he keep that from you as well?"

"He will be here in his own time," said Holtzclaw, dusting off the dirt from his bottom, where he had been sitting on the stoop. "You may want to harvest what you can."

Turnip tops and corn stalks waved back at them. "I think I will leave it for the birds," she said.

"That's your choice, of course. I do hope, though, that you'll be discreet concerning our transaction. I have a few more lots to purchase, here and there."

"Why should I keep it a secret?" said the widow Smith Patterson, caressing a coin.

"Because your neighbors might take it on themselves to be greedy, beyond the value of their lands. Then, I will have a difficult choice. I would have to pay them more than I paid you. And they wouldn't deserve it. You have been more clever and productive than they have. Why should they have the reward?"

Holtzclaw tried to make the speech sound fresh and life-like, though he'd asked the same of every landowner he'd met in his career. The widow nodded her understanding; she wanted justice just as much as he wanted cheap land.

The deal was done; Holtzclaw could not linger. He'd extracted her promise of discretion, but promises are not worth much. The weight of his traveling satchel pleased him as he hefted it back over his shoulder. It held less gold, but more wealth.

Holtzclaw borrowed a ride back up the hill from Clyde and his turnip wagon, parting with him at the main road. Clyde was not going to town, but to a merchant's barn, where turnips were bought at wholesale. Holtzclaw turned south, further down into the valley, along the road that he assumed was the Post Trace.

So far, this lumpy end of the state had done little to endear itself to him. In the Wire-grass, every hummock in the road provided a view of gentle fields where homes bloomed like tiny white flowers. It was a tamed landscape, a garden of a hundred thousand acres, and Shadburn found that pleasing. "They have plowed it down and raised it up," he would say as they traveled between claims, passing farms with neat corn rows and fences at right angles. Shadburn loved the industry; Holtzclaw, the order. Here and there sprouted old plantation homes, and one could be assured of country refreshment, a mint julep served by a pale woman in a white dress. The mountains, though, had yet to offer him a julep of any sort.

But the mountain valley did share one essential trait with the Wire-grass: every inch was owned. Holtzclaw's map showed claims by Ode Peppers, Luther Wages, and Pigeon Hollow—the last, Holtzclaw hoped, was not a personal name, but a geographic one. And if every inch was owned, then every inch could be bought.

Something caught the corner of his eye. Holtzclaw paused midstride and looked down. Between his feet was a coiled snake. Holtzclaw leapt into the air, kicking and flailing; the snake sprang, too, striking out, making contact with Holtzclaw's leg. He felt fangs sink into his flesh, and he landed to a wince of pain. The snake was a green flash streaking into the underbrush.

Holtzclaw's heart beat faster, and a jolt of agony streaked up his leg. He rolled his trouser cuff and lowered his stocking to reveal his swollen and angry ankle. Seeing the wound sent a fresh spasm of pain shooting out. But the pain must be put aside. If it was a poisonous snake, then he had to act. In his traveling satchel were a few implements which, he supposed, could be turned to surgery: a knife, a quill pen, a small flask of high-proof claret. But most necessary was water, which would be needed in great quantities to flush out the poison.

Holtzclaw looked for a stream or a spring near him, and instead, he saw a small post: "water" and an arrow. This wasn't luck, but inevitability; such sources were never more than a hundred paces away in this water-logged valley. He hobbled with as much speed as his injury would permit.

After just a few paces on the side path, the landscape had been transformed. Old chestnuts loomed overhead. Tree trunks were coated on the windward side with a verdant moss, layered like ice. A cool, wet breeze blew against his cheeks. The contrast with the fiery pain of the poison made both sensations sharper.

The frosted path widened into a clearing, and a narrow beam of sunlight illuminated a spring. Rough rocks were built up three feet high to enclose a pool thirty feet across. In the center of the spring was an irregular island. In a more refined garden, it would have been topped with an Italianate gazebo and connected to the mainland by an arched Oriental bridge, but here, in the wild, the island was deserted.

Holtzclaw removed the shoe on his affected foot. He noted the ruined polish and a deep scuff mark along the saddle. Even if he survived this journey, the shoe would not. Sitting on the rock wall, he plunged the wound into the water. The cold water brought relief, but Holtzclaw knew that this was only a surface cure. Inside, the poison was working its baneful duty. Holtzclaw could hear the hissing of the corruption in his blood.

He glanced again at the island and started in surprise. A girl was perched there, her bare feet submerged and splashing in the glassy water. He'd overlooked her, preoccupied with mortal matters. Had she been reclining, so that her silhouette followed the curve of the island?

"I am very sorry to have stumbled into your bath," said Holtzclaw, through gasps of pain. "And if circumstances were other than they are, I would leave. But you'll have to excuse me. It's a dire situation. If you have delicate sensibilities, you may want to look away. I am about to perform a surgery on myself to remove the poison of a snakebite, and the waters will run red with my humors."

"Where were you bitten?" The girl came nearer, stepping through the shallow water. She was so calm in the face of Holtzclaw's imminent death; this must be the sorry life of the mountain-folk.

"It isn't proper, mademoiselle," insisted Holtzclaw. "The scene will be gory, and time is short. Please, give me space, and do not mind me if I scream. The cries are necessary, since there is no ether to be had."

"There, on your ankle? That's not a snakebite." She sat down on the rock wall next to Holtzclaw and drew up his foot by the big toe. "The swelling and color are wrong. A snakebite would have turned black. And you haven't been bleeding, either. The fangs would have opened a wound, and the skin here is intact."

Holtzclaw glared at the wound. It was red, but from irritation. There were no signs of bleeding punctures. The pain, which had risen as high as his breastbone, ebbed.

"But I saw the snake..."

"What color?"

"Green. Bright green, with a yellow belly. It's fixed in my mind."

"There's no green snakes here that are poisonous," said the girl. "We have copperheads and rattlesnakes, but they're not green. But it doesn't matter. You weren't snakebit. You leapt up when you were startled and twisted your ankle when you landed."

"I suppose that could be possible," admitted Holtzclaw. "But if you're wrong..."

"If I were wrong, you'd already be dead. The best cure for you is cold water. Sit as long as you like and let the swelling go down. It'll be easier to walk."

Holtzclaw let the affected part relax in the spring waters. He felt an immense relief, then an immense embarrassment. The girl fetched him a wooden cup and he filled it from the spring water, bringing coolness to his addled brain.

"You're right, of course, mademoiselle," said Holtzclaw at last. "I've had a day over-filled with exertions. Then there was a snake, and the surprise of it all led me to certain hasty conclusions. I'm sorry for disturbing you."

The girl dismissed his apologies with a wave. She was young—Holtzclaw took her for fifteen or sixteen. The skin was tight on her face, especially around her eyes and brow. Her eyes were set deep; her cheekbones were strong; her eyes—green? blue? A long curtain of black hair, streaked with silver uncharacteristic for her youth, fell down her back. Her clothing was cut in the rustic style Holtzclaw had seen worn by the widow Smith Patterson, but the fabric was cobalt blue.

"May I trouble you for your name?" said Holtzclaw.

"Princess Trahlyta," she said.

"How lovely," said Holtzclaw. "Mine is James Holtzclaw, at your service. 'Princess' as a given name is popular right now. Your parents picked a fashionable one for you."

"Pleased to meet you, James. Princess isn't my name. It's my title."

"Princess, eh? Where is your kingdom?"

"This spring and the others like it," she said. "The valley. An hour upriver; the same downriver. And thousands of miles beneath my feet."

"You own all that?" said Holtzclaw.

"To be princess doesn't mean to own it," she said.

Holtzclaw's respect for her calmness and command of natural lore turned to contempt at her childish answers to his questions. She was playing a game with him, trying to draw him into her fun. It was a waste of time. A small pocket of gratitude resisted these annoyed thoughts, but it was overwhelmed. The girl had not saved his life; she'd only splashed a little cold water on his face. She'd done nothing of consequence.

"Well, Princess Trahlyta, I suppose that I should leave you to resume your ablutions. I have work to do concerning those who are owners of land, not merely titleholders. Thank you for letting me share your spring."

The girl examined her wet toes, then started with sudden remembrance. "I have a present for you." She skipped across the water like a flying stone, coming to only a momentary pause beside a thicket of leaves and brambles, and then returned with the largest peach he had ever seen. It was colored like sunlight. Holtzclaw had to accept it with two hands.

"A piece of customary hospitality," she said. "For the journey."

Holtzclaw left the spring and continued towards Auraria. His wounded ankle did not let him hurry, much against his will. The sun was setting, time was slipping.

For a long while he ruminated about the peach, since it took a long while to eat it. There must be some trait in the water, the soil, or the climate of the Lost Creek Valley that produced such fruit. Peaches like these would be sought after in Milledgeville, not only for the novelty but also for the dramatic color. After a few appearances in the cornucopias of prominent families' tables, every party host would want a bushel from James Holtzclaw, sole supplier!

But how to deliver the peaches at the peak of their freshness? A peach couldn't withstand a bumpy cart ride out of the valley. He would need a train line. To lay the rails, he'd have to invert mountains into valleys, carve winding serpent tracks upon sheer cliff faces, blast tunnels through the granite hearts of the mountains—just to transport a few wagonloads of peaches into Milledgeville. Even the most novice speculator would find the financial calculations unfavorable. Ah, but peaches could just be the start. What if the whole valley were turned to industry? Cotton gins, saw mills, furs and game. Add a mail car twice weekly, and a profit could be made. One of the rail companies may even invest, lessening the capital risk. Could this be what Shadburn had in mind for Auraria? Fruit?

Holtzclaw wrapped the stone of the peach in his handkerchief and slipped it into his breast pocket. Perhaps he could yet make some success from this stone, whether Shadburn participated or not.

These thoughts of a peach empire were not the first that Holtzclaw had entertained about putting his own name to a business. When he was not much more than a boy, Holtzclaw had become enamored of a new industry that was just beginning to bloom in Georgia: silkworms. The foothills of the Appalachians bore an uncanny resemblance to the silkworm's native Chinese provinces. The weekly magazines were crammed with inspirational stories of success, and even the academic journals and agricultural reports that Holtzclaw perused were bullish. He would have been a fool not to join in, especially since he could bring a certain precision and discipline to the practice. From his research, he prepared a precise list of necessary items, and with his small inheritance, he bought the following items:

> *10 acres, southern exposure sloped land in region of mild climate, hot summers, little frost, and low-moderate precipitation*
> *15 mulberry shrubs*
> *125 silkworm cocoons*
> *Qty. wood, glass, nails, etc. necessary for construction of hothouse, dimensions 30' by 20' by 8'*
> *1 dwelling for self*
> *Qty. articles of necessity and comfort for the furnishing of dwelling*

As his fragile charges gained strength in their strange home, he would replace the meager comforts of this budget with the riches of fine native Georgia silk. Holtzclaw and a hundred others purchased property near each other, and the earliest arrivals named the fledgling town Canton, after its Oriental model. The town was a vile smear on a hill overlooking the Coosa River, overstuffed with a young, rough people and the sorts of businesses that they frequent: taverns and boarding houses, a barber's shop, and other places of ill repute.

Holtzclaw had been settled six months in Canton, long enough to see his finances shrink more quickly than his silkworms were maturing—owing, he supposed, to three months in which precipitation, as he measured, was between one-quarter and one-half inch below the expected. A revised plan showed that, at historical rates, he could anticipate a gap of four months between the end of his capital and the beginning of his profits. The weather forecasts heralded no improvement, thus he supposed the gap would widen over the months, rather than narrow. These circumstances were untenable.

Holtzclaw carried out these calculations on a dozen papers spread out on a table at the Eagle Tavern. He often repaired there for supper, because it was the only place in town that stocked a decent claret. He was attempting to solve a tangled and discouraging equation when he was interrupted by a targeted clearing of the throat. Holtzclaw looked up to find a tall man with a hard cleft chin. He wore his hat indoors, a white bowler with a black band and narrow brim, but this breech of etiquette was excused by excellent cufflinks, in monogram order: hSe.

"My name is Hiram Ebenezer Shadburn, of Milledgeville. May I offer you a claret, Mr. Holtzclaw?"

Holtzclaw nodded. Shadburn did not arise to inquire at the bar, but pulled a bottle from a traveling case, uncorked it, and pushed the vessel towards Holtzclaw. Drinking straight from the bottle would not have been out-of-character for any other denizen of the Eagle, but Holtzclaw motioned to a circulating servant to bring an appropriate glass, reprimanded him for bringing the kind suited for aged liquors, and resigned himself to a white-wine glass. During all of this, Shadburn was silent. When Holtzclaw's nose was inside his glass of claret, Shadburn spoke.

"I don't wish to waste time, yours or mine. I buy land for development and resale. Your land is of interest to me, and I want to buy it, this evening, for cash."

The lack of preamble or pretense was a little shocking, but not altogether displeasing. "I have improvements and possessions on the land. Investments. Expectations."

"Do you mean, the silkworms? They are dying, the poor creatures. They don't belong here. I cannot put the value of your expectations into my offer." Shadburn passed him a folded piece of paper. The written sum, while less than Holtzclaw's initial investment in land and capital, was not inconsiderable. Holtzclaw pushed aside his other documents and worked out his calculations in front of Shadburn.

The complexities of his equations related to change. A man who no longer wants to be a shepherd will take a lower price for his flock of sheep. Shadburn's offer had caught Holtzclaw at the very moment when his own wish to change was at its peak. This value, input into his equations, solved it in favor of selling. Holtzclaw signed the short document that Shadburn presented.

"I do hope, Mr. Holtzclaw, that you'll be discreet concerning our transaction. I have a few more lots to purchase. If their owners know that someone wants them, they will inflate their prices. I do not want to pay them more than I paid you. You should have the best of it; you saw reason first."

"What you pay other people doesn't matter to me. I've agreed to a fair price."

"That's sensible, Holtzclaw." Shadburn folded the document and put it into his pocket.

Holtzclaw was upset to see his land treated so casually. "If you'll pardon my frankness, Mr. Shadburn, you must guard that deed more carefully. It's precious. You should treat it like gold. Do you have a portfolio or a satchel of some kind?"

"I do not," said Shadburn. "I've never cared for such things."

"I could manage them for you," said Holtzclaw. "For a time."

"Could you now? Would you like such employment better than raising silkworms?"

"I have very little affection for the silkworms themselves."

Shadburn approached many other property holders in the following days; Holtzclaw followed along to sort the deeds and organize the paperwork. Most of Holtzclaw's generation held out. But a sudden cold snap caught Georgia's Canton unaware. Silkworms died by the thousands, their entire civilization extinguished. Men who had turned up their noses at five hundred dollars before the cold spell were glad to take fifty and a train ticket to somewhere far away from their failure. Before the end of six weeks, Shadburn owned forty percent of the Canton region, all of it on the high ground above the Coosa River. He never made overtures towards the land along the riverbed, even though it was better for farming. Something was afoot; Shadburn was too purposeful to make such mistakes.

Holtzclaw followed Shadburn back to Milledgeville, where he kept his offices. The employment was meant to be temporary, to tidy the books and file paperwork from the Canton project, but in Milledgeville, Holtzclaw found a great many books that needed tidying. It took three months to put all the paperwork in order. As he was nearing the end, he read a remarkable headline in the business papers. The Coosa River Company had just been organized to build a flood control dam. When they closed the gates, the impounded river would form a lake that would trace the borders of the land Shadburn purchased in Canton.

Now, instead of owning forty percent of a failed experiment in American silkworm farming, Shadburn owned the entire shores of a beautiful, shimmering lake: thousands of acres of newborn farm-land, kissed by water and served by the railroad spur that the Coosa River Company had built to move supplies to their dam site. The cheap high ground was made valuable in an instant by the touch of water, and Shadburn pocketed a fortune.

Holtzclaw felt a touch of bitterness than he had not held out to see the profit for himself. How had Shadburn done it? Was it backroom deals, prior knowledge? He didn't think so; Shadburn did not seem subtle enough. A lucky stroke? Not this, either. The next six projects all turned out just as well. Holtzclaw accompanied Shadburn at every meeting, keeping notes and leading negotiations himself. Every deal was profitable. Shadburn had perfected the alchemy of creating gold from paper.

As Holtzclaw reminisced, the sun dropped below the mountains, which rose up to meet it. The Post Trace—if it was the Post Trace, and not some nameless path—doubled and redoubled on itself as it descended. Holtzclaw didn't know if he was any closer to Auraria, where he would find his bed, supper, and most importantly, his luggage, with a change of shirt and shoe polish. A hateful thought occurred to him: in his musing about an empire of peaches and silk-worms, he'd missed a turn. Another error, hours slipping away. He should have been in town by now; he should have been winning the affections of the local government or making quiet deals with the key shop owners. Instead, he was lost in the woods.

He considered turning around; if he made no more mistakes, he could return to the widow Smith Patterson's house. The laws of country hospitality would oblige her to put him up for the night and provide supper as well. Even if her instincts for hospitality were weak, the promise of another gold coin left beside his plate would inspire her. But then he would have no evening coat, smoking jacket, or gentleman's robe. Nowhere to wash his face but some crockery bowl, or, worse, an old bedpan. He had no shaving kit in his traveling bag; the widow would give him either a bread knife or an old piece of metal dulled by her former husbands' cheekbones. He would have to forgo his evening claret, without which Holtzclaw could not even aspire to restful sleep. And all of these discomforts would be compounded by the knowledge that his schedule would be slipping even farther behind. He pressed on.

Only a narrow strip of purple sky was visible above. Pale emanations rose from mossy rocks and branches. A bright green glow, like a signal lantern, flashed twice from a rocky monadnock across the valley. Fireflies telegraphed their messages from ridge to ridge.

The road ended at a creek; Holtzclaw heard the water, but could not tell where it flowed until he had stumbled into it. He picked his way through underbrush, following the current downstream. The creek joined with several others into a larger flow, and as it did, a cold wind struck him. The flow of the water pulled the heat from the air. The mountain waters were radiating their chill vapors. His breath came out as white clouds. The green glows of the flora and fauna faded away. Even the light of the moon above was occluded, whether by the tall tops of chestnuts or by the cold mist, Holtzclaw couldn't say.

His ears caught an indistinct sound that was not quite singing, yet not quite speech. It was too faint for him to understand. Holtzclaw peered through the foliage, towards the noise, which came from a wide place in the river ahead. Shimmers of water rushed over large, flat rocks, catching the little bit of light that penetrated into the valley and throwing it back with a strange metallic sheen.

In the water, there were six human forms. They were bathing in the stream. It made Holtzclaw shiver just to watch them; the cold slapped at his cheeks, and he could not fathom how they could endure the water. Yet the figures seemed undisturbed. They dashed over the rocks, pursuing one other, splashing, cavorting.

Their limbs were too long and lean. The shapes that stood for their heads, too, were distorted. But it was too dark to understand anything for sure; at this distance, in this light, he could not trust his eyes.

At last, Holtzclaw risked calling out to them. He did not want them to think he was leering.

"Hello there!" he said, hoping that he would not startle them. "I am so sorry for intruding; I assure you, I am so bold only because I need your help. I'm a visitor, I've lost my way, and if you could..."

The air snapped, as though a photographer's flash bulb had burst. Where there had been six people bathing, there were now ripples across the water. A warmer breeze coming from the forest pushed away the cold air. In an instant, the scene had vanished from all of his senses.

Holtzclaw emerged from the underbrush and walked to the edge of the stream, perplexed and alone. Where had the bathers gone?

"Hello, James."

He whirled towards the voice. Just at the edge of the creek was the little girl from the spring, who'd called herself Princess Trahlyta. He'd overlooked her; she had looked like part of the landscape.

"Don't leap out like that! You'll give me an apoplexy!" cried Holtzclaw. His surprise turned to irritation. "Have you followed me, princess? All this way?"

"What do you mean? The spring where we met isn't more than a stone's throw away. On the other side of those poplars." The princess was spreading sheets of blue fabric out on the rocks, but Holtzclaw did not know why—they would not dry in the mist and moonlight. As she finished this work, a light rain began to fall. The waters of the stream were broken into uncountable expanding circles, dispelling the sheen that had floated across the water.

"That can't be true, princess. I've been walking all day."

"I'm the native," she said, "and you're the visitor. You've lost your way."

Holtzclaw wished he were the kind of person who could offer a rude gesture, but a hard-etched decorum restrained him. He cleared his throat, which was meant to cover the sound of swallowing bile. "So, you were you out for a swim with your friends and I just chanced upon you? It isn't the right weather for a swim."

"They are happy for a bath in any weather," said Trahlyta.

"Very fast and very skittish, too. An odd lot, princess. Are all of the inhabitants of Auraria like them?"

"Oh no. Some are just the opposite."

His questions were taking them in circles, and Holtzclaw no longer wanted to be lost.

"I was trying to get to Auraria, but I've somehow missed the right path," he said, using his negotiator's voice. "Would you be so kind as to point me in the right direction? Or, if the town is very far away, can you tell me of some other place where I could spend the night? I would be happy with a little yeoman farmer's barn, so long as it is clean and dry."

The princess giggled. "Auraria is just over the ridge. You are so close, James." She indicated a break in the foliage, where a path led downhill. This was more preposterous than her earlier claim, that he'd come just a hundred feet in an afternoon of walking. He peered down the tree-lined tunnel, but nothing recommended it above any of the other footpaths that led away from the clearing.

"Well, go on," she said. "You'll catch a chill, out here in the rain. You're not used to our climate."

Holtzclaw sighed. If he had to spend the night in a hollow log, so be it. The logs on this path would be just as damp as on any other.

In half a hundred yards, before even his sour thoughts ran themselves out, the rain had ended and the local storm dispersed. The chestnuts corrected their stooping posture and reached upwards; the sky became lighter. Around him, the darkness was fading, not to morning, but back into evening, still tinged with fireflies and luminescent mosses.

Holtzclaw broke from the forest and onto a dirt street. Buildings and homes were scattered before him, and the Lost Creek split the town in two. He'd arrived in Auraria.

Embarrassment sullied the relief of reaching his destination. The small triumph of buying the widow's land was a poor recompense for an afternoon lost to hysteria, wandering in the woods and stumbling upon some local bathers. The pace of the project was off now; he would have to move double-time tomorrow.

CHAPTER III

Progressing from Milledgeville to Gainesville to Dahlonega to Auraria, Holtzclaw had witnessed the gradual fading of civilization. Milledgeville, the glittering old capital, had given way to upstart, industrial Atlanta, which had in turn given way to functional Gainesville, a busy agricultural center and home to several vegetable canneries. Dahlonega, though smaller, was at least a county seat, with a courthouse, a clock tower, and a railroad depot. Auraria could be called a town only because of tradition.

At its heart, Auraria was a grassy square, bordered on three sides by dirt roads and weathered storefronts and on the fourth by the Lost Creek. A few streets emerged from the square, like shaggy threads hanging from a spool, tying together a disordered collection of simple houses.

The first structure that Holtzclaw passed was typical of the location: a two-story building slowly collapsing under its own weight. The upper porch tilted forward, and columns splayed out like branches. Holtzclaw thought that it wouldn't take much effort to demolish the place once he'd purchased it. A good rain might do the trick.

Half the houses in Auraria had weeds growing over them. Most of the storefronts were empty. Above them were deserted offices, their window frames filled with broken glass.

The only signs of life in Auraria were flickering yellow lights clustered on a neighboring street. Three buildings, standing opposed to each other, all had the look of guest houses: wide porches, worn stairs, and bald patches in their gardens where feet had passed in idle pacing. One house emitted loud fiddle music; in another, a solo piano played. The third was silent. None had any signs or nameplates that Holtzclaw could see, so he did not know which was McTavish's, where he hoped his possessions had been delivered. He needed to shine his shoes before continuing on; he felt awkward negotiating in dirty shoes.

The silent house disturbed him, and he was too weary to endure a ribald fiddle-house. Holtzclaw chose the piano music, even though it was lifeless, mechanical playing. He saw the reason for this where he entered the guest house. There was no player at the piano; it played itself.

Five small tables, two occupied, sat beneath dozens of daguerreotypes in the dining room. A high counter, attended by six empty stools, served as a bar. Many years of boots had worn the floors smooth. Someone had etched and re-etched tally marks into the wooden beams.

A red-haired woman in a white apron emerged from a back room. Her curls framed a round, young face, and her eyes appraised Holtzclaw, her dining room, and her guests. She was thin and short. With her red hair, she reminded Holtzclaw of a matchstick. He thought her a little plain and common—again, like a matchstick. But what passed for common in Milledgeville might be great beauty up here in the mountains.

Between her freckled hands, she carried two copper mugs and two bowls of soup, which she laid on one of the occupied tables, in front of two identical men. She executed this crisp delivery and then turned to address Holtzclaw.

"A new face!" she said. "Muttonchops, too. From the city? That's always good for few minutes' entertainment. Welcome to the Old Rock Falls! Not that there's a New Rock Falls. This one has been old from the start."

The other table was occupied by a very fat man and a very thin one. They sat beside their hats; Holtzclaw, in his confusion, had neglected to remove his own. Doing so now added to his embarrassment.

"I'm terribly sorry. I believe I'm engaged at McTavish's house. My trunk was sent ahead. The guest houses were unsigned, and I didn't see anyone to ask."

"Running off?" said the red-haired woman. "Did someone warn you about the sweet potatoes here?"

"No, not about the sweet potatoes, but about certain other phenomena," said Holtzclaw, remembering the warnings of X.T., the carriage driver.

"It's only the sweet potatoes that are dangerous," said the woman. "Ours here are so full of sugar that if you cook them too long, they'll burst into flames. I explode one every now-and-then, just to test the harvest. I'll explode one for you, if you buy it. But if you're not the kind of person who can take a sweet potato, then, I'm afraid there's little I can do for you for supper. Mrs. McTavish's place is the quiet one across the way."

Holtzclaw bowed, in preparation to take his leave.

"You may be back sooner than you think," said the woman. "Mrs. McTavish lets you wash her Highlands recipes down with water or buttermilk. No spirits. Not even sweet milk."

These predictions of his culinary future did not help to allay Holtzclaw's anti-Scottish prejudices. "I think I can become acclimated to sweet potatoes, if they're well-prepared," he said, placing his hat on one of the empty tables.

"Not that one!" said the red-haired woman. "It's occupied." The woman looked flustered. "Now I must apologize to you, mister...."

"Holtzclaw. James Holtzclaw."

"Abigail Thompson, charmed." She lowered her voice. "I don't know if you are familiar with small towns. They have traditions. Folk ways. I won't call them ruts, out of respect for current company." Abigail glanced over her shoulder, but not at her customers; she looked at the piano.

"I'm sorry," said Holtzclaw. "I don't mean to upset any one." He let Abigail lead him to another empty table.

"Now, what is it that I can get you for supper?" she said. "Fair warning: everything has sweet potatoes in it."

"Whatever's hot is fine by me. Among your alternatives to water and buttermilk, you wouldn't have any claret, would you?"

Abigail walked behind the bar counter. A key turned in a lock, then she lifted up a dusty, age-darkened bottle. The label was yellowed and foxed; an illegible name was handwritten in an ornate script. The style of cork at the top didn't correspond with that of the Bordeaux vintners—at least, not of this century. At the bottom, sediment in suspension was swirled upwards by Abigail's handling then drifted downwards again like a lazy ghost.

"Oh, this isn't claret," said Abigail, perusing the label. She replaced the bottle and took out another, which Holtzclaw recognized even at a distance as a common and modern. It promised a familiar, if unremarkable, drink. Moments before, the rare and ancient bottle had inflamed Holtzclaw's imagination; now, he could think of nothing better than the comfort of a known vintage.

"It came in the delivery last week," said Abigail.

"You have a regular delivery of claret here?"

"We're fond of all sorts of anti-fogmatics."

"I wouldn't think that your clientele would be the claret kind."

"Do you think we drink just white lightning and corn liquor in the mountains?"

"That came out wrong, Ms. Thompson," said Holtzclaw. "I'm out of my natural element."

"You don't say." She brought out a heaping plate of food without delay. There was a bowl of stew, thickened with sweet potatoes, and a plate of biscuits; Abigail left it with a curtsey, then disappeared into the back room. Holtzclaw devoured the meal with no time to mind the silence. Halfway through, he remembered he was not alone. Taking with him his glass of claret, Holtzclaw approached the table at which sat the thin man and the fat man; the twins presented a more formidable barrier to a stranger. "May I join you, gentlemen?"

"My associate and I were about to discuss this year's turkeys," said the fat man. The thin man nodded in confirmation.

"Are you farmers, then?" said Holtzclaw.

"We are aggregators," said the fat man. "Aren't you involved with poultry?" When Holtzclaw confessed that he was not, the fat man began a lengthy and candid explanation of his business. The turkeys, raised in small clutches on family farms, were driven down from the hills into a pen on a rented town lot. Here, the turkeys were kept until all the year's stock could arrive and be bought by the aggregators.

It was a story that ceased to be fascinating just a few minutes into its telling, and Holtzclaw regretted his decision to talk with these two, who owned no property and had little influence in town. The twins leaned in towards each other for some whispered words, and then arose to depart. The clattering of the front door caused the fat man to interrupt his speech, and Holtzclaw was able to interject a question. "Do you know those men who just left?"

The fat man said, "They're like us, but for gold instead of turkeys."

Abigail returned to the dining room. "When was the last time anybody found treasure worth keeping?"

The thin man spoke up for the first time. "Six months ago Ode Peppers found that nugget the size of a squirrel turd." This gave everyone pause. "Did you know," continued the thin man, "that a turkey's foot makes an excellent raking tool, and a thousand turkeys' feet so much the better? That after a herd of turkeys is driven over a promising area—say, the wet bank of a creek—that the sand is churned up, loosened, made ready for the wise man who comes back later with a pan, or better still, a rocker box, to wash that sand away and find a little gold left behind?"

It was too complicated, to raise turkeys just to make gold mining easier. But Holtzclaw did not share his doubts with his companions. "It's a clever scheme," he said.

"Not half as clever as how we really use them," said the thin man. At this, the fat man walloped the thin man with his hat.

"Are you still looking for that cave?" said Abigail.

"Maybe we are and maybe we aren't," said the fat man.

"Spanish caves! Soldiers' caves! Miners' caves! Misers' caves! If every story about treasure caves were true, you'd all have gold nuggets the size of squirrel turds," said Abigail.

"Course they're not all true," said the thin man. "Just a few of them are. That's all we need. Only two or three fabulous fortunes, not six or ten."

"Well, it's good to know you're not greedy," said Abigail. She tallied up their bill. The fat man withdrew a small pouch and poured out a quantity of gold dust onto a set of balances. Holtzclaw had seen its like only among jewelers and herbalists, never in a tavern.

"They are good men," said Abigail to Holtzclaw, after the turkey drovers left, "and hardworking, even when they're digging for gold."

"I've heard this is a universal fascination among your townsfolk."

"They dream of nothing else. They dream of gold even when they are awake."

The piano in the corner began an uptempo number that had been popular a decade ago.

"I should be on my way to McTavish's," said Holtzclaw. He paid for his supper in ordinary federal coins, which Abigail accepted without complaint. He looked inside his hat for several moments longer than necessary to be assured that the crown contained no enemies or poisons. At the threshold of the house, he turned back and called to Abigail. "I think your player piano may be a bit out of tune. May I take a look?"

"It's not a player piano," said Abigail. "I wouldn't touch it if I were you. Mr. Bad Thing is rather particular."

Ignoring her, Holtzclaw lifted the lid of the upright piano. Inside, there were no gears, no mechanisms at all, just the ordinary contents of a piano. "How does it work, Ms. Thompson? Did you get this from some novelty catalog to amuse your guests?"

"Just because you don't know how it works," said Abgail, "doesn't mean that it can't work. Mr. Bad Thing plays just fine."

The tune jumped to a minor key, then cut off. A shiver ran over the crown of Holtzclaw's head. A pale fear tickled at his feet; they cried out for him to flee.

"See, you shouldn't have touched it," said Abigail.

Outside, Holtzclaw's head swam with claret and discomfort. The night air cut into his thoughts. The most rational explanation would be some kind of spirit; how else could the piano play with no mechanism? And fill him with such a sudden dread?

Ah, but these were the improper workings of a wearied mind; he himself was going out of tune, if he were entertaining such preposterous notions. Somewhere, there was a trick whose explanation, for the moment, eluded him.

It wouldn't be proper to keep on with his mission in this state. He should find his correct quarters and make it an early night. If he tried too hard to solve the matter now, on a depleted constitution, it would pollute his dreams.

He opened the front door at the guest house that he now knew to be McTavish's. He was greeted by an immense globe of a woman. Her head, feet, and arms were undifferentiated from the purple sphere of her body.

"You're Mr. Holtzclaw, yes? X. T. left off your trunk earlier this afternoon, and I made him haul it up to your room. I'm glad you made it safe; I was fixing to worry about you, and I wouldn't have felt right to charge you for a room you weren't to sleep in, but I guess, since your trunk's already up there, you are occupying it. What brings you to Auraria?"

An excellent lie occurred to him. "I am a dealer in scrap metal. You have a great deal of it in your old mines, and I would like to buy and remove the larger pieces for better purposes." He was quite pleased by this story; it would excuse his behavior and wouldn't inflame too many suspicions.

"As good a call as any," said Mrs. McTavish. "Most folks come to dig for gold, too. Figure you'll be doing that at some point? You could hardly say you'd seen Auraria unless you looked up at it while kneeling in the sand of the river!" Mrs. McTavish made this remark from memory. She had perfected the melody of the joke while neglecting this meaning. Still, Holtzclaw performed his duty of issuing a slight chuckle.

"Now, are we going to be getting you some supper?" she said.

Holtzclaw confessed to his blunder and that he had already eaten at the Old Rock Falls Inn.

"Why would you trust a skinny innkeeper?" said Mrs. McTavish. "With that red hair, she looks like she has Irish in her."

When Holtzclaw awoke, it was mid-morning. The claret had been too fragrant, the sweet potato stew too heavy, the wear on his feet and mind too taxing. He'd fallen into the feather bed at McTavish's and had not stirred until a chickadee at his window began tapping in an unintelligible code.

It was a rotten start to a day that was burdened with tasks. If he didn't make at least six visits today—from the Striklands through to the Sky Pilot at some place called the Terrible Cascade, he might as well surrender the project; he would be too far behind schedule. Shadburn said that these six properties, plus the widow Smith Patterson's, were the most essential—geographically, politically, socially. It would have to be in a day, too; procrastination would make the prices go up, perhaps too high to be overcome.

Holtzclaw put on the shoes that he had not found time to polish the night before and ate an unsatisfying breakfast in McTavish's parlor. She offered hard rolls, garnished with marmalades imported at great distance and expense, and a glass of buttermilk. Holtzclaw first tried to eat the buttermilk with a spoon, as though it were some breakfast custard, before her glare corrected him. He took a glass of water instead, and this was the only restorative part of the meal. The water was cool and sweet and fresh.

Before leaving town to make his first visit of the day, Holtzclaw decided to purchase a few needed effects from local stores. In his *trousseau de voyage*, he had mirrors, ablution bowls, shavers, basins, ewers, powders, pill cases, and an array of bottles, sprinklers, and spritzers, in addition to a gentleman's wardrobe—none of it was useful. He needed a pair of boots and a walking stick so he could cover the terrain before nightfall; a hat in the local fashion might help prevent townsfolk from instantly marking him as an outsider.

Holtzclaw walked from McTavish's to the center of town. Around the open lot that constituted the square of Auraria were several merchants, though twice the number of empty storefronts. By their signs, Holtzclaw recognized a tailor, a barber and tonsor, a store for dry and general goods, a confectionary (a curious find in a small town), a pharmacy, and most germane to his purposes, a seller of readymade clothing and cloth.

He went inside, where the proprietor, Burton, directed him towards a display of boots. Holtzclaw selected a workhorse pair. Of the hats, Holtzclaw asked Burton's opinion.

"Well, if you're looking for a farm hat," said Burton, "then most folks would go for the straw one, with the wide brim. Keeps the sun off your neck best it can. But you can't wear that if you're off visiting folks. You'd look like a hayseed. Most folks buy something like this,

AURARIA

if they want a traveling hat." Burton indicated an array of low-quality
bowler hats in brown or grey felt. "People like this one, even though
it's more expensive." He held it out to Holtzclaw. "Dark lining and
the bowl is stiff, so you can turn it over it for a quick pan if you happen to see colors in the water."

"But then isn't your hat wet for the rest of the day?"

"With the right strike you could buy any number of hats, wet or
dry. You could buy a whole store full of hats."

Holtzclaw bought the gold-panning hat, along with the boots. No
walking stick was to be had, though. "Folks don't buy a thing like
that," laughed Burton. "Plenty of sticks out in the forest; you can
make it yourself."

After outfitting himself sartorially, Holtzclaw aimed to stop at
the confectionary and purchase two tarts—one for now, as a supplement to a hasty breakfast; one for later, to give him some extra
vigor on the road. At the door of the confectionary, he met Abigail
Thompson, exiting.

"Victuals for the Old Rock Falls's dining room?" he asked. "Or a
treat for your dear Mr. Bad Thing? Don't let the syrup gum up the
piano keys." Beneath his jokes, he felt a strange shudder.

"He doesn't much care for sweets, Holtzclaw, except for sweet
potatoes. If he did, he wouldn't have such a temper. They say no one
who eats sweets can have a sour disposition."

"I'm not sure that's true," said Holtzclaw.

"Just how are you keeping busy here, Holtzclaw?" asked Abigail.

"I have some visits to make to various old mines. Recover some
scrap metal, if the price is fair." The lie felt hollow the second time,
either because of the repetition or because he had a higher opinion
of Abigail than of Mrs. McTavish. "It would be an easier journey if
I had a walking stick, but the shopkeeper said that I'd have to make
my own."

"I have one you could borrow," said Abigail. He followed her, for-
getting about the confectioner's shop. She led him back to the Old
Rock Falls; on the way, he modeled his new hat for her. "It's a proper
Auraria hat," she said. "It's got gold on the brain."

45

Just inside the door of the Old Rock Falls was an umbrella urn containing several walking sticks. She selected one and gave it to Holtzclaw. It was made of pale wood, without the knobs and twists of a walking stick made from a fallen branch.

"This one belonged to my uncle," she said. "He was out walking though some brush when a copperhead started coming for him. Most times a copperhead will flee like you're a bear, but this one wanted blood. My uncle held up his walking stick, and the copperhead's fangs got caught in it. There it was, thrashing and crashing on the end of that stick, biting it over and over, and the snake didn't quit even when my uncle dunked the end of the stick in the river. The copperhead just kept struggling until it drowned. Then the stick began to swell up. When you get bit by a copperhead, your leg will swell up—that's the poison. Well, his walking stick had got the poison, and by the time he got home, he could hardly carry the stick anymore—it was a log bigger than a railroad tie. Ten feet long, two feet around. I saw it! But my uncle liked that walking stick. So, he spent the next two weeks whittling and planing that walking stick back down to a size he could use."

"So he carved himself a walking stick from a bigger walking stick?" said Holtzclaw.

"That's why it's special," said Abigail.

"And you don't mind if I take it?"

"I'll mind if you don't bring it back."

The beat of the walking stick measured the miles as Holtzclaw ascended the Fiddlehead Trail. Beneath the high canopy of chestnuts, an unbroken carpet of ferns strained for light.

Holtzclaw was confident enough in his boots and walking stick that he ignored the path and instead reviewed his notes on the acquisition. He hoped that they were more accurate than the notes concerning the amalgamated empire of the widow Octavia Smith Patterson.

He arrived at a two-story cabin, covered on the sides with clapboard and painted white, and was admitted into the farmhouse of Edgar and Eleanor Strikland by the former. Inside, the bottom story was one large room; a ladder in the corner led upstairs. Small feet scurried overhead. Three brooms of various lengths were hanging by the door—two pointed downwards and a short-handled one pointed upwards.

"Begging your pardon," said Edgar as he shook corn husks off a cane-seat chair. "The house has been a bit of a mess since the wife died."

"I am very sorry for your loss, Mr. Strikland," said Holtzclaw. "When did she pass?"

"Oh, about a year ago, I suppose," said Edgar. "Yup, that would be about right."

A woman in an apron entered from the rear door of the cabin. Holtzclaw stood as the lady entered and came towards them.

"That's nobody, just ignore her," said Edgar. "That's my wife's ghost. She's been fluttering aroud here ever since she died."

Holtzclaw was in a quandary. Propriety demanded that he introduce himself to the lady of the house, but this risked offending Edgar, who was insistent about his odd marital spat. Holtzclaw decided on a middle way. He bowed slightly towards the lady, with his hat touched against his breast. The lady said nothing, but curtsied in reply, which was a very un-ghostly response.

In Holtzclaw's experience, those who reported encounters with ghosts usually described subtle, ambiguous events—rattling doors or pans, tapping inside walls, faint whispering. These subtleties made them easy to emulate. Shadburn had once expelled a stubborn family by giving a pack of street urchins ten cents each to hide beneath the foundations of a home and whisper the bloody details of their murder to the terrified inhabitants above. This particular trick Holtzclaw did not think very sporting, but Shadburn had excused it by giving the family a good deal of money for their land.

This ghost-wife appeared neither subtle nor ambiguous, but like an ordinary mortal. Beneath her apron, she wore a long, bone-white dress that ended in lace at the collar, cuff, and floor hem—not fitting for farm work. Her raven black hair tumbled below her shoulders. Had she been in the kitchen or fields, she would have put it up in a bun or braid, away from her work.

"As I was saying," continued Edgar, "since Eleanor died, I've had to do the housekeeping, or make the children do it, and I'm not very good at either. I'm lucky to get any kind of supper turned out. Folks were nice to us right after Eleanor passed. We ate real well after the funeral, real well. Then they didn't keep it up. I think Eleanor scares them. I wish she would move on! Silly ghost! Get going!" He waved his arms at his ghost-wife as though he were trying to shoo chickens. Eleanor's expression was unchanged.

Three faces appeared, spaced along the ladder. "Is that momma you're talking about?"

"Who else?" said Edgar. "You three, come meet this man. He says his name is Holtzclaw. He wants to talk about the farm here."

The three children presented themselves in a ragged line for Holtzclaw's inspection. The smallest, a girl, had a corn husk doll. "Momma made it for me."

"I hadn't seen that before," said Edgar, taking it from her. The doll had a long, dirty-white dress, fringed in rough fabric that resembled lace at the collar, cuff, and floor hem. Black thread stood for hair that tumbled below its shoulders. It was the spitting image of its supposed creator. "Ain't that a thing?" Edgar gave it back, and the child clutched it to her chest.

Eleanor turned to watch the children return up the ladder. In the dark of the cabin, a milkiness of light clung to her skin. She was so pale that she seemed brighter than her surroundings.

The two men and the ghost-wife took seats around the kitchen table, which held, among the remnants of a past dinner, a reed basket of porcelain doorknobs.

"It's for the chickens," said Edgar. "If they're not laying, they get lonely, and that makes them even less likely to lay. Then they're restless; they walk around and maybe drop the egg in some secret nest, in a bush. So you put a doorknob in their real nest, in the coop, with the pointy part down and the smooth part up, so the chicken thinks it's sitting on an egg. If you're a rich person, you can buy a real porcelain egg for your chicken, but poor people have to make do with some old doorknobs. Doesn't work as well. They know the difference. Chickens aren't laying right now, haven't had more than a dozen eggs since Eleanor died. She gives them the fright! See some white lady stalking about in the bushes in the dead of night. You wouldn't lay, either."

Eleanor placed her hands on the table. Her slender fingers were capped by translucent nails.

Holtzclaw presented his scenario about scrap metal and inquired if the Striklands were willing to sell. Edgar invited an offer with a sweep of his hand. As Holtzclaw enumerated the various monetary values of the property, Edgar remained silent. He did not grimace at particular sums, nor did he correct Holtzclaw to say, "We just put a new roof on that corn crib" or "What about the chickens? You didn't count the chickens." Edgar's chief interest was the running tally. When Holtzclaw's running total exceeded a certain sum, Edgar leaned back in his chair and sighed.

Eleanor turned away, her face in profile against the window. Her hair was up in a bun now; Holtzclaw had not seen her do it. The sharp angle of her nose was softened by the sunlight.

"So, Mr. Strikland, do we have a deal?" said Holtzclaw.

"Where do I sign?" Holtzclaw indicated a number of places on various documents. When Edgar had finished making his last mark—a curious pattern of geometric shapes that, while bearing no resembles to a cursive rending of his name, was actually more complicated—Holtzclaw counted out a stack of bills.

"What do you think you'll do with your money, Mr. Strikland?"

"I have plans, yes, very definite plans, Mr. Holtzclaw, now that I've got your money and you've got my land. You've got some new plans, too. You get to deal with all the corn coming up; some you got to feed to the chickens and some you got to feed to yourself and some you got to cart down into the valley and try to sell it for sugar or coffee. And then you've got to wake up the next morning and do it all again, and there's never an end in sight." Edgar gesticulated toward an empty chair; Eleanor sat on the opposite side of the table. "When your wife dies, then you get to deal with a farm house and all the washing and the cooking, too, and sweeping out the house because you get dirt and spiders and evil spirits—can't keep 'em all away, least of all your ghost wife. And you got to try to make it all mean something, doing the same work day after day with never an end in sight, thinking if you could save a penny here or a penny there you could get out, try to do make it big, but you never do."

Eleanor's eyes fixed on his husband. Her mouth was hard set. A red flush spread to her pale cheeks.

"We're gonna move," said Edgar. "We'll go to California or maybe Alaska, where they still have gold. Strike it rich. We won't be saving pennies any more. Buy a mountain of sugar, buy a ton of coffee. Move in to the city and have twenty butlers. They still have butlers in the city? Somebody told me about it once, but that was a long time ago. A maid, too, and some golden slippers. They don't have to be real gold, because that would be heavy. Just gold colored. And expensive."

Edgar stood up, scooping the money into his pocket. "If you'll excuse me, Mr. Holtzclaw, I've got to get ready. We have to load the wagon. Hitch up the children. Shake off all these old ghosts."

Holtzclaw went to the door, and Eleanor followed beside him. He tipped his hat to her, but she did not return any courtesy. She looked at him with sadness welling in her eyes.

"I am sorry for any trouble I have caused you, ma'am," he said, with as much tenderness as his profession would allow.

Eleanor took the small broom that hung upside-down and swept his dust from her house.

CHAPTER IV

Despite the strange welcome and strange sendoff he'd received, Holtzclaw was happy. It mattered little to him what Edgar Strikland did with the money that Holtzclaw had paid him; the strained relations between Edgar and Eleanor, ghost or not, were unimportant to his mission. Holtzclaw's interest in the matter ended when Edgar signed over the deed.

The next property was at the head of the valley, farther upstream, at the foot of Sinking Mountain. Today's road proved much less bewildering than yesterday's. After a half hour's walk, Holtzclaw arrived at a property owned by Shadrach Bogan.

On Holtzclaw's map, Shadburn had written, "vast empty swath of useless cleared land leading to empty mine tunnels," but this was incorrect. The land was covered in close-packed pine trees, thick scrub, and patches of laurel and mountain hemlock.

Holtzclaw found the property's owner sitting in front of a crack in the mountainside. He was carving a new handle for a pickaxe from a tree branch. The knife he was using was far too large for the job, and yet, Bogan whittled and whistled.

"Help you?" said Bogan.

"I am hoping we can help each other," said Holtzclaw. "You are in possession of a piece of land, and I may be interested in purchasing it." Shadburn's direct method, Holtzclaw had found, was universally appropriate when facing parties that held large knives. They did not care for verbal tricks.

"What do you need it for?" said Bogan.

"I am a dealer in scrap metal."

"Well, there's a ton of it down there under Sinking Mountain," said Bogan. "Mostly gets in my way. Want to go take a look?" He gestured with his head towards the crack in the mountain. The passage was not braced up against collapse. Loose boulders were stacked to each side. "It used to have another way in, over on the widow's side of the mountain, but I had to blast my own way in. Imagine, blast into my own mountain, 'cause I didn't buy a front door! Look what I got instead."

Bogan got up and scurried over a line of boulders. On the other side, there was a lake.

It was the last thing that Holtzclaw expected to see; he did not think lakes could emerge from hiding so suddenly. It ambushed him with its beauty.

The lake was filled at one end by a waterfall and drained at the other end through jagged rocks. Stone, blasted into a crater, embraced the body of water; the side-walls were deeply concave and fifty feet tall. The water was a deep blue, darker than a summer sky. Within the water, a vein of paler color—robin's egg blue—concentrated in one shaded pocket and then diffused in thin tendrils.

"It's astounding," said Holtzclaw. "Does it have a name?"

"'Course it has a name. Every hump and hummock has a name. Get two horses pissing next to each other, and someone will name the river they make. This started out as a fat spot in the creek. Some fellows were getting good pans just below here and then nothing higher up stream, past where the waterfall is. So they figured—smart fellows—that the gold must be right in here. They took some dynamite...what am I saying, some? They took a mess of dynamite and packed it all around here. Boom! Sudden lake, or sudden hole for a lake, and it doesn't take the water long to fill it in. They must have blasted down into a spring to get that color. So they called it Cobalt Springs Lake."

It would be pleasant to own such a piece of property, thought Holtzclaw. He would put a cabin on the ridge, with a wide veranda that overlooked the waterfall. Perhaps he could persuade Shadburn to set aside this piece, which had no evident commercial value, and Holtzclaw could reinvest a part of his salary into this retreat. A cool place for his health to be sheltered from seasonal miasmas.

"It's a wrong lake," said Bogan. "Unnatural. No fish in it. No bugs even. Bluer than the sky; nothing should be bluer than the sky. I hike up to the top there, past the waterfall, to fill my water skins. I want to drink from an honest pond: brown, muddy, filled with skeeters and crayfish, frogs singing on the edge of it. This Cobalt Springs Lake—it's an accident."

That the lake was a product of industry only made it more attractive to Holtzclaw. He ran his fingers in the current—the water was cool and left his fingers tingling.

Bogan continued his narrative. "Worst of it was, after those fellows set off the dynamite and made themselves a lake, they couldn't find a bit of gold, upstream or downstream. You can try it with that hat of yours. You can run the sand three times through the rocker box. Completely empty, not a cent in the whole lake. Boy, was that the biggest news here in Auraria for months! What most people figured was that, when they opened up that spring—the Cobalt Spring—all the gold got washed away. Whoosh! Like some flood. But I figured that that gold had a tunnel that it was running out of, and when the fellows made their lake, they closed up that tunnel, and the gold stayed stuck in Sinking Mountain. Maybe even built up, like it was sediment. When the old owners absquatulated, they sold me this here Sinking Mountain, and the bottomlands where they had their camp, and Cobalt Springs Lake—they wouldn't sell it without the lake, even though I didn't want it. That's enough about lakes. Are we going to go look at some scrap metal?"

Holtzclaw eyed the precarious passage into the mountain. If he wanted to maintain his cover story, he had no choice. He nodded, and Bogan handed him a lantern.

"Always check it for fuel before you go in. See, that's got plenty in it. Take some matches and candles. Don't want to run out of light—you'll never get out! I got ropes, though we probably aren't going to need them. Got some water and victuals too—couple peaches."

"Will we be gone that long?" said Holtzclaw.

"Never know," said Bogan. "We might find a treasure tunnel. Might sprain our ankle." They passed through the narrow crack and into the darkness under the mountain. Within a few paces, the light from the outside world was gone. Two lanterns floated in the gloom.

"You'd probably have to widen this part up a bit to bring up any of the larger pieces," said Bogan. "I can help you with that. It would take some careful dynamiting. That's what I've been doing for ten years now, careful dynamiting."

Holtzclaw kept his lantern close by. Its feeble light did not penetrate the darkness very far. The entrance corridor continued for two hundred yards. The floor was uneven and jagged, as were the walls. Numerous side tunnels cut off to the left and right.

"Those look like tunnels, but they only go a few feet. Those were my mistakes. Took me eight months to make it through here. I didn't want to bring the mountain down on me, so sometimes I had to feel out if the ceiling was going soft, and if it was, I had to back up and come another way. I was looking for the mine shaft, too, and if I felt like I was getting away from that, I would have to come back and rethink. Of course, the real aim was gold, so a few times I chased a seam of quartz for a bit. Didn't pan out, though! Sorry, that's miner humor. Hey, here we go! I made this part nicer, so I wouldn't need to pull out a rope every time I came through."

The tunnel veered left ninety degrees and descended on a set of rough-hewn steps, and then it opened up into another tunnel of a very different character. It was eight feet square with a smooth floor, along which ran a narrow gauge rail.

"If you head left, you'll get to the end of the old tunnel and then into my diggings. Not much there for a buyer like you. We'll head to the right. You could pull up all this rail line here. I don't need it. You might leave it until the end, though, because it would help you move the bigger pieces."

"Bigger pieces?" said Holtzclaw, though he hardly needed to encourage the garrulous miner to continue.

"Like this mine cart up ahead here. All metal, even the sides. Wheels still turn. Not rusted because I've kept it out of the water. A solid piece of equipment."

The mine cart straddled the narrow gauge track and filled the width of the tunnel. Holtzclaw squeezed past it along the far side, inspecting it for show.

"Whoa, whoa, whoa!" Bogan grabbed Holtzclaw's arm and pulled him back. Holtzclaw's lantern revealed a pit large enough to swallow up an inattentive miner.

"I near fell in that one myself," said Bogan. "I was pushing a different cart along here, moving some rock out of my way. Well, the track had bent whenever this hole was made, and I didn't see that. The cart flipped over. I had the good sense to not fight it, to let it go. The whole mine cart just disappeared. I never even heard it hit the bottom. A big, heavy thing like that, imagine! Not even a clatter."

Holtzclaw kicked a rock over the precipice. It bounced twice off the sides of the drop. He stood listening for a minute, but no sound reported the depth.

"I leave that cart there to remind me about the hole. Sometimes you get sleepy down here. Only takes one mistake."

Bogan edged past the cart on the opposite side from the pit. They turned down a side passage. Holtzclaw placed his hand against the wall to steady himself. The wall was cool, slick, and damp.

"Is there a spring here?" asked Holtzclaw.

"Springs everywhere. Painter's Creek running over our heads, down the side of Sinking Mountain. All the mountains here are filled with water. It's because there's a layer of some hard stone above us that this tunnel stays dry. The water's got to find a different way to go. Where the water goes, that's where the gold goes, too." Bogan's feet disappeared into blackness and tossed up a sloshing. Holtzclaw waited at the edge.

A rumbling, wheezing sound was followed by a rush of water. The water level in the passage was falling. Already it was low enough that Holtzclaw could step into it without dampening his trouser cuffs.

Bogan was standing beside a rust-covered system of metal, an industrial rendition of an octopus, with long, flat pipes extending in various directions through an open cavern. He was spinning a crank attached to the side of the machine.

"Where does the water go?" said Holtzclaw.

"I'll be blasted if I know," said Bogan. "Through this pipe, I guess, and then down into the mountain. I think the machine was here before the mine. The miners didn't make this cave. Why would they?"

Holtzclaw walked the length of one of the flat arms extending from the humming machine. It was not a simple tube—numerous smaller channels branched from the main and branched again. The machine was very well suited to the purpose of removing water, but Holtzclaw doubted that was its whole purpose.

Bogan stopped twisting the crank on the machine. "It's more scrap metal for you," he said.

"Don't you need it to keep the tunnels dry?"

"Can't keep them all dry, and you couldn't keep all the water out, no matter what you do. Have you seen enough yet to make me an offer on the scrap?"

"Could we return to the surface to continue?" said Holtzclaw. "My eyes are somewhat weak."

"The way I figure it, while I got you down here, I might get another few bucks as a tip," said Bogan. "You know, for being your guide. There's the rails, six pumps like this one—I'll keep the one nearest my diggings—ten mine carts, then the statue, the beds, the huts, the chandelier, all of those cups and pipes and troughs." Holtzclaw raised an eyebrow at the mention of such variety. "You would think there's not much down here, but every tunnel is filled with so many things. Glance up and down the big tunnel, and it might look empty. Look down the side passages, on the other side of the mine cart, and it's like the shelves of a store."

"There is another matter," said Holtzclaw. "To bring all this selection up to the surface, I will need room on land. Space for a camp, a smelting and refashioning operation, even as a staging area for some other reclamation projects in the area."

"So you want to buy the land, too? Couldn't let that happen. I have ten years of digging here."

"I don't mean to buy your diggings. You'll retain the mineral rights to the mountain—at least, the parts of the mountain that are on your own property. I need only the trees, or rather, the earth on which those trees stand."

"Well, my stars, I didn't know that you could just buy and sell the outside and leave the innards. I wouldn't have bought all that up there. Empty, rocky lake? Scrubby trees? What do I care? If you want it, Mr. Holtzclaw, you can have it."

Bogan held both lamps, which provided just enough light for Holtzclaw, bearing down on the rusted pump, to perform his tallies.

Bogan argued over the prices Holtzclaw assigned to the various pieces of scrap, most of which Holtzclaw had not seen, but he said not a word against Holtzclaw's price per acre for the surface land. Holtzclaw regretted not reducing his offer to offset the concessions he was making for scrap iron.

"And what about the mineral rights?" said Bogan as Holtzclaw was completing the contract. Holtzclaw appended a standard clause to the contract, asserting that any minerals to be discovered below the described property would remain the property of Bogan. It was a powerful clause not because of what it asserted but what it lacked. For example, it was not incumbent upon Shadburn to conduct any mining operation or even to let Bogan enter his tunnels. The idea of "below the described property," too, was vague and advantageous to the buyer; gold found inside the mountain, while underground, may be twenty feet higher than a chasm or sinkhole somewhere else on the land. Was this "below" the property, then?

Bogan and Holtzclaw began to retrace their steps out of the tunnels. "Did you see the bats?" said Bogan. "They always come back to the same place every year. If one is missing, it's not because he's found a new home." Bogan held up his lantern three inches from a crevice. Inside was a small, warm creature, softly breathing.

"You're going to wake him up," said Holtzclaw.

"Hasn't happened yet," said Bogan.

At the threshold of the outside, Bogan bid farewell to Holtzclaw and turned back into the mines. Holtzclaw stepped alone into the sunlight, then crossed over the rocky slope again to inspect his new lake. The sun had travelled behind a high ridge of Sinking Mountain and its thick cover of trees, bringing a premature afternoon to the hollow. The cobalt blue water took on a deeper hue.

Splashing in Holtzclaw's lake was a familiar face. The young woman from the spring sat beside him on the fallen tree. Her black and silver hair was dripping wet.

"Hello, Princess Trahlyta," said Holtzclaw. "What a coincidence."

"How is your ankle, James?"

"Well enough to walk on, thank you. How have you happened to come here?"

"I'm making my rounds," she said. "A royal tour."

Holtzclaw chuckled. "And what do you think of this part of your domain?"

"It is an accident of explosions, greed, digging, ruptures, fractures, mixing, melting. That it is also beautiful is very unfortunate."

Holtzclaw was taken aback. His affection for the lake grew into something more tender and wounded. "I couldn't make a better lake myself if I gave it all my effort."

"That is the only way to make a lake in Auraria. They are made by rainwater that has filled an abandoned mine pit, or they are ponds dammed up by a farmer to water his cows. All of them unnatural. A spring should not be made by blasting. It should emerge where it pleases."

"Water has no will," said Holtzclaw, "and I don't have time for philosophizing over it. I'm leaving, and I'd thank you to leave as well. This is private property now. My property."

The princess curtsied, but she did not move.

She was harmless, he thought. There was no need to chase her away. Lot by lot, he would buy all of her domain. It would be his kingdom...or rather, Shadburn's.

His next purchase was halfway back towards town. On the plat map, the property was listed as a small farm containing a cabin, barn, and spring house. As he neared, he was struck by a chill. The weather had turned cold; Holtzclaw wished he had brought an overcoat to guard against the wind. Strange, that an eastern exposure site should be cooler than its neighbors! The suddenness of the chill reminded him of the bathers from the previous night, but the air felt different. The teeth of the wind gnawed at his fingertips, and he shoved his free hand into his pocket. The other hand gripped the walking stick.

Holtzclaw reached a break in a split-rail fence that marked the property; the fence was rimed with frost, a remnant of cold dew. The ground was crisp, and a hundred paces onto the property, Holtzclaw slipped on snow.

The farm resembled a Currier and Ives winter scene, but without the human comforts. No roaring fires or sleds or roasting chestnuts. No smoke puffing from the farmhouse or unseasonable greenery decorating the eaves. The roof of the farmhouse was layered with snow several feet thick, and its walls groaned under the weight. Only a few of the thickest tree branches remained intact, and even these bore a load of ice. A drift of snow had piled against the sides of the barn so high that one could have walked up on to the roof, but once on top, his companions would have been a few chickens, frozen solid. A lean mule roamed the farmyard, digging holes in the snow with a scrawny hoof.

Holtzclaw knocked at the farmhouse, but there was no answer. He braved the icy blasts and continued across the property, searching for the owner. The source of the cold was a small structure in a grove of ice pillars that had once been trees. He recognized this as a spring house. Rural people, lacking iceboxes, dig down several feet around a spring, then build a small hut over their diggings. The roof of a spring house stands three or four feet above the earth, but inside there are eight feet of shelves, filled with turnips, potatoes, hams, apples, peaches, and other produce, between the mud floor and the ceiling. Some even pack up winter ice in layers of straw. As long as the door of the spring house is shut, the dark and damp conditions keep the crops cool.

The door of this spring house had a gaping hole in it. Holtzclaw could not approach to investigate. Looking at the spring house was like turning towards the storm. A well-equipped polar expedition could come nearer, but Holtzclaw was dressed for mild Southern weather. He pressed on to find the owner.

The creek in the rear of the property flowed at a trickle among the ice-covered rocks. A reedy figure dipped a pan into the feeble flow, swirled its contents, and then tipped them out with disgust.

"It's terrible weather we're having, isn't it?" said the man. "Name's Moss."

"Holtzclaw, delighted to meet you. The weather is peculiar to your property, Mr. Moss. Down in the valley, it's a pleasant day."

"Well, don't that beat all. Seems like it's been snowing hard ever since I can remember. It's that spring house, I reckon. Always cold in there, and I know I let it out. It's that door. I'll fix it some day, but I'm always too busy." He held up the pan.

"You mean to say that your spring house is responsible for this blizzard?"

"I wouldn't know any other reason for it. It's cool and shady in there—or was, before that door got left open. Now, it's frozen solid."

Realizing that the conversation was turning against him, Holtzclaw changed tactics, hoping to make a deal; the explanation and solution to this bizarre weather would have to wait. Holtzclaw gestured towards Moss's pan. "How's your luck today?"

"Not so good right now. The funny thing about luck is that it likes to change on you. The more bad luck you get, that's just the more certain you'll get some good luck soon. The Five Forks Creek hasn't given up all that it's got."

At the edge of the creek was a hole cleared in the ice. Moss scratched in it with blue-tipped, clumsy fingers and loosened a few handfuls of half-frozen black mud, which he transferred to his pan and worked with practiced motions. But either the creek was over-zealous in its work and carried away the gold downstream, or, more likely, there was no gold to find in the black mud.

"I have a business proposition that you might consider a turn of luck," said Holtzclaw. "Is there a warmer place we can discuss it?"

"I'm fine here," said Moss.

"Yes, but I wasn't prepared for a blizzard," said Holtzclaw.

"That's a personal problem," said Moss. He was intent on his work.

Holtzclaw shivered again as he watched Moss dip another pan into the creek and wash its contents downriver.

"Do you care to hear my business proposition?" asked Holtzclaw.

"Will it cost me anything to listen?"

"Of course not. I would propose to buy from you, at a fair price, your farmlands and pay immediately in federal notes, or, if you prefer, gold coins." He spoke quickly, hoping to get back to more seasonable weather.

"Buy the farmlands? You want to get in before the harvest. We have a good crop of corn coming up this year."

Holtzclaw had not seen any corn, frozen or fresh. "We can make allowances for future crop yields, structural improvements, and mineral rights."

"You'd buy the gold still in the ground?"

"I haven't seen any gold, but if you had other provable minerals, like coal or iron, those can be considered."

"What do you need my farm so bad for, that you'd just walk up and buy it with coin?"

"It is a convenience, not a necessity. I deal in scrap metal, and we are excavating a few of the abandoned mines here in the Lost Creek Valley. To move the scrap, we need a right-of-way, and it would be easiest to run through the land of your farm." It was nonsense, but it would have been more convincing if Holtzclaw's teeth were not chattering.

Moss did not look up from his panning. "What do you think you'd pay for a place like this? Only because I'm curious."

Holtzclaw began his ritual of tabulation. He may as well have been quoting tonnage rates on cotton or rainfall rates in the desert for all the impact that the figures had on Moss.

"I just couldn't do it," said Moss, interrupting. "One good strike here in the creek and I'd have half again as much as that."

"You've been digging here for how many years? Five? Ten?" said Holtzclaw, his frustrating rushing out. "And what have you found? I don't even seen how there could be gold here. Where would the vein be? How would it wash into the creek? Yet it doesn't stop you from looking. Your crops are dead, your lumber trees are bare sticks, your farm is frozen over because your head was so filled with saw dust that you couldn't remember to fix the door on your spring house—or so you say. Here comes a rare chance, a piece of good fortune such as you haven't had in all your years here. I am offering you gold, man, gold! You can pretend that you found it digging and panning, because it's almost the truth. Instead, you tell me that you're going to keep the property, all this ice and dirt, because you've found nothing."

"Yes, that's why I can't sell, sir. Because I've found nothing yet."

Furious and freezing, Holtzclaw stormed away. How could Moss not take him up on his offer? Of all the owners that Holtzclaw had met, Moss should have been the most eager to sell his worthless, frosted property. And the absence of gold was not evidence of a future reward—that's the gambler's fallacy. But Holtzclaw couldn't persuade Moss by pointing out his irrationalities. Moss lived in the midst of one.

A sheet of snow began to fall upon Holtzclaw's new hat, dampening it. He plotted his next move. It would be interesting to see Moss's change of mind if he were to find a piece of gold on his property. He might redouble his digging efforts, chasing the next nugget, because one is never enough, and work himself into a pneumonia from which the property might be wrested. Or Moss might trade the nugget for a bellyful of drink, and from that state find himself landless.

These possibilities gummed up in the small moral caramel of Holtzclaw's brain: the sweet, sticky morsel that was to blame for occasional sentimentality in difficult situations.

Still, hiding a piece of gold on a man's property—giving him a gold nugget! This could not be considered a crime. It would break the impasse. He could not use a gold coin from his collection. A jeweler could melt one into a convincing lump, but Holtzclaw doubted he could find a discreet accomplice on short notice. Holtzclaw could try melting coins in his fireplace. When would Moss be absent from his creek? Could Holtzclaw endure the wintry blast from the spring house for long enough to plant the nugget a few inches deep?

Holtzclaw had travelled a quarter mile along the road and into warmer winds, before he heard frantic calling behind him. "Wait, sir, wait, wait!" He turned around to see a flushed Moss rushing towards him. "Is the offer still good? Will you still buy?"

"I suppose that in ten minutes, little could happen to the land that would change the offer."

"Everything's changed. I took the luck from it." Moss thrust a piece of metal towards Holtzclaw. It was gold—a thin, reedy piece.

It did not resemble other nuggets that Holtzclaw had seen, which were globular and smooth, like candle wax dripped into a bucket. But however unusual it was, Moss's nugget was larger than a squirrel turd and would be celebrated in the local taverns.

"You found this in the dirt, where you were digging?" Holtzclaw struggled to suppress the excitement in his voice.

"Just about three pans farther down. Hoo boy, it finally happened!"

"And you want to sell now? Your auriferous creek? Your gilded muck and golden sand? Now that you know there's gold there?"

"There's no luck in the land now. You can dig and dig there all you want. You could dig until winter, dig until the creek freezes over, dig until the world freezes over. You're not going to find anything. I knew there was one good strike in that farm, and I struck it, and now I'm going to move on."

"Well, if that is your decision, sir," said Holtzclaw. "As you say, there's no more luck in it. You know you're not selling me any gold, just some land. But land is all I needed, land for the right-of-way. Would you like the sum remitted in federal notes or gold coin?"

"Doesn't matter. I got my gold. You can pay me in notes for the farm. Better for traveling anyway."

Both men were filled with glee—Moss at what he'd found; Holtzclaw at what he hoped to find. And the promise of the land was enhanced by the thrill of success. He'd had never bought a lake and a gold-bearing creek in the same day. Even Shadburn would think it remarkable.

From Moss's farm, Holtzclaw bounded along the shore of the Five Forks Creek, which flowed cool and free outside the influence of the spring house. When the air had warmed back up to its usual temperature, Holtzclaw paused to rest on a fallen tree that extended into the creek. His fingers were chapped, but they were flexible again. The bite of frost at the end of his nose was healed. Nothing could be more splendid except for a bit of something to eat and drink.

He had been hurrying the whole morning, and a dull hunger rumbled in his gut. He should have bought something at the confectioner's shop, but he had been distracted by Abigail, and now he was short on provisions. He would have to stop in town for some sustenance, if he did not want to expire on the road. One of the properties he had to buy was back in town. If he aimed for this one now, he would be able to have a little dinner and not cause too much delay. With everything on schedule, he could afford the slightly circuitous route.

Holtzclaw stopped for a moment on a fallen tree that extended into the creek. He bent down for a handful of water; when he lifted his head, he saw was not alone.

Princess Trahlyta sat on the log beside him, dangling her feet into the flowing creek. She had followed him. She had become a special familiar.

"What is it that you want, little girl?" said Holtzclaw. "Why are you pushing your nose into my business, the business of my employer, the business of those that I choose to do business with?"

"I had a gift for Moss. It's not my custom to give away gold. It does so little good. But this is a special chance."

"You hid that nugget on his land?" said Holtzclaw.

"Gold is not rare, James, it's just shy. It is happiest in the darkness, and it's very angry when it's pulled into the light."

Holtzclaw felt pity for the poor addled girl. Whose money had she given away? Would she be punished? "What did you think you'd accomplish with your gift?" he said.

"Moss is a forgetful man," said Princess Trahlyta. "He wouldn't fix his spring house door. Here, all the mothers say, 'Young man! Close that spring house door! You're letting the cold out! Are you trying to freeze over all of outdoors?' He couldn't be trusted to keep watch on the spring house. He was distracted enough to let his farm freeze over; in time, it would have been the entire valley. He didn't need to own the spring house any longer."

"What will happen when I demolish the spring house? Won't the cold rush out in one burst?"

"There are a thousand springs here in the valley, James, and they don't change our weather. It's only the spring houses, with their shade and cellars, that get so cold. They are an unnatural mark on

the land, and they have unnatural consequences when they are left
open."

Holtzclaw folded his arms. "You're talking as if this explains why
I would find a piece of permafrost in the north Georgia mountains.
Spring house doors are left open by careless children across the
world. Why here, in the Lost Creek Valley, does a springhouse make
a blizzard?"

"Our cold springs have a lunar iciness, because our days have more
moon that most."

"The laws of nature are general, not particular. The sun sets no
earlier in one valley than in another."

"The deeper the valley, the shorter the day," said the princess.
"Higher mountains, longer shadows."

Holtzclaw had not considered this.

The princess slid off the fallen tree into the creek. Water rushed
past her knees. "Moss would have found that nugget, but not for
years. We all would have been so cold."

She had helped him, thought Holtzclaw. It was a strange way to
help—not profitable, certainly. But the money had not been his, or
Shadburn's, and so what was it to him? The end result was just what
he wanted.

"Well, I suppose I should be grateful to you, princess," he said.
"You paid off Moss, got him to sell his property, and now, my employer can now do something useful with that land. We won't let it
go to frozen waste."

"I hope so. Do you want to buy many properties?"

"My employer has charged me to buy several."

"And you want to please your employer?"

"Else he would not long suffer me to be his employee."

"I have employers, too. They always want to be pleased. And they
are not pleased by gold."

"Then they must be even stranger than you, princess. What do
they want instead?"

"They want to leave this valley with less than they came with.
They want a healthful holiday."

"So, they are tourists?"

The princess nodded. "We have good water here."

"Where do they stay? At the Old Rock Falls? It has at least one peculiar inhabitant already. That trick piano."

"Oh, James. It will take you much longer to settle in if you keep fighting with Mr. Bad Thing. You'll never settle in to the valley if you insist on doubting what you see here."

"I don't mean to settle in. I want to finish my tasks and then depart."

"You've already started to settle. You've drunk our water. You saw a boy catch a wild wonder fish from the mist. You've met several ghosts, even tipped your hat to them. You've seen my employers— their bathing habits, their old passages. You shielded your ears from a wind blowing out of a spring house, a wind like you've never felt before. And you were not perturbed. Here we are, having a nice chat."

Holtzclaw leaned towards the creek and brought up another handful of water. He examined it in his cupped palms. It looked like ordinary water, clear and fresh. He sniffed it; a slight metallic whiff, but many springs and resorts praise their water's mineral content. He tasted it, musing over the flavors as he would a fine claret. There was nothing to surprise him here.

"Perhaps these things that you've mentioned are only tricks," he said. "Perhaps they are spirits. Blavatsky's children. It sounded like hokum, but one never knows. It doesn't much matter, does it? My employer's money still spends the same here as it does anywhere. The gold, even better. My purposes are the same, whether a bit of land is covered in sweet potatoes or supernatural frost. I choose not to be bothered, because it will only interfere. There's no profit in being perplexed."

Holtzclaw looked to the princess, to judge her by her face. She seemed happy with his words, but he hadn't meant for them to please her.

"That's a start, James."

The princess left him with a curtsey at the edge of the Five Forks Creek. She sauntered across the flowing face of the water as though it were a paved pathway. It was a curiosity, to be sure, but Holtzclaw repressed any astonishment. Local spirits are bound by land deeds, just like any other soul.

CHAPTER V

Holtzclaw arrived in town ravenous and went straight into the Old Rock Falls Inn in search of dinner. Abigail looked up from her work.

"Well, you are a sight!" she said. "What sort of trouble did you find in your scrap metal dealings?"

Holtzclaw looked down at himself. His boots were caked in mud, his traveling clothes damp and wrinkled. There was a green vegetative stain across the seat of his trousers, left by moss or slime.

"It must have happened when I sat down on a log to talk to someone," he said.

"Who?"

"Oh, no one. A strange girl. I've met her several times along the road. "

"Do you mean Princess Trahlyta?" said Abigail.

"You know her?" said Holtzclaw. "She isn't an actual princess, is she? Maybe she's the daughter of a rich man and thus feels entitled to wander where ever she will."

"I don't think she's anyone's daughter. I've never met her parents, even when we played together when I was small."

"How could that be? Aren't you older than she is? You look to be at least ten years her elder."

Abigail scowled at him. "Even in Milledgeville, it's rude to draw attention to a lady's age."

Holtzclaw was abashed. "I apologize. My confusion is overwhelming my better instincts."

"Things around here take a little getting used to, or so they say. I was born here, so I haven't had to acclimate. Where did you see the princess?"

"She and her strange habits have followed me all over the valley. I saw her up near the Cobalt Springs Lake, and then again at the frozen tundra on Moss's property."

"What were you doing on Moss's farm? No scrap metal there," said Abigail.

"It's part of a right-of-way," said Holtzclaw, quickly.

"To where?"

"I'm afraid I don't have the whole map in my head," said Holtzclaw. "I'm just an agent, and I can't think the best if I haven't had anything to eat. Did you have some hot food on special today?"

"No specials, only ordinaries."

"I would be very content with ordinary."

Abigail left him in his flustered state and returned with a bowl. "It's a sort of stew," she said. "Sweet potatoes, pickled cabbage, turnips, beef fat. We call it a miner's dinner. Nobody wanted to play the cook or gardener while everyone else was working the creeks. So nobody did, and when mealtime came around, they made do. Folks around here got used to it."

"Even the greatest cuisines have humble roots," said Holtzclaw. "French peasant dishes or Italian festival foods. A chef of promise elevates them, and then they are all the rage in the city."

Abigail excused herself to wait on other customers, then vanished again into the kitchen. Holtzclaw had extracted the last of the broth from the bottom of his own bowl before she returned.

"I am surprised that you don't have any help here," said Holtzclaw. "No maid or waiter or cook?"

"My father managed by himself."

"And your mother?"

"My mother was a miner," said Abigail. "Not a hard rock miner. They wouldn't let a woman into the tunnels because there were too many places in the petticoats where a woman could hide gold dust, and it wouldn't be polite to check them all. She worked the gold pans."

"Did she find much gold?"

"You can pan the rainwater coming down the roads here and come up with a few flakes."

"I didn't know one could get rich from rainwater."

"Do we seem rich?" said Abigail. "As I said, it's only a few flakes, which buys you less than a full supper. Almost any work would be better."

"Like tavern keeper?" asked Holtzclaw.

She placed a bottle of claret on the table; Holtzclaw indicated with his fingers that he wanted a small pour. "Still some visits to make this afternoon," he said. "I would prefer to sleep, of course, after eating, but I shouldn't encourage it." Holtzclaw had never napped in his adult life, save during a bout with a lowland fever.

Abigail smiled. "A small glass, then, Holtzclaw."

"Many thanks, Ms. Thompson. How's business?"

"There are enough visitors like you and the turkey men to keep the rooms filled."

"Then profitable?" asked Holtzclaw.

"Are you aiming to be a business partner? You're not the first."

"Just making conversation," said Holtzclaw. "Unfortunately, men like me often turn our conversations into business matters. We can't help it."

"Profits are a very small thing," said Abigail. "Even if the Old Rock Falls had no paying customers, I could keep it going. I'd have to. Our many guests would be displeased if there were no more Old Rock Falls. They might forget the happy hours they've spent here and get into mischief."

She gestured to one of the artifact-covered walls. A dozen daguerrotypes showed the outside of the Old Rock Falls and a parade of different figures standing in front. Holtzclaw recognized a smooth-cheeked Bogan, leaning against a mattock as tall as himself. Moss, too, was there; he held a shovel. A boy wore a gold pan inverted like a hat. His makeshift headwear covered his hair and eyes, but Holtzclaw's interest was piqued by a certain familiarity to his chin.

The daguerreotype that held Holtzclaw's attention the longest depicted the Old Rock Falls at a point of high water. The dirt court in front of the inn had become a frothy river. A number of men stood on the porch and watched the disaster flow past; the women watched from the branches of a huge tree. On one of the lowest branches, dangling her feet in the water, was Princess Trahlyta. Or, if not her, then a mother or elder sister, for the princess did not look much younger in the picture than she did now. The piano had been moved from the dining room to the porch, and an old, bent man sat at the keys. Sitting on top of the piano was Abigail herself, not long out of swaddling clothes.

Most of those pictured in the daguerreotypes clutched some dear possession: a gun, a book, a quilt. Some held the reins of a prized animal. Children held corn-husk dolls or spools of thread or pressed their hands to their sides, having been warned against putting them in their pockets.

"No one is smiling," said Holtzclaw. "Are you sure they're happy?"

"Have you seen anyone smile for a picture? It hurts your cheeks to smile for so long. They are content, at least. Comfortable."

"And you, Ms. Thompson, are you happy, or content, at least? As a tavern keeper?"

"I suppose I am. What other choice do I have?"

"Even if you felt compelled to stay in the family business, you could have forgone the tavern and been a miner, like your mother." Holtzclaw was examining one of the smaller daguerreotypes, which hung crooked on the wall. He straightened it and saw a row of smudge-faced people standing in front of a long rocker box on the shores of a creek. Just as many wore laced-trimmed bonnets and ground-sweeping, homespun dresses as brown bowlers and canvas trousers.

Abigail tilted the daguerreotype of the miners until it hung just as crookedly as before. "My mother spent the entire day in the mountains on our own claim. I'd play in the river while she worked, and we would stay out for as long as there was light and often longer. Mother said that the gold would shine out in the darkness like points of sunlight, but that never helped her find much."

"It's like gambling—all luck," said Holtzclaw.

"No, not luck! For some people, gold is a certainty."

Holtzclaw thought of Shadburn. Even the worst of his projects brought some small profit in the final calculation. He knew just how to pan a nugget from the poorest sand; one quick flick of the wrist, and Shadburn came up with gold. The dam at Canton. A magistrate seeing reason for Franklin's land. The silent partner who had invested in the railway spur when they'd bought the mill race at Baxley. A hard-hearted soldier's change of heart in Fitzgerald.

"But my poor mother," continued Abigail, "might have been three feet from a major vein, six inches from a nugget the size of her fist. Her hand would slide over a stone as she was climbing from a creek bed, and under that very stone was a fortune!"

"How did you know?" asked Holtzclaw.

Abigail looked embarrassed. "To some people, gold is a certainty."

"Do you mean, you could see where the gold was, in the ground?"

Abigail said nothing.

"Well, if that were the case," said Holtzclaw, "you would have told her where to dig, and there would have been no need to earn your living at the Old Rock Falls."

"That's just it, Holtzclaw. I said nothing because my mother was a miner, but why should she be, if we had already found gold? My father was an innkeeper, but why should he be, if we had enough money to provide for us? A person can't find a fortune one day and be the same person the next."

"So, Ms. Thompson, you'd rather that your fellow townsfolk dig for gold but not find any? That's a cruel slavery to wish for them."

"Oh, they could find a little. Find enough to keep them fed and happy. But we are a town of poor diggers, not rich idlers. The only profit my father took was in kindness. It's why we have so many guests here, even if not all of them pay for a meal or occupy a bed. Some just play the piano."

"Oh, there's no piano today!" said Holtzclaw. The silence had not struck him before. The piano was silent in the corner.

"Mr. Bad Thing doesn't get up until four o'clock," said Abigail.

As he left the Old Rock Falls, the door to McTavish's flew open, and the large woman puffed down her front stairs.

"Begging your pardon, Mr. Holtzclaw," said Mrs. McTavish, "I don't mean to intrude. But seeing as how you were on your way again without so much as a 'hallo' to me, I must. See, this came for you. Byers got back from Dahlonega an hour ago and had this with him. I thought you'd be in the Old Rock Falls, so I've been keeping an eye out for you. You've been real friendly with Ms. Thompson instead of eating here, where you're booked. Not that I mind, Mr. Holtzclaw. She's a pleasant young woman and I'm a hairy old bat. I cook a sight better than her, though. Can't trust a matchstick girl to cook."

Mrs. McTavish handed him a folded letter. Shadburn's seal was impressed against the flap, but the seal was broken.

"Did it come to you unsealed?" asked Holtzclaw.

"Yes, it came like that. Byers said the man gave it to him unsealed. It broke when he was fiddling with it and the man said there wasn't time to redo it."

Holtzclaw thanked Ms. McTavish and turned away to read the letter:

Need yr assistance regard railroad. Come to Dah-ga this instant. All land bought? -S

Why did Shadburn need to be so curt? It wasn't a telegram; Shadburn was not paying by the word. The messenger would have carried a letter with several paragraphs written upon it for the same price. Had Shadburn written in full sentences and standard grammar, he might have included some vital information, such as a meeting time, or what sort of assistance was needed, or clues about this mysterious new railroad project.

Holtzclaw bristled, too, at the accusing question mark in "all land bought?" He had visited four properties between yesterday afternoon and this morning. He'd acquired hundreds of acres of land—a cobalt-blue lake, a gold mine, a frozen creek where a gold nugget had been found, or rather, hidden. But these four properties did not make up "all land." With one mark of punctuation, Shadburn turned Holtzclaw's efforts thus far into a disappointment.

The worst of it was the interruption in the work, the delay! While Holtzclaw was gone in Dahlonega, word of his purchases would soon leak to others, and the prices would soar. Nothing could be so important in Dahlonega that it would counter-balance such a fundamental error.

It was all so foolish, so unlike the wisdom that he usually saw from his employer, that Holtzclaw wondered if there hadn't been a mistake. Perhaps Shadburn had meant the letter to go to someone else. At this very moment, a Milledgeville law clerk was musing over the significance of "Dear Holtzclaw, smashing job so far. Keep up the excellent work. I shall trust you to make all acquisitions in a reasonable and prudent time. Take care of your knees and have a good breakfast every morning." But this was a wishful thought.

Holtzclaw decided that he could not leave now. The risk was too great. He would finish out his day—three more properties. That would be seven, enough to stand in front of Shadburn and not be ashamed. If they were the most essential, as Shadburn had claimed, then perhaps the surge in prices would be mitigated somehow. After acquiring the Terrible Cascade, Holtzclaw would find transportation back to Dahlonega. He would have to travel overnight. It was not a prospect that he relished, but he saw no other way to fulfill his employer's command.

CHAPTER VI

The town house that was meant to be Holtzclaw's next acquisition was a flat-fronted, white rectangle with four glazed-over windows, two per story, which did not interrupt the monotony of the edifice. It was distinguished from its neighbors only because it was freshly painted. Holtzclaw could not think why Shadburn considered it an essential purchase.

Holtzclaw knocked on the door twice and stood with his hat already in his hands. A hatless man belongs inside, and the person answering the door is meant to resolve the impropriety by inviting the visitor inside. The door was answered by a rail-thin woman, whose hair was pulled back in a working style. She held a broom, but her boney arms continued so naturally into the handle that it seemed she had straw for hands.

"Help you?" she asked.

"Good day, ma'am," said Holtzclaw. "Could you tell me if Mr. Ignatius Walton is within?"

"I think so," said the woman. "Hold up. Beluhah? Do you know if Mr. Walton is home?"

"I think so," called back a fainter voice from above. "Hold up." A pause. "Cannie says so, but she didn't check with Dan cause he's sleeping."

The first woman returned to the door. "Cannie says so," she said to Holtzclaw.

"Might he be summoned to receive a visitor?"

"Nah, I don't think he'd come down. He's a very busy man, you know."

"I have some very important business to discuss with him."

"Well, if it's important you might come in and find him yourself. He might talk with you. But don't tell him I let you in. If it's not important, he might get mad. I used to try to guess what was important and what wasn't. I let in some people that looked important, but Mr. Walton said they were nothing. I drove off some fellows one night who were lying up a whorl, but Mr. Walton said they were folks he needed to see. Wonder he hasn't fired me. And stars forbid if I tried to clean up around here. Mr. Walton would say, 'Arma, Arma, what do you think you're doing? Don't you know that's an original copy of the birth certificate for King Paul of Poland, gnawed by the very rats that later gnawed his bones?' and I'd say, 'No, sir, I did not.'"

Arma stepped back from the door and admitted Holtzclaw with a sweep of her hand. The plain exterior of the house gave way to an utter chaos of possessions inside. Holtzclaw recognized an abacus, a framed print of a Turkish ruler, and several whittled representations of various produce: a sweet potato, a peach, and a fruit that looked like an eggplant, but fatter. The chief ingredients of the chaos, though, were books and papers. Holtzclaw did not want to remove any of the volumes from the mass—some were load-bearing—but he read a few titles from spines that happened to be visible. *The Medicinal History of Virginia Waters* and *Historical Alabama Resorts.*

An object crunched beneath his feet. Under his heel were the smashed remains of some acorns. "I hope those were not important," he said to Arma.

Arma shook her head. "They were either the last known seeds of the Tree of Life or something the vermin dragged in. And even if I knew which, I still couldn't tell you if they were important or not."

"Mr. Walton would be where?"

"Upstairs, of course. You can see he's not here."

Holtzclaw climbed to the next level, which was no less cluttered than the previous. A full skeleton of a cow was the primary attraction. The cow skeleton was several feet too long, given the ordinary proportions of the animal. Had this unfortunate long cow dwelt upon the earth, then had its anatomy collected as a medical curiosity? Or had the skeleton been assembled post-mortem into a showpiece intended to deceive? Holtzclaw was inclined to believe the latter.

There was no sign of Walton, or any human, on this floor. He must then be in the garret, below the roof. Holtzclaw ascended the stairs and was doubly surprised—first by the enormous round face of a woman too close to his own, then, once he had cleared this inquisitive gaze, by the architecture of the room. It was not a slope-roofed garret, but a squared-off, full-height story identical to those below.

"You the one Arma let in?" said the face. "I'm Beluhah."

"She said that Mr. Walton was upstairs."

"Yes, we all think so."

"But aren't I already as high as I can go? I counted two stories from the outside."

"Well, you know how some houses are," said Beluhah. "They look small from the outside, but they're bigger inside. How were you counting? By the windows? That's not a very good way to count. What if someone forgot to put in a window, or put in an extra one? I had some neighbors once that made up a passel of fake windows because they wanted us to think they lived in a ten-story house, as though it would make them better than us because we only had one story and a loft."

"The laws of physics wouldn't permit a ten-story house in the space I observed."

"I can be certain in telling you that this house doesn't have ten stories. That would be too neat and clean for Mr. Walton. Too round! No, he'd want to have one hundred seventeen and a quarter, if he could."

"Could Mr. Walton be up that high?" he said.

"How should I know?" said Beluhah. "I've never been above fifty-five."

The architects of this dwelling hadn't the sense to build one set of spiraling stairs that travelled both upwards and downwards. Instead, they adopted the simpler alternating method, which forced the ascender to cross the entire room every time he wished to gain a story.

Holtzclaw picked his way through the debris of the third floor, which featured an inordinate number of rocks. Limestone, shale, quartz, obsidian, and granite were represented by stones the size of a house cat. Crossed pine branches covered another display. As Holtzclaw walked past, a hissing noise emerged from beneath the branches, and Holtzclaw gave the display as wide a berth as the towering stacks of paper would permit.

A woman named Cannie welcomed Holtzclaw to the next story, which was uncharacteristically empty. The room also felt smaller than the previous ones. It was a trick of the eye, given the emptiness of the floor. Still, Holtzclaw thought that his frames of reference—the windows, the staircases—were nearer each other than they'd been on the first floor.

"Be careful where you step, sir!" said Cannie, and she pointed towards the floor. "Oh, not there! Anywhere but there!" She knelt beside Holtzclaw's shoe and rapped on its toe twice with the knuckle of her index finger. Holtzclaw lifted it and contorted himself into a one-legged pose that enabled him to stoop lower without further moving his feet. The apparently empty surface of the floor was covered with piles of dust. Each of the ten or twelve piles that Holtzclaw could distinguish were different. Here was a blue tint or pinkish hue, large granules or fine-sifted crumbs like flour.

"I think you have stepped right into the arsenic powder and blown it to the four corners of the world," said Cannie. "I don't know I should ever sort it out from the sulfur."

"Such a collection would be better placed in vials or bottles," said Holtzclaw.

"It's not a collection of bottles," said Cannie.

"No, I would imagine that collection is somewhere upstairs."

"Maybe. I've never seen it."

On his tiptoes, Holtzclaw managed to cross the room without further scorn from Cannie. He climbed the stairs, which should not have led anywhere, but found himself in another full-sized story, and across the room was another staircase. It was impossible and astonishing, this proliferation of space under a single roof, yet somehow disappointing, too—it was only more stories in a house. A very modest wonder.

But disbelief would only slow him down. Holtzclaw could shut his eyes, beg for rationality, but this infinite house would still be here, and Mr. Walton would still be inside. Besides, when he convinced Mr. Walton to sign over the property deed, Shadburn would own this house, and it could be demolished if the laws of nature were too offended.

On this higher story, the aforementioned Dan was still asleep. This seemed as impossible as the house itself, for the species of clutter unique to this story was by far the loudest. Musical instruments of all sorts filled the room to the rafters. Dan was sleeping on top of a closed piano. When he turned, he jostled the neck of a banjo, which fell on top of a violin with a painful crash of wood and tuneless ringing. Two rotating musical disks, like one would find in a dingy nickelodeon, competed for supremacy with tinny melodies. Several standing clocks counted off unsynchronized minutes. When one would strike the quarter hour, as happened five times during Holtzclaw's two-minute sojourn across the room, the other musical instruments in the room joined in sympathetic vibration.

As Holtzclaw's head pushed into the higher story, two children looked up from their stations. They sat in an avalanche of paper—maps, deeds, land lottery tickets, stakes, claims, and surveys.

"Would either of you be, by chance, Mr. Walton?" said Holtzclaw.

"I'm Flossie, and he's Ephraim," said one.

"And you wouldn't know, then, the whereabouts of Mr. Walton, owner of this property?"

"We trade a lot of properties," said Flossie. "That's how we pass the time. See all these papers? They're land lottery tickets and maps and deeds. So Ephraim's got his stack, and I've got my stack. And I say, 'Hoy, Ephraim, I will trade to you the Moss farm if you'll give me the Pigeon Roost mine.' And he will say, 'Hoy, Flossie, if you think I'll give you that on face, you are batty. You'll need to add in those bottomlands by the Amazon Branch, and two springs besides, the Lifsey and Taylor Springs.' And I'll say, 'I'll give you the Amazon Branch and the Lifsey Springs. Taylor I want. How about the Wright place?' And he'll say, 'That's nothing but twenty acres of cut-over woodland.' And I'll say, 'Then we'll have a whole new deal. For the Pigeon Roost mine I'll give you the deed for the Terrible Cascade, all the way from the Sky Pilot's down to the Beaver Ruin.' And he'll say, 'You can't give me that cause I already own it. I got it from you two weeks ago!' And I'll say, 'Show me!' And we both go digging in our papers. Turns out that I did own the Terrible Cascade, just like I said, because he sold it to me for the Pigeon Roost mine two days ago!"

"You mean to tell me you own all that?" said Holtzclaw. "Or Mr. Walton owns all that?"

"Well, he has maps and papers and tickets," said Flossie. "But he doesn't live on it."

"If you have the right papers, then you own the land. It doesn't matter who lives on it."

This made Flossie turn pensive. Still, Ephraim did not avail himself of the chance to get in a word.

"Can I see your game pieces?" If they were real, he could buy the whole valley right here in this room.

Flossie handed over a few sheets of paper. They looked very old, and Holtzclaw didn't recognize the signatures. Important survey notes were missing. Perhaps they were original deeds that had since been surpassed by more accurate records. It would not make sense for all of Auraria's deeds to be here. They were too precious. Their owners would keep them, or they would be filed in the county seat. They would not hold in court as a mark of ownership.

He gave them back to Flossie, who clutched them close to her heart. Still, there was a great deal of paper, and some of it could be useful. Maybe somewhere here was a deed or two, or even old maps that would offer leverage in property disputes. Perhaps Walton could just sell him the room, as a whole, and he could peruse the contents at his leisure, after getting back from his nighttime trip to Dahlonega.

On the next story, Holtzclaw was met with a collection of chairs, which he found far less interesting than the land deeds from below. All the chairs were scratched, and dusty. Most had seats woven from corn husks. One of the chairs, a rocker beside the window, was filled with a large woman who called herself Gertie.

"Mr. Walton?" said Gertie. "He's downstairs. In the cellar."

Holtzclaw teetered on the edge of an apoplectic fit. "You must be mistaken. The others told me upstairs!" said Holtzclaw.

"No, I am quite certain," said Gertie.

"I shouldn't go just a little higher and ask Hiram or Immajean or Jessie?"

"Well, we haven't seen Hiram in ages. I think he's been lost. The rest would just tell you the same as me. Mr. Walton is downstairs. He said he was going to the cellar, and that was hours ago, and we haven't seen him come back up since."

"Hadn't I better check just a few stories, just to see if he's right above?" said Holtzclaw.

"What's a few stories? Two, eight, thirty-six?" said Gertie.

"How many could there be?"

"I don't know. I've never been higher than forty-four. That one is pretty tiny. I couldn't fit myself up the staircase past that. You know the rooms get smaller, right?"

Holtzclaw had noted that on Cannie's story, and Gertie's felt smaller yet; the windows were half a pace nearer each other.

"So you say that I should go back down?"

"I would insist on it." Gertie rose from her chair and stepped in front of the ascending stairs.

There was nothing for it. He descended the staircases and crossed the rooms again, past Flossie haggling with the still-silent Ephraim, past sleeping Dan and his cacophony, past Cannie hunched over a pile of powder and holding her breath, past Beluhah rearranging the limestone, shale, and quartz boulders, and past the skeleton of the long cow.

When he reached the ground floor, Arma was surprised to see him so soon.

"I climbed as high as Gertie," said Holtzclaw, "but she told me that Mr. Walton had gone downstairs."

"Gertie is a rotten liar!" said Arma.

"Still, hadn't I better check the cellar?" protested Holtzclaw.

"You'd be the worse for it. It's dark down there, and for every floor we've got up here, they've got two down there." But Arma did not bar his way.

Holtzclaw descended the stairs into the first level of the cellar and, in the twilight, blundered into a small, soot-covered man. His thready hair hung past his ears, and his collar was uneven—turned up on one side but folded over on the other.

"Hullo, there, can I help you?" said the grubby man.

"I am hoping against hope that you can tell me, please, where I can find Mr. Walton, and that you are not a Zebulon or a Bertram," said Holtzclaw.

"Then I am pleased to tell you that I'm Walton. I'd just popped down to select a bottle for afternoon refreshment. Would you care to join me?" Walton held out a magnificent claret, of a vintage that belonged to a nobler century.

"Nothing would give me more pleasure," said Holtzclaw, not believing his luck.

Walton sat down on one of the stairs and, using a field knife from his boot, hacked off the corked end of the bottle. The glass neck flew into a dark corner. Walton pulled a large mouthful of the rare and ancient claret directly from the bottle then passed it to Holtzclaw. "Careful where you put your lip! Sharp edges," said Walton.

A desecration! Such a wine should be enjoyed with all the proper ceremony and respect: the glass, the temperature, time to breathe, the proper chamber, the proper attitude. To drink claret still cool from the cellar, sitting on a dirty stoop, in subterranean half-darkness, was a horror. Holtzclaw would have been content even with a champagne flute. He felt an emotion that others would call anger begin to rise towards his face.

Still, he took the bottle and drew his own mouthful of the claret. It was symphony of mature flavors. Yet how much more harmonious if given a stage, rather than a streetcorner!

"It's good, sir," said Holtzclaw. So good that Holtzclaw contemplated a rash act—he could flee with the bottle, present it at the Old Rock Falls Inn, and enjoy it seated in a chair, in Abigail's not-unpleasant company. A quick hop over Walton, past the deceitful Arma, and he'd be out the door before anyone would be inclined to pursue.

Holtzclaw's fugue was broken by Walton's snapping fingers. He wanted another drink. Holtzclaw handed the bottle back.

"So, you've spent an hour finding me," said Walton. "What is it that I can do for you?"

Holtzclaw explained his mission—the acquisition of scrap metal from certain mines in the area.

"Why, I have a great deal of scrap metal myself," said Walton. "Not for sale, of course, but you might appreciate it as much as I do, if you are dealer. It's upstairs somewhere. Would you like me to show you?"

"No! No, thank you. I have a tight schedule today, and I'm afraid I'm already behind. I am inquiring if you are interested in selling your dwelling here. It would make a suitable and spacious temporary headquarters for my operation."

"This place is cramped," said Walton. "Above one hundred floors, the space is fit only for thimbles and thread. I think it is a fundamental flaw of the vertical model. A problem of gravity."

"I should think that fifty floors or fewer would suffice for my needs," said Holtzclaw.

"And what possessions do you have to offer me, in return for my house?" said Walton.

"Well, there is a certain standard formula for these transactions. We consider the dimensions of the property, apply certain transformations and regularizations, and the result is a dollar value that I can offer."

"That is all one possession, merely differing in quantity," said Walton. "Dollars! I have dollars already. I have a room with dollars from every year that they have been printed. What else do you have?"

"I have some of unusual gold coins," said Holtzclaw.

"That is more interesting," said Walton. "People here love gold coins. They want to keep them in their own pockets and not trade them with me."

"Then I will pay you in gold coins."

"Again, you are speaking about quantities, not diversities, Mr. Holtzclaw," said Walton. "Show me the coins that you have."

Holtzclaw opened his satchel and withdrew the bag of coins. He held it out to Walton, who reached in and pulled out one coin at a time. After inspection, he placed the coins in groupings on a higher step.

"These are all Harrison Brothers' coins!" said Walton. "You know the story, yes?"

Holtzclaw thought it wisest not to answer, but to take another sip of the magnificent claret.

"Thirty years ago, in better times," said Walton, "the Harrison Brothers minted their own coins, right here in Auraria, from the local gold. They only did it for a few years before the federals came in and confiscated the Harrisons' stamps. Such a travesty! The brothers would have resisted, if they had found a way to profit, but I think they saw the raid as a relief. They could quit without shame."

"How could they not have profited on gold, of all things?" said Holtzclaw.

"The miners and panners wouldn't tolerate any metal lost in minting, and they wouldn't pay any exchange fees. Could you blame them? They'd sweated for every flake. And the folks here in Auraria still cling to those coins in their tight fists. They won't give them up. I don't have a one here, among my things. How did you get so many?"

Holtzclaw told the truth, seeing no value in a lie. "They came from my employer, who has authorized me to spend them as needed."

"Here's a one dollar, two dollar, three dollar, and a five, ten, and twenty, all stamped with the same month! That's clever. And if you'll notice, here's four one dollars, siblings of sequential years. What lovely pictures, too! Did you know that the Harrisons stamped a groundhog on their two dollar piece? The younger Harrison loved groundhog. Who doesn't? Good and greasy, wipe it off your chin. Lovely. Do you have a groundhog coin in there?"

Holtzclaw inverted the bag of gold coins onto the floor, and both men rummaged through them. After a few minutes, Holtzclaw held up two coins that featured a crude groundhog stamped on the obverse.

"I only need one," said Walton, "and this is the finer of the two. So, these coins then, for the house and lot?" said Walton.

Holtzclaw added up the face value of the coins Walton had selected. It was a fine deal, very fine. If Holtzclaw considered the square footage of the structure, the deal was legendary—how could one put a price on infinity?

"If you are sure, I will draft a deed," said Holtzclaw.

"It will be an opportunity to get more space for my possessions. A warehouse all on a single floor. Acres and acres under one roof. I could have an indoor railroad that would carry me about to different departments. Wouldn't that be nice?" Walton's face radiated pleasure.

Holtzclaw executed a bill of sale; Walton signed with an elaborate flourish.

"And Mr. Walton, one more matter. Like you, I am a collector. I have a personal collection of documents. Your Ephraim and Flossie guarded some that I should like to have for my own curiosity. Maps, land lottery tickets, old surveys, et cetera. As your future plans include relocation, would you see fit to sell any of those papers, one collector to another?"

Walton mused. "What would Ephraim and Flossie play then? They do so love their trading game."

"With their bickering over territory, they might like chess. Or they could have a spelling game out of blocks. Flossie has many words to share with Ephraim."

Walton shook his head. "I cannot do it, Holtzclaw. I cannot sell any of my possessions, I am afraid," said Walton.

"You did sell the house," said Walton.

"That is not a possession. It is just a place to keep them. A possession must be movable, because if you leave it behind, it is no longer in your possession."

This rich man had no more sense than Moss raving about taking the luck from the land. Holtzclaw tucked the land deed into his traveling bag, alongside the others. Such papers did not need aphorisms to make them valuable.

After leaving the Walton tower, Holtzclaw headed for the town's druggist. He needed a remedy that would reinforce him through the last two properties that he had to visit before sundown. While Holtzclaw's feet were accustomed to walking—his occupation compelled him to travel many miles, and not all of them on horseback or stagecoach—his knees were not accustomed to the mountains. A mile on a fifteen degree slope, whether ascending or descending, required as much strength as a dozen miles in the level Wire-grass or pine barrens. Walton's steep staircases had only exacerbated his condition, and now he suffered from an acute ache that would slow him down if it weren't addressed with medicine.

Entering the druggist's shop, Holtzclaw was further surprised to see that the store contained, not an array of frog's eyes and bat tails and pine bark and other folk remedies, but a fine selection of *ars medica* in colored bottles and vials, and in front of them a man in a broad mustache.

"Something for the barking dogs, eh, stranger? Well, you're no stranger here. My name's Emmett, and you are?"

"James G. Holtzclaw."

"Welcome, Jim!"

"This is your store?" said Holtzclaw.

"Yes, my very own," said Emmett.

"Do you own the building?"

"Ah, no I do not. I would rather put my money and my efforts into the aid of my fellow man. No, the building belongs to the doctor."

"The doctor? Is that an honorific or an occupation?"

"Doc Rathbun, and he's a real doctor. Looks at your bones and everything. Sends me patients. We work well together. The barber will look at your aches and pains, too, but the doctor and I don't get on so well with him."

"I suppose your connection with an actual man of science somewhat explains your selection of wares," said Holtzclaw. "Given your rural location, I had expected to see some more rustic offerings in your store. Witch hazel or what have you."

"Some of it's pure and true. A sprig of ginseng will do you good! Smash up some ginger and put it up the backside of a mule, and he'll run like lightning. Nothing fake about that. Can't fool a mule!"

Now Emmett leaned in close to the counter, lowering his voice as if to avoid being overheard, although there were no others in the store.

"Jim, there's some pumpkins of good in those cures. But folks around here aren't going to buy them from me, and why would they? A fellow says, 'Emmett, I don't need to buy any ginseng from you. I can go out in the woods and get as much as I like; it's just lying around.' Well, it's not as easy as that, but I don't argue with him.

I say, 'Fellow, you're right! You don't need that common stuff. You need Dr. Pep's Double Cure! Two blended medicines for all your complaints. Insomnia, sleepiness, fevers, chills, headache and heartache, ruddy complexion or paleness in the cheek. And that same fellow, he'll buy that right away. Comes in a pretty bottle that he can put a daisy in for the missus. Nice label on it that proves all of what I'm saying. I get them printed down in Gainesville. And what are those two medicines that a fellow paid me fifty cents for? Well, Jim, I'll tell you. It's ginseng and clear liquor. Ginseng to cure 'em, and liquor so they like it."

"So, you're fooling your customer?"

"What's fooling? He gets better; he's happy. I get paid; I'm happy. The missus gets a flower vase; she's happy."

"But he could have just found some ginseng in the woods."

"Ginseng doesn't cure like Dr. Pep! Ginseng doesn't have a label."

"And would Dr. Pep help my pained knees?"

"Dr. Pep would do most anything for you if I told you it did," said Emmett, "but I think the hog may be out of the sack on that one. For you, friend Jim, I would prescribe the scientific cure. I have an excellent and popular substance for which I am the sole local supplier. Effervescent Brain Salts! Good for pained parts, but where it shines is in the mind. Cures mental enervation and excitement, excessive study, mania, and over-brainwork. Says so on the label." Emmett tapped it in front of Holtzclaw's nose.

"I suppose I'll try it," said Holtzclaw.

"You won't be disappointed, and if you are, I'll tell you why you're wrong. Shall I wrap it up for you, or will you be taking the remedy now?"

"Wrap it up, please. I'll take it farther on the road."

As Emmett wrapped his purchase, Holtzclaw studied a gorgeous lithograph hanging on the wall, which showed a smiling man in an Egyptian headdress. The man in the image held a red tin that depicted the same smiling face. Behind him, three Pyramids rose like mountains from a desert landscape. Golden letters proclaimed the name of the product.

"What's Pharaoh's Flour?" said Holtzclaw.

"Why, Pharaoh's Flour is the best I have, and it has the best speech, too. Let me give it, and see if you don't leave with a tin or a wagon full." Emmett cleared his throat and began to speak before Holtzclaw could protest. "Pharaoh's Flour! The laughing face of Amenhotep III promises the highest quality flour, used for millennia by pharaohs and queens and your very own mother. Its natural sweetness is discerned by even the choosiest tongue. Rolls are fuller and crusts are crisper. Of the last ten winners at the Great World Exhibition of Culinary Arts, all ten chose Pharaoh's Flour. But it's not only for the kitchen! Pharaoh's Flour is used in locks to help an old key turn and in door hinges to eliminate creaks. Scatter half a box in front of a heavy chest, and it will slide along the floor, just as the ancients moved the Pyramids' great stones. Pharaoh's Flour is most useful in the marriage bed—but you already know that, you clever girl! Mix Pharaoh's Flour and water into a pure paste that can plug insect holes or even repair a leaky roof or sinking boat. To ward against nighttime thieves, scatter fresh Pharaoh's Flour around your rooms and in the morning look for footsteps leading to the guilty. Poured onto dirty snow, Pharaoh's Flour will restore the look of a virgin winter's night. Pharaoh's Flour, brushed onto lilies, saves their springtime freshness until summer's end. Pharaoh's Flour has a fresh, sharp scent to drive away all evil spirits and malicious ghosts from the corners of your home. Other brands have no command over shadows of the dead. Use Pharaoh's Flour for divination and fortune-telling—consult the forms designed by scattered grains. Like sand sculpted by the wind, Pharaoh's Flour holds ancient secrets. Pharaoh's Flour promises the full fidelity of your husband and the eternal good behavior of your children—not only because the delicacies that you create with it can never be forgotten, but also because Pharaoh's Flour bakes into every cake and pie the ancient spells and curses with which the pharaohs guarded their undisturbed homes and descendants into Eternity. And the ancient spells and curses, once guarded by the wise and wealthy, are now available in your kitchen. Pharaoh's Flour! On every grain dances an ancient maiden. Pharaoh's Flour! At every reputable store."

Emmett made a little bow, and Holtzclaw conceded that it was an excellent speech. "How much does such a wondrous product cost?"

"What a crass question! I should take offense. How much is purity worth to you, Jim? What price do you put on freshness, taste, and ancient secrets? A thousand men died to protect these secrets, Jim, and ten thousand to bring them to the light and put them into tins in my humble shop! If I said a dollar a pound, you would still gladly pay it. But for you, it is fifty cents, and I couldn't sell it for a penny less, not even to my own mother."

It was a foolish price for flour, but not all flour comes with ancient maidens or elaborate speeches. After so much effort on Emmett's part, Holtzclaw would have felt abashed not to buy. "Well, I'll take a pound then, along with my Effervescent Brain Salts, even though I don't need it weighing me down."

"Why, you won't even feel it. A pound of Pharaoh's Flour is light as a feather."

"Spoken like a consummate salesman," said Holtzclaw. Emmett beamed.

CHAPTER VII

Holtzclaw's next acquisition, the next-to-last of the day's essential properties, was a place called the Amazon Branch, a fork of one of Auraria's many waterways that all flowed into the Lost Creek itself. When he arrived on the property, he found it deserted. A stone chimney rose up from a scorched place. The owner's cabin must have burned recently.

Blast it! thought Holtzclaw. He should have done reconnaissance before hiking out here. Had the owner died in the cabin fire? Nearly everything on Shadburn's map had been out-of-date—so, too, was the information about the Amazon Branch. Without giving too much away, he could have asked Abigail or the garrulous Emmett for confirmation, but he'd been in too great a hurry, and now, he'd wasted a trip.

Holtzclaw's head ached, as did his feet. He began to make a circuit around the property, to see if there were some signs as to how he could rescue this mission from failure. The land sloped downwards and met a pleasant brook that crossed through the property. It was shallow, clear, and fast—all excellent for the thirsty traveler. He remembered the cure he'd bought in the druggist's. Holtzclaw took a draught of water, then a capful of Effervescent Brain Salts. It was sweet but with the sharp, metallic bite of carbonation. The salt crystals hissed and popped inside his mouth. The taste was lively, in a way more literal than is usually meant, and he did not dislike it.

His field of vision flashed with green light, and there was a rush of bubbles in his ears. He blinked the occlusion away, but not every point of light faded. In the creek, a thousand points of yellow brightness lit up in the electric flicker. Holtzclaw would have recognized gold even if Auraria had another name and reputation. Perhaps he'd taken too great a draught of Effervescent Brain Salts, or maybe the water was not as fresh as it tasted. But these questions were lost in the sudden wonder of gold.

What luck, then, that Holtzclaw now possessed a genuine Auraria hat, whose special genius was its inner gold pan! It would be a shame if the hat were used only for its sartorial potential. He waded a few steps into the creek, balancing on flat stones that broke from the surface of the water. He bent down and collected a handful of gravel and mud, which he then carried back to the bank and deposited into his inverted hat. Then, grasping opposite sides of the brim, Holtzclaw lowered the hat into the stream. A few of the smaller stones floated, and the mud swirled below the brim, but little else happened. Holtzclaw supposed that shaking was required, so he shook the hat to and fro, first below the water, then above it. This was less effective than the plunge. Holtzclaw stirred the mud and gravel with his fingers, cupping the bowl of his hat with his other hand. That felt even less useful. But he persisted through his ineptness, because the yellow flakes winked at him like so many alluring eyes.

"This is private property!" called a woman's voice from behind him. Holtzclaw whirled and saw a tall, slender woman in a riding suit. Her golden hair was drawn back and capped with narrow-brimmed straw hat, encircled by a blue and white ribbon. She wore boots, gloves, long sleeves, and a high collar. Her face was shaded by her hat, and a small glimpse into the shadow revealed deep-set, dark eyes.

Holtzclaw felt a pang of lapsed decorum. He should have doffed his hat for the lady, or at least tipped it, but Holtzclaw was not wearing his hat; it was filled with mud.

"I stopped for a drink, you see, and something was gleaming in the river," he said.

The woman's face softened, and between the narrow red fissure of her lips, Holtzclaw saw perfect teeth. "I shouldn't been too concerned," she said. "It doesn't look like you know what you're doing. At best you would have carried away a few rocks, and my creek would have been cleaner."

"I confess that, by trade, I'm not a miner."

"What is it that you do?"

"My name is James G. Holtzclaw, and I'm an agent of the Standard Company. My chief tasks here involve preparation for the extraction of scrap metal."

"Scrap metal?"

"Yes, old narrow-gauge from the mines, ore carts, pumps, stamps, weights, and the like."

"Has metal become so rare that you'd rather have it covered in rust than fresh-melted from the earth?"

"Ah, but that requires miners, purification, and refinement. It's sometimes better to obtain metal already worked, even if decades old."

"Oh, you do go on, Mr. Holtzclaw," said the woman. Holtzclaw recognized her well-practiced tone from conversation circles. It was a manner of speech cultivated to betray neither interest nor boredom.

"We have no one here to make introductions, thus I'm afraid I will not learn your name," said Holtzclaw.

"It's Elizabeth Rathbun," she said, "or, now that we're introduced, Lizzie."

"Are you a relation of Dr. Rathbun?"

"His daughter."

"Is he the owner of this property, the Amazon Branch?"

"No," she said. "It's mine."

Holtzclaw fidgeted with his cufflinks. "Well, then, it's good luck that I found you here, since you're the owner of the land. I must speak with you regarding a business proposition. As I said, I'm an agent of the Standard Company..."

"You looked such a fool panning a few minutes ago," said Ms. Rathbun. "Shall I show you how it's done?" Holtzclaw, silenced, gave over his hat.

First, she plunged Holtzclaw's hat into the river and emptied it of its prior contents. Then, scrabbling at the bank with her gloved hands, she packed the hat with black sand. A few steps down the creek, she located a still eddy of water formed in the shadow of a rock. She lowered the hat into the water, but did not submerge it. Water swirled in counter-clockwise circles inside the crown of the hat, catching the lightest material. Ms. Rathbun dipped the hat into the water again, and the worthless sand from the upper layers floated away. Holtzclaw's eyed followed.

Again and again she worked the pan, her movements becoming more delicate as the material that remained was washed down to no more than a spoonful. Her last circling motions were only subtle turnings of the wrist, but these were the most glorious; they revealed a few shining drops of gold in Holtzclaw's own hat.

Ms. Rathbun, flushed, returned the hat to Holtzclaw. "This is called powder gold," she said, "because each flake is so small. Each flake is called a color. It would take four times ten thousand colors of powder gold to melt an ounce of free gold. And in your hat, you have ... eight. Eight colors."

"But there's gold here? In this creek?"

"There is gold in every drop of water. Gold in the lakes, gold in the seas. If you were to pan your bathwater, you might see a color or two. There aren't many places where panning is worth your while, though. Here, it's too much work for too little reward."

"You are quite knowledgeable, Ms. Rathbun," said Holtzclaw.

"I wish I wasn't. It's impossible not to know about these things in Auraria. I can't make a living on the Amazon Branch as a gold panner, and if I tried to take a little money from it, the cost would be much ravaging on my poor hands. They are not hands meant for work, are they, Holtzclaw?"

She took off one of her gloves, which she had not removed even when panning. From wrist to fingertip, her hand was a soft, unblemished white. Her palm and the back of her hand were distinguishable from each other only by the curve of her fingers.

"And what is it that you should want money for, Ms. Rathbun?"

"I want to leave," she said. "Auraria is a sad place, an old place. Where is it that you come from, Holtzclaw?"

"My offices are in Milledgeville," he said.

"Ah, the old capital! I hear that it is so much more dignified than Atlanta. Better people. Older money. Do they have fancy-dress galas there? Do women color their faces and have gowns without sleeves? And do you go as well, Holtzclaw, with shoes polished so well that they shine like the moon?"

"You have romantic words for it, but yes, every night there is some occasion for dancing. Not every evening is as fine as another, but often they are quite enchanting."

"Oh, I should like to be a part of that," said Ms. Rathbun. "But I'm tied to this land, and in any case, I have no money of my own with which to establish myself."

"I might then be of some assistance to you on both accounts." Holtzclaw opened his purse where he kept the Harrisons' gold coins. Ms. Rathbun's eyes brightened, reflecting the color inside.

"I would need enough for travel expenses," she said, "and several months lodging and board at a reputable guest house."

"My conscience would not permit you to leave with less than sufficient for your comfort," said Holtzclaw. She wanted to sell. He needed to find her price.

"Add to that enough for a ball costume, from shoes to gloves, even if modest."

"I would think you would need at least two or three different outfits," said Holtzclaw.

"Perhaps even a few more, and some jewelry besides, so as not to appear impoverished at these galas. I have to overcome the natural disadvantage of my rural education."

"Four outfits, then?" That would be enough for a fine lady.

"Seven! Seven outfits! Because there is a ball every night of the week, and it would be improper to repeat within the same week, wouldn't it? The other ladies would know, and I would be quite embarrassed. There's a singer ... what's his name? Dasha Pavlovski? A perfect Old World charmer. If he comes to town for a spectacle at the odeon, I would need suitable clothes."

"Then seven outfits." Holtzclaw added another line to a running total that he was creating on a sheet of ledger paper. He realized he was tallying her expenses, not the features of the property.

"And how do the ladies amuse themselves when not at a gala?" asked Ms. Rathbun.

"They play faro or dominoes," said Holtzclaw. "But we've started these negotiations incorrectly..."

"I have a set of dominoes, but they are made from cow bones! Can you imagine? It would be a laughing stock," said Ms. Rathbun. "Would I not need a set of ivory dominoes?"

"Why, every woman in Milledgeville already has a set."

"Then you would put me at the mercy of the charity of others? I suppose I should beg my own food, then, too. My sole word in defense of my character would be that my patron, Mr. Holtzclaw, did not provide me with enough."

"No, do not say I am your patron, nor the Standard Company. Tell the truth—that you are a woman of means from Auraria, who came by her wealth in honest dealings over land."

Holtzclaw then quoted a price for her land that did not seem extravagant until it left his lips, and then he could not make the words die from the air.

Ms. Rathbun smiled despite herself. "Oh my, what a generous offer."

The ache returned to Holtzclaw's head; the cure of the Effervescent Brain Salts had been too short-lived. "Well, you have a new life to start in the old capital of our fair state," he said, "and starting a life cannot be done with pennies."

Shadburn had warned him countless times against the traps that sellers lay for buyers: social entanglement, pity, and nostalgia. Did this land deserve a higher price because its owner was young and beautiful? Was a farm worth more because its owners were poor? Was a homestead that reared a dozen children more valuable than if a bachelor owned those acres? No! But Holtzclaw had been snared. He'd paid an exorbitant price for the Amazon Branch, and paid not with his own money, but with Shadburn's.

At least, Holtzclaw consoled himself, the money would go towards that establishment of a new star in the Milledgeville social heavens, and not into the pocket of a hoarding miser. She was quite beautiful.

Deeds were signed, because Holtzclaw could not turn back on his word. He counted out stacks of bills and coins that left his purse much lighter than moments ago. The weight of the new deed was small compensation.

"Well, now you can pan as much gold as you'd like," said Ms. Rathbun. "Best of luck, Holtzclaw."

Holtzclaw had no hat to tip as Ms. Rathbun strode away. It was sopping wet from its bath in the river and still held eight colors of gold. The flakes looked pathetic compared to the wealth that he had surrendered. But these eight colors were gold—real money. He couldn't let them float away.

Holtzclaw tried another dose of Effervescent Brain Salts, mixing them with creek water from the Amazon Branch. No green light filled his vision, but as he drank, he heard a splashing noise. He did not need to raise his head before greeting the princess.

"Are you the Amazon after which this branch is named?" said Holtzclaw to Princess Trahlyta.

"No, that's an old legend," she said. "Some mining party was attacked here by a woman wielding an ax. A prospector lost his head."

"I can't see it, princess."

"You're right, an ax is not in my nature. Besides, one was not needed to separate your head from your shoulders, James. Ms. Rathbun did that rather nicely."

"I suppose she did. My employer will be put out, but then, he usually finds some cause to be put out, no matter how much good I do for his enterprise. At least, I managed to get her land."

"What have you bought, James? A woman's name on a piece of paper. How do you know it was hers to sell?"

Holtzclaw blanched. "I'll sort it out," he said. "It can be done. There are courts. Lawsuits. Social pressure. I will at least be able to get my employer's money back. It's one small part of the valley—perhaps not even an essential one."

"Why do you think your employer wants all this land?" asked Trahlyta.

"It isn't hard to guess," said Holtzclaw. "He would only undertake such a project if there was a promise of tremendous profit. I think he has some new strategy to extract gold."

The princess brightened.

"Yes, so much gold that one bad deal wouldn't wound the final profits," continued Holtzclaw, rhapsodizing. "Imagine some sort of powerful water cannons that would wash away the hillsides and bring minerals down into the river, and a mill that would pulverize the runoff and let us take out the gold."

Trahlyta face fell. She shook her head. "It wouldn't work. Your water cannons would wash away the entire mountain before you carved into the deep deposits. And I can't let the waters be bent to such work."

"I'll do what's asked of me by my employer. If he wants to move a mountain and take out the gold, then I'll make it happen, whether you wish it or not."

The princess mused about this for several moments. She knelt in the creek. The waters rushed past her waist. Her hands scrabbled in the mud before her; she withdrew them and held them up for Holtzclaw, he saw they were covered in flakes of gold, as though they had been gilded by a jeweler. Then, she returned her hands to the water, scrubbed them together, and they were clean.

"To find gold is so simple," said the princess. "Ridding ourselves of it is much more difficult."

Holtzclaw stepped forward. The creek rushed over his shoes, flooding his toes. "Show me how you did that, princess."

"It can't be taught," said Trahlyta.

"It's a trick, then. Sleight of hand. A hidden cache in the river. Are you trying to buy me off, like Moss? Are you plying me with fool's gold?"

"Gold can't help if it's found by a fool. As I said, you'll never settle into this valley if you are always looking for tricks."

"I would vastly prefer if, instead of speaking to me in slogans and sayings, you would tell me the plain truth instead."

"Would you believe me?"

"I would try."

"Let's give it a little more time. Have another drink."

She crossed to the far side of the Amazon Branch, splashing from rock to rock, and vanished into the woods. She moved with a lightness he could not hope to match. His clumsy feet would never catch up.

♣

Leaving behind the Amazon Branch, Holtzclaw headed southwest, to the last property he meant to purchase that day. He heard the land before he saw it; as he approached the Terrible Cascade, his thoughts were drowned by the waterfall.

The Terrible Cascade was a confused tumble of water, a steep series of cataracts rather than a simple drop. The Lost Creek entered a narrow channel, gaining speed and anger as the gorge walls narrowed. Water leapt into space and fell against a jagged line of stones, made more perilous by a pike line of branches and metal detritus. The frothy waters raced for another hundred yards over boulders before crashing into a solid wall of granite, then turned like a hairpin, first to the north and then back to the south. Beyond this turn, the river regained its tranquility, as if all its rage had been shaken out in the journey. In the half-mile that Holtzclaw could survey of the gorge, the waters fell at least two hundred feet. Here was the end of the mountains and the beginning of the spreading lowlands.

At the horizon line of the falls was a hut, and in front of the hut was a man. He was an amalgamation of clothing scraps that were held together by leather straps. Bandoliers supported knives, a bow, a quiver, and a long-barreled rifle. He looked like he was wearing boots, but upon closer inspection, Holtzclaw saw a thick crust of mud that coated his legs halfway to the calf. The man wore a soft hat that shielded both his eyes and the back of his neck.

"Are you the Sky Pilot?" asked Holtzclaw, shouting over the noise of the waterfall.

"That's what I call myself, and other folks picked up the habit," said the man, shouting back.

"What does a sky pilot do? Are you a balloonist?"

The Sky Pilot shook his head. "I would never climb into such an unnatural thing. Doesn't even have wings. A man came through here with a balloon one time. He wanted to take pictures. Thought he could see from up there where some gold was buried."

"Did he see anything?"

"Don't know. He and his balloon fell out of the sky, right into the gorge. The current got his body. They found it two miles down river at the Beaver Ruin. That balloon basket was pinned against some rocks for months, until a freshet broke it up."

"I've heard many stories in your town," said Holtzclaw, "but yours is the most morbid yet."

"Why, I've got half a hundred of them that are worse. What would you like to hear? Folks die in all kinds of ways."

"What I'd prefer to discuss," said Holtzclaw, "is a business matter. My name is James Holtzclaw; I'm an agent of the Standard Company. May we retire to your cabin for discussion?"

"If you like," said the Sky Pilot. "Makes no never mind. It's not any quieter, and that's how I like it."

The Sky Pilot's cabin was little more than a corn crib. The chinking had been removed from between the logs, so that the walls of the structure did little to separate the inside from the outside. Wind and sun blew through the structure, and the roar of the Terrible Cascade below was undiminished. A pleasant consequence of this drafty construction was that the Sky Pilot's cabin did not possess a foul odor. Nature was allowed to sweep it out. There was no chimney nor hearth, nor tables and chairs, nor even a bed. But the absence of such cultural niceties was compensated by a plethora of savage artifacts. A variety of rifles and weapons were suspended on the walls; Holtzclaw was intrigued by one long-barreled gun onto which had been lashed a double-bladed woodsman's axe.

Among the clutter, Holtzclaw could not locate a place to rest. The Sky Pilot sat on the skeleton of a crocodile that had been nailed onto a wooden scaffold.

"Did you kill that crocodile?" asked Holtzclaw.

"Where would I kill a crocodile? This is the Lost Creek, not the Nile. I got it from a roving tinker. I traded him a gorilla skull for it."

"Are these objects part of the trade of a sky pilot?"

"No, just a hobby. A sky pilot's work is to go all the way up to the top of the mountains; I know how to get up there and I know how to get back."

"What do you need at the top of the mountains?"

The Sky Pilot leaned forward. "Ice."

"Ice?"

"Ice."

"Just ice?"

"What's 'just ice?' Everyone needs ice."

"Well, it's only water, is all, of which your valley has plenty. And I've met another man that has no shortage of ice," said Holtzclaw.

"You mean Moss? That's frost, not ice. Frost is what happens with rain and wind and snow. It piles up in drifts. It's a powder. It doesn't stay frozen."

The Sky Pilot approached the corner of his windy crib and cleared away debris and possessions to reveal two wooden strongboxes, made of burled maple with copper ornaments, that were much finer than their surroundings. Inside, protected by layers of straw and blankets, were cubes of ice. They measured a handspan in each dimension, and each surface was as smooth as if cut by a jeweler. The ice had no internal blemishes and only the faintest color. It was truly fine ice. But, it was still just ice.

"In the other box?" asked Holtzclaw.

"Ice, too," said the Sky Pilot. "But a different ice." He did not open it.

Holtzclaw broke the stillness. "I did say that I had some business to discuss. It is a matter of land. I represent the Standard Company, and we have a potential interest in the property that you own. I had wondered if you had considered the possibility of making your land available to me for purchase."

"What do you need a place like this for?"

Holtzclaw could not think of a reason that corresponded to his cover story—nor any use at all. The property was no good for transportation, since the Terrible Cascade was unnavigable. Agriculture was impossible and mining unsuitable, given the proximity of the water table. The Terrible Cascade's sole advantage was as a geographical oddity—it was the neck of the valley, given the narrowing of the watercourse, the high walls of the gorge.

Holtzclaw told the Sky Pilot a slanted truth. "I don't know why my employer wants the property. I'm a lower man, a functionary, and I'm not always told the full truth. My employer says, 'Buy, Holtzclaw!' and I buy."

"I am glad I don't have an employer," said the Sky Pilot.

"It's not a curse," said Holtzclaw. "He's a good man, a visionary."

"I'm sure."

"If you sold your lands here, Mr. Sky Pilot, you could afford to buy some other lands. Better hunting grounds."

The Sky Pilot shook his head back and forth. "I don't believe I would give up this place."

"Your land here is not vital to your profession," said Holtzclaw. His voice betrayed more urgency and weariness than he wanted. "Your ice comes from somewhere else. Your catfish hunting is done somewhere else. If these are pursuits you wish to continue, even once you have a good supply of funds, then you could continue them in more comfortable surroundings."

"Makes no never mind," said the Sky Pilot.

"Do you have some special connection to the cascade? Were you raised here?"

"It's the meanest waterfall in all the world. Plug-ugly. If I never saw it again I wouldn't cry."

"Then what is your attachment? Why will you not even listen to my offer?"

"I have a friend here. He lives in a cave down in the gorge. He means no harm to anyone."

Holtzclaw nodded. "And your friend wouldn't move? He can't be very comfortable in a wet cave."

"He has lived in the same place for as long as I've known him. I think the cave suits him."

"Do you think I can talk with your friend?"

The Sky Pilot thought for a very long time. He closed his eyes and dropped his head. Holtzclaw was at first worried that the man had fallen asleep, and then that he had expired, but just as Holtzclaw was contemplating reaching out his hand, the Sky Pilot stirred.

"No, I don't believe that you should talk with him," said the Sky Pilot. "I think that you had best leave."

"I didn't mean to offend you, sir. I speak for my employer, and I'm endeavoring to complete my duty to him. Please, let's talk a little longer."

"I don't care," said the Sky Pilot. "It is a rotten duty if you need to disturb my friend. Now, please leave."

"I have federal notes, real money..."

"Nope."

"How about gold? Local coins with pictures of groundhogs and bathing beauties?" Holtzclaw fumbled in his traveling satchel and pulled up a handful of the bright metal.

"I don't care a whit about it. Gold is not my friend. It has no songs."

"What do you mean, no songs? Gold can keep the piano playing all night."

The Sky Pilot shook his head again. He pointed towards the door.

Holtzclaw did not want this last property to escape him, but he eyed the long-barreled rifle ornamented by the double-bladed axe. If he persisted, he might provoke the Sky Pilot to employ it. What could Holtzclaw do but leave as commanded? It was too much to hope that every landowner would sell on the first visit. His easy tricks were exhausted, and all of the more persuasive maneuvers needed time, of which Holtzclaw had none. Shadburn had recalled him to Dahlonega, and it seemed he would have to go without the deed to the Terrible Cascade.

"Holtzclaw, you blasted fool!" Shadburn's words echoed inside his head, drowning out even the roar of the Terrible Cascade. "You blasted, blasted fool."

❧ CHAPTER VIII ❧

I t was suppertime, already dark, when Holtzclaw returned to Auraria from the Terrible Cascade. He should find a carriage back to Dahlonega, report as summoned, and hope that Shadburn's displeasure would be diffused by the six land deeds that Holtzclaw could present, rather than the one that he could not. But he knew he'd take a drubbing over it—any failure overwhelms any success.

From within the Old Rock Falls Inn, a warm firelight glowed. Abigail was no doubt preparing some roasted dish. At McTavish's, a greasy, wet smoke rolled from an open window. Mrs. McTavish had created a culinary miscegenation, and Holtzclaw didn't want to eat it. At the Grayson House, there was a chorus of what sounded like eleven fiddlers. He had not been inside there yet. Taking a meal there would be invaluable scouting for future negotiations, and perhaps he would hear how much the people of Auraria knew about his mission. It would be a half-hour well spent, and the delay would make no great difference to Shadburn. Besides, Holtzclaw would better face his employer's wrath if he were fed.

A man was napping on the Grayson House's porch. It was Dan, the man who'd been asleep on the floor of Walton's tower that was crammed with musical instruments. The fiddle music, crashes, and clinks from within the Grayson House were a fine lullaby for him. Holtzclaw stepped over the sleeping figure and into a whirl of motion.

Two dozen people capered in the room, which served as bar, dining area, and gaming parlor. In the crowd, Holtzclaw saw familiar faces—Moss, from whom he'd bought the frosted spring house; Bogan, the miner; Emmett, the druggist. It was dangerous that Moss and Bogan were together in the same place. Each, on his own, might be discreet about his transaction, but if they began to converse between themselves, they might discover that they had both sold their lands in the same day, to the same stranger. This was why it was so foolish to leave Auraria now.

"It's Jimmy!" called Emmett the druggist, approaching Holtzclaw. "Hi there, Jimmy! How were those Effervescent Brain Salts?"

"I think they may have impaired my judgment," he confessed.

"Well, either you didn't take enough, or you took too many," said Emmett. "Supposed to work wonders for what ails you. Says so right on the label. In the meantime, we are having quite the night here. Moss over there is treating folks, which is right kind of him."

Holtzclaw felt a sickening pit form just below his spleen. "Did Moss say why he's being so generous?"

"Said he made a strike. Found some gold in his river. Can you imagine? He's been digging for years and never got more than a sprinkle of powder, and now he's talking about a nugget that he dug up, right by the Five Forks Creek."

"A nugget? Well, I'll be," said Holtzclaw. "That's a fine discovery, isn't it? Goodness. Moss say anything else?"

"He might have, but I disremember. Finding a nugget is the biggest news there is. What could top that?"

"Has anyone else been free with their purse tonight?" said Holtzclaw, hoping that the question itself was not too suspicious.

"No one's had to be," said Emmett. "Moss is setting everyone up."

"Oh, a buffet? What's on the offering? I'm famished."

"Setting up means drinks, Jimmy. You still got to buy your own food. See, buying someone a drink doesn't insult their poverty. Everyone likes getting a drink. But you buy somebody food, and he gets offended. 'You think I can't buy my own food?' he says. If you want food here at the Grayson House, this is what you have to do. You put out a bit of gold dust for yourself on this spot here."

Emmett motioned towards a burned indentation in the surface of the bar. Each stool had such an indentation in front of it.

"Sampson's shy, and the mistress says she'll do whatever makes him comfortable. Put ten cents down for you and ten cents down for me. That's just enough gold dust to cover up the spot."

"I have eight colors in the brim of my hat."

"Eight colors will buy you about eight beans," said Emmett. "You got federal money?"

Holtzclaw found two dimes in his breast pocket. He placed one on his own spot and one on Emmett's.

"What did I just tell you about insulting poverty?" said Emmett. Holtzclaw moved to retract the dime, but Emmett laughed. "You're a soft touch, Jimmy. If you want to buy me supper, I won't be upset. Now, Sampson's real shy, so you don't want to stare at your money, otherwise you'll never get fed. Just turn around and look out in the crowd. Watch Nimrod play the fiddle a bit."

"What if someone takes my coin off the table when I'm not looking?"

"You'd think that would happen in a place like this?" said Emmett. "Well, you'd be right. So glance back every once and a while, and if your money is gone but there's no food, then yeah, you got robbed. Maybe you'll just have to steal a little back from the fellow at the next stool over. But most people get fed on the first try."

Holtzclaw and Emmett turned to watch a dice game that was taking place at a nearby table. Holtzclaw knew that it was chuck-luck, a game that was not unique to Auraria. It was played in every tavern from Lexington to Savannah. Dice were more reputable than playing cards, but the most refined people amused themselves with dominoes.

"What are the shooters dipping their fingers into?" said Holtzclaw.

"Why, Pharaoh's Flour, of course! Before I started to carry Pharaoh's Flour, it was cornmeal, but now, they all buy from me. Soaks up the sweat, gives a clean release on the dice, imbues them with the spirit of ancient Hittite warriors. Gives the shooter more control over the toss."

"Aren't dice throws supposed to be a matter of chance?"

"No, no! That's not a game then. No skill, no merit. Chuck-luck isn't like gold mining. If you keep digging, you're bound to find a nugget, but unless you've got the knack, you're going to lose that nugget over dice. You'll lose it to a better player, who uses all the advantages he's got."

Holtzclaw turned back to see if his money had been taken. It was gone, but in its place was supper. Three steaming bowls had been placed at each stool. The largest held a creamy soup; another, breaded frogs' legs; the last, a grayish pudding.

"What's in the small bowl?" asked Holtzclaw.

"Squirrel brains. Even people that don't like the taste of squirrel still like the brains."

First, Holtzclaw gave each bowl a thorough visual inspection. Second, a complete olfactory profile, to ascertain the freshness of the ingredients. Third, a vigorous stirring, to investigate the murky depths. Fourth, a hesitant bite, followed by a prolonged pause to sample for fast-acting poisons. And finally, a substantial morsel.

"These are all quite good!" said Holtzclaw, who proceeded to dig into the bowls with delight.

Emmett scraped up the last from his bowl of grey pudding. "These squirrels died happy. You can tell because these brains are sweet. Not bitter, like they are when you shoot your own squirrel. I don't how Sampson does it. The lady would keep him around just for the squirrel brains, even if everything else were blinky."

Holtzclaw ate until all traces of the soup and the squirrel pudding were gone. The frogs' legs were also cleaned to the bone. While the Old Rock Falls Inn offered more pleasant company, the Grayson House won on culinary merit.

The fiddler struck the opening notes of a new tune, and a whoop made Holtzclaw turn away from his empty bowls. An excited Moss flailed his hat above his head and leapt from one leg to another.

"Chickens are crowing up on Sourwood Mountain!" sang Moss, somewhere near the tune. "Hi-o diddle-um day!"

Moss had imbibed enough to loosen his tongue. A large enough drink might push him past the phase of total candor and into a less talkative mood.

"What's the most powerful thing served here?" Holtzclaw asked Emmett.

"That would be moonshine.'

"Wouldn't that make it too easy for the revenuers to intercept your home brew, if you sell it in your tavern?"

"No, you're thinking of white lightning. Moonshine doesn't have liquor in it. You don't even drink it."

"And it's enough to knock a grown man flat?"

"I've never seen a one stay standing," said Emmett.

Then it would serve his purposes, thought Holtzclaw, whether it was a liquid or powder or unguent. Holtzclaw excused himself from Emmett and approached Moss, who had taken a seat on a long bench.

"Hello, Moss!" said Holtzclaw.

"Why, hello, stranger! I'm Moss."

"Yes, pleased to meet you, Moss. Your friends tell me you've had a piece of good fortune."

"I should say so! Been digging for ten years, twenty years. I was owed. I was due! Name's Moss, by way."

"Can I help you celebrate, then? What would you like? Moonshine, maybe?"

Moss nodded, then continued to nod, then flung his head so wildly back and forth that he fell forward from the bench. Holtzclaw picked him up again. It may not take a dram of moonshine to finish this man for the evening, but better to over-fill than under-fill.

A short man with an apron was scurrying around, filling mugs from behind a wooden bar and delivering them to chuck-luckers, dancers, and idlers, and spitters. Holtzclaw caught the edge of the bartender's sleeve.

"Sir, we'd like a mug of moonshine, or a cup or shot or however it comes."

"Bowl, comes in a bowl. Silver bowl," said the bartender. He returned bearing a heavy metal bowl and pitcher, which he placed on the table with a thump that was heard above even the noise of the fiddler tuning up. Many heads turned to see the bartender pouring the contents of the pitcher into the bowl. A shimmer of starlight, rising from the silvery water, filled the tavern.

Moss, holding on to the edge of the table, peered into the bowl. He started to say something, but his knees gave out. He slumped to the floor, dazed, mouth moving but no sounds coming out. Two patrons caught Moss by the armpits and lifted him up. Holtzclaw, astounded but pleased with the results, resisted the urge to look himself—if the sight of the contents of the bowl was enough to flatten Moss, he was sure it would do the same to him.

"Now he's got to sleep it off," said the bartender to Holtzclaw. "You want to pay for a room, too?" Holtzclaw counted out money into the waiter's waving palm. The bowl of moonshine had cost more than an acre of timber, but buying Moss's silence for another day could prove far more valuable.

Bogan sat alone at a corner table, drinking a bottle of Dr. Pep. Without a character like Moss to draw the words out, Bogan wasn't likely to spill the news of the land sale.

"Who's got poppy rocks?" called out the fiddler. "I need some."

"The lady doesn't like it, Nimrod!" replied a voice from the crowd. "They wake her up from her beauty sleep."

"She's not even here!" said the fiddler. "She's up visiting daddy."

"Naw, she's upstairs," said someone from the crowd. "She came in the back way few minutes ago."

The fiddler whooped and took a crystal from an outstretched hand. He put it into his mouth and bit down. A terrific bang shot from between his lips, complete with sparks and a sulfurous smell. "Why, howdy! That'll wake you up!" He bit again, and another bang jolted his head to the side. Smoke drifted from his nose. Some of the spectators started to cheer. Others slipped out of the exits.

"Boys, just what is going on down here?" A woman's voice cut through the hoots, hollers, explosions, and clatter.

The room fell silent, except for one voice that said with a stage whisper, "I told you she was here! I told you she came in the back way."

Ms. Rathbun appeared from the kitchen. She was wearing an evening dress, narrow-waisted with voluminous skirts, black, trimmed with red ribbons that spiraled up her forearms. Her head was uncovered. Her blonde hair had been taken out of its tight coil, and it rolled in loose waves.

"Beg your pardon, ma'am," said the fiddler. "I didn't think you were here."

"It shouldn't matter if I'm here or not. We have rules at the Grayson House about poppy rocks. It's not the noise, but the vapors. The place smells like Waterloo. Makes me wrinkle my nose, and if it wrinkles enough, the wrinkles will stay there. Plus, that sulfur ruins the aroma of Sampson's delicious food. You wouldn't want that to happen to Sampson, would you?"

"No ma'am," said the fiddler.

"Let's have it, then," said Ms. Rathbun, who held out her handkerchief. The fiddler opened his mouth and extracted the saliva-covered artifact. He placed it into Ms. Rathbun's hand, and as he withdrew his fingers, she squeezed. A deafening thunderclap tore through the tavern. Men cowered, covering their ears. Mugs tumbled. Furniture shook apart. Beards were curled. Boots came untied. Holtzclaw's ears filled with duff notes that resolved into the murmurs and whimpers from the assembled spectators.

Ms. Rathbun's voice cut through the din again. "Now, what song will you play for me as I leave?" she said.

"I can play 'Liza Jane,'" said the fiddler, tugging on his ear.

"Why, that sounds delightful."

Accompanied by the strains of fiddle music, Ms. Rathbun glided towards the doorway from whence she had come, into a small alcove out of the din and bustle. Holtzclaw intercepted her at the foot of the stairs.

"Why, if it isn't our resident agent of the Standard Company!" she said. "Welcome, Holtzclaw! Did you have any more luck at the Amazon Branch?"

"I didn't," said Holtzclaw. "Someone else did."

"It is not an easy creek for gold," said Ms. Rathbun. "For you, I mean. But I'm sure you'll find some purpose. Some higher and better use."

"Now that I know your character, Ms. Rathbun, I should not have been surprised to find you proprietor of a place like the Grayson House. When you were telling me about your dreams of making a new start in Milledgeville in its good society, you didn't tell me about your decadent empire here."

"How is it decadent?" said Ms. Rathbun. "I look after these boys, and I give them rules. No poppy rocks, because they rot their teeth. No cards, because of paper cuts."

"But as much food and drink and dice and fiddle music as they can buy?"

"There are worse ways they could part with their money. The worst is to hoard it, lose it to time or to thieves. Better they spend it as they get it. I help them change money, which is cold and heavy, to pleasure, which is warm and light. I hope that our transaction this afternoon has brought you happiness, Holtzclaw."

"I have a suspicion that the land is not yours to sell."

"Who told you such lies?" said Ms. Rathbun. Her voice was unchanged, as light as ever.

"Princess Trahlyta," said Holtzclaw.

"That water-logged child? Who did she say owned it?"

"She didn't say, but she implied..."

"You assumed that she was telling you the truth. You believed her ludicrous tales. Why? Because they were ludicrous?"

"I've encountered several phenomena here in the valley, Ms. Rathbun, that are not easily explained," said Holtzclaw. "And it's been said to me that I should not attempt to understand it all."

"Those sound like the words of those who are trying to manipulate you. Do you want to abandon your reason? Have you gotten this far in life by believing in folk tales and nonsense?"

Ms. Rathbun turned away from Holtzclaw and climbed a single riser, then stopped. She was taller than Holtzclaw now by half a head.

"My father gave me the Amazon Branch, as a birthday present. He got it from an immigrant named Millan, who had a catarrh that my father cured with spring water. Millan bought it from Bowlin, who won it in the lottery. It's all in the courthouse, if you care to check when you file your deed. And that is no folk tale."

She stood in profile, pensive, with a hand on the bannister and a graceful arm arcing upwards from there to a shoulder angled back towards Holtzclaw. Even this casual pose seemed practiced.

"Now, did you want to cancel our deal?" she said. "Did you want a refund? I will give it to you, if you believe that moist maiden over me."

"No, it's not that. I just wanted to inquire. My curiosity is satisfied." Holtzclaw turned to go, with a deferential tip of the hat.

Ms. Rathbun called after him.

"I heard that you bought Moss's property, and for a lot less than you paid me. I find that flattering."

"That is a private transaction," said Holtzclaw, spinning around, "and I would thank you to keep it such."

"You've bought many other properties, too. Strikland. Bogan. Patterson. Walton. You've told them all your lies about scrap metal business. We both know there's no money in that. Why are you really buying them?"

"My employer has his own motives," said Holtzclaw.

"Why, a creature like that is not going to share our interests," said Ms. Rathbun. "You ally yourself with those who are least likely to reward you. Tell me, Holtzclaw, have you thought of buying some of these lands yourself? Before your employer gets to them? You have money of your own, I presume, and so do I. If we were to find a few key parcels of land ahead of your employer, there would be a good profit in it. I'd perform the negotiations; he wouldn't know about us."

"I am not going to betray him."

"We wouldn't thwart his plans, just place ourselves to benefit from them. A little foreknowledge, a few hard bargains, and it adds up to a tidy profit for you and me. Should you decide that you have any information to share, Holtzclaw, I may be persuaded into a partnership."

Holtzclaw watched her exaggerated ascent up the narrow staircase. Her motives, so transparent, made more sense than many of the things he'd seen in the Lost Creek Valley. At the top of the stairs, Lizzie Rathbun paused, as though considering a last word of parting, but she said nothing. Her blonde hair fell in loose waves against the midnight of her dress.

Holtzclaw had not found a carriage driver in the Grayson House, and now, it was risky to inquire there. Secrets were already seeping out. He didn't want to hasten the leak with his own questions. Abigail would be more discreet. He crossed to the Old Rock Falls and was enveloped by a jaunty piano tune.

There were no visible customers at the Old Rock Falls. Mr. Bad Thing tinkled on the piano. Abigail worked behind the counter. "Need some supper, Holtzclaw? It's the same as dinner—sweet potatoes. I'll get you a bowl."

"I've already eaten, Ms. Thompson, thanks." He threaded his way through the tables and leaned across the counter. "Actually, I'm in a bit of a predicament. I need to find a ride back to Dahlonega tonight. I must be there by morning. Do you know where I could find a driver?"

Abigail walked past Holtzclaw to the corner of the dining room to fetch a broom. She started sweeping under the tables. "Folks here don't like to drive at night. X.T. won't go. Byers won't go. Even the Sky Pilot won't go."

"Will anyone?"

"I'm not sure," she said.

"Then I shall have to go by myself."

"That's a fool idea," said Abigail.

"Why is that?" said Holtzclaw. "What dangers lurk out there?"

"There's the plat-eye," said Abigail.

"And what is a plat-eye?" said Holtzclaw. There was bound to be some spirit on the roadway; he wondered how this one was peculiar.

"The shade of a man," said Abigail. "This particular one was named Hulen Holmes. He used to have a farm in Hope Hollow. Hulen didn't take to being dead, though. He doesn't sleep sweetly."

"So, the road is haunted? It wouldn't be the most unusual thing I've seen here so far. I can endure it."

"When a place is haunted, there's no real worry," said Abigail. "Furniture flies around. Footsteps, whispers, piano plays itself. It's eerie when it starts, but then you get used to it. The ghosts are playful. They love a place so much they don't want to leave it just because of death. Sometimes they had a bad time there at the end; that makes the ghost want to stay all the more. They want to fix their memories, try to have a good time again. A plat-eye, though, is wrathy. He feels alone, especially in death, and it fills him with despair. If you're a stranger, a new face that he doesn't know and love from his life, he'll try to take your head off your shoulders."

"I suppose it isn't as simple as steering around Hulen's old home-stead," said Holtzclaw.

"You could meet him a few miles up the road or at one of the springs if you stop to water your horse. If you'd resolved to go, I'll have to take you."

"Ms. Thompson, you'd venture out against this plat-eye?"

"Well, he likes me. It won't be a cheap fare, though. If you need a horse, that's extra."

She quoted a price, but Holtzclaw did not think it outlandish, given the sudden departure and the late hour. He agreed to it and departed to collect a few essentials from McTavish's.

When he returned to the Old Rock Falls, Abigail was going through her closing routine. Certain regulars had to be appeased. On the counter, she laid out five bowls and filled each with a different substance. In the first, she poured an entire bottle of Dr. Pep. In the second, she poured a bottle of cream.

"For the cat?" asked Holtzclaw.

"She doesn't drink cream. She wants butter because it's easier to eat. Lazy thing."

Abigail opened a small mahogany box and withdrew a geometric form wrapped in red silk. As it was unwrapped, Holtzclaw saw that it was ice, of the quality that he'd seen at the Sky Pilot's cabin. Abigail placed the blade of her kitchen knife above the smoldering ashes of the hearth fire, then she cut off a perfect slice, leaving all the edges as smooth as before.

In the last two bowls, she poured out the contents of two ewers. The liquids were colorless, but one gave off a distinct metallic odor, while the other reeked of sulfur. "Mineral waters," said Abigail. "Some need the chalybeate and others the yellow sulfur."

After sweeping the kitchen and dining room, Abigail poured out a handful of Pharaoh's Flour onto the floor around the counter. "This is the most important part, because it shows all the guests who went to which bowl. No one can lie and say, 'I never got any ice!' There's evidence."

"Ah, that's clever," said Holtzclaw.

"The worst part of the profession," said Abigail, "is dealing with disputes between the customers. When I was younger, there was more fighting. Now, the wilder spirits have settled somewhat."

"Like gold at the bottom of a pan," said Holtzclaw.

CHAPTER IX

They rode side by side towards Dahlonega, under a splendid moon. Holtzclaw chatted about recent gala events held at the Governor's mansion, making special mention of ball gowns, dance forms, and musical selections. One gala, which he had not attended, had been a fundraiser for the southern highlanders.

"The organizer made some claim about the squalid schoolhouses of the mountains," said Holtzclaw, "and how one is as likely to find a bucketful of dung as a bucketful of coal for stoking the furnace, and that snakes will come pouring out of the floor."

"It's poppycock," said Abigail. "The only time snakes will come pouring out of the floor is if you build a home on top of their nest. It happens sometimes, which is why, when you light the first fire in a new house, you make sure that the blankets are tucked in tight, so nothing that's woken up by the warmth will slither in. I suppose these organizers told their snake stories to make us mountain folk appear more pitiable. That's poppycock, too."

"I've seen more first-rate claret here than in the restaurants of Savannah," said Holtzclaw. This stirred a memory in him, and he described to Abigail many of the fine and healthful meals that he'd consumed over the years: various game birds, in assembled or disassembled forms, served roasted, chilled, raw, or stewed; organ meats cut thin or served as pates; turtles in broth; rare oriental fruits served a single slice at a time from ancient porcelain. But he dedicated the most detail to a rustic meal that had been prepared for him by a troupe of Hungarian immigrants that had settled near the Alabama line. Rabbits and sausages roasted over a long, open fire. A massive iron cauldron, transported with great effort into the wilderness, held a steaming goulash. Alas, the Hungarians did not stay long. The changing financial fortunes of the region, combined with political pressure relating to the manufacture of their native spirits, conspired to evict the Hungarians from their small territory. The families moved to the Ohio coal fields, leaving only a weedy cemetery with the name "Budapest" written in wrought iron above the gate.

"I picked up a few words in Hungarian from them," said Holtzclaw. "Have you studied any foreign languages?"

"All the little girls in Auraria learn Chinese, in between lessons in butter-churning and gold panning."

Holtzclaw waited for a moment to see if Abigail would say a word in Chinese. But when none came, he risked a brief chuckle; the moonlight on Abigail's face revealed this to be the appropriate response.

"But I do believe that gold panning is part of your universal education here," said Holtzclaw. "In my travels today I met a young woman who was as practiced as any grizzled prospector."

"Who was that?" said Abigail.

"Ms. Rathbun. In the old capital, that sort of woman would only know about gold in its final, highest form—the cufflinks of a lover or the necklace of a rival."

Abigail's face soured. "Yes, I guess you're right. A very lazy woman like her would only care about gold if it helped her judge people. Who's worth her time, who's not. Are cufflinks and necklaces really the highest form of gold?"

"When men and women dream, do they dream of simply sitting upon piles of gold? No, they dream of what they'd buy. Fashionable clothing, a spread of land, fine cuisine at a ball, attending servants, a life of leisure. They dream of using gold, not finding gold."

"Those are dreams of rich idlers. In Auraria, we are miners, even in our dreams. When I'm asleep, I follow the hillside that leads up from the Five Forks Creek, and in Fowler's Gully is a loose boulder, and underneath the boulder is an iron pot in which are buried fifty gold double eagles. Or I wade into Painter's Creek until I step in an eddy, where there is a golden head with pearls for eyes and an emerald set in for a tongue. Or I'm following a tunnel that leads to an open cavern with a village of stone houses and a palace over them, gathered underneath a stone sky. I descend a staircase that falls straight down into the mountain and ends at an underground sea, and there is gold piled there in drifts, as though the river carried it down like waste. And when I press all of my fingers against the warm metal, I wake up."

"And do you then set out with your pick and shovel?" said Holtzclaw. Perhaps Auraria could inspire prophetic dreams, or perhaps if one dreamed often enough in a place as rich as the Lost Creek, then one of those dreams was bound to come true.

"I've never had the need," said Abigail.

"We are very different people, Ms. Thompson."

A mile past midnight, when they were still not out of the Lost Creek Valley, Holtzclaw asked Abigail if they could stop for a drink. She nodded. They were following a road that paralleled the course of a running river; Holtzclaw could hear the flow somewhere in the darkness below. But they rode for several minutes before Abigail brought her horse to a stop.

"Here it's easy enough to get down to the water," said Abigail. They left the horses on the road, hitched to a post. A path led down to the water, and as Holtzclaw followed Abigail, he was surprised to find the path transformed into rough-hewn steps. The farther they descended, the colder the air became.

The path ended at a waist-high wall, likely the remnants of a mill race, and just on the other side of the wall was the river. Holtzclaw leaned over and found that the far side was rimed with frost. The wind was laden with ice, and when Holtzclaw put his cupped hands into the flow, they shivered. He tried to sip the water, but his lips recoiled.

A flickering silver light made him look towards a bend upriver.

"Oh, I didn't think they'd be out tonight," said Abigail.

"Who is that?"

"We call them moon maidens, but I don't know if they have their own name for themselves."

Holtzclaw mind raced. "I need to see them. Again. Can I see them?"

The first time he'd encountered these creatures, he'd seen only shadows. Now, he was in stronger spirits, with more of his wits about him, and he had been prepared by two days spent among the strange sights of the valley. He needed to know what sort of people commanded the service of Princess Trahlyta—terrestrial or supernatural.

Had Abigail offered some excuse why Holtzclaw shouldn't seek the moon maidens, this would have been its own proof. Instead, she said, "Go ahead, if you want. Try to be quiet, or you'll frighten them away. Pretend that they are some gentle animal at a spring."

Holtzclaw could not find a clear path leading upstream. The bank was overgrown with bracken. His progress up the river was slow; he broke twigs underfoot, pushed leafy branches from his path, and navigated around a thorny laurel bush until he cleared the bend.

Five women bathed in the middle of the ice-cold stream. He had seen this before, when he'd been lost getting to Auraria for the first time, but now, he was much closer. The bathers were clad in blue fabric; the thin garments would not protect against the cold. Two of the bathers were stretched supine on the rocks, letting the crystalline water flow over their shoulders. Three others waded in a waist-deep pool, cavorting and splashing. Their skin was pale, and their long, straight hair was white or silver or a very fine blonde.

Holtzclaw huddled against the wall, stealing a peek at his quarries. Now he was just twenty feet from the moon maidens, and he could see their faces. All had small noses that ended in an upward turn; their ears were long and folded at the top.

One of the cavorting maidens dove below the water's surface and reemerged at a rocky pool just a few feet away. She turned towards the wall where Holtzclaw was hiding and made a call that was halfway between a bird whistle and a mammal's rooting. Her companions froze and fell silent. The only sound was the moon maiden's sniffling and the cracking of ice. She ran her nose along the river side of the wall; the elongated tips of her ears were alert and anxious. Holtzclaw could not hope to flee, so he pressed himself against his own side of the wall, hoping the cold would confuse his scent.

The moon maiden was not fooled. She leapt onto the wall and leaned over, upside down, just above Holtzclaw, her face inches from his. She had no color in her eyes; they were black from edge to edge. The expression on her face was alien and inscrutable.

Then she vanished so quickly that the air snapped and quivered. Holtzclaw sprang up from behind the wall to see the soles of feet patter across the slick boulders of the river and then disappear into the underbrush.

Already, the air felt milder, and starlight flickered on the face of the water. The peculiar influence of cold and water and light was broken, slipping away like a sweet memory. Nothing else was like them in this sublunary world.

With the moon maidens gone, the place was an ordinary stream, and Holtzclaw found no reason to tarry there. He picked his way back through the underbrush, and when he stumbled back to the base of the wide staircase, he saw Abigail in conversation with Princess Trahlyta. They stopped when Holtzclaw neared. Abigail was playing with a small rock between her fingers, twirling it up and down across her knuckles.

"Hello, James," said the princess. "What do you think of our valley now?"

"Blizzards and haunted pianos are a poor way to introduce it," said Holtzclaw. "You should start with something spectacular and unequivocal, like your moon maidens."

"My employers are not a side show for your amusement," said Trahlyta.

"Are there many of these maidens, or only the five that I saw?"

"They take their holidays in smaller numbers now, as is the fashion," said Trahlyta. "Still, they keep me busy. They demand excellent streams, piping springs, comfort and company."

"Company? What do they have to say?"

"We talk about the weather, mostly, and shaking off the lunar chill. No matter what weather we're having in the Lost Creek Valley, it's always warmer than on the moon."

"All tourists talk about the same things," said Abigail, "no matter where they're from." She cast away the rock which she'd been twirling. Holtzclaw saw it glitter in the starlight before it ricocheted off a boulder and sank beyond his sight.

"Was that gold?" said Holtzclaw, the moon maidens all but forgotten. "Did you throw away a nugget of gold?"

"It was a rock," said Abigail. "Gold is a rock."

Holtzclaw turned to the princess, but she was fixated on a moonbeam reflecting from a puddle and had lost interest in earthly matters. He unlaced his boots and removed his traveling coat, then stepped into the rush of the river. The water was still bitterly cold, but he ignored the discomfort. He had splashed out to the point in the river where he'd seen Abigail's discarded stone fall. The riverbed was pocked with deep holes and crevices that had been scoured by the course of the river. He plunged his arm into one of the deep holes, but his hand did not touch bottom. In another, he found a slimy flank of some aquatic creature. Something nipped at his fingers, and he recoiled.

"It's gone, isn't it?" said Holtzclaw. "The nugget?"

"No, it's not gone" said Abigail. "But you can't get it. It's too deep. Perhaps you'll stub your toe against an even bigger find, on down the road. Come out of there, and let's move on."

"Will you help me find it?" said Holtzclaw. "It could mean great fortune for both of us."

"You need to get to Dahlonega, and I need to be back before the chickens want feeding."

He protested to no avail, until a sharp wind shook him from his revelry. If he still wished to be employed in the morning, then he must meet Shadburn, as summoned.

The princess did not wish them goodbye. She studied the advancing path of moonlight against the earth. Of all the wonders Holtzclaw had seen so far, the most perplexing was a nugget of gold, carelessly tossed into a stream, and two poor souls who did not care a whit.

Holtzclaw and Abigail rode on. He was uncomfortable in his wet clothes. The night air was still cold, though its lunar inhabitants had fled.

"How long have you known the princess?" said Holtzclaw, controlling his jaw against a reflexive shiver.

"We used to play together," said Abigail, "when we were small. When I was small. We'd play Bonaparte Crossing the Rhine, or mermaid, or sometimes washer-woman, but Trahlyta didn't think that one was very fun."

"I don't think she likes me," said Holtzclaw.

"She didn't even mention you."

Holtzclaw found this hard to believe.

"We were trying to remember all the rules of our mermaid game," continued Abigail. "How long you had to hold your breath, how many rocks you had to bring up, what colors counted for how many points. It was a very complicated game."

"Did you get more points for nuggets of gold?"

"That would make the game too easy."

Holtzclaw drew up his horse. "Abigail, this isn't some joke that you play on foreigners? A fish you dangle in the mist to bait them?"

Abigail seemed puzzled by his turn of phrase. "Why would I?"

"To disrupt my employer's mission."

"Why would I care about scrap metal?"

Holtzclaw shook his head. "It's not scrap metal. I don't know what it is."

"I didn't think so," she said. "I couldn't see the profit in scrap metal."

The moon was no longer overhead—it had vanished behind the steep walls of the valley. The silvery tinge on the trees was gone. Leaves rustled in the darkness. Abigail pulled the reins of her horse, drawing him to a sudden stop.

"He's abroad. We might have avoided him if he were in his hollow or hunting on the other side of the ridge."

"The plat-eye?" asked Holtzclaw. Abigail nodded. "Do we flee, then? Do we fire at him? I didn't bring a rifle, but I think I could make a speedy break."

"None of those would do any good. Listen, if he sees your head, he'll try to take it. Because he doesn't know you. Because he's in a place of bad memories. So, he mustn't see your head."

Abigail instructed Holtzclaw to undo his overcoat. She pulled it up by the lapels so that the collar now surrounded the crown of his head, and then she fastened the top button against Holtzclaw's forehead. She left the third button undone, which provided a window through which Holtzclaw could peer with a single eye. He was forced to hunch his shoulders towards his ears, and his arms could not hang in their natural position.

"Don't say anything, and for your own sake, don't show your nose." She tied his horse to hers, and the train staggered up the road for a few paces.

Holtzclaw heard a swirling noise, then a voice that, a dozen years ago, could have been pleasant, but was now inflected by the wheeze of decay.

"Why, it's Abby Thompson!" said voice. "I'd tip my hat to you, little miss, but ... aha!"

Holtzclaw turned his bound torso and caught sight of the speaker. Muddy boots, spattered trousers, a hatchet held across his chest, and above the shoulders—nothing. Where his neck should be was a smooth place, unmarked by gore or scars. It didn't look like he was missing a head, but rather that he had never had one at all. Holtzclaw had never met a headless man before; it was disconcerting to him. But he had never climbed the stairs of an infinite house before, nor found a blizzard blowing from a spring house. Then Holtzclaw remembered that he himself, buttoned up inside his jacket, would look headless to the rest of the world. He'd joined the ranks of the fantastic.

"Hello, Hulen," said Abigail. "How's the hunting?"

"Oh, I cannot complain ... got no mouth! Aha! Tavern business treating you well? How's your father?"

"Still dead," said Abigail.

"That's right," said Hulen. "I keep forgetting. Just slips out of my mind ... aha! Such a nice place, the Old Rock Falls. Do you think I could come for a drink? For old time's sake?"

"It would be splendid, Hulen. Mr. Bad Thing would be thrilled. But you'd have to promise not to tear off any heads."

"Who's your friend there?"

"Traveling salesman of some kind. Came down from Dahlonega yesterday and now he's heading back. Tight schedule so we're traveling at night."

"He's got no head, either?"

"No, no head."

"Poor fellow. It's not an easy life. I'd cry all day about it..."

"But you've got no eyes?" said Abigail.

"Whose head is he trying to take?"

"No one's."

"And he was at the Old Rock Falls?"

"Had dinner and supper there."

"If some traveling salesman can do it, then old Hulen can do it. Say, do you have any of that Sour Mountain whiskey? That was always my favorite."

"It wouldn't be, any more. Old Joe went out west. His brother took over the still, and it doesn't run as sweet for him. We have Blood Mountain whiskey now. Almost the same, but not quite."

Hulen muttered a series of nonsense oaths.

"You're not the only one, Hulen. Nobody likes the change, but it was forced upon us."

"How about Cold Valley?"

"Plenty of that."

"Mix it with Porter Springs mineral water, put it over a stone of the Sky Pilot's ice—that was fine drinking. Fire down your gullet! Of course, I don't have a gullet ... aha ..."

"Doesn't matter, Hulen."

"No, no I suppose it doesn't." Hulen had no chin to rub, no head to scratch, but Holtzclaw detected the same sentiments in his posture. "Well, you'd best be careful, Abby. There's ghosts out, you know. Headless ghosts. I've seen 'em with my own two eyes ... aha!" Hulen made a bow from the waist and turned back into the wilderness. Abigail waved goodbye.

The linked horses stumbled forward for a quarter-mile, then Abigail at last permitted Holtzclaw to unbutton himself from his high collar and resume control of his own mount.

"That was not as terrifying an experience as you made it out to be," said Holtzclaw.

"You were with me, not alone," said Abigail. "But it did go very well. I don't think Hulen expected to meet another headless horseman."

"Why do you call him a plat-eye, if he doesn't have any eyes at all? Aha!" said Holtzclaw.

"Don't you start."

"Would he have tried to take my head off, like you said?"

"He wants a head so badly. He's shown me other heads that he's tried, and they don't look right. I've told him an animal head might be more suitable, but he hasn't been able to kill one big enough. Once he came out of the woods wearing a squirrel head, and it was all I could do not to laugh."

"You'd trust him to come back to your tavern, given his head-collecting proclivities?"

"We don't allow that sort of behavior at the Old Rock Falls, and he wouldn't desecrate the place."

"Why doesn't he try to take your head?"

"I like ghosts," said Abigail, "and I'm a face from his happier life."

"And if I liked ghosts, he wouldn't try to kill me?"

"I don't think you could make friends with a spirit. Just see how you treated Mr. Bad Thing. Most people can't leave behind the ghost stories and come to know the ghosts."

Chastened, Holtzclaw fell silent for a few moments. He brooded, then could not hold back. "How does he speak, if he has no head?" he asked.

"How does he eat, or drink, or see, or breathe?" said Abigail.

"It is not natural," said Holtzclaw.

"It's perfectly natural for a ghost," said Abigail.

CHAPTER X

Morning broke over Dahlonega just as the pair rode into town. The clock tower at the railroad depot read six o'clock. Abigail escorted Holtzclaw to the door of Shadburn's temporary offices and departed, her second horse hitched up behind the first. He brushed as much of the dust of the road from himself as he could, then knocked at Shadburn's door.

"Not a minute too soon!" said Shadburn. "Why, you are a frightful sight. Grubby. Most unlike you."

"I came directly when I received your message, Shadburn," said Holtzclaw, glossing the truth. "Rode through the night. I haven't slept. I haven't breakfasted. I haven't had a moment to tidy up."

"It's a hard life, Holtzclaw, it surely is. Well, we shall get you a cup of coffee on the run. The railroad men are already here."

"At six o'clock in the morning?"

"Railroad time! These men are busy, very busy. They have a seven o'clock train back to Atlanta, so we must present our case now."

"Our case? What is our case?"

"The land, the town, the dam, the lake, the hotel, the railroad, clearing the town, the whole of it! There is no need for secrets with these men."

"You haven't told me anything about this." Holtzclaw rubbed the top of his head, where something gnawed at him.

"There's hardly time now," said Shadburn. "Already it has taken us two minutes to cross this foyer. The railroad men must think we have fallen into a pit, and their coffee has gone cold. Will you get them a fresh pot, Holtzclaw, then come straight in?"

Shadburn vanished through a door at the end of the hallway, closing it behind him.

Holtzclaw stood helpless for a moment, not remembering where the kitchen was. He opened doors at random, first into a closet stacked with brooms, overcoats, and hats, then into a workroom that was overgrown with papers. From one of the remaining doors a serving boy emerged, carrying a coffee pot on a polished tray. Holtzclaw took it from him with profound and repeated gratitude; he even fished into his pocket for a coin. Holtzclaw took the coffee into the salon, where Shadburn, standing, was in conversation with two men on a settee. Holtzclaw recognized them. They were the twins that had dined at the Old Rock Falls Inn when he'd first arrived in Auraria.

"At last!" said Shadburn. "Holtzclaw, my associate. Please allow me to introduce Misters Johnston and Carter, from the railroad. Holtzclaw has come to freshen your coffee, gentlemen."

Pouring the coffee into their outstretched cups, Holtzclaw wished that he had let the servant do his job. The twins—Shadburn hadn't specified which was Johnston and which was Carter—accepted the hot beverage. They tipped their heads and offered their hands to Holtzclaw, as though meeting him for the first time. Holtzclaw supposed that that was proper—in the Old Rock Falls, they had not been introduced.

"Gentlemen," said Shadburn, "I hope you'll forgive if we dispense with the pleasantries. We are all busy, I'm sure. There is a town a few miles down the road. Its name is Auraria, and my associate and I have been acquiring property in the town and the surrounding Lost Creek Valley with an eye towards a major development project. There is promise in that place. Wouldn't you say so, Holtzclaw?"

"Oh yes, great promise," said Holtzclaw. "I have seen it. Very much promise indeed."

"I have a vision of a recreational center that would take advantage of all the natural advantages of the valley," said Shadburn. "The area is rich in timber and game, so it is a natural site for sawmills and tanneries, neither of which it has now. These natural resources are also enjoyed by the tourist. The high climate is both healthful and scenic. It is also a wet place, wouldn't you say, Holtzclaw?"

"It's the dampest place I've ever visited that wasn't underwater. Never have I dipped my fingers in so many creeks."

"But it's a healthful dampness, yes?" said Shadburn.

"It's not a swamp. There are many springs and tributaries, all swift. Many of these paint a sublime picture for the tourist's eye." Holtzclaw was thinking of the Cobalt Springs Lake.

"It sounds a proper treat," said either Johnston or Carter.

"What do you need from us?" said the other.

"Industry and tourism cannot develop until there is a railroad," said Shadburn, "and the railroad will not run until there are industry and tourism. It is that old dilemma, the chicken and his house."

"Chicken and egg?" offered Holtzclaw.

"Yes, exactly. Which do you eat first, the chicken or the egg?"

"The egg, because it is breakfast," said either Johnston or Carter.

"The chicken, because it is tastier," said the other.

"If you are hungry, gentlemen," said Shadburn, "Holtzclaw will fetch you something from the kitchen." Both men shook their heads to decline. "Well then, I propose that you build a railroad from Dahlonega into Auraria. You will be the egg, and then the chickens and the timber and the furs and the visitors and the mail will come later, much to the profit of all."

"You are not the first developer we have spoken with, Mr. Shadburn," said Johnston or Carter.

"Every landholder believes that his land is suited to riches," said the other.

"I am prepared to bear a greater cost, gentlemen, than your average developer," said Shadburn, working his thumb into the cleft of his hard chin, "and my vision is grander. We will build not just a railroad, but a dam, too, to form an enormous and beautiful lake, with a fine hotel. The Lost Creek Valley will be the Lost Lake."

Shadburn paused for a moment, as though hoping for an audible gasp, but none came. Either his pronouncement was too predictable, or, as Holtzclaw decided, he'd flubbed the delivery.

"Wouldn't this flood the town?" asked Johnston or Carter.

"Destroy every house in the village?" asked the other.

"Oh yes, and many farms, too," said Shadburn. "That's essential. The whole valley and its old ways will be underwater. All who are now living at the bottom must be moved to the shores. We'll put them up in modern company housing. A first-class hotel and series of minerals baths will be located right on the water's edge, and that will be the chief industry, but Auraria has much promise for other development, too."

Holtzclaw caught a shining dream in Shadburn's eye. It must be the thought of gold. Hotels, sawmills, tanneries—the profit here was much smaller and more difficult. Why didn't Shadburn list gold among the valley's resources? Maybe he meant for it to stay a secret, but he didn't know the secret was already out. The railroad men were acquainted with Auraria.

"It is a lot of land," said Johnston or Carter.

"Expensive to acquire," said the other.

"My associate has already bought these key properties, and many besides. Half the town is already in our possession. Yes, Holtzclaw?"

"For a few of the properties," said Holtzclaw, "negotiations are ongoing, very near the end, with only a formality or two to conclude." Now was not the time to confess his failures.

"Persuasion is our speciality, as railroads and dams are yours," said Shadburn. "You built the dams at Toxaway, Burton, and Rabun."

"We caused them to be built," said Johnston or Carter.

"We did not ourselves pick up shovels," said the other.

"Of course!" said Shadburn, chuckling a bit, though Holtzclaw was not sure that Johnston and Carter were joking. "My plan calls for a dam that is a sight higher than Toxaway. The lake would be deeper and longer, too, though narrower than Lake Toxaway, because of the shape of our valley. The lake I've drawn is somewhat less than a mile at its widest point, two-and-a-half miles long, sixty feet deep at the dam but seventy or eighty in certain hollows, and covering seven hundred acres at full fill. A perimeter road of seven miles, accounting for arms and branches that result from the natural geography."

Holtzclaw was surprised to hear Shadburn quote numbers. It showed more forethought than usual; Shadburn was accustomed to diving into projects, trusting to inevitable success, and leaving the figuring to his protege. Holtzclaw could not check the math in his head, but he felt the figures were dubious. Was it mathematically possible for a lake of seven hundred acres to have a boundary of seven miles and rough dimensions of one mile by two-and-a-half miles?

"And the lake is necessary?" said Johnston or Carter.

"It's an immense effort," said the other.

"A lake is essential," said Shadburn. "First, for leisure. When the wealthy people of Milledgeville, Charleston, and Chattanooga take their leisure in this modern age, they want water sports and recreation. Hunting and hiking are good enough, but the allure of boating, fishing, and swimming are greater. Second, for power. The flow of the Lost Creek has, heretofore, been wasted. There is hardly a water wheel propelled by it now. Our powerhouse will drive a host of electric wonders in the hotel, which are necessary for its profitability. Finally, for aesthetics. For every leaf that Nature bursts into color or for every cupola that we polish on the roof of the hotel, the mirror surface lake creates another for free. You will forgive me, gentlemen, if I am effusive about the virtues of the lake. It is just that I see it as the heart of the project, and without it the rest is doomed to failure. I would abandon the whole enterprise right now, in total, rather than to give up on the lake."

"Mountains must be sheared off," said either Johnston or Carter.

"Tunnels excavated," said the other.

"Who will pay for the expense?"

"Who will own the lake and dam and rails?"

"The rails you will own," said Shadburn, "including the whole of the profit for every passenger, bag of mail, and ton of cargo that passes along. I don't care for those revenues if you will build and service the line. I will pay for the construction on the dam, every penny, if you'll build it for me. I want the highest quality, spare no expense."

Holtzclaw sputtered into his cooling coffee. Shadburn had promised them mountains of money, and what could he hope to get in return?

"That is a generous proposition," said Johnston or Carter.

"But not without risk to us," said the other.

"We could build the rail, but it could sit idle and rust."

"No trains, no passengers, no cargo."

"My associate and I have studied the capacities of the valley well," said Shadburn. "I believe that we could commit to certain minimums. You can run ten cars of lumber, three times daily. What else, Holtzclaw?"

"Well, that is, I do not have hard statistics, but if I were to theorize..."

"We need numbers, not theories," said Johnston or Carter.

"You've worked this out, we assume," said the other.

Holtzclaw wrenched inside. He would like nothing more than to figure out the answer. But Shadburn had taken from him the pleasure of discovering the truth, replacing it with the discomfort of a lie.

"Seventeen. Seventeen cars per day, except Sundays," said Holtzclaw. This answer must have been acceptable, because it did not stir any emotion, either positive or negative, on the faces of the railroad men. "Should there be any remaining space it could be filled with products of various small industries. For instance, while in Auraria, I ate the most impressive peach that I have ever eaten. These peaches would be a sensation in the cities."

"And how many cars for passengers?" said Johnston or Carter.

"Including their luggage and mail?" said the other.

"An average day," said Shadburn, "would see at least five hundred passengers arriving or departing."

"Five hundred?" Holtzclaw sputtered.

"In the summer season, the traffic will be more," said Shadburn, "and in the off season, less." He must have simply invented his ridiculous number, much as Holtzclaw had invented his felicitously plausible one.

"You've met with no serious objections thus far?" said Johnston or Carter.

"No one who will buy and hold any of the essential lots?"

"Even if every detail of the project were printed on broadsheets and tacked up in the square," said Shadburn, "I cannot imagine that we would have any opposition. All in the valley will benefit, and thus no one will oppose."

"I think we've heard enough," said Johnston or Carter.

"We'll build your railroad and your dam," said the other.

"You won't regret it. It will be a splendid profit for the people in Auraria," said Shadburn.

"And for you," said Johnston or Carter.

"An excellent profit, if all goes well," said the other.

"Oh, I suppose so," said Shadburn, "after a time. Our first expense is a retainer for you, as a deposit on the construction costs. Holtzclaw, would you fetch the strongbox?" He pointed to a stained blanket in the corner of the room.

Holtzclaw removed the covering to reveal several strongboxes. So poorly guarded! The first that Holtzclaw opened was stuffed full with brown leaves.

"That is tea," said Shadburn. "I do not think these gentlemen would take that as a deposit."

Holtzclaw opened a second one, confirming that it contained more customary currencies, then brought it to Shadburn, who removed fistfuls of federal notes. The railroad men had not come prepared to receive such a sum, so Holtzclaw fetched a potato sack from the kitchen. Once the dirt was knocked out of it, the potato sack was very suitable and inconspicuous.

"I'll start with a standard form contract," said Holtzclaw, "then we will append our specific requirements."

"These gentlemen haven't time for even your hastiest contract, Holtzclaw," said Shadburn. "You went on too long about your peaches."

"For a transaction of this magnitude," said Holtzclaw, "with so many promises made and major constructions planned, each party would want some kind of protection, or written understanding, or even a reference, in case we can't recall that we promised to deliver five hundred people and their mail every day."

"We will not let you forget that," said Johnston or Carter.

"We will hold you to it, even without a paper" said the other.

"I think that we can take the word of these gentlemen," said Shadburn, "which is built upon the substantial reputation of their railroad."

"At the very least, a receipt!" said Holtzclaw.

"No, Holtzclaw, it's not necessary," said Shadburn. "Let us shake on it and consider the matter finished, or rather, just begun."

Handshakes were exchanged from all sides—between Shadburn and the railroad men, between Holtzclaw and the railroad men, between Shadburn and Holtzclaw, between the railroad men, and even with the servant boy who came into the room with fresh coffee just as all were rising to leave.

From the porch of their offices, Shadburn and Holtzclaw watched the railroad men disappear into the foot traffic of the awakening town. A train whistle sounded from nearby and a plume of steam rose into the air. The clock tower chimed for seven o'clock.

"Well, that went well," said Shadburn. "I'm famished. Let's eat."

Shadburn refused to address Holtzclaw's agitation until both men were seated in Elmer's Provender. The server, without taking their order, brought them plates of pan-fried poultry cutlets and scrambled eggs and hash browns topped with onions.

Shadburn smacked his lips. "It's tasty enough," he said, "but in Auraria, they serve the hash browns with wild forest mushrooms, butter poached. You'd never seen that flourish in Dahlonega, and they would think you funny if you asked for it. Marvelous, isn't it, the regional differences in a cuisine. Here we are, not ten miles from a place, and the kitchen manners are as different as if we had traveled to the Orient."

"That's an overstatement," said Holtzclaw. "Whether you're in Auraria and Dahlonega, it's still potatoes."

"You didn't have Auraria's hash browns with mushrooms, then? You'd feel differently if you'd eaten them."

"So, this is why you're so passionate about this dam, this lake?" Holtzclaw rapped the table with his knuckles. "Your stomach has given you away. This is not just any tiny hamlet. You've been there before. What, is it your home town?"

Shadburn smiled. "It's a very humble place, and I am proud that I have risen from it. And now, that I have reached my peak, it is time to repay those origins. I have raised many waste lands to higher and better use, bettered their people. But for Auraria I have reserved the greatest boon. But we must be very careful about it. It is more perilous than any other project we have tried before. Full of buried secrets. Some forces conspire to spoil us."

"Some! Half a hundred! Since you are so familiar with them, why didn't you warn me? Red fish that jump up from lakes of mist. The girl who calls herself the Queen of the Mountains. Houses with infinite interior space. Farms frozen over by their spring houses. Moon maidens. Plat-eyes out to rob travelers not of their goods, but their heads."

"Every hill and dale has its particular boogeymen. There is supposed to be some kind of skunk ape that lives in the Okefenokee, but did that matter to us when we were buying logging rights down there?"

"I don't believe that, Shadburn. I think that you find these phenomena problematic, and I propose that your real purpose in flooding their valley is to drive all these phenomena away, or drown them."

"On the contrary. Most of them I consider endearing. The lake isn't meant to destroy spirits. It's meant to destroy an industry, or rather, replace it with a better one."

"Which industry?"

"Gold, of course! Did you see men neglecting their fields to pan at the creekside? Did you see men becoming moles, living underground, chasing seams that they've never seen? Did you witness old women toss away their hard work because they caught a glimpse of gold coins? It's a sad occupation, all caprice and luck, and all its fortunes are unnatural."

"I can't believe you would try to wipe out something as profitable as gold mining."

"That's just it, Holtzclaw. It isn't profitable." His fist rapped the table twice. "If it were, don't you think that the valley would be crawling with commercial mines? Did the people of Auraria look like they were bathing in gold dust? Yes, you're about to say that you saw plenty of gold dust up there. From time to time, someone strikes a nugget, but that makes matters worse. A hundred dollars worth of gold, spent in an evening, inspires those poor people to throw away a million dollars of good work, rich land, tall trees, fat animals."

"And if you flood all the mining tunnels, then the people of Auraria will have no choice but to do something more productive?"

"We'll show them the way. Sawmills, tanneries, but most importantly, a hotel and resort, which will attract the best people and convince them to leave their money in the valley."

"It's like nothing we've done before."

"We built a lake at Canton," said Shadburn.

"You were in the right place when someone else built a lake at Canton. That's a distinction that makes all the difference! You bought and held the property—not the whole basin, just the shoreline—and sold it as the water came up. There was no construction, no relocation, no development at all after the dam gates were shut."

"Of course, yes, you're right," murmured Shadburn.

The table fell silent. Ravaged plates of hash browns congealed before them.

"Was this the only meeting you had in mind?" asked Holtzclaw. "Am I permitted to go back to Auraria now? Time is wasting, Shadburn."

"We'll both go. All the land is bought, yes, except for a few trifles? We're ready to move to the next phase."

"Am I supposed to have bought a whole town already? I did the best I could with a day and a half. It's more than I've ever bought in such a short time."

Shadburn frowned. "How far did you make it down the list I gave you, then?"

At last, Holtzclaw had to reveal his failure. "I bought the lands of the widow Smith Patterson, the Moss farm, the Strikland farm, Bogan's lands but leaving the mineral rights, though that is solved easily enough. The Walton house with its many floors and alphabetized employees. The Amazon Branch; I fear that I overpaid for it, but that does not appear to be a concern of yours on this project. The last I tried was the Sky Pilot's house. Despite my best pleadings, though, he has not yet sold his parcel at the top of the Terrible Cascade."

"You've missed the most important piece!" said Shadburn. "The Terrible Cascade is the site for the dam. The Sky Pilot's cabin will be beneath a hundred thousand tons of earth."

"I will dislodge him yet," said Holtzclaw. "You haven't even given me to time to visit his house a second time."

"I can't understand it, Holtzclaw. You explained to the Sky Pilot the value of the project, didn't you?"

"How could I have told him? I didn't know your plans myself. I invented some story about wanting to recover scrap metal from the gold mines, but the Sky Pilot wouldn't hear it."

"I wish you hadn't mentioned the mines at all," said Shadburn.

"I was careful not to stir up any hopes. I didn't say that I was starting any diggings. Only that the mines contained certain pieces of scrap in which the Standard Company had a passing interest. I did see some elaborate workings, too, in the tunnels. Pumps, ventilation, tracks, carts. Some could be quite valuable, Shadburn."

"You were in the mine tunnels, too? Holtzclaw, this becomes worse and worse! You did not have time to persuade the Sky Pilot to sell, but you crawled through the mud of the mine tunnels looking at scrap metal. Have you succumbed to gold fever, too? I must go back with you to Auraria, to make sure you aren't distracted."

"Give me a little more time. Let me go back and finish what I've started."

"It's decided, Holtzclaw. In truth, it's a matter of mushrooms. We started talking about Auraria's cuisine, and now, another Dahlonega breakfast does not appeal to me in the least."

"You're making business decisions based on mushrooms? We're not in the mushroom business now, are we?"

"Would that we were!" said Shadburn.

CHAPTER XI

That afternoon, for the second time in three days, Holtzclaw found himself being driven by X.T. over the Great Hogback Ridge and into the blue mist of the Lost Creek Valley. Holtzclaw's eyes were very heavy, and his head nodded against the sidewall of the carriage, only to be slammed by violent rocking as the carriage bounced over a rock or rut. For all the miles he'd traveled, he was back on the same rocky road.

"I am sorry about that, misters!" said X.T. "We had a storm this morning that was to wake the dead! That is, if they weren't already awake. Positive torrents of rain. Makes the road a mess."

Holtzclaw's head banged again into the side of the carriage. "Blast it!"

"There's no need for such language," said Shadburn.

"Sorry. It was a moment of inattention. I was half asleep."

"Then it is more disappointing. It tells me that such oaths are your natural speech, and you must defend against them with your waking mind. When those defenses are lax, then your true words emerge."

"I am a litany of disappointments to you."

"A jeweler doesn't polish the faces of the stone that have naturally cleft smooth. He polishes the rough edges."

The carriage came to a stop in front of a total washout. The Carver Creek had become the Carver Cascade. Brown water tumbled from the hillside, through a funnel created by boulders.

"Never seen that sort of freshet," said X. T. "Wasn't here before. Can't get through."

"What are our choices, then?"

"It's back up the Great Hogback about a mile, then we'll take the Salamander Trail, then down Erwin's cart track. But that's a road we take only in the best weather because it's muddy, and this isn't the best weather. If there's a washout on the Great Hogback Road, then I'd wager Erwin's will be a mudslide."

"Can we ford this washout, then?" said Holtzclaw.

"It's running fast and I don't know how deep," said X. T. "I don't have spikes on my wheels."

"We're not moving yet?" said Shadburn, emerging from inside the carriage and onto the running board. "Ah, I see."

Holtzclaw followed Shadburn's gaze and saw Princess Trahlyta. She occupied an island in the center of the muddy freshet, where the current broke around a fallen rock. She let her feet bob in the rush.

"Hello, Shadburn," said Trahlyta. "I haven't seen you in a very long time."

"Hello, princess," said Shadburn. "You're looking well. A little older. You've met my associate, Holtzclaw? I thought you two might get along."

"James and I have been across the valley several times together. He's very loyal and obedient. A model employee."

The princess sprang forward from her perch, head and arms disappearing behind a crashing wave. With an arc-like motion she was again on top her rocky island, now holding an enormous fish. She supported it under its mouth with one hand and beneath its tail with another—its ruby body extended a full two feet. The scales shimmered, set off by a cross-hatched pattern of dark lines and accented with gold; no other accent would be appropriate in Auraria. Its eyes were gold; its barb-like fins were gold; its tail was shot through with golden lines.

"You remember the wild wonder fish, don't you, Shadburn?" The waters quieted so the princess could be heard.

"I may have eaten one, once," said Shadburn.

"A wild wonder fish is not food. He's not caught with a fishhook or a line run through his tongue. His outsides are armor, and on the inside, he is metal."

Trahlyta stroked the head of the fish, and it opened its jaws, gasping. They were toothless, and the cheeks, as far as Holtzclaw could see, were fleshy and pink. She aimed the fish at Shadburn as though she were leveling a rifle. One of its side-facing eyes was fixated on Holtzclaw.

"Fish are so fragile," she said. "Always so near death, and yet they are the most vengeful of creatures. Their spirits come to you in your dreams, Shadburn, because they can swim through the night as though it were river water, and they sit cold and clammy upon your mind."

"You are threatening me with a fish?" said Shadburn. "What can they do, princess? Will they gum my toes? Flop out of my dreams and soil my slippers? Of course you would threaten us with a fish, because you could not command anything more fearful. No waves of fire for you, no falling stars. You are a local spirit. Leave that fish alone, princess. It's already suffering, the poor thing."

The wild wonder fish gave a shudder through its body and vainly flapped its tail. Trahlyta knelt on the muddy island, sheltered behind the rock, and lowered the fish back into the water. Holtzclaw couldn't see the fish itself, just the disturbance made by its passing. It swam twice around the island, then against the current, up the hillside, and away.

The princess's face brightened. With four light steps, she traveled the muddy flow from her island to the shore. "I don't want anything more than fish and streams. It would be such a strain. I don't care for booming pronouncements and vague threats, either, but my employers and subordinates sometimes expect it."

"Well, it doesn't impress me," said Shadburn.

"I assume there are grand plans?" said Trahlyta, much more cheerfully. "Dams and lakes and such?"

"Holtzclaw told you?" said Shadburn. "He insisted he knew nothing about it!"

"He didn't, but his mission was clear enough from the places where we chanced to meet."

"We met at every stream and brook," said Holtzclaw. "I am surprised that I did not see her in my wash basin or chamber pot."

"We've only just been acquainted," said the princess.

"Are we finished here?" said Shadburn. "Will you let us pass?"

The flow of the current slackened, and the Carver Creek was soon passable.

"I forgot to tell you the most essential fact about the wild wonder fish," said the princess.

"That it is delicious with browned butter?" said Shadburn.

"That his teeth, when he shows them, are spades."

Twilight was already deep by the time the stagecoach arrived in Auraria. The narrow ribbon of purple sky overhead did little to light the streets, and the green foxfire and fireflies were more atmospheric than luminous.

In the grassy square at the center of town, a yellow tent had been erected, lit from within by lanterns. Holtzclaw spotted it before Shadburn, who was editing an advertising piece with a pencil, holding a candle so near the page that Holtzclaw was nervous of fire.

"Shadburn, what is that?" asked Holtzclaw, pointing out the window.

"What do you think about this?" he said, ignoring Holtzclaw. "'A paradise for those lithe of limb and sound of lung.' Too ornate?"

"It's overwrought. Even for a club publication."

"Yes, but I want it to sound mystical, even fanciful."

"We can work on it together, later," said Holtzclaw, "but in the meantime, there's the matter of this yellow tent."

Shadburn looked up. "It's for a circus, an election, or a controversy. It's not the season for the first two, which leaves only the controversy, and I believe that we—or rather, you—are the most likely topic."

Holtzclaw seethed. All his haste had been for naught. He'd worn out his knees and had drugged himself with some mystical medicines, and it had made no difference. "If I'd had another day," he said, "I could have finished up the purchases, or at least a good portion of the important lots. But you needed me in Dahlonega. Why, Shadburn? What did my presence accomplish?"

"I think that your firsthand experience, from the field, was most impressive to the railroad men."

"They had their own firsthand experience. I meant to tell you. I saw them in the Old Rock Falls Inn. Abigail said they were miners."

Shadburn's face clouded over. "This is bad, very bad," he said. "Why didn't you tell me this before? We have given these gold seekers license to climb over our valley with their machinery."

The stagecoach stopped just outside the meeting tent, which was crammed with townsfolk and hummed with indistinct speech. The tent reminded Holtzclaw of a wasp's nest, and he was not eager to approach it any closer.

"And how do you think we should proceed?" said Holtzclaw.

"I think that you'd best go explain yourself," said Shadburn.

"Must I do it? How much? The lake, the hotel, the new town?"

"Might as well. It will all come out in the wash."

"We'll never have that property at the Terrible Cascade now, and everyone else will triple their prices. I shouldn't wonder that yesterday's customers will want to tear me to pieces unless I pay them off."

Shadburn shrugged. "Don't let it concern you."

"The prices will be ruinous to you!" said Holtzclaw. "Don't you care for profits?"

"Of course I will, but not for the moment. Tell them you are here to help them help themselves. They will listen and they will believe."

"I don't think..."

"Stop thinking, Holtzclaw, and start talking! Get out there!"

Holtzclaw tumbled from the stagecoach, compelled by Shadburn's insistent tone as if by his boot. In his haste, he had forgotten his hat. It was still inside the stagecoach, on the seat. Shadburn had turned away from the window and was much surprised when the door opened again.

"Holtzclaw, I asked you..."

"I needed my hat." Holtzclaw placed it upon his head and shut Shadburn inside.

Holtzclaw wedged himself into edge of the crowd. Because of his local hat, the distracted townsfolk did not immediately mark him as an outsider.

In the center of the tent a wooden platform had been built. Holtzclaw was gratified to see that it was not a gallows, just a dais for a central speaker. The dais was occupied by three people—Emmett, the garrulous druggist; Abigail Thompson; and an older man that Holtzclaw did not recognize.

"So you haven't seen him since you took him up to Dahlonega?" the older man asked Abigail with a precise voice that cut through the muttering din of the crowd.

"Not since I left him at the Tanner building just off the square, Dr. Rathbun," said Abigail. "He said they were offices that he'd rented. He seemed pleasant enough to me."

"Did he ask questions?" said Dr. Rathbun.

"Not too many," said Abigail.

"Emmett, you saw him twice at least," said Dr. Rathbun.

"He came in the store, and then I saw him at the Grayson House. Sold him Effervescent Brain Salts and a box of Pharaoh's Flour. He wasn't looking for anything strange. Fellow said he had a powerful headache, but he looked like he was feeling better by the time he showed up at the Grayson House. He had a bit of a long talk with your daughter there, Dr. Rathbun."

"Did he? She didn't confess that," said Dr. Rathbun. "Untoward advances?"

"Just saw them talking at the foot of the stairs," said Emmett. "You know how loud it is in there. Couldn't hear a word two feet away."

"Ms. Thompson? Did the stranger make any untoward advances to you?"

Abigail shook her head.

"Did he tell either of you what he wanted?" said Dr. Rathbun.

"There was some bull story about scrap metal!" shouted someone from off the dais.

"Yes, I heard that's what he told Bogan," said someone else.

"There's no mine on the Moss farm," chimed a fat man. "Moss doesn't have so much as a tin cup for scrap metal."

"I had a gold nugget!" said Moss, shouting from across the crowd. "That is worth a lot more than a tin cup or any scrap metal, which is all you'll ever see."

"You had a gold nugget, but you gambled it all away in one night!" said a raspy-voiced woman.

"That's my business!" answered Moss.

"You are all going to simmer down," said Dr. Rathbun. "We don't run an inquest by shouting. Raise your hand and you'll be asked up here to have your say."

Holtzclaw raised his hand. Recognition spread out from him like a ripple across the surface of a lake; concentric rings of heads turned toward him.

"That's him! The one that bought up my land!" This voice was unfamiliar, young and wavering.

"That fellow?" said the fat man. "Wasn't he supposed to have a shock of red hair, and a beard?"

"Be six feet tall with a limp?" said someone else.

"Mary said it was two men, twins, with clean black suits," said a trim woman who looked like a schoolmistress.

The crowd shrank back from Holtzclaw like skin from a wound. He climbed the two steps, and his shoulder was caught by Abigail. She whispered into his ear, but there was too little voice behind her whisper and too much noise from the crowd. "I'm sorry," he mouthed, hoping that she would understand. She sizzled as she strode away.

"Now, let's all calm down," said Dr. Rathbun. "We want to hear what this fellow has to say, don't we? Go ahead, Mr. Handclaw."

"It's Holtzclaw," he said.

"The consensus was Handclaw," said Dr. Rathbun.

"I said, 'Holdcow!'"

"No, 'Wholecloth!'"

"No, it's Holtzclaw," said Holtzclaw again.

"Abigail was right then," said Dr. Rathbun. "Go ahead, Mr. Holtzclaw. Settle them down and say your piece."

Holtzclaw tried a number of rhetorical gestures to capture the attention of the crowd. He cleared his throat and begged their pardon, but these small tricks were lost in the noise. He held up his arms in an expansive Y-shape, as he had seen politicians do at the culmination of their arguments. Even the Asheville Attitude was ineffective, though it had no real hopes of success in this environment, one against many. In desperation, Holtzclaw stomped his boot against the wooden plank of the dais. The footfalls rang out like shots, echoed by the hollow space below, but these explosions did not disrupt the crowd.

"Just start talking," said Dr. Rathbun, "and those that want will listen."

Holtzclaw sketched in broad strokes, which was as much as he understood it, the plans for the future of the Lost Creek Valley. "We have planned a great transformation for your valley. Your buildings are crumbling in the weather, your fields are frozen, your mines empty. And your response to all of this was to bury your noses in the earth, looking for flakes of gold. You have let your other natural resources go to waste, because you were obsessed with gold. Soon, all of that will be scrubbed away. The Standard Company is buying the valley. We mean to own all of it, from the river to the mountaintops. At one end, we'll put a dam, and the river will become a beautiful lake. On its shores will be a grand hotel, populated by the best people in all seasons, with splendid cuisine and gala dancing. The railroad will arrive from Dahlonega, bringing passengers and mail and such exquisite things to buy—things from the city and from across the sea. The railroad will carry back the results of your industry and reward you with money to buy these luxuries. It's the beginning of a new age of prosperity. Honest, good-paying work will be available at the hotel we're building, in the gardens, at the depot, and at sawmills and tanneries. Any who lose their livelihoods will gain better ones."

He paused for gasps or applause, but the angry noise of the crowd persisted. Even Holtzclaw wasn't positive that any of these promises could be realized.

"He talks like a book, and lies like one too! A fairy-tale book!" yelled someone close to Holtzclaw's ear.

"The whole matter will be clearer in the morning," said Holtzclaw. "I can bring you some charts. On a map, you will see how it is all to work. We are here to help you."

"Who is we? This Standard Company?" said the schoolmistress.

"Who do you work for?" said the fat man.

"My employer came with me tonight," said Holtzclaw. "This is his plan. His name is H. E. Shadburn, of Milledgeville. No, of Auraria."

"Here I am, as summoned."

Heads turned as the name was invoked. Shadburn stood above them all. He had put on new cufflinks of bright silver. His shoes were polished, and his hands were tucked into his suit-coat pockets, to show his ease. When he doffed his cap and held it to his chest, his baldness was proud and shining in the lantern light.

All the assembled crowd looked up to him, the rich man.

"Hiram, is it you? Hiram?" The widow Smith Patterson addressed Shadburn. Her voice quivered, and Holtzclaw imagined that he could see tears welling in her eyes, lit by the fires all around them.

Shadburn nodded.

The widow Smith Patterson grabbed his ear and pulled, forcing Shadburn to bow. "Where have you been, Hiram? Where have you been?"

Book II

Negotiations with the dead had come to a standstill. The dead sat on their gravestones and refused to move. Holtzclaw's hired gravediggers idled on the perimeter of the cemetery, shovels in hand, but sentiment and superstition prevented them from digging up coffins while being watched by the occupants.

Holtzclaw was annoyed at the impasse; it was yet another expense, more wasted money. They had spent so much already. After the tent meeting, Holtzclaw had thought that he and Shadburn would be run out of town—loaded into a turnip cart and pulled back up the mountainside. But Shadburn had sent Holtzclaw forth with a pile of money: federal notes, gold coins, shining promises. Such treasures softened their hearts. Holtzclaw was authorized to spend whatever was necessary to unseat the owners. It rankled him, to be so undisciplined, and yet, these were his employer's orders.

For those who had concerns beyond money, Holtzclaw could promise them housing and jobs in the coming hotel. A neat company town was taking shape above the flood line. There was a gleaming set of offices for Dr. Rathbun, a three-story guest house with a large sign announcing the new location of McTavish's, and two dozen pretty white houses with wide porches and well-swept front stoops. Nothing had yet been set up for the Old Rock Falls yet; Holtzclaw had other plans for it.

It had taken months, but now, all the living landowners had been bought out, save one. The Sky Pilot was still obstinate, but Holtzclaw and Shadburn had an arrangement to proceed despite him. In any other of Shadburn's ventures, this would have been the end of the project. Shadburn and company would have delivered a bound fascicle of land deeds to the client who'd contracted for their services and left the construction—the realization—to him. In imitation of their usual ritual, Holtzclaw had ceremoniously handed just such a bundle to Shadburn: a hundred land deeds, formally executed and notarized. Shadburn set a coffee mug on the papers and asked Holtzclaw where they stood on the construction of the dam.

That should have been his primary concern—dramatic, geological work. He did not need more troubles from petulant dead.

"Who is in charge here?" said Holtzclaw, passing the gravediggers and addressing the dead, who were sitting on their stones, squatting on his land.

"There is no authority," said a man whose beard tangled around his bare feet. "There is only the wind."

"I meant, someone who can negotiate for you," said Holtzclaw. "With whom can I speak?"

"You may speak with any of us," said a woman, calico-clad. "So few do. We would be glad of the company."

"But whom can I speak with who can authorize relocation?"

"There is no authority. There is only the wind."

"Well, who has been here the longest?" said Holtzclaw.

The dead pointed blue fingers at a small girl. Her gravestone was a crude boulder, and she huddled on the top with her knees drawn to her chest. Like the others, her skin was clammy, and her face was streaked with dirt. She looked as though the rain had eroded her, left her smaller and more worn than she should have been. Around her eyes and mouth were folds that should not have been found on a young girl.

"Hello," said Holtzclaw, in as neutral a tone as he could muster. She looked like a small girl, but if she were the earliest laid to rest, then she was many dozens of years his elder. It was a delicate situation that was not addressed in etiquette manuals.

The girl drew her knees closer and began to turn away.

"Hello, there. My name is James. What's your name?" Holtzclaw's voice softened.

"Emmy," said the girl.

"Hello, Emmy. How old do you think you are?"

"Six," she said.

"Six, that's almost grown up! Your friends say that you have been here the longest. Is that right?"

Emmy nodded.

"So if you asked them to do something, do you think they'd listen?" Holtzclaw hoped that she would not wax oracular about the authority of wind, but Emmy only nodded again. "I have a problem, Emmy, and you can help me."

Emmy uncurled her legs and let her feet rest on the earth, so that her gravestone was now a stool.

"Emmy, my employer is very mad at me."

"What's an employer?" said Emmy.

"I suppose it's like a father, but for your work," said Holtzclaw. "Did your father or mother have work?"

"They were farmers. They were always very busy. They didn't have fathers for their work. There was no one else here."

"That must have been nice," said Holtzclaw. "You could do whatever you wanted."

"It was lonely," said Emmy. "It was very lonely for a very long time until the rest of the family came here." Emmy looked over a row of gravestones. The family resemblance among their occupants was noticeable. "Why is your work father mad at you?"

"Because I cannot do my work," said Holtzclaw.

"Sometimes I didn't do my work," said Emmy. "I was being lazy or sleepy or I was dead. You should do your work."

"Did you have any chores like feeding the chickens? You took the corn out to the chickens, but the chickens wouldn't come in, or the chickens wouldn't eat? Was it your fault that the chickens wouldn't eat? You did all you could, but the chickens got you in trouble!"

Emmy laughed.

"Well, my work father has told me that I need to clear this graveyard. So it will be cold and dark and not pleasant at all. It will be under water!"

Emmy curled up again on the pinnacle of her stone.

"I know, it is scary. You and your friends don't want to be here when that happens. So we have a new home for you. There are men with shovels there who will take the dirt and bones up the hill and to a new field, which is very lovely."

"Is it far away?" said Emmy.

"At the top of the hill up there." said Holtzclaw. "Do you want to come with me to see it? Can you come see it? No one will disturb anything while we are gone. I promise."

Emmy fiddled with string around her neck and drew out a leather pouch. She descended from the gravestone and scratched at the base with both hands until she had loosened a mound of earth and dust. She filled her pouch with this earth and hid it again beneath the collar of her dress.

She held up a hand to Holtzclaw. It was gray with the grave dust. Holtzclaw hesitated for only a fraction of a moment, then took it in his own, and they began walking.

The town was soon behind them. They followed a narrow path made by occasional foot traffic. Holtzclaw had learned, in his four months in the Lost Creek Valley, that the roads and cart paths were often the least direct routes. A complex series of lesser pathways, made by the desires of valley residents, were far more expedient. The architecture of these desire paths was historical, not logical. They had been made by friendship, enmity, and courting.

Holtzclaw and Emmy turned from the path that led from Harbin's old turkey pasture to McConnell's fallow fields, where the birds could forage without fear. For a while, they followed a route that the Lawrence children had taken to Snell's barn. On Saturday nights, Snell shooed his pigs and put up a dance floor, charging a penny a head and selling pies and lemonade. The dances had not been popular with the Stones higher on the ridge, so to continue their ascent, Holtzclaw and Emmy took an old fur traders' trail, very old but so worn by the frequent passing of big men that it was still passable. Near the top of the ridge, they came under high-canopy forest, where the underbrush had been cleared by Trip's pigs rooting for mast.

Emmy clapped her hands and ran to the base of an oak tree, knelt down, and brushed away the leaf cover. A perfect yellow trumpet poked up from the soil. Emmy plucked it and gave it to Holtzclaw.

"I was always the best mushroomer," said Emmy. "I could see them before any of my brothers or sisters."

"Well, it looks delicious," said Holtzclaw. "I will be glad to fry it up in butter when I get home."

"You can eat them fresh," said Emmy. "There's more goodness."

Holtzclaw looked over the yellow trumpet which now did not look so perfect. The cap had a white smear, and an unknown fuzziness clung to the gills. Emmy looked on expectantly, so Holtzclaw popped the mushroom into his mouth.

The mushroom had a nutty taste to start, like an almond, then finished with a fruit-like lingering akin to an apricot. The mouthfeel was not unpleasant. In his mind, Holtzclaw drew on the stock of adjectives refined by years of claret. To Emmy, he said, "Oh, very tasty."

"Let me find you some more."

Their progress on the last quarter mile was much slower. Emmy scurried from tree to tree, hole to hole. She looked under rocks and beneath fallen limbs, and by the time they emerged into the grassy field that was designated for the new graveyard, Holtzclaw's pockets were stuffed with a dozen kinds of mushrooms: red-capped, spotted, black, yellow, stemmed, rounded, flat, tall, puffy, reedy.

"You'll have a lovely lunch," said Emmy.

"Did you ever look for ginseng?" said Holtzclaw. "I was told that was a popular occupation."

Emmy looked down at her feet. "I don't like ginseng. He looks like a little man, and he cries when you take him out of the dirt. Mushrooms don't mind getting picked. The real mushroom is down under the ground, and what you pick is just a tiny piece. You can come back later, and the real mushroom under the ground has made a new sprout for you to pick. You can be friends."

The forest broke into a bald at the top of Green Mountain. A rocky promontory afforded a view to the north. One could look down into the forest and see a breeze meander through a canopy of leaves, and the sun would not be harsh here, nor the rains hard and driving. All of this Holtzclaw explained to Emmy.

"And you could go into the forest for mushrooms whenever you like," he concluded.

"We don't roam very much," said Emmy. "It is not our time. But it is beautiful up here. Where will the lake be? And the town?"

Holtzclaw indicated towards the south and west, but taller trees blocked the view of the sites.

"So far away? Now we are in the middle of town. We see everyone that walks past."

"Yes, but that is not the modern model. You might prefer a quiet place, away from the bustle, where you could reflect in tranquility."

"Where we would not bother the living. Where no one would have to think about us."

"No one could visit you if the graveyard were at the bottom of the lake. Here, you will have some visitors. I will come visit. We can go mushroom picking."

Emmy squeezed his hand, and Holtzclaw regretted his lie. It was not yet a lie, he decided. He would visit, at least once, before the Auraria project was finished.

Holtzclaw and Emmy turned back towards the valley.

"I don't know if this is a polite question," said Holtzclaw, when they had passed under the forest canopy, again into the smell of leaf and mushroom, "but do you ever tell how you passed away? How you died?"

"Yes, we talk and remember. Some of us died very badly, others sweetly."

"How did you die?" asked Holtzclaw.

"Poison mushroom," she said. She gave him another one, taken from the leaf litter at the base of a majestic chestnut—orange, bi-lobed, with a creamy swirl.

The Sky Pilot and Holtzclaw met on a rock jutting out over the Terrible Cascade. The Sky Pilot had put two chairs onto this precarious promontory, but Holtzclaw's first act was to move his chair from its adversarial stance to a position right next to the Sky Pilot's, on the same side of the table. The noise of the waterfall would have made any other configuration impossible.

"Since we've sat down so many times," roared the Sky Pilot into Holtzclaw's ear, "I thought you would enjoy a change of scenery."

"I promise this will be our last negotiation," said Holtzclaw. "We are prepared to accept your refusal. The railroad men have assured us that the alternate site is acceptable. We don't need your property, Mr. Pilot."

"But here you are."

"Acceptable does not mean ideal. Here is what you're forcing us to build, because of your contrariness. On the one side of your property, the upstream side, you will have a dam, rising sixty feet above your head, and on the other there will be a dry gorge. The water will be carried from the dam spillway through a wooden flume. We are going to put the river in a suspended wooden chute and carry it through the air for a mile, over your head, to the other end of the gorge and into the powerhouse. Imagine that! What acrobatics of engineering! There will be not a drop of water through the Terrible Cascade."

"You can manage all this with touching my soil?"

"Yes, we can. We have spent a great deal of time on these alternate dam plans," said Holtzclaw. "A great deal of additional expense, too—engineering, scouting, construction. It took buckets of money, just buckets."

"Money comes in buckets?" said the Sky Pilot.

"It does not come in buckets, but it leaves in them. We can put these plans aside, Mr. Pilot, if you are willing to sell. With your co-operation, we won't need to build this foolish and fragile chute; our dam can have a normal cascading spillway. As it stands, you will be the only person to get no money from this project. It is deeply disturbing to Shadburn. Everyone else in town will be compensated in some way—many have gotten paid for their land, and even those that had no land have the promise of new industrial and service jobs that are much more reliable than farming and mining. Everyone has his reward, Mr. Pilot! But if you don't sell, you'll get nothing. You will get less than nothing—you will lose even the water and sunlight that you have now."

"I cannot leave my friend," said the Sky Pilot. "As long as he is here, I will not be moved."

"Yes, your friend. Will your friend not be persuaded to relocate?"

"He has special requirements," said the Sky Pilot.

"We have made spectacular accommodations for others. Can I talk with him, please?"

The Sky Pilot thought for several minutes. He stared into the crashing waters falling.

"I suppose that he won't like it if the Cascade goes dry," said the Sky Pilot. "That won't do for him at all. You had better talk to him. I cannot make decisions for him."

"Yes! Let us go see your friend. Can we go now?" said Holtzclaw.

"I will get the rope," said the Sky Pilot.

Minutes later, Holtzclaw dangled from a rope harness and was being lowered into the gorge by the Sky Pilot. His feet dangled in space above the churning current of the Terrible Cascade. With his eyes only a few feet from the cliff face, Holtzclaw could see that wall was a complicated network of fractures, outcrops, crevices, and slides. Tiny trees clung to the face of the cliff, growing in teaspoons of soil that had found their way into depressions. The spray of the falls kept them moist.

Holtzclaw had been so focused on his white-knuckled hands that the arrival of the ledge beneath his feet came as a surprise. The ledge was still a hundred feet above the water, but he did not need to descend any further. Holtzclaw stepped out of the loop seat and tugged on the rope three times, which was the signal that the Sky Pilot could let it go slack for a time.

The ledge provided access to a rocky fissure, which opened into a cavern fifty feet wide and twenty feet tall at its highest point. Entering, Holtzclaw felt coolness, caused not just by the twilight. Water gurgled unseen through the rock. The floor was glass-smooth and slick from moisture. The ceiling was domed, like an odeon. The space would make an interesting dance hall if it weren't so difficult to reach. To one side of the cavern, Holtzclaw saw silk-and-straw wrapped bundles—the Sky Pilot's store of ice.

Holtzclaw called out a hallo. From the deeper shadows of the cavern came a scrabbling noise, then the sound of an enormous weight being dragged along the stone surface. A leathery head emerged into view, and behind it, the idea of a shell that filled the cavern, floor to ceiling. "I am the Great and Harmless and Invincible Terrapin that Lives Under the Mountain."

"I am James Holtzclaw, pleased to make your acquaintance."

"Welcome, little morsel! I will tell you a story. Long ago, when the world was soft and had not yet been baked hard by the sun, I was a small terrapin. The sun began to blaze, and I fled from its heat. I burrowed into the mud, and as I grew I made larger and larger channels. I came to this place where the rock was soft and the valley was cool and dark, and I have lived here ever since. I am old here."

"Well, I am new here," said Holtzclaw. "We are developing this valley."

"What does it mean, develop?" said the Great and Harmless and Invincible Terrapin.

"We are going to build a hotel, a company town, and bring in industries," said Holtzclaw. "We are going to flood the valley and turn it into a lake."

"Long ago, a flood came over the lands. Much more than the valley was underwater. The whole world was underwater. The land became soft again, and I pushed my head out from the top of Sinking Mountain, which in those days had no name. I saw the Great Bird fly over the earth, looking for dry land, and his wings pushed up mountains and pushed down the valleys, and they were filled then with men and creatures."

"Were they men and creatures of ordinary size? Or were they all as big as you?"

"No, long ago we were all small. Many died before they could become large. Those of us that lived on became Great. Not all who are Great are Harmless or Invincible. I think that the Armadillo is also Great and Harmless and Invincible. The Great and Harmless and Invincible Armadillo and I once ventured to the vast southern desert together. The sun had been hanging over that land for many years, and the earth was scorched into a red clay that burned the tender parts between our claws."

"But you said that you are invincible."

"Just because I am Invincible does not mean that I do not suffer pain," said the Great and Harmless and Invincible Terrapin. "I suffer the pain of many, many long years spent under the mountain."

"Then perhaps you will be receptive to my offer, because we would like to remove you from under this mountain and give you a new home."

"Where would my home be?"

"Wherever the Sky Pilot chooses to live, I suppose," said Holtzclaw.

"He will go where I choose. Long ago, a Great Serpent lived in the mountains to the north. He was an acquaintance of mine. He was also Invincible, but he was not Harmless. He ate many creatures, including men, whom he enjoyed because they were soft on the outside and crisp on the inside. The Great Serpent and I quarreled, and he departed the mountains. He made this terrible valley as he descended. That is why it is so crooked and narrow and deep, because of the passing of his Serpent body."

"Why didn't you follow him?"

"Below here are the flatlands, and there are so many tracks on the flatlands. The Great Deer ran across them in the time before the sun baked the earth. The Great Bird covered them over with fallen seeds. The Great Roly-Poly pushed them flat with his rolling and polling, so that I could not see where the Great Serpent had gone. I was not yet Great, and I could not roam forever looking for the Great Serpent. So I stayed, where I could last see the signs of his passing. Now I am like the Serpent. I am Great. There is one who follows me, who is the Sky Pilot. Where ever I will go, he will go. That is my choice and his destiny, until he is Great or dead. Will my cavern be flooded when you have made your development?"

"No, it will be dry," said Holtzclaw. "There will be no more water coming through the gorge."

"That will be a sadness, but weeping will not make it wet again. I shall continue to live here."

"If there is no other cavern to suit you, we can build one. We can blast it from the rock with dynamite and bring in pumps to make wet or dry, for your comfort."

"I do not need your little fireworks to make a home," said the Great and Harmless and Invincible Terrapin. "My beak is sharp and my claws are strong. My shell can raise the earth. I can bring down any mountain that I choose. I do not want another cavern. I will stay here and wait for the Great Serpent, or I will wait until the Sky Pilot or some other man becomes Great."

"I find your mythology very confusing," said Holtzclaw.

"Listen, little morsel! It is very simple. A long time ago I came here. A long time from now I may leave. As for now, I and my friend will stay. Now, I will play the Song of Parting for you."

The Great and Harmless and Invincible Terrapin lifted up its head, which revealed a patch of pink skin along its throat. The skin vibrated as the terrapin wheezed. Its breaths became deeper; a long tone began to issue from its nose. Above and below this note, others began to sound from within the shell of the Great and Harmless and Invincible Terrapin. Ridges and fissures and gaps modified the tone; flexure of muscles changed the rhythm and pitch. When the pipes of the Great and Harmless and Invincible Terrapin's internal organ were sounding at their full volume and pace, the Song of Parting had a jolly, jaunty swing—the sound of a mazurka, not a dirge.

CHAPTER XIII

S hadburn's office in Auraria had developed a peculiar aroma during the months he'd occupied it. A plate of hash browns, piled high with mushrooms, exuded its vapors into the atmosphere. A kettle, hung over the fire, whistled steam. The leaves had lost much of their freshness, and the unwashed cups had acquired a patina that leeched into the cup and overpowered the tea with a musty, warmed-over scent. These were not the worst smells: a man sitting in a room too long fills it with various emanations and eructations.

Had they set up their offices in Walton's infinite dwelling, the worst of these odors would have diffused among the many stories. But Shadburn had insisted on a different space, any space. He had spent too many unproductive hours in the Walton house, he'd said. Instead, he and Holtzclaw had occupied a second-story warren of rooms above an abandoned storefront.

"Come in, Holtzclaw," said Shadburn. "Excuse the mess. Have a seat." To emphasize his order, Shadburn pointed to a chair that was already occupied with papers. "I've finished with those. You can dump them out," said Shadburn.

Holtzclaw removed a few sheets from the top of the pile.

"I did not say examine them," said Shadburn.

"These are receipts, bills of sale," said Holtzclaw. "They should be indexed."

"The work has been done and the money paid," said Shadburn. "Why keep them?"

"In case there is some dispute," said Holtzclaw.

"It is useless jetsam," said Shadburn. "In a true knock-'em-down dispute, each party will produce contradictory receipts and claim the others were false. They are easy to falsify."

Shadburn took the receipts that Holtzclaw was holding, tore them into pieces, and cast them into the fire. Rising cinders extinguished themselves against the cast iron of the kettle.

"You have a few thousand others here," said Holtzclaw. "Will you burn them, too?"

"I'll burn the whole building. It must be destroyed, just like all the others, before the floodgates are closed. Now, be kind enough to take a seat."

Holtzclaw lifted the back of the chair, and the pile of papers fell forwards onto the floor. A stain on the fabric disconcerted Holtzclaw; he stooped to inspect it and was relieved to find it was likely tea and in any case long dried.

"Alas, I have not offered you anything to eat, Holtzclaw!" said Shadburn. "The best I can give is the remainder of my lunch." He extended the plate containing the half-eaten, mostly cooled mound of mushroom-topped hash browns. With his other hand, he wiped a fork against his trouser leg.

"Would you believe I have had my fill of mushrooms today?" said Holtzclaw. He recounted his visit with Emmy and his hopes that the dead would soon be persuaded to move.

"If they do not want to cooperate, then we may have to proceed past them," said Shadburn.

"Do you mean, not relocate the graveyard?" said Holtzclaw.

"We can move the stones without permission from the ghosts."

"The trouble is that the dead are sitting on those stones, and my men are not brave enough to approach them and remove the stones from underneath."

"Then we can order new stones," said Shadburn. "Marble ones, or granite. Whichever you think. Have them engraved appropriately, with names and dates."

"Then we do not move the bodies?"

"I don't care, Holtzclaw. Do it however you think best. Only, do not hold up the matter any further. Now, did you talk with the Sky Pilot?"

Holtzclaw nodded. "More significantly, I talked with a large terrapin, who is the Sky Pilot's conscience on the matter."

Shadburn sighed. "That fat turtle..."

Holtzclaw nodded. "Our conversation did not accomplish much, and at the end, it played for me a song that emphasized that it will not be moved, and by extension, neither will the Sky Pilot. I am not sure what other legal recourse we have. Some kind of condemnation proceedings?"

"Too slow," said Shadburn. "We'll put the dam upstream, as we said."

"But the cost..."

"Another strongbox arrived just this morning from the Bank of the Ozarks. Half of it I've already paid out to the railroad men, but there is still money, and a good many more boxes besides."

"Money in, money out! I am afraid, Shadburn, that your affection for your hometown is leading to ill-advised business decisions. If any project were to drain your coffers, it would be this one—a project with high passions and mysterious happenings, into which you are willing to pour every penny without any trace or plan."

Shadburn, using two fingers, lifted a mushroom from the cold plate of hash browns. He lowered the grey, butter-slathered thing onto his outstretched tongue and drew it into his mouth. "I didn't get all of this money to spend on dams and lakes and marble headstones by being bad at business, did I? I didn't win your loyalty by being bad at business, did I? Have you known any of my projects to fail, in the final calculation? We are spending for a better cause than most."

"If you run out of money before you see your project through, then no one will ever benefit."

"Then I will take care not to run out."

Holtzclaw kicked over a tower of receipts. "You don't even know how much you've spent today. How much gold has fallen from your fingers."

Shadburn turned away, back to his lunch.

Holtzclaw pressed his anger and confusion into a little knot, a gallstone, and what was left was an emptiness that resonated with hunger. He hadn't had lunch; that should be a simple enough problem to solve. The palaver with Shadburn had parched him worse than a morning spent climbing the valley slopes. Outside of the Old Rock Falls Inn, a new fruit hanging from a shrub attracted Holtzclaw's attention. It was difficult to ignore—the smell was unpleasant, and the noise worse, but no one was tending it. The shrub had been only a woody passel when Holtzclaw had first noticed it, but it had grown quickly.

The locals called it a sheep-fruit plant. It had been agitated by the work in the valley, and its fruits had come out early, over-plump and strained. They resembled eggplants, including a purple skin, and they were covered with a fine white fuzz that made them more closely resemble their namesake. And like their namesake, the sheep-fruit bleated to express their content or displeasure, and in this late season, the fruit had become much more vocal. Their angry cries affected the sleep of the townsfolk, even those inured to barn-yard noises.

This shrub had five or six sheep-fruit hanging from it, and they were very disturbed about the presence of another—a twisted, half-rotten husk that had clung to the vine for too long. The better sheep-fruit bleated and whined, clucked and snuffled. They made such a fuss that it was a wonder anyone could pass by and not act. Holtzclaw grabbed the rotten fruit at the top and yanked. It came free easily; there was not much strength left in its stem.

The demeanor of the other fruit changed. The offender was no longer in the realm of their senses, which did not extend beyond the shoots and leaves of the shrub. One of the fruit purred, like a cat. Others gently rocked on their vines, mewing.

"What are you going to do with that?" A boy at Holtzclaw's elbow gestured to the rotten fruit that he held.

"With this awful thing?" said Holtzclaw. "Throw it into the woods."

"Let me have it," said the boy.

"Why? Are you going to smear it in your sister's hair? Put it on the school matron's stool?"

"I'm going to put it up as preserves."

"Come now. You can think of a better lie than marmalade."

"It's not a lie," said the boy. "Chop it up fine, then put it up with some wood berries. Sweet. Old folks like it too."

"Do the ripe ones taste better than the rotting?"

"I've never tasted the ripe ones. They go on pleading and bleating right up until you stew them up in butter and even a little past. Sometimes they moan on the plate. Other boys will eat them, but not me. I don't want to kill an innocent creature."

"You'd kill a chicken," said Holtzclaw.

"A chicken has wings—it could have flown. It has claws and a beak—it could have fought back. A sheep-fruit is helpless. That's why I only eat the rotten ones. They don't suffer."

"Well, even if it isn't true, it is a good enough story to earn your prize. Have it."

The boy pressed the narrow end of the fruit between his fingers. A brownish softness oozed from a hole in the skin. The boy got it on the side of his finger and put it into his mouth.

"Tastes like relief," said the boy, but he did not offer any to Holtzclaw.

"I've already put the fire out," said Abigail as Holtzclaw entered the dining room of the Old Rock Falls. "I don't have any food for you."

"No biscuits or stew or fried meats?"

"Nothing warm," she said. "I suppose you could pluck one of the sheep-fruit and have it on bread."

"I'd prefer not. How about a glass of claret?"

"Our supplier hasn't made the run since the railroad construction started. He can make a better wage running chuck up to the crews, which leaves us short on certain vital commodities, like claret."

"I can speak to Shadburn about that. He does not want the town to be in want. We could award a small subsidy for deliveries to you and other townsfolk, to stay competitive with the other enterprises cropping up."

"Such a heroic action," said Abigail. "A small subsidy to the rescue."

"It would only be temporary, and the permanent solution is on the horizon. When the railroad is running, you will have access to such an array of goods as you've never seen before, and at better prices, too."

"When the railroad is running, the Old Rock Falls will be drowned," said Abigail.

"There is a site uphill ready for your new construction," said Holtzclaw.

"That's no substitute. Do you think my guests would be so ready to move? Would Mr. Bad Thing settle into a new home? He was so accustomed to this place that even death could not separate him from his routine."

"I have become a bit of an old hat at persuading ghosts to relocate. Just this morning I ate mushrooms with the leader of the dead; I took her by the hand and we walked together. I could speak with Mr. Bad Thing and any of the others that are reluctant to exchange their old haunt for a new one."

The piano, which had been softly tinkling in the background of their conversation, ceased.

"He's not interested," said Abigail.

The piano started again with a new tune: a loose interpretation of the Song of Parting. One could hardly expect the same sort of performance from a haunted piano and from the shell of the Great and Harmless and Invincible Terrapin.

"You know that the centerpiece of this project is a hotel, yes?" said Holtzclaw. "I thought it would be right and proper to honor local traditions within that hotel. We would have local lumber, local stone. Decorations evoking the past of this valley—though the gold mining history is to be absent, per Shadburn's orders. A taproom that is the spitting image of the Old Rock Falls, even. Your bar and floorboards and tables. Hulen's stool. The row of mugs and photographs on the wall."

"Wouldn't your fine guests want something more plush and luxurious?"

"There can be two dining rooms," said Holtzclaw. "One will have crushed velvet and brass finials, and one will have a piano for Mr. Bad Thing to play any tune he wishes."

"What if the occasional shadow came unfixed and flew about the room? What would your guests think of that?"

"They would call it character," said Holtzclaw. "They might even enjoy it. Of course, to ensure the success of the whole operation, we would need an experienced hotel manager. You would be my top choice for such a post."

"Not Lizzie Rathbun?" said Abigail.

"The kind of establishment she keeps is out of line with the expectations of my employer and his anticipated clientele."

Abigail removed some copper mugs from a wash basin where they had been soaking. "You would sound less awkward if the hotel had a name," she said.

"It does not, as of yet."

"You can't make one up?"

"No, I wouldn't venture. What would you call it?"

"The Auraria Hotel," said Abigail.

"I think that Shadburn will be downplaying that name. It is difficult to clarify without reference to gold. But, to add to what I was saying, you would have the advantage of a regular salary."

"As long as there are any guests," said Abigail.

"The hotel is bound to succeed. Shadburn is at the helm, and he has yet to fail on any project that I have known. He has a Midas touch."

Abigail laughed. "He is turning us to gold, is he? I thought he wanted to turn the gold into anything else: spring water or corundum or tannins or sawdust or corn meal. At least, that's what I gather when he's here eating his sweet potatoes and ramps and hash browns with mushrooms."

"Isn't he taking his meals in his offices?" said Holtzclaw.

"Not all of them," said Abigail. "He can't be a hermit in his hometown."

"It's just that if he's abroad, my job is more difficult. I don't know whom he's seen or what he's promised."

"Trouble between the two of you?"

"Not in the least. He has my complete faith." The words were perfunctory and automatic; Holtzclaw hoped they did not sound that way to Abigail.

"It has never mattered to me if the Old Rock Falls is successful," said Abigail, "but I suppose after the lake is in, it will."

"How do you mean?"

"In the valley, there is money under every rock. A nugget beneath an eddy. An iron pot with a few old grains lost in rust at the bottom. Colors pour down the streets when it rains. But when it's all underwater, who knows? Will I ever dream about gold again?"

"If you want to recover some of this money, I can outfit an expedition," said Holtzclaw. "You should undertake one scouting trip, at least, while you have the chance. If only to satisfy your own curiosity. Else, you would never know if you dreamed true."

"My curiosity does not need satisfaction," said Abigail. One conversation would not be enough to reveal her secrets. The closer she held them, the more valuable she must believe them to be.

CHAPTER XIV

When Holtzclaw, still unfed and dissatisfied, stepped out of the Old Rock Falls, the sky was clouded with an even, featureless grey that promised rain. While rain was not unusual, the princess often neglected the clouds. Drizzle fell from the ribbon of clear blue sky. The clouds were reassuring; they promised a natural rain.

He crossed over to the Grayson House, where there was sure to be some hot food, but a series of flashes from the mountain caught Holtzclaw's attention. Pops of green light signaled across the mountainside—two or three, then a dozen. He thought first of lightning, then foxfire. The light was too regular for those phenomena, yet too bright for railroad lanterns. The lights fired in patterns: first a line from right to left, then left to right, then a staggered wave, then every second, every third.

Then a green light hovered just in front of him. The central orb, floating at eye level, was as tall and broad as Shadburn's. A second, smaller orb floated behind, slightly out-of-sync with its partner. Flitting across the surface of each orb was a complicated pattern of green lines, like shattered glass, but its crazed surface was in flux. Orbiting these two main spheres were a dozen smaller, brilliant green lights. They varied in shape, speed, direction, and number from moment to moment. Two or three would squeeze into narrow streaks and make several quick equatorial orbits, but then a slow-moving glob would cross their path, and three lights would smash into one, careening on a wild zigzag above the surface of the large orb before dividing again.

The will-o'-the-wisp emitted a confusion of hums, buzzes, snaps, and discharges. Holtzclaw couldn't tell if the noises and lights were random, or if they were part of some complicated pattern language beyond his understanding. He tipped his hat in greeting to the orbs, but they did not change their display.

"If you are an ectoplasm belonging to a dead and vengeful spirit," said Holtzclaw, "negotiations are being conducted with your kind through a mushroom-loving little girl. If you are a spell or astral projection, I will need to know your master, with whom I can speak.

If you are a weather phenomenon, I would ask you to kindly wait your turn—we are dealing with several already. If you are a plat-eye and seek to remove my head, I must ask you to refrain, because I still have need of it. If you are related to rabbit-faced women from the moon, then I would direct you to a different party here in the valley. And if I haven't guessed it, please make some sort of sign, so that I can serve you right."

The will-o'-the-wisp wavered in front of Holtzclaw for a moment, then floated backwards, away from him. It came to a stop thirty feet away, off the road, above the turkey drovers' field.

"Am I to follow you?" Holtzclaw called to the retreating object. He walked towards the orbs, which held their position over the same bit of earth. As Holtzclaw neared, the will-o'-the-wisp dipped low and touched the ground. The earth sizzled when touched, and the green light backed away from the burned spot.

Holtzclaw picked up a stick and scratched at the earth, which yielded to the makeshift spade. Ten inches down, the spade met a solid obstacle, a flat rock that he pried up and flipped over. On its underside was a crude etching of a lizard-like creature with six clawed feet.

Beneath was a depression, lined with cloth, that held a hodgepodge of artifacts. A piece of red clay pottery that had been glazed over with a grey finish and painted with interlocking squares. A bear carved from bone. A wooden spool wound with three different color threads. A tin spoon. It looked like a child's hoard, but a child's hoard does not often contain gold coins. They had been wrapped inside a faded paper label that had been removed from a bottle of Dr. Pep. There were two coins, very old, both with Spanish markings.

The owner of these goods had chosen a very poor hiding spot. This assuaged the small guilt Holtzclaw felt slipping the gold coins into his own pocket. The remaining items—treasures only to their collector—he concealed again beneath the stone and filled over with the dirt. The spot was still very conspicuous. Disturbed earth and scorch marks made by the will-o'-the-wisp were plainly visible.

"Are you a cousin to the moon maidens?" asked Holtzclaw. "Have they sent you to me? What do you want in return for this treasure?"

The green lights blinked in their strange code from the hillside, and the will-o'-the-wisp dimmed and brightened in response. It blinked six times, then popped, like a soap bubble. It reappeared ten feet away, blinked three more times, and then disappeared again. Holtzclaw swiveled his head, spinning in place like a top, but he could not see where the phenomenon had gone. He kicked at the ground over which the will-o'-the-wisp had last hovered, but the earth was packed hard, and he could not dig to any depth.

A loose chicken sidled up beside Holtzclaw and scratched at the ground with its beak.

"What do you think you'll find, little bird?" said Holtzclaw. "Something to eat?"

At the Grayson House, there were no fiddlers, no festivities, no poppy rocks. The chuck-luck wheel was still. At a few tables, men rolled dice. The bone cubes tiptoed along the tables to the gentle tune of coins.

"Hey there, Jimmy," said Emmett the druggist. "Life treating you all right?"

Holtzclaw joined him at a stool at the bar, placed his money on the spot in the table and then turned his back on it, as he'd been taught. "Too much work to do to waste time with complaining."

"That's me, too, friend," said Emmett. "I have scads of fiddly bottles to move up the mountain. Got to wrap them all up so they don't bust. Just this morning I knocked over a couple by accident when I was pulling them from the shelves. Some of them spilled on the floor and got mixed up. Then there was a purple cloud and I woke up two hours later. There's time lost."

Holtzclaw glanced back towards the bar counter and was relieved to see, at last, a plate of food put before him. He tucked in to the reddish brown stew and parsed the flavors of rich meat, caramelized onions, good measures of salt and pepper and woodland spices, and, happily, no mushrooms.

"Will you tell me what am I eating here, Emmett, or is it better to enjoy it in ignorance?" asked Holtzclaw.

"It's groundhog stew. Not real groundhog. Can't get real groundhog right now. The blasting and hammering up on the ridge scares them away. Sampson's had to make do with imitation ground hog. It's beef with extra fat. He puts in all the right spices, and that makes the stew taste right. He could probably make turkey meat taste like groundhog. It's this bit right here that makes the stew." Emmett reached into Holtzclaw's bowl and extracted a gravy-soaked leaf. "You don't want to eat this whole. It just gives flavor."

"What is it?"

"They call it cut-gut, turkey pea, or goat's rue. It's got three names because people can't decide if it's good for you or not, or what it's supposed to do for you. I keep some at the shop. A few folks will come in and want it for the shivering fits, dropsy, the vapors, chronic bubo, the squirting johnnies, or spider kiss. The rest want it for groundhog stew. But I'm an apothecary, not a greengrocer!"

Holtzclaw ate shovelfuls until he found the bottom of the bowl, then he sopped up the remainder of the stew with torn pieces of bread. He wondered if this dish could be exported from Auraria. In flavor, it could stand with the best of city cuisine, but Holtzclaw doubted it could survive a change of atmosphere. A bowl of groundhog stew served in a mountain tavern is a very different dish than a *ragout de marmotte* served in a china bowl to a wheezing aristocrat.

The lady of the house, Lizzie Rathbun, entered from the kitchen. Her hair was up and her sleeves were rolled to her elbows.

"Ms. Rathbun," said Emmett, shocked, "are you staffing the kitchen today?"

"Goodness, no," said Ms. Rathbun. "I was only passing through. Why, Holtzclaw, it's a pleasure to see you. You've been scampering all over the Lost Creek Valley like a squirrel trying to keep his brains out of the pudding."

"Enchanted, Ms. Rathbun, I'm sure," said Holtzclaw.

"Holtzclaw, I have a business discussion to continue with you, if we could retire to somewhere private."

Emmett's face, for the first time that evening, cracked into a broad smile. "Say no more, Jimmy! I release you." He scooped up his bread and bowl and alit in a chair near the dice game, casting a sly glance back at Holtzclaw.

"Your intimation has tarnished my reputation," said Holtzclaw to Ms. Rathbun. "Do you think Emmett there is the most discreet of your customers?"

"If your reputation is going to suffer a tarnish," said Lizzie, "you may as well deserve it and claim your few minutes in the pleasure of my company. You may find it profitable."

Ms. Rathbun's rooms occupied the highest story of the Grayson House. Her private stair and corridor were not shared with any of the guest rooms. At the top of her landing was a fine wooden table, likely French, on which stood a painted vase, decidedly not French. It had two large loop handles that fancifully doubled as ears and applied clay decorations that represented bulging eyes, a bulbous nose, and a thin-lipped but toothy grin. A bouquet of flowers in pinks, purples, red, and yellows stuck out of its head.

"Do you like it?" said Ms. Rathbun. "One of the mountain men gave it to my father, in payment for medical services rendered."

"It's charming, in a rustic way," said Holtzclaw. "What kind of flowers are they?"

"Oh, beautiful ones. I don't collect them. For all I know, they grow from this fellow's head."

Ms. Rathbun opened a set of double-doors into a long room. One end was set for dressing and conversation, and here Ms. Rathbun bade Holtzclaw take a seat. The other end of the room held her nighttime furniture. A large bed, as wide as it was long, was guarded by four posts and veiled by white gossamer. From a hook on the wall hung a silk sleeping gown.

Ms. Rathbun did not sit beside Holtzclaw. She sat down in front of a large mirror, facing away from him. From a silver ewer, she poured a measure of water into a silver basin.

"What sort of water is that?" said Holtzclaw.

"The wet kind," said Ms. Rathbun.

"Yes, but I mean, which of your local springs is it drawn from?"

"All the water comes from the same mountain," said Ms. Rathbun, rubbing her temples. "Some of it leaks from rocks, some of it flows down the hillside, some of it comes from upriver. It all mixes and mingles and flows out through the cascade, and then the people below us do not care a whit where it came from."

In the mirror, Holtzclaw could see her ablutions. Ms. Rathbun lifted a hand and unfastened the top two buttons on her collar, which fell open to reveal the flesh at the base of her neck. She applied a dampened cloth across her forehead and down her cheeks.

"I can step outside, Ms. Rathbun..."

"Do you think you could see fit to calling me Lizzie?"

"I suppose I could try. And you may call me James."

"I don't believe that I will, Holtzclaw. It does not hang on you well. Some people simply do not suit their given names. Neither you nor your employer."

"He's not a Hiram, is he?" said Holtzclaw. "It was suitable for his boyhood in Auraria, but it's not a name for a businessman."

Ms. Rathbun patted her throat and re-fixed her buttons, then joined Holtzclaw at the cluster of furniture designed for conversation. Ms. Rathbun collapsed into an overstuffed club chair, reclining as though it were a fainting couch. She exhaled deeply.

Holtzclaw ventured to interrupt the silence. "Tell me. Ms. Rathbun, Lizzie, have you ever been beset by a set of orbs?"

Ms. Rathbun flushed. "How do you mean, Holtzclaw?"

"Outside just now, I met a creature that the Romantic poets would call a will-o'-the-wisp."

"Oh, yes. Once one clung to the edge of my windowsill for the better part of a late night hour."

"Did it lead you anywhere? Did you follow it?"

"I put a pillow over my eyes and tried to sleep," said Ms. Rathbun. "Anyway, you don't need the promises of forest lights to become rich. How large is your share in your employer's company? Thirty percent? Forty?"

"There is no share," said Holtzclaw. "I have a salary."

"Do you mean that he doesn't include you in the profits? Holtzclaw, that's unconscionable!"

"It is an excellent employment that has kept me in good stead, professionally and financially."

"With all his rhetoric about giving better jobs to the people of this town! You're the one scampering through the valley while he stays tucked up in his office. The rich are the laziest of men. They pay others to do the hard work."

"That is not Shadburn's philosophy," said Holtzclaw.

"Of course he says that it's not his philosophy," said Ms. Rathbun, "but what is his practice? Who is drafting contracts, or pleading with widows to surrender their family homesteads, or driving away sweet potato farmers? And he pockets the profits, of course. You get your ... salary." She made the word a small and contemptible thing. "And why do you care if it's profitable, if you are not owed a portion of the profits? Because success is its own reward? Because you enjoy the beaming glow of completion, and the pat on the back of a job well done? Are they redeemable in coin, Holtzclaw? Can you cash them in for comfort in your old age?"

She lifted herself from the reclined position and leaned forward, arms crossed, elbows on her knees. Her voice dropped to a whisper, and Holtzclaw, despite himself, leaned forward, too. "We have an opportunity to earn our own riches. And you can be a full partner."

"I can't work against my employer."

"Ah, loyal Holtzclaw. His failure would be a loss to everyone, but you can make a side bet on his success. The men down there at the chuck-luck wheel sometimes put down money on numbers that aren't their own."

"What is this opportunity?" said Holtzclaw, "and what do I purchase by my participation?"

"My plan requires a piece of land with a border on the new lake," said Ms. Rathbun, "and some construction capital. I'll put up my own money, too, for an equal stake."

"And what will you do with this land? Sell it? Hold it?"

"No, Holtzclaw. We'll build. Something useful. Something of our own."

There was money in her voice. "What? What will we build?"

"That depends on the kind of land you acquire," said Ms. Rathbun. "We'll conform our plans to its geography."

Holtzclaw nodded. "The land will be the hardest part," he said. "Shadburn wants to own it all."

"Have you turned over all the deeds? Must his name be on all of them? Would his plans be harmed if he owned only ninety-nine percent of the lakeshore, rather than a stifling hundred?"

A bit of competition would benefit everyone, conceded Holtzclaw. It may whet Shadburn's appetite for profits again, make him more of a Shadburn and less of a Hiram.

"Find me a piece of shorefront," said Ms. Rathbun. "I would be happy with even the smallest slice. We will put up our own establishment, a guest house, be it ever so humble. There is plenty of profit, even in that."

She held out her hand, not horizontally to kiss, but vertically, as for business agreements. A clock in the room counted three seconds. Her hand trembled slightly from the exertion of extending it over the chasm between them. It was a trick known as the Toledo Tremble—a splendid tool because it exploits the social compunction to take any hand that is offered. Impossible agreements have been reached because a single hand looks lonely. Holtzclaw recognized that this trick was being employed against him, and his esteem for Ms. Rathbun rose.

When Holtzclaw's hand met hers, he was surprised to feel an exhilaration within him, a new animating purpose. If the dice came up for Shadburn, as they always did—then for once, he would profit, too.

CHAPTER XV

The hydrocannon filled an entire boxcar, and Holtzclaw spent much of the day supervising its unloading, transport, and installation for its first test. The bulk of the cannon was canvas hose, carefully sewn in a long, tapered shape. At the river end, where the water was collected, the opening was as wide as a man's shoulders; a thousand feet later, at the end where the cannon nozzle was fitted, the hose diameter was only a palm spam.

The cannon nozzle was made of twenty feet of brass. Its operation was simple: a large lever controlled an internal valve, and eight handles allowed four men to lift and aim the cannon. The only adornment was "Lawson Foundry," stamped in raised letters along one fitting. The catalog from which Holtzclaw had ordered this cannon has offered various decorated forms, the most fanciful of which was a dragon maw that bellowed water, not fire. The operators held on to various spikes, wings, and horns. Perhaps some tyrant might order the dragon's maw edition to obliterate the ancestral terrain of his enemies—wash it into the sea.

The target for their hydrocannon was a knobby outcropping called the Hag's Head. From certain angles, the rock did resemble an old woman's profile. A smooth wall, peaked at the top, was her cowl. Craggy ledges formed her cheekbones and nose. A peculiar jut, high enough that a trail could run underneath, represented her chin, and a tuft of hanging roots were the hairs of her wart. Holtzclaw felt a tickle of joy at being able to reduce the ugly image to gravel.

Johnston and Carter, the twin railroad men, had come out to see the operation of the hydrocannon. They had recommended this device to clear the valley, extolling its excellent cost efficiency and reputation for rapidity. If all went well with these tests, the hydrocannon could be turned to general cleaning work. Swathes of small trees, brush and bracken, and even houses, fences, sheds, and spring houses could be washed away.

A runner took the message down the length of hose that the operation was ready to start, and soon the hose began to plump with water. The four men at the brass nozzle braced themselves. The weight of water behind the canvas tubing bucked and swayed, and the operators struggled to hold on to the device. Inside, it was ready to explode. Holtzclaw gave the order to open fire.

The force of the water cleanly decapitated the Hag. Her nose, eyes, and the top of her cowl came down as one piece, then were shattered by a second blast from the hydrocannon. Holtzclaw was stunned that the formation fractured so neatly. He wondered if it had been solid rock, after all. The hydrocannon filleted the mountain face, cutting like a chef's best knife. Granite boulders tumbled through the valley. Trees, severed at the trunk, rolled down the mucky hills. Geysers of mud splashed back to drench the hose operators, spattering even Holtzclaw and the railroad twins standing at a distance. Gravel like grapeshot ricocheted around their ears.

Then, like someone turning off a spigot, the jet of water ceased, and the operators stumbled forwards.

With the creek powering the cannon at a constant rate, the pressure shouldn't have dropped. The only explanation was a leak, then, or the sudden disappearance of the creek. Holtzclaw was relieved to see water pouring forth from a tear in the hose a few hundred feet away; it was simpler to repair than an angry water princess.

"You've sprung a leak, Holtzclaw," said Johnston or Carter, who followed his gaze.

"Popped a fountain, positively," said the other.

Holtzclaw excused himself from the presence of the railroad twins and went to investigate. A hundred yards away, in the shaded copse, he found the split. The wound was not at a seam, nor was it ragged. The fabric had been cut with a blade.

It was unlike Princess Trahlyta. An ax was not in her nature. Perhaps Abigail had done it, or Lizzie Rathbun, although he could not figure their motives.

Then, one of the taller bushes whispered to Holtzclaw. He peered around the leafy mass to see Shadburn, a long knife tucked into his belt.

"Blast it, Shadburn! What are you doing?" said Holtzclaw.

"Putting a stop to this. When you said you had a water cannon, I thought you were clearing some topsoil. I didn't think you were going to explode the mountainsides."

"And you had to ruin my cannon? You couldn't have just waved your hat at me, asked me to stop?"

"No time. You were digging too fast."

"That was precisely the point, Shadburn."

"But there are hollows below. Tunnels. Our railroad friends might think they have treasure in them."

"Do they?"

"Those railroad men are trying to trick you. They are using you to dig for gold. Auraria has had enough of that already. Why, there are people down in the valley now, putting themselves in harm's way from the rocks and boulders that you are throwing off. They want to catch the gravel that you are washing down the hill. If there is any chance that there would be some gold among the ruin and danger, then they will wade halfway out into the river to catch it in their hat."

Shadburn lowered himself on to his haunches. His bones cracked and popped. He took a handful of wet earth and squeezed. Mud came oozing from between his fingers—in that mud, there was a sparkle of quartz or mica, and, too, a color of gold.

"If a few more months do not ruin them, they will be safe. But these are the most dangerous times of all. Railroad men with shovels all over the hillside. Explosions. Surveys. Scrutiny of every crack and hole across this valley, even places that had been all but forgotten. Frantic men and women with washtubs and apron skirts—anything that will sift a color—lowering themselves in muddy construction debris because they hope that they can find a twinkle of gold. Well, they should have better than that! I'll give them better than that."

Holtzclaw had listened with his arms crossed. "Are you quite finished, Shadburn?"

"That is a rather impertinent tone."

"It's a weary tone. I don't know what I'm supposed to be doing—building a lakeside resort or stuffing the pocketbooks of your childhood friends. If it's the former, then I should use the hydrocannon to accomplish the job as quickly and inexpensively as possible. If it's the latter, why not just pour out all your strongboxes directly in their gold-loving palms?"

Holtzclaw turned to walk back up towards the former site of the Hag's Head, where the railroad twins and their men were waiting. From this slight distance back, he could see how completely the hydrocannon had transformed the place. The Hag's Head had been inverted into a three-story grotto. Men stood inside of it, chatting. Holtzclaw heard their voices as though they were right at his ear. His first thought was that some new spirit had gotten loose, but then he realized that the hydrocannon had made a perfect acoustic resonator. The men's voices echoed forth, magnified by the shape of the rock.

Shadburn slinked away into the underbrush from which he'd come. Holtzclaw returned to the railroad twins, offering excuses for the failure. He told them that the streams of Auraria were too powerful for the factory stitching on the canvas tubing. The railroad twins asked if it could be repaired; Holtzclaw doubted it, but he would consult with the better seamstresses of the town. There was much agitated grumbling about unnecessary expense, unforeseen delays, and Holtzclaw was entirely sympathetic to their plight. But what could he do, if Shadburn was abroad with a blade?

The hydrocannon was carted back to the workers' camp in Asbestos Hollow. The hose was a nasty, knotted mess. Holtzclaw hated the sight of it, a good tool now ruined and chaotic, and he excused himself while the men were still trying to wrestle some of the slippery loops out of the tracks made by the coal wagons.

Then Holtzclaw turned to look downhill, and a wondrous vision awaited him. Large boulders had been trapped against a harder ridge of granite. Small stones, gravel, and mud had caught in this jam and formed a promontory. It was large and flat, at least a quarter acre.

New land had been made! No survey map showed it, nor deeds yet written to describe it. It had no owner, and thus it belonged to Holtzclaw, as the first to discover it. He had no flag to plant in it, but in his office, he had the paper to draw up a deed, which was the surer way.

A soothing peace filled Holtzclaw. Now, he was not only working for Shadburn. He was working for a new vision—his own. He could it see: a grand structure of some kind, with his own name. He should have pressed Ms. Rathbun for more details. The form arising in his mind's eye, upon the little promontory, was hazy.

The dam must be built! The lake must rise! And if Shadburn could not find the money to finish it, then Holtzclaw would.

Holtzclaw's intended route back into town—a well-trod path descending from the Brightwater Creek to the Needle's Eye—was blocked by less felicitous tailings from the hydrocannon. He picked his way instead down the valley slopes, towards the Lost Creek.

At the riverbank, Bogan and Moss were working a rocker box. Bogan, using a shovel, loaded muddy runoff into a hopper. Moss operated a wooden handle that agitated the hopper, forcing the heavier material into a series of baffles. Periodically, one man would fetch a pail of water from the river and pour it over the ridged surface. Most material was washed over the edge of each subsequent terrace, but some—a heavy, rich, black sand—was caught against the terrace edges. When the washing was done, Bogan and Moss scraped the recovered sand into their pans and took it to the river, where they panned out a star field of gold.

"Looks like a good pan," said Holtzclaw.

"Yeah, it's been good panning all afternoon," said Bogan. "Whatever you were exploding up there had plenty of metal in it."

"We were clearing a ridge for the railroad line under the Hag's Head," said Holtzclaw.

"Aw, the Hag's Head?" said Moss. "I used to go courting up there. She makes every other girl look better."

"Is that what you told them, Moss?" said Bogan. "'You're not as ugly as that hag?' Is that why no one wants to go courting with you nowadays?"

"No one's courting with me. I'm too busy working before Mr. Moneybags drowns all the good spots."

"Flakes like this are just chips off the big block," said Bogan. "No one is going to get rich on this runoff. There's no nuggets, no coins, no ingots. We'll have some good eating and drinking tonight, for sure, but we'll be so weary that we'll hardly be able to enjoy it."

"We're not profiting any by jawing," said Moss. "Now, Holtzclaw, are you going to pick up a shovel or are you going to go away?"

Holtzclaw demurred. If there were no nuggets or coins or ingots, then his daily wage from Shadburn was greater, and the promise of the new land was richer still.

The next day, Holtzclaw accompanied Lizzie Rathbun up the ridge to survey the land that he had acquired for their side bet.

She clasped her hands. "Oh, Holtzclaw, it is perfect!" she said. "You didn't even have to compromise your moral principles very much to get it."

"Better land could be had, I suppose," said Holtzclaw, "but not so cleanly. I put only your name on the deed, Ms. Rathbun. It gives me a measure of deniability, in case Shadburn should run across it."

"It's not necessary, but I think it's wise," said Ms. Rathbun. "Now, this piece of land—it will have a part of the lake shore?"

"By my projections, we are the owners of a peninsula that will jut nicely into the shimmering waters of Lake Trahlyta."

Ms. Rathbun and Holtzclaw promenaded the length of the promontory. She continued to the very edge, a point of land that jutted above the steep slope of the valley.

"Is it large enough, do you think, for building?" said Holtzclaw. "I suppose our enterprise will have to be suited to the land, rather than vice versa. I doubt we'll have another property dropped into our laps." Holtzclaw dropped to his haunches and examined the lay of the terrain. He had done this many times before with more care, but he made a show of it now for Lizzie's benefit. "We can't build upwards. The land isn't stable enough to support it. No three story structures, I fear. A guest house and tavern of no more than ten rooms. We can charge a premium for the intimacy and proximity view to the lake. It is modest, but I could be happy with that."

Ms. Rathbun laughed. "Oh, Holtzclaw, that's not ambitious enough! Your employer, despite his other flaws, at least dreams big."

"Ambition cannot exceed the extents granted by Nature," said Holtzclaw. "We cannot build into empty space."

"But we can!" She gestured out into the emptiness of the valley. "We'll float our hotel. We only need a dock on the promontory. A steamship, larger than any of the barges on the Mississippi, with two paddle-wheels to bring it to the dock and back out into the middle of the lake. Stately cabins, dining rooms, and gaming areas. The novelty! A white and brass mansion reflected in the crystal waters of a mountain lake, cheery white steam puffing above like clouds, and the sound of soft paddling, laughter, and the clink of glasses filled with fine spirits. That's ambition! Not some tiny guest house, but a floating palace."

"How can we build it?" said Holtzclaw. "There is no room here for a dry dock, and we could not bring in the boat from upriver or downriver. The cataracts to the north and the gorge to the south isolate us from navigable waterways."

"We build the base now, before the lake is made," said Ms. Rathbun. "When the floodgates close, our floating hotel with rise with the lake waters. It need not all be finished. Just enough structure to make it seaworthy. All the furniture and supplies and decoration can be added when the hotel is floating at the dock."

"Shadburn may even consider it a favor," said Holtzclaw, striding to the end of the bit of land. "He promised five hundred passengers per day to the railroad twins, and his plans, grand as they are, could not hope to achieve that goal. If we built a modest hotel, it would not much help, but a larger project, with its own advertising and attraction, could make a significant contribution. The whole area would be given a boost."

"You see?" said Ms. Rathbun. "The success continues to flow without a single threat to your moral principles or loyalty." Then her brows fell, and a watery substance like tears gathered at the inner corners of her eyes. "Only, I fear, a project of this nature needs more money than we have at present. What we have between us, Holtzclaw, is enough to get started, even to finish out the frame of the boat and float it up to the dock if we are careful, and a dock is not expensive. But to finish out the inside in style..."

"Needs a far greater investment," said Holtzclaw.

"How shall we get it, then?"

"Give me a little time, Lizzie."

"There is so little already, Holtzclaw. Like money, we have none to waste."

Holtzclaw had already seen the white and brass mansion floating on the lake, puffing cheery smoke into the air. He had seen himself, the master, in the crystal waters. From the other shore, the green lights signaled to him, but their language was only pattern and mystery.

CHAPTER XVI

Holtzclaw's traveling satchel, while containing still half a bottle of Effervescent Brain Salts and a dusting of Pharaoh's Flour, had run out of currency, both gold and federal notes. The railroad twins had needed an immediate payment towards day laborers. He needed to resupply from Shadburn's stock.

In his offices, Shadburn was consumed with letter writing. "I am putting out our advertisements," he said. "All the major Eastern publications will have announcements. We'll have a full complement of the best people in our resort for the upcoming season."

"Your yet unnamed resort?" said Holtzclaw.

"No longer! I have the perfect solution. We'll borrow a native name and apply it to the lake, village, and hotel, like Saratoga or Chautauqua. Colors of ancient mystery. The hotel will be called The Queen of the Mountains, on the shores of Lake Trahlyta."

"Have you asked permission from the owner of that name?"

"I would think she would be flattered."

A red woolen blanket covered two dozen strongboxes stacked in a corner. Holtzclaw removed the covering with a flourish and broke the wax seal on the front of one of the strongboxes. When he opened it, he was astounded. It was filled with sand, and on the top, an envelope.

"Shadburn, you have been honey-fuggled! Sandbagged, or sand-boxed!"

Shadburn didn't look up from his correspondence.

"There's a letter, perhaps from the culprit," said Holtzclaw. It was sealed with wax, too, and marked "To H.E. Shadburn - Personal and Confidential." Holtzclaw opened it.

"'Esteemed Mister Shadburn,' it says, 'your request for withdrawal from deposits held by our institution cannot be completed. Your account was closed and the full balance delivered over three years ago. Copies of correspondence and bills of travel and transfer are included. We send this weighted strongbox in lieu of actual currency to spare you any embarrassment that might result from an unanswered

request for funds. We appreciate your past patronage and anticipate future deposits, which we will hold in the strictness security
and confidence. Yrs truly, and with profound regards, etc., Absalom
Fredricks, President, Second Sportsman's Bank of the Mountains,
Springfield.' Shadburn, this is extraordinary! You have been robbed
at the bank. I know that the Second Sportsman's Bank account held
at least twenty thousand dollars. I wrote this request myself after
verifying it against the account books."

"Oh, did you?" said Shadburn.

"This correspondence is dated three years ago. We were working
on the Calhoun lumber project at the time, near Waycross, and that's
where the deposits were delivered."

"Was that the sawmill in the swamp?"

"Yes, the cypress and pine on some of the Okefenokee islands."

"Then I know where the funds were spent. There were some immediate concerns about transportation and flooding from Calhoun's
backers, and the deal was dying. Money was needed to drain a few
canals and to build a plank road for the importation of machinery.
Our client was getting cold feet; he was thinking about giving up. I
invested in the project so that the deal would not turn sour."

"So you spent twenty thousand more than the ledgers showed?
We cleared eleven thousand on the project, and I thought it a triumph. These new expenses would place the project at a nine thousand dollar loss."

"So it would, Holtzclaw, by the rules of arithmetic."

"You lost money, Shadburn." Holtzclaw waved the letter at his
employer.

"Is it a crime? You should have realized by now that not every
project can be perfectly profitable."

"How many of these strongboxes are empty, Shadburn? How
many times have I reported a profit for a project when it was actually
a loss?"

Shadburn's mouth moved faintly. A cloud fell across his face. "I
can't remember. There have been a few. Honestly, Holtzclaw, the
redness in your face is an overreaction. Did all of Vanderbilt's proj-

ects pay off? Was there not some land deal gone bad? I am not an infallible Midas, whose every work is golden."

"On paper, you are."

"What shall I do, Holtzclaw? Issue an apology? File amended paperwork? We have no investors that have been misled."

"No investors?" Holtzclaw threw up his hands. "Shadburn, I am an investor! I've put in the best years of my life." He walked to the edge of the little room, to the fireplace. "Do you remember the silkworm land you bought from me? In Canton? What happened there? Did you pay for that dam?"

Shadburn relaxed in his chair and looked up at the history writ on the ceiling. "You and your kind were wasting your lives in silkworms, these little foreign pests. Their sole use is that their excretions are fancied by the rich. You silkworm farmers—you were just like these gold-seekers here. You toiled away, and for what? Dead bugs! You, Holtzclaw, most of all, should be thankful, that I turned you to productive work."

"I didn't need rescue," said Holtzclaw.

"He is stuffing the Lost Creek Valley with gold, like a festival turkey," said Holtzclaw to Abigail as he studied his reflection at the bottom of a bottle of claret.

"The valley doesn't need stuffing," she said. "It's already groaning."

"Then it's all the more foolish that he is doing it," said Holtzclaw. "I opened two more strongboxes filled with sand before I found one with any money in it. How near is he to running out?"

"Men like him never run out of money," said Abigail.

"That is what the poor always believe about the rich," said Holtzclaw. "But it's untrue. They can lose their fortunes very quickly, when their manias take them. He is calling in all his strongboxes, even if they are filled with sand. And there is still half a dam to built. His money may last until then, but then what? There is a hotel to run. Sawmills and tanneries to outfit. Money will be needed to pay all of your townsfolk until these businesses are operating on their own power, and that takes time. As soon as the lake begins to rise,

Shadburn will be the only employer in the town, and what if he cannot meet his obligations? All that we have promised will be broken. And Auraria will dry up..."

Holtzclaw trailed off, wistfully. He hoped that he had not oversold the matter, but Abigail was a nostalgic sort.

"Dry up?" she sniffed. The tone of her voice was not entirely encouraging. Holtzclaw should have considered that she was an tavern keeper, and thus accustomed to people at their most maudlin and manipulative. Still, he persisted.

"Yes, dry up," said Holtzclaw. "Wither, I mean. I wish that we had an investor who cared about the future of this town. Who could reinforce our capital should the unthinkable happen, should we run out."

"I don't have anything, Holtzclaw."

"You have dreams! You don't even have to put down money. You can put down knowledge, which is free and not diminished in the giving. I will dig where you tell me to dig."

"You'd pin all your chances of success on a dream? That's not good business."

"I think it is the only sort of business that is worthwhile," said Holtzclaw.

Abigail stalked away, behind the counter. She polished glasses that were already polished.

"Will you consider my proposal, Ms. Thompson? It is a matter of some urgency."

"Drink your claret, Holtzclaw. You've said enough already."

Even after claret, Holtzclaw felt a pain through his midsection. It was a mild affliction, to be sure, given the gamut of troubles in life, but Holtzclaw still found it unpleasant. He thought a bath might do him some good, but not in Mrs. McTavish's old iron basin. Seeking a bath in the other two guest houses might have consequences and entanglements that he, in his discomfort, didn't want to face.

He walked upriver to a place called Sugar Shoals. The current swirled through a maze of boulders and kicked up white froth, which settled in eddies and shadows of rocks.

Holtzclaw doffed all the clothing that he dared, leaving a striped garment that reached from his knees to his elbows. He kicked at one of the foamy mounds, which burst into airy nothing at the passing of his foot. The water was pleasant, not too cold. He stretched out along a flat ridge and let the water pool behind him. It ran past his ears and toes. He moved into deeper water.

Beneath him, the rocks were slick. He lost his footing and came down hard on his tailbone. He stood and fell again, but was not deterred. On his hands and knees, he crawled towards the center of the river. A funnel of water coming between two rocks sculpted a natural sofa. Holtzclaw placed himself into this basin and let the water crash around him.

The water in his natural spa turned cold. Crystalline fragments of ice pricked at his skin. In the sugary froth that accumulated in the eddies of the river, there were flakes of gold. He reached out to scoop up the colors, but the foam vanished before his fingers. His skin had acquired a golden hue, which faded towards green. It looked sickly on his skin; he felt sickly, and the recurring pain throbbed stronger than ever. He plunged back into the waterfall channel, but the water there was thick and oozing. He rolled back the extremities of his undergarment, and beneath, the stain was worse. He stood up, turned, shook himself, and shivered.

"Not the cleanest swimming hole, James," said the princess.

On hearing the girl's voice, Holtzclaw and his uncovered limbs scrambled into one of the deep wells. He was compelled by modesty. The icy waters fixed the golden residue against his flesh.

"Don't dive too far," said the princess. "There might be snakes down those basins."

Holtzclaw scurried out of the pit and shielded himself behind a rock. His face was hot from embarrassment and chill from the water. He chattered and burned.

"James, you're such a pitiable sight," said Trahlyta. "Come out from there."

Holtzclaw withdrew himself from behind his rock.

"What's happening up the river? What's happening to me?"

"The moon maidens, like you, decided that the best cure for their ills was a bath. Sadly, you're suffering from their run-off."

"How can ... how can that be? What's this on me? Can I see them?" Veins of waterborne gold twisted downriver.

The princess shook her head. "Why? They are in a bad humor. The singing tree was supposed to perform for them, but he's been unreliable of late. Their whole holiday is off, thanks to you. Even the current doesn't wash as well as it once did. You've made it worse, with all the money you're pouring into the water. Excuse me; I have tidying to do."

A light rain started to fall. Wild wonder fish came to the surface and nibbled at shiny flakes; a larger catfish trawled the bottom with his whiskers.

"I don't understand, princess. Why do you want to be rid of gold? Isn't it as natural as any other rock?"

"It doesn't belong in this valley. We should have springs and rivers, not mines and treasure tunnels. Gold is an unwelcome visitor. It works against the acclimation of people to the land."

"I think that is a sentiment that can only belong to unearthly creatures," said Holtzclaw. "We terrestrial people will never refuse gold, never say it's unwelcome."

"You won't, will you? Ask Shadburn his opinion. And here you are, shivering and covered in gold, and you want more?"

"I want it as coins, as nuggets, not as residue. I can't spend this. I can't give this away. I can't even get it off me."

"How shall any of us get clean if the baths are dirty?" said the princess. "Scrub up with Pharaoh's Flour, I suppose. That's the best I can recommend. Go on, then."

Holtzclaw hied back to his room, where he kept a tin of the stuff. The cure worked better than expected. A thorough dusting of Pharaoh's Flour followed by vigorous scrubbing took all the undesired metal off of him, and with very little stinging. But, the cleansing work had left him as impoverished as ever. For all his discomfort, all his work, he did not have even a single flake of gold.

CHAPTER XVII

Three months later, on a grey morning, Holtzclaw and Shadburn stood on a dais high above the valley. It stood at the center of an iron bridge that spanned from the Great Hogback Ridge to Sinking Mountain. Originally, the dedication ceremony was only for the bridge, but Shadburn had insisted that it serve for the dam as well. It was time to close the floodgates and let the lake begin to fill.

Holtzclaw thought it was lunacy. Once the waters started to rise, the old town site would be underwater in a week, and the rest of the valley gone in a month. Far too soon! Holtzclaw had too much work still to do—for Shadburn and for Ms. Rathbun. He had yet to find any investors or any of Auraria's promised fortunes. He did not have the capital to see either hotel to completion.

"Shadburn, it's not too late to postpone the flood," he said to Shadburn, standing beside him on the dais, while Dr. Rathbun swelled to a rhetorical flourish in his remarks to the crowd. "There's no shame in waiting, only prudence."

"First, Holtzclaw," replied Shadburn, "I don't want to endure the indignities and expenses of two opening ceremonies. One rocket and two barrels of fruit drink will suffice for both of them. Surely you would approve of such frugality. And second, an unstoppable deadline always inspires the best and most rapid work. Set a fire. Start a flood. Place the explosives and light the fuses."

"It is irresponsible," said Holtzclaw. "I have hurried as much as our resources will allow."

"And even then, it is too slow. Soon they will have fishes spawning in their chimneys."

Around the dais were only a handful of spectators. More would have come if the event had been better catered, but when word spread that only fruit drinks would be offered—no cakes, no liquors, no roasted meats—many would-be attendees stayed home. Those who did attend seemed to regret their decision. A woman in a yellow bonnet yawned broadly. Two men in matching cravats studied each other's shoes. The handful of children, too bored to play with enthusiasm, tugged at the hems of their clothing.

Holtzclaw looked over the valley below. It was a ledger of unfinished tasks and failures. Holdouts needed to be evicted and relocated up the mountain. Buildings and homes needed to be burned so they would not interfere with navigation on the lake. Farm fields had food in them still. Harvesters would take what was large enough to grasp—tomatoes, berries, young corn—and leave the rest for stray turkeys. Most troublesome was the grey bulk of a shot tower, improbably uncovered during the clear-cutting of trees; it was a hateful, late imposition into Holtzclaw's schedule.

The unfinished outline of the Queen of the Mountains glared impatiently at him. Columns and poles and girders stuck out at awkward angles. The hotel's lawns and gardens were only mud fields. Springs ran untamed; pavilions to cap them had not yet been built. It did not look much like a first-class hotel, but a first-class mess.

The Lost Creek Valley, over which the Queen of the Mountains was meant to preside, was no longer sublime nor picturesque. Forests had been harvested for the flume of the dam, the hotel, the company town, and many thousands of railroad ties. Stone and earth had been borrowed for the dam, leaving strange depressions and open wounds of mud. Even an ugly lake would be a welcome disguise for this scarred landscape.

A silver streak far down the valley caught Holtzclaw's eye. It was the hull of his side project, Ms. Rathbun's floating hotel. Holtzclaw had deflected questions by telling the railroad men that it was part of the hotel, by telling the hotel crew that it was part of a civic water source, and by telling those responsible for pipes and springs that it was an integral part of the dam's construction. Making the hull had required a great deal of his personal capital, and nearly all of Ms. Rathbun's as well, but they had made a seaworthy beginning. He hoped that the result would be worth the effort. Had he not been trying to administer two projects, perhaps he could have had the valley cleared by now, perhaps the shot tower would have been toppled. But his efforts would do no good if he could not find more money. The empty shell of a boat will attract very few visitors.

In the distance, the dam bottled up the far end of the valley. At the top, the dam was twenty feet thick and stretched three hundred feet from rim to rim of the gorge. At the bottom, the dimensions were nearly reversed. Because the gorge walls came together, the dam was only a hundred feet wide at its base, but to resist the concentrated weight of the water, the dam was two hundred feet thick— thicker than it was wide. Large boulders were manhandled onto the lake-facing surface of the dam to protect the earthworks from tides and currents. The open side, facing towards the Terrible Cascade, was shielded with gravel as a protection from rain.

During construction, the Lost Creek was channeled into a narrow watercourse that passed below the body of the dam. Now, permanent floodgates were being lowered into the channel. Permanent plugs of rocks and earth would be added for reinforcement. The railroad twins swore that this was the only possible method, given the size of the lake. No screw or hinge yet made would resist the force of such a large body of water, they said. If storms came, regular floodgates could blow out, emptying the lake into the lowlands. Thus, the design of the dam required that it empty itself, at both normal pool and storm surge, through the spillway. The wooden flume that carried the water away, over the head of the Sky Pilot and down to the powerhouse, was invisible over the dam's horizon.

A smattering of applause issued from the crowd. Holtzclaw joined reflexively but was startled when Shadburn approached the podium. Shadburn had forgotten his hat. The low sun did not give him much need of it, but it was indecorous to parade his thinning hair and balding head in front of the crowd. Shadburn modestly put a hand on top of his own pate and then gave up the farce.

"In a few months we have done much for you," said Shadburn. "Now we are nearly finished. You have a dam that will soon make a place to fish and sail. You will have a fine hotel to which the best people will come to be refreshed. You have a railroad to bring you wonderful things to buy. And best of all, you now have better work, which comes with salaries."

Shadburn walked away from the podium, accompanied by polite clapping. Then no one stood at the podium for a while. Dr. Rathbun leaned over to Shadburn and whispered. Shadburn looked startled. He passed the message to Holtzclaw.

"Holtzclaw, I am supposed to open the bridge. How do I open the bridge?" said Shadburn.

"I suppose you loudly declare it. Throw up your hands or some such."

"I don't want to do that. Can it not just...be open, without being opened?"

"Evidently, the people expect a gesture," said Holtzclaw.

Shadburn stood. He straightened his jacket and aligned his hat appropriately with his ears. Then he stepped to the podium, threw out his hands as if he were embracing the valley, and roared, "I declare this bridge open!"

There were only a few, slow claps. Someone in the crowd said, "What's its name?"

"It needs to have a name, too?" said Shadburn. "What shall it be, Holtzclaw?"

"I wouldn't venture a guess."

"Let's call it the New Bridge," said Shadburn.

"But there was no old bridge," said Holtzclaw.

"The name doesn't have to be explained." Shadburn turned again to the crowd and repeated his gesture, this time calling, "I declare this bridge, the New Bridge, open! And the dam, too! Say hallo for Lake Trahlyta!"

There was some fumbling behind the dais. A match was struck, and then a rocket launched into the sky. It exploded over the valley, letting off a rain of green sparks. They were only visible for a moment against the gray sky, then there were lost in the daylight. If the men at the dam has seen their signal, they were sealing the floodgates now, but it would have been easy to miss such an unspectacular display.

Wooden barrels filled with fruit drink were wheeled into the crowd. Men and women drank the red, red stuff from tin dippers. Burbling conversation soon subsided; in its place was disquiet.

"Why is no one leaving, Holtzclaw?" asked Shadburn. "Do they expect an all-night entertainment from me? I've forgotten how to swallow fire, and my legs don't know how to jig."

Holtzclaw didn't know; he asked Dr. Rathbun for an explanation. "The matter," said the mayor, "is the folk tradition that the first to cross a new bridge is soon to die."

"Many people crossed it when it was being built," said Holtzclaw. "I walked it end-to-end two dozen times, inspecting. The workmen ate their lunch on one end and relieved themselves from the other."

"Yes, all well and good," said Dr. Rathbun, "but that was just a span of wood and metal, not a bridge. A plank laid across a creek is not a bridge. This structure, now that is has been opened, now that it has been named, is unequivocally a bridge, and you have on your hands a boodle of over-cautious people, none of whom want to be the first to re-alight on land."

"I suppose the only recourse is for one of us to be the first man across," said Shadburn. "We must lead by example."

Shadburn linked elbows with his assistant and began walking, with Holtzclaw stuttering and shuffling to match the pace of his taller employer. Just at the end of the bridge was a warped board that curled up an inch. It interrupted Shadburn's stride; he was forced to take a short step to avoid coming down on top of it. Holtzclaw's left heel landed on earth a moment before Shadburn's right.

On the lake-facing side of the dam, a painted red line on the closed floodgates marked the natural level of the river. The water already ran a handspan above the line. Quiet tides lapped against the metal. On the obverse of the dam, though, where men were reinforcing the gates with rock and clay to prevent a future disaster, there was a frenetic scene. The Sky Pilot harangued the workers, tossing pellets of ice. The ground rumbled, throwing workers to their knees and shaking apart the barriers of clay as they were curing behind the sealed floodgates.

"They're on my land!" said the Sky Pilot to Holtzclaw. "Every time one of them puts a foot across this line, they're on my land, and I have the right to pelt them with ice. And that's because I'm a kind soul. I could shoot them in the back as trespassers or punch them clear through the ribs, and I'd feel clear in my conscience."

"I don't think a jury would uphold you shooting a man in the back because his foot slips into your land," said Holtzclaw. "What is it that you want?"

The Sky Pilot threw a cube of ice at a young worker that had come too close. The ice hit the boy on the shin; he cried out in pain and scampered back like a wounded animal. His companions glared across the dividing line at the Sky Pilot. Holtzclaw worried that, if he had not been present, the workers would have invaded the property and made their revenge, against all claims of trespassing.

"This dam cannot be removed now that is displeases you," said Holtzclaw. "If you are holding out for money, it is too late. I have no money to give you. So, what do you want?"

"I want you," said the Sky Pilot, stabbing his finger into the space between Holtzclaw's second and third ribs, "to talk with my friend. Since you've turned off his river, he weeps so much."

For the second time, Holtzclaw was suspended from a rope harness and lowered down to the cave of the Great and Harmless and Invincible Terrapin that Lives Under the Mountain.

The dam workers had paused from consoling the injured boy to warn Holtzclaw about putting his life in the hands of the crazed enemy, but Holtzclaw didn't think that the Sky Pilot would drop him on the descent. On the return, though, if he could not come to an agreement with the Terrapin, then Holtzclaw would request that someone else belay him.

No spray splashed at his feet. The tiny scrub pines that had clung to life in the crevices were starting to yellow. In place of the constant roar of the falls, there were the cries of men, the chirping of birds, the settling and stretching of the earth.

Holtzclaw alit on the ledge, removed the rope harness, and entered the cavern.

"Little morsel, I am sad!" said the Great and Harmless and Invincible Terrapin. He trundled his claw-tipped legs against the stone of the cavern, and the mountain quaked.

"I am sorry," said Holtzclaw. "What can I do?"

"The mountain is pressed. The rocks are complaining. There is too much quiet. I miss the flow of the waters over the rock. They were many voices in excited conversation."

"So you would like the men up there to make more noise? Talk more? We will have them play at bowls or bring out a fiddle. I could have them set off an explosion on the half-hour."

"Long ago," thundered the Great and Harmless and Invincible Terrapin, "when the world was not yet baked, there was a great river that followed across the world, end-to-end, and back around to itself. And when the Great Hog and the Great Turkey, and even I, the not-yet-Great Terrapin, were thirsty, we came to the river to drink the fresh, sweet water. And when the Great Sweet Potato and Great Corn were thirsty, they stretched out their roots through the soft earth and drank, too, from the river. But the Great Beaver could not master his instincts. He gnawed through the children of the Great Pine and the Great Chestnut and the Great Poplar—the children wailed as they fell across the river, and the Great Beaver sealed them together with sticks and twigs and mud. He dammed the single great river! And when the water could no longer flow downstream, then it could no longer loop around to itself and feed from the top of the stream, and the river became a dry canyon. There was great thirst in all the land because there was no water, no water. And there was no more roar of the cataracts and waterfalls. No more bubble of the streams. The world was quiet, except for the wails of the thirsty."

The Great and Harmless and Invincible Terrapin sobbed.

"I look out of my cave and I see the dry river and I hear no roar and I am reminded of the terrible sadness, long long ago, when all were thirsty and quiet. I think about the Great Hog. His shiny bristles turned dull and fell from his skin, and he grew small and became a naked pink creature of no significance. I think about the Great Corn. He was tough and noble, a hard and useless and proud thing that grew where ever he wished. Now, he has been made fat and sweet. He hides in his little silken house. He is a fancy dandy, a rich idler, as your people say. Oh! And your people raise his children by the thousands and grind them into your bread. It is a terrible fate. I have too many memories, too many stories."

"You enjoy telling them," said Holtzclaw. "You would go on for hours if I let you."

"It is necessary to tell them! Long ago, there were more stories, but they have been forgotten. They were not told, and they went away into the earth. Or they were told only to a few, like seeds that are scattered too thinly across a field. They cannot take root. The weeds of other, lesser stories choke them."

"Then I have a solution," said Holtzclaw. "Listen, terrapin! I'll build you an amphitheater. I will put it here, just at the entrance to your cave, with a staircase leading up to the gorge rim. All day and night, visitors will come and listen to your stories—they will jabber among themselves like all people on holiday, and it will be like a babbling brook."

Holtzclaw attempted to calculate the costs of such a promise. Building steps in vertical rock, bringing wood for benches: these were not easy projects. To make a promise is inexpensive and easy—for the moment, it needed only to be made, not fulfilled.

"There would be many people?" asked the Great and Harmless and Invincible Terrapin.

"There would be as many people as you like," said Holtzclaw. "We can advertise your names in all the best weeklies, and you will have a constant throng of admirers. Families will bring their young ones, mouths brimming peanuts and sweet pies and yelps of glee and boredom and affection. They will applaud thunderously, like a waterfall. Or we can invite only the finest guests, sell a very few tickets very dearly, so that any who buy them would treat the same experience with deep reverence. The women will wear long gloves and the men will put on tails. After your stories, they will clap primly, and the mingled sound of their appreciation will be the babble of a gentle stream."

"And what must I do to receive this boon?" said the Great and Harmless and Invincible Terrapin.

"It is very simple," said Holtzclaw. "You and your companion, the Sky Pilot, must not trouble my works nor undermine the dam. Leave it alone, and you will have your audience."

"It is agreed," said the Great and Harmless and Invincible Terrapin.

The Sky Pilot appeared behind Holtzclaw during his last monologue. He had climbed down to see if Holtzclaw had appeased his friend, and, if not, to obtain more ice to throw at trespassers. The Great and Harmless and Invincible Terrapin lifted his head, and his beaked face, streaked with leathery lines, cracked with recognition.

"Friend, I am glad," said the Great and Harmless and Invincible Terrapin. "This little morsel has promised that he will bring me people to hear my stories. They will sit on something called an amphitheater and they will listen."

"I've heard all your stories," said the Sky Pilot, "and I would gladly hear them again. Do you need more friends who will listen? Am I not enough?"

"You are not a roaring stream. There must be a Great and Wide and Infinite River from the Mountain. But you are my good friend."

The Sky Pilot ran to the terrapin; he embraced the terrapin around a keratinous claw.

"Now," said the Great and Harmless and Invincible Terrapin, "I will play the Song of Comfort." A simple scalar melody lilted from the turtle's shell. The terrapin rocked the leg to-and-fro, fore-and-back, and the Sky Pilot, still embracing, swayed in time. He smiled like a child about to sleep.

Mother Fresh-Roasted sat on the front porch of her riverside cabin. In her lap was a broken banjo. It had no strings, but she strummed the air above the scoop and fretted the neck as though she were playing, teasing some sound from it. She had sold her land readily enough, but had put off the move, blaming the mules. They were too comfortable in their present home.

"Mother Fresh-Roasted, the water is rising!" Holtzclaw called out to her as he approached.

The woman cast aside the banjo in a rough way, which explained how it lost its strings. "I saw a wet hen run smack into a wet dog this morning. Guess they had both been at the spring house and when they were coming up here to get their feed, they got all tangled up. Usually means a storm's coming, but I guess this time it meant flood. Is it minutes, hours? You are so winded; you must have hied like lightning to tell me."

Holtzclaw panted, but it was an act—he had not hurried, and his knees were now much more accustomed to the mountain roads, so that he hardly needed any Effervescent Brain Salts to take away their aches.

"Well, it will be four weeks until the whole lake it filled," he said, "but your stables will be underwater in a few days. You must move now."

"Graciousness! It's lucky, then, that Emmett sold me a solution for the mules." She ducked into her cabin and rummaged. Holtzclaw heard the sounds of metal on metal, glass on glass. Something shattered, and heavy piles slid and tumbled. Mother Fresh-Roasted emerged with a glass bottle.

"I normally like to mix up my own," said Mother Fresh-Roasted, "but none of my brews made those stubborn mules get up their get-up." She uncorked the bottle, filling the air with a strong smell of alcohol. "Emmet called it highlife and said I should put a dab just so. I need you to lift up his tail. Don't hold on too tight!"

She dunked an index finger into the bottle as Holtzclaw grasped the switching tail of one of the mules. He lifted it, and Mother Fresh-Roasted placed her dripping finger at its base. The mule brayed fiercely, lurched forward, and galloped into the sloppily cut underbrush. Holtzclaw was left holding several tail-hairs.

"I told you not to hold on too tight," said Mother Fresh-Roasted.

"How does he know where to go?"

"I sent the singing tree up there already, to tidy the place up. They'll hie to his voice."

She approached the next mule; Holtzclaw barely held the tail between his two fingers and Mother Fresh-Roasted's finger gingerly touched just the base. This mule, too, was shot through with vim and courage, barreling away uphill into the woods following the beaten track of its brother.

"That is some strong stuff," said Holtzclaw.

Mother Fresh-Roasted upended the bottle into her mouth and took a long swig. "It's all right," she said. Holtzclaw waited for her to explode into green sparks, but when he saw only a small shiver, he reasoned that the special effects of the highlife were confined to either mules or topical application.

"Your mules will be all right on their own, with just a singing tree to look after them?" said Holtzclaw.

"If you're worried, we can put a little highlife under your tail, too, and you can catch up with them."

"I would prefer not!" said Holtzclaw. But he took a sip from the bottle that she held out to him. It burned clear and tasteless—a fine spirit.

"Besides," said Mother Fresh-Roasted, "the Admiral will keep them in line and pick them up if they get lost." Hearing his name, a grey mop-like dog snuffled between Mother Fresh-Roasted's feet. "He executes my orders and all the animals follow."

The Admiral wheezed and spun around in place half a turn, pursuing his tail until it escaped him.

"Only trouble is, sometimes he gets to chasing after ghosts. He doesn't like them, even if they never harm anybody. So I have to put a glass button around his neck to stop him. Oh, Admiral! You've lost your button. It's a good thing that mushroom girl hasn't been by here. You wouldn't have given her any peace, would you?"

Mother Fresh-Roasted knelt down and removed the lowest button from her dress. She tied it to the Admiral's collar with a piece of thread drawn from her pocket.

"There, now you'll stay on task. Keep those mules moving, sir!" The Admiral wheezed and plodded towards the trees.

"He needs some highlife, too," said Holtzclaw.

"The Admiral is a teetotaler."

They went next into a shed that served as a shelter for the chickens. The coops themselves were built into a wheeled cart—ten coops long, four high, two abreast.

"Eighty hens, and each one has a window seat," said Mother Fresh-Roasted. "They've been so cold lately, so cold. I bring them into the house at night in the worst weather and put them right in front of the hearth, but they're still laying snowballs." She lifted one of the hens and withdrew a packed clump of snow, oval just like an egg.

"How do they cook up?" asked Holtzclaw.

"Tastes like ice cream," said Mother Fresh-Roasted.

"That could be a very profitable treat to sell by the roadside, when there are more visitors to the valley, as long as the weather cooperates."

"It may not be the weather after all. It may be unnatural fraternization with the cows," said Mother Fresh-Roasted. "We have seen the strangest signs. Rainbow-colored clouds in the sky. Ghosts and cats playing chuck-luck. My pond spring has flowed with gravy on two occasions."

The wheeled coop was hitched to a brace of oxen, and Mother Fresh-Roasted set this ungainly creation on its way with a clicking of her tongue.

Behind her cabin, in a stand of trees, were beehives. "My proudest creation," said Mother Fresh-Roasted. She lifted the lid of a hive and a green light shown forth. Holtzclaw approached the swarm without hesitation, drawn by light. When he peered inside the hive, he saw that each bee pulled behind it, through the twilight and shadows, a firefly-like lamp.

"I have made a marriage," said Mother Fresh-Roasted. "A firefly has a light but no purpose; a honeybee has a purpose but no light. Their children inherit the best talents of their parents!"

"This is not unnatural fraternization?" said Holtzclaw.

"No, not in the least. Can you imagine a more natural pairing? The fire-bees can work in the dark and make a double-crop of honey. When the honeybees gained illuminated tails, they lost in recompense their stingers, which is a boon for the hides of my visitors."

"So you have left your sweet and lucrative creations defenseless?" said Holtzclaw.

"On the contrary," said Mother Fresh-Roasted. "I have a gun, which is better than any stinger ever devised by Nature."

"How will you persuade them to move ahead of the waters?" asked Holtzclaw. "They have made a home for themselves here."

Mother Fresh-Roasted motioned for him to stay put, then walked to a copse of chestnut that had not yet been cleared. Leaves rustled, and a smaller tree staggered forward. A deer, adult-size but swayback and knock-kneed, carried a blooming peach tree from her back. The tree was not held in a pot of soil, but grew from the deer's back, at an angle just off straight, so the deer had to lean on its right legs to keep balance. The tree was in excellent health—shiny green leaves and bright white blossoms, even in this late season.

"That odious Sky Pilot shot her with an arrow he took from a peach tree, but he did not kill her," said Mother Fresh-Roasted. "I could do little for the poor creature. The peach-wood arrow had already taken a root inside her, and to try to remove it would cause a bleed that I couldn't stop. The peach tree and the deer are one creature now. The tree shares the mast that she forages and the water that she drinks. The deer sleeps beneath a continual cover of share and forever has a source of leaves and petals and fruit, in season."

"No one has tried to chop her down?" asked Holtzclaw.

"As I said, I have a gun," said Mother Fresh-Roasted. She clicked sideways out of her mouth, and a boy came out from the woods. He wore overalls and a straw hat, and he was covered in dirt across his body, but his hands and face were clean. He held a fishing pole, but he let it fall when he stood next to Mother Fresh-Roasted, who inspected his hands and face approvingly.

"Keeping them clean; that's a good lad," said Mother Fresh-Roasted. "Do me a kindness and lead our lady up to the new farm. You remember where it is?" The boy nodded. "It's a hard walk for her so she'll need your help."

"We can let her rest her middle on the wheelbarrow and then she will have a wheel, and I can pull up on the handles and help," said the boy.

"Why, that is a splendid idea, and worth twice the pay." She withdrew from her pocket two silver coins and two walnuts. The boy gobbled one of the walnuts quickly and placed the other three objects into the pocket of his overalls. He placed his hands on either side of the deer's face. Her eyes, weary and wary and sad like the eyes of all deer that Holtzclaw had seen, regarded the boy, then a black tongue emerged to lick the boy's hands. The boy laughed, the bees hummed, and the amalgamated creature—boy and bees and deer and tree—rounded the edge of the barn and disappeared.

Mother Fresh-Roasted's turkeys lifted their heads and opened their throats to the sky, as if expecting rain. Their alien warbling filled the air.

CHAPTER XVIII

When the workers cleared Skunk Cabbage Hollow, they discovered a tower. It was a rude gesture from the land directly aimed at Holtzclaw. He was hurrying from Mother Fresh-Roasted's farm to another small freehold, and his route took him past the site. Holtzclaw offered a rude gesture of his own towards the abandoned structure.

The tower was revealed only when workers toppled the soaring chestnuts around it, and the last thing that anyone expected to be hidden in the copse was a thirty-foot stone structure. The workers battered it with their hammers, but it would not topple.

A little dynamite would make short work of clearing the tower. Holtzclaw requisitioned it from Atlanta, scrounging the money for it by omitting some rock work at the dam. The explosives would arrive in two days by train, and that would be the end of the matter.

He was about to round the path and put the tower out of his sight again, but something shining from within caught his eye. It was a green light. All at once, the tower was no longer an imposition, but an opportunity.

He had not seen a will-o'-the-wisp in three months. Perhaps he'd offended it when they'd last met. He was determined to act more boldly this time. It might lead him to a cache of treasure that would solve all of his problems.

The tower was square and windowless. At the ground floor, a small archway with a free-swinging wooden door permitted entrance. The walls were made of rough-hewn, irregular stone. It was functional, but not a thing of beauty. The grout had cracked in several places, and green light spilled out through the gaps.

Holtzclaw stepped inside the entrance, and the green light shifted. Now, the will-o'-the-wisp was far below him. The floor of the tower was a small deck, just a few feet square. The rest was water, and far below, in the deep, the green light beckoned.

He had looked inside the tower before, of course, but there had been no treasure light then, and so he had not explored the depths of this murky pool. What was down there, in the water? What did the green light promise? He knelt at the water's edge, expecting the standing water to be a foul liquid, the soup of stagnancy and decay. But it smelled fresh.

The pool was part of the function of the tower. It had belonged to a shotmaker. A staircase led upwards. At the top was a hearth and a perch, from which the shotmaker could drop molten metal by teaspoons. Falling, the lumps of metal achieved a shape that was spherical enough for ballistic purposes. The pool at the bottom caught and cooled the spheres without deforming them, and the shot would come to rest of the bottom. To retrieve them, the shotmaker needed to empty the water from the pool.

Holtzclaw looked for the mechanism that would do this. Slimy stone steps showed that there was a way down—down where the will-o'-the-wisp shined through the water—but there must also be some way to drain the water, a valve attached to a drainpipe. A filament, no larger than a strand of silk, caught his eye. At one end was a tiny ring, covered in rust. He pulled it, and a sharp click from below made the waters explode into foam. A grinding of gears, a wheezing of bellows, whistles, clicks, and gurgles mixed into a roar.

With the water, the green light drained, too. The will-o'-the-wisp divided into two primary bodies, each circled by two dozen frenetic satellites, then recombined into a near-solid whole—its surface glazed over like darkened glass, then fractured into shimmering points. None of its antics arrested its descent. The will-o'-the-wisp came closer and closer to the floor, nearing the mouth of a drain pipe, and then—ploop!—it was sucked through.

If Holtzclaw had not offended the will-o'-the-wisp before, it was sure to be irate now.

But he was not dismayed for long. In place of the treasure light was a small glint of gold. Holtzclaw scurried down the damp stairs. In the middle of square floor was a rounded depression, about a foot deep. Water was already collecting here and brimming over the sides. The tower had been built on top of a spring! The shot maker could empty the tower, and the spring would refill it. Some slow leaks or drains at ground level kept the tower from over-filling. The constant renewal kept the water from turning brackish.

The glint of gold came from inside the depression, the source of the water. Holtzclaw reached into the depression and withdrew three spheres, the size of bullets. They felt like pure gold. Why the shotmaker had experimented with golden bullets—and then why he had abandoned them—was unclear.

"Did you taste the spring water?" said Princess Trahlyta.

Holtzclaw had not heard her approach. His first instinct was to pull the golden spheres close to his chest.

"This is my gold to take, princess. It was abandoned on my property."

"Take it, if you want. I asked if you'd tasted the water."

"Why should I?"

"To satisfy your curiosity."

Holtzclaw transferred the three golden spheres into his left hand, then dipped the right into the brimming spring basin. The water was warm. He sniffed the waters, but they had no special odor. He touched them with his lips, and the flavor astonished him. He spat it out, but from surprise rather than distaste. He took another sip, better prepared for wonder, and teased apart the flavors. It was a fine claret—aged, nuanced, smoky—that lingered on the palette but did not overstay its welcome.

Holtzclaw turned to face the princess, who was skimming across the tower floor on her bare feet. The water from the claret spring had risen high enough to put a thin layer of dampness across the surface. Between the stones were small pellets of lead shot, smoothed pieces of metal, algae and slime; these, too, were glistening.

"Tell me, princess. Is this one of those springs that flows with whatever the taster most desires? That would be fitting for a fairy tale. Would Shadburn taste mushrooms, and Abigail taste sweet potatoes and you, when you drink, taste ... I don't know ... more water?"

"Oh, no," said Trahlyta. "This spring always tastes like claret. I like your idea of an every-flavor spring, but they have already been invented. I think you call it a restaurant. Are you not building half a dozen of those?"

"Two," said Holtzclaw, "or none, if Shadburn runs out of money."

"Well, it's lucky for him that he is in the Lost Creek Valley, of all valleys. Here he can take as much gold as he likes. As for you, what are you going to do with these morsels? Are they enough for your floating hotel?"

Holtzclaw tried to hang a puzzled look on his face, but he succeeded only in making the princess smile. "It's hard to hide a steamship, James."

"No, it's not enough money," said Holtzclaw, dropping his facade. "These will only outfit a cabin or two. Drapes, linens, eider down, Persian rugs. First-class. But not the whole boat."

Holtzclaw slipped the three golden spheres into his inner breast pocket. The princess giggled.

"And why is it funny?" said Holtzclaw.

"Because if it not enough, why take it at all? Don't spoil your appetite by nibbling at scraps."

"I need every scrap, princess. I'll only ever have these tidbits, never a feast. I'll beg for scraps and orts and hope to be sated at the end of the meal."

This caused the princess to quake with laughter. Her voice careened from the stone walls. The earth itself was laughing at him, in the round.

"Perhaps you would be so kind to show me, then," said Holtzclaw, "where the big banquet is laid. I will leave these morsels here and take as much as I need in a single helping."

"Ask your friends, James!" said the princess, wiping tears from her cheeks. "They know where it is. It is so funny that you fret and pine for something that is not only common, but not even misplaced, not even wanted."

"I am asking you, princess. Show me where I can find the gold."

"It is everywhere, James! Everywhere."

"You've given me these trinkets, but it's not enough. I can't be bought as cheaply as Moss. If you want to save your valley, you will have to give more. It is a little disappointing that you would stoop to these levels. I thought that you would resist us more dramatically. That the dam would have been attacked by typhoons, or that the workers would have been drown in mud. But I've faced no rainstorms, no mudslides, no interfering fish. It has been a cake walk, princess. Perhaps you are powerless after all. A local spirit. A little girl."

The princess had stopped laughing, but her manner was still light. "Oh, James. Do you think that you would have gotten the gates on your dam closed if I hadn't wanted it? You may think I am yielding, that I can be bottled and controlled. That is the way of water. It seeks the easiest channel, but it is powerful when released. Rather than splash around like a child playing in a puddle, I will run cool and still. And when I please, I shall open the mountain and let the waters out."

Holtzclaw was choked with anger; he could not get out a retort. He stormed from the tower and back into the denuded forest. He stopped when he heard the sound of rain. It did not fall on his head, but on the tower and the hillside above it. Great torrents of water poured down, as though a spring had exploded from the firmament. The ground softened. Stones slipped from their places and tumbled down the face of the hill. Mud and rubble oozed towards Holtzclaw.

The tower shivered. Its footing was fast flowing away. A boulder slid from the high ground and knocked against the structure, and though it was not a hard hit, it was enough for the weakened foundations. The shot tower fell cleanly into its own pit, a puzzle placed back into its box.

The evening was thick in old Auraria. There were few lights left to dispel the dark. All but four or five of the inhabitants had taken up lodging in the new town or on new farms higher on the ridge. High on the valley, around the Queen of the Mountains, yellow lamps twinkled from behind new glass.

Abigail still slept in her room at the Old Rock Falls, but the kitchen was closed. She had relocated her essential relics to a storage building near the Queen of the Mountains, but she wanted to stay in her traditional place for as long as she could. Sampson, too, had relocated from the Grayson House, so there was little opportunity to eat. Holtzclaw had been making his suppers from Effervescent Brain Salts and Pharaoh's Flour.

Shadburn and Holtzclaw kept their living quarters at McTavish's for convenience, even though Mrs. McTavish had been among the first to set up a new establishment on the high ground. There was no sign hanging in front of her old house, and no cooking in her kitchen, Scottish or otherwise. Shadburn's windows at the McTavish house were dark. His office, too, was dark. Evidently he was spending the night elsewhere.

Holtzclaw was happy to see that there was a light glowing from within Ms. Rathbun's rooms at the Grayson House. He decided to give her the golden bullets he recovered from the shot tower before retiring. They were a trifle, to be sure, but any tribute was sure to please her.

He crossed the open, muddy space that used to be the town's square. There was a scratching sound; a turkey must have wandered from its master. His stomach rumbled. If he caught the turkey, he could convince Ms. Rathbun or Abigail to prepare it.

He crept forward with his head hunkered down. The noise was coming from the bottom of a twelve-foot hole, and Holtzclaw peered down. He was disappointed. Instead of a turkey, though, Bogan was at the bottom, flinging shovel-loads of dirty water upwards and outwards.

"You've struck the water table," said Holtzclaw, dodging mud.

"The water table's struck me," said Bogan. "I was digging where I was supposed to, and then the water started coming in higher and higher." Bogan made a face. He withdrew some artifacts from his pocket and tossed them up to Holtzclaw. A bear carved from bone. A wooden spool wound with three different threads—red, black, and yellow. A tin spoon. Holtzclaw recognized these things. He had found them and left them behind at the direction of the will-o'-the-wisp.

"Surely you have a better occupation," said Holtzclaw, "than to be knee-deep in mud?"

"Surely I don't," said Bogan.

❧

"It is such a little money," said Ms. Rathbun, when Holtzclaw showed her the golden spheres he had taken from the shot tower.

"Yes, but it will do to outfit a few cabins, won't it?"

"We need more, Holtzclaw. Ours would not be much of a pleasure boat with only two staterooms. Doesn't your employer have money?"

"Some," said Holtzclaw. "I don't know. Maybe a lot, maybe nothing."

"You need it now."

"I won't steal from Shadburn."

"Of course you wouldn't. I am not asking it. Perhaps, though, he'd consider it a good investment. It is going to a project that, after all, can only serve to benefit the reputation of his hometown and the resort he's making in the valley."

Ms. Rathbun's quarters in the Grayson House was stripped to necessities. The dressing table had only a comb, a basin, and a crockery ewer. The canopy over the four-poster bed was gone. Her bed had a single coverlet of red and white checks.

Ms. Rathbun unwrapped a piece of cheese cloth to reveal one cold johnnycake. She offered it to Holtzclaw, who for reasons of propriety could not accept it. Ms. Rathbun tore off bite-sized pieces and chewed them.

"I would fix supper, but all the pots have been moved," said Ms. Rathbun. "Sampson, too. He's left my employment and set up on his own."

"That is a blow," said Holtzclaw. "I'd hoped he would staff the kitchen on our floating hotel. His cuisine could be famous in the right venue."

"The worst of it is," said Ms. Rathbun, "he's plying his art from a chuck wagon. He flung some pots and pans and spices into a box on wheels, hitched it to an ox, and drove it up to the railroad camp. It's a waste of talent."

"We could woo him back," said Holtzclaw.

"That would take even more gold," said Ms. Rathbun, "and we have so little now."

"I have the scent of a much larger strike." He was thinking of what the princess had said, and what the will-o'-the-wisp promised, but he did not want to share the origins of his optimism. Ms. Rathbun would consider them unreliable.

"I've heard this all before," said Ms. Rathbun. "I think we need another partner. I'll ask Shadburn myself. Shadburn's a rich, successful man; he can never run out of money."

"No! Don't mix him into this. Give me a few more days."

"Why, you sound like my customers when their bill comes due. 'One more day, Ms. Rathbun, I swear it, I'll pay it all in full when I have the money.' Where is this strike?"

"It is buried in the heads of certain friends. They are an unnatural lot, Lizzie—I cannot quite understand them. They are sitting on top of mountains of gold, and yet they have no interest in bringing it out. I must convince them to dig it up for me."

Ms. Rathbun leaned back in her chair. "Our methods are not so different, Holtzclaw."

CHAPTER XIX

In the morning, Holtzclaw went up the mountain to the camp of the railroad men. Their camp was set into Asbestos Hollow, against a vertical face of Burnt Rock Mountain, the better to shield them against wind and rain. Holtzclaw's ostensible purpose was to recruit a wrecking team to clear the remaining houses in old Auraria, but he was also drawn by the promise of Sampson's cuisine, which he could smell from a half-mile away. Holtzclaw waited his turn at the chuck wagon, where the ritual inherited from the Grayson House was carefully observed. A customer placed his piece of gold on a burned wooden spot and turned away; moments later, a bowl of stew was in its place. This morning, it was a variant of groundhog stew, spiced for breakfast with cinnamon and nutmeg and decorated with a raw egg cracked on top of it.

As Holtzclaw waited his turn and then ate his breakfast, he surveyed the camp. The men were mostly imported. Holtzclaw recognized only a few faces, Dan and Moss among them. Morning fires still smoldered from where men had warmed themselves after a cold night. Some who'd lost their pay in gambling cooked a poor breakfast of beans rather than buy a bowl of groundhog stew. Gaming paraphernalia was in evidence—illustrated decks of cards, dominoes, a standing roulette wheel.

From one of the caverns above the camp, a man staggered out, supported by two women. All were still in evening clothes. One of the women tried to manage a parasol while handling the slumping figure; the other did not pause to pick up her hat when it slipped from her head.

The man raised his face and looked out at the world through bleary eyes.

"Shadburn!" cried Holtzclaw. "Hiram Shadburn!"

"Is it Holtzclaw?" he said. "I can barely see through this fog. Holtzclaw, if it is you, give these good women some money. I made a pest of myself last evening, and I could not adequately recompense them. My billfold was lighter, you see, than I had thought."

"Perchance you were robbed when you were in some indisposed condition."

"Oh, he was not indisposed, but quite in his right mind," said the first woman, tugging on Shadburn's arm to thrust more of his weight onto her back.

"A rich man!" said the other woman, who had missed her hat. "I like rich men."

Holtzclaw withdrew a pouch of some loose gold dust from inside his vest pocket and poured a measure into the outstretched palms of the two women. They released their charge at the sight of money. Shadburn could not keep his footing under his own power; he slumped into a heap.

Holtzclaw had two men fetch a wheelbarrow. They loaded Shadburn into the vehicle while Holtzclaw rounded up the wrecking crew that he needed.

"Bella and Isabella did a number on your fancy friend there, Holtzclaw," said the pilot of the wheelbarrow.

"Which number?" said his companion. This was met with uproarious, suggestive laughter.

"Gentlemen, a little respect," said Holtzclaw. "Your Bella and Isabella are professional flatterers. That Shadburn, a naive soul, could not resist them is a virtue, not a flaw. He is only trying to do right for you; to uplift this valley."

"Well, he has contributed to the uplift of those two women," said the driver of the wheelbarrow.

"His own uplift, too!" said a man with a mattock over his shoulder.

At the edge of the camp, the railroad twins stopped Holtzclaw's small party. The twins were impeccably dressed; they made Holtzclaw feel ashamed of his own rumpled, road-stained clothes. The morning sun gleamed off of their gold cufflinks.

"We have a pressing audience with you, Holtzclaw," said either Johnston or Carter.

"You have not been taking our meetings," said the other.

"I am sorry for that," said Holtzclaw. "There have been many things to do, you see, and very little time in which to do them. We have a fixed schedule. The lake is rising!"

"This makes our request all the more pressing," said Johnston or Carter.

"Some work must be done before the flood," said the other.

"What work is that?"

"You promised us sawmills, Holtzclaw," said Johnston or Carter.

"You promised us tanneries, Holtzclaw," said the other.

"I will build them," said Holtzclaw. "I mean, I will not myself pick up a shovel, but I will cause them to be built."

Shadburn flailed in the wheelbarrow, inverting the position of his arms and legs.

"But a dam and a lake are enough, don't you think for the moment?" said Holtzclaw. "When they are finished, we will start the next phase, the grand hotel. Then, in good time, the sawmills and tanneries. I would crave your patience, gentlemen."

"We can no longer be patient," said Johnston or Carter.

"Some preparatory work must be done now. It should have been done weeks ago."

"I understand your concerns, gentlemen," said Holtzclaw. "Trust us that your investment will be turned into a profit, though you have demanded so much capital from us that I fail to see how you could be operating at a loss."

"We can aid you in your obligation," said Johnston or Carter. "Let us start clearing certain sites."

"We will dig some pipes, so that the sawmill can have a good supply of water."

"Are these blasted moles trying to dig something up?" said Shadburn, stirring from the wheelbarrow. "Are these dull-eyed groundhogs looking for a tunnel?"

"Please, Shadburn, be quiet," said Holtzclaw.

"You'll let them swindle you, Holtzclaw. You'll let them swindle you out of the best piece of land, and they'll go digging, and it will all be ruined. You're a fool, Holtzclaw."

"I am doing my best for you, Shadburn, and our interests, and the interests of these gentlemen, too," he said. "When the lake is filled and the hotel is underway, we will put all our resources into industrial development."

"You have the funds for these plans?" said Johnston or Carter.

"A man that cannot pay his companions cannot support his business," said the other.

"Now listen to me, gentlemen!" said Holtzclaw, puffing his chest. "Any building that is built or digging that is done will be at my direction, in my own time, and you will not act upon my land—my land!—without permission, which I will not give until the lake has reached full pool. If there is a delay, if your trains do not run at capacity for awhile—well, these are the risks of business."

The railroad twins responded with oaths and interjections before turning back towards their camp. Holtzclaw hastened their departure with a derisive waving of his hat, as though he were airing out an odor. Holtzclaw's crew jeered and hooted.

"That's a smashing spirit, Holtzclaw," said Shadburn.

"Quiet, you!" said Holtzclaw.

Holtzclaw deposited Shadburn in his chambers to sleep off his debauchery, then met Abigail at the Old Rock Falls. It was time for a last inspection, then to have the structure cleared, before the rising water turned it into dangerous debris.

"I'm not sure whether to be disappointed or impressed," said Abigail, after Holtzclaw told her the story.

"Disappointed," said Holtzclaw. "Very, very disappointed. I have made enemies of our business partners in order to support his strange mania. It's terrible business."

He and Abigail began at the kitchen of the Old Rock Falls, then continued up through the guest rooms. The Old Rock Falls was stripped to a shell. The good wood had been salvaged for the Queen of the Mountains. Shadburn had acquiesced to Holtzclaw's plan for two dining rooms. The main one would be luxurious, as befitted a first-class hotel, and the second would be authentic, as near a recreation of the Old Rock Falls as could be managed, using the original materials.

Abigail checked the corners, the cabinets, and the caches. She lifted floorboards to reveal hiding places already cleaned out. She pried up secret paneling. Only once was there a moment of excitement, when a tin of Pharaoh's Flour was discovered under a floorboard. Abigail opened it—it was empty. She grasped a bookshelf with two hands, and it swung open to reveal a passageway. Abigail and Holtzclaw went inside, hunched over. It was a dusty room with no furniture, artifacts, or spirits.

"Who lived in this one?" said Holtzclaw. "Mr. Bad Thing?"

"No, he couldn't have opened the passage. This was a special suite that we kept for adventurers and children, who wanted a bit of mystery instead of an ordinary room."

In the attic, they found a large wasp's nest. Thirty of its inhabitants flitted perpetually perturbed around their home.

"These little ones want to travel," said Abigail.

"You can't mean to install them at the Queen of the Mountains," said Holtzclaw. "A decent hotel cannot be infested with wasps."

"They've been here longer than I have," said Abigail. "One time, there was a rough rider that came into town. He got stung on the nose and moved along. He could have been trouble."

"So you will reward these wasps for instinctual action performed by their ancestors years ago?"

"It's the history of the world," said Abigail.

Abigail took the wasp's nest from its perch in the eaves. Between her hands, it was very fragile. She pressed on the two far ends, and the nest yielded in the middle along a natural fault. Twice more she was able to crease it until the nest was no larger than a folded handkerchief. The wasps permitted this. "I'll put them somewhere above the water, at least."

Holtzclaw and Abigail could only examine the dining room by peering through the doorframe—the wooden floorboards had been removed and put up in storage near the framework of the Queen of the Mountains. The basement gaped from below. Across the void, two daguerreotypes still hung on the wall. One was the ten year-old boy wearing a gold pan like a hat above his hard, cleft chin. The other was the Old Rock Falls at high water.

"We'll fetch them," said Holtzclaw. "I'll find a ladder."

"It's not worth the trouble," said Abigail. "I remember them well enough, and I suppose I'm the only person who would find them interesting. There are plenty of others for the New Rock Falls."

"Oh, I think that a fair number of visitors to the Queen of the Mountains would pause and look, if only because the images are somewhat unusual. That is, if there are ever any visitors, if the hotel ever opens."

"This argument again," said Abigail.

"I promise, this is my final plea," said Holtzclaw. "Shadburn's capital has dwindled. I am afraid you may be the manager of an abandoned palace, Ms. Thompson. No guests at all. I warned you about this months ago. And with the water rising, the gold that you see in your dreams—which you have taken for granted all these years—will be flooded very soon and forever beyond your reach."

"You told me Shadburn had Midas's touch," said Abigail.

"This time, I think the object was too large to alchemize. He couldn't wrap his arms around this one to work his transforming power—anyway, I'm getting lost in the metaphor. The plain fact is that he hasn't the money to finish what he's begun. I am certain of it now. He may soon spend his last dollar, whether on wages for the dam builders or trinkets for his female companions, I'm not sure. We have cleared acres of trees for no purpose. We have drowned mines and farms without setting up any compensating industry. Shadburn's money so far has gone into the lake, not into factories. We have gutted your beloved inn for nothing."

Abigail put her the palm of her hand against a wooden beam.

"I know that Auraria has rich veins," said Holtzclaw. "If Shadburn will not avail himself of the resources this land provides..."

"You mean, if he won't fill his pockets with gold," said Abigail.

"Gold that is on his own land! Gold that he is about to drown forever! Gold that he is spending not on himself, but on the betterment of his own people!"

"It's altruism all the way down," said Abigail.

"If Shadburn will not take it, then I must," said Holtzclaw. "As his trustee. I will recover it and put it away for him. For you, your traditions and legacy! When the hotel porters come for their wages or when the railroad twins demand a sawmill to fill their freight cars, like they did this morning, Shadburn will turn to me horror-stricken, and I will say, 'Certainly, gentlemen, we can satisfy your needs,' and it will not be a boldfaced lie."

"Why do you need me? Haven't you been chasing a will-o'-the-wisp for weeks now?"

"I have found a piece or two of gold," said Holtzclaw. "One can hardly help it. In Auraria, as you have said, there is gold in the gutters after it rains." Holtzclaw thought of his excitement at his first discovery—the eight colors of gold that had been enough to put aside his reason. "But my particular treasure light is angry or defective. It gives me too little to fulfill the promises that have been made. I know there is a much greater treasure, Abigail, somewhere."

"I've never been there," said Abigail.

"But you could still take me, yes? We'd take only what we need. We don't mean to enrich ourselves, to become rich idlers—though that could be done easily enough, and without having to run it first through a scheme of dam and lakes and resorts. We only need to finish what we have begun. To decorate the Queen of the Mountains in fine style, worthy of succeeding the Old Rock Falls. To keep our employees fed until the hotel is self-sufficient."

"Don't pretend it's all loyalty to Shadburn or charity towards our town, Holtzclaw. You have your side bet. Your pleasure boat. That's why you need gold. For your own profit."

"You're right," said Holtzclaw. "But I'm not going to put the money into my pocket. I will do something useful with it. Putting it into the floating hotel is for the good of the valley, too. It's another place of employment, another draw for visitors. It's in line with all of Shadburn's wishes, even if it not under his ownership."

"What he wants is to seal the gold under the lake," said Abigail.

"And if he succeeds before we've taken up a little more of that gold, then the Old Rock Falls will be at an end. Auraria will be at end. You are your own last hope, Ms. Thompson."

As they exited the Old Rock Falls, Abigail gave a nod to a crew that floated nearby. Her silent instruction released them, and they set to the building like a wave. They crashed against supports and smashed against walls. Axes came through windows. Pry bars caught against stairs, against panels, against frames and fixtures, which lifted and shattered in the swell. The building shuddered from the tide; it fell into a drift of boards, splinters, and fragments.

"It's a shell," she said. "There is nothing sad about a shell."

The can-man sloshed kerosene onto the rubble, and his companion, the fire-bringer, threw on a torch. The rubble burned with a cheery, even flame that first glowed blue, then red. The sound was a low crackle, comfortable, like a cooking fire in a hearth.

The fire signaled Dr. Rathbun, with whom Holtzclaw had an important appointment. Some of the buildings still standing in Auraria, against all good sense and the rising river, remained inhabited. As mayor, Dr. Rathbun had the moral authority to discharge these squatters and ensure that their possessions were cleared ahead of the wrecking crews. His permission was not required for demolition, but it was a prudent cautionary step—the burning of a town, by outsiders or even by estranged sons, is bound to be a delicate matter, and the approval of the beloved mayor would have a palliative effect.

He emerged from behind the Grayson House, waved to Holtzclaw, and threw a thumb over his shoulder towards the structure he'd just left. The wrecking crew lifted mauls, mallets, and flame.

Dr. Rathbun exchanged bows with Abigail. "You will be all right, won't you, Ms. Thompson? Where are you staying until your new hotel has lodgings for you?"

"At McTavish's," said Abigail. "If I hurry, I may be able to make dinner."

"You can't take the Sugar Shoals road," said Dr. Rathbun. "I tried to come that way this morning, and the water is already too high over Arman's Ford. I had to come by way of the Patterson track."

"Then I will be too late for dinner," said Abigail. "Perhaps there will be a cold biscuit to be had, somewhere."

She bowed slightly to take her leave, and Holtzclaw watched her go, to see if she would cast any backwards glances. Her path was aimless, only generally upwards and outwards. Then, a purpose flitted into her boots, and she strode off resolutely in a direction that would only take her farther into the valley. Where could she be going? Holtzclaw considered it an encouraging sign.

Dr. Rathbun and Holtzclaw started their slow patrol through the empty buildings of Auraria. The commercial blocks came first. In Emmett's pharmacy, several shattered bottles had spilled their brightly colored potions. Emmett had not bothered to mop up. Next door, the dry goods emporium, where Holtzclaw had bought his combined hat and gold pan, was empty and merited only a cursory glance.

The third store in the block was a confectionary shop. Holtzclaw had been surprised that a small town supported such a specialty shop, but then, Auraria's obsession with food rivaled its obsession with gold. Still, he'd never managed to visit it while it was in operation. It was neglected in the whirl of other tasks. Holtzclaw met with the owner at the Old Rock Falls; money was exchanged there, and no cakes or pies were proffered in the deal.

"Plaxton took his marble countertop, I see," said Dr. Rathbun, entering the store, "but not his decorations."

Behind the counter were shelves stacked with tins upon tins of Pharaoh's Flour. The laughing face of Amenhotep III was duplicated in an evolution of styles and poses a hundred times over. On the facing wall were advertising cards for Pharaoh's Flour. Amenhotep embraced the sun which rose like a golden loaf over the bleached desert. Amenhotep loomed over a pyramid-shaped tartlet, about to consume it. Amenhotep stood with his arms folded across his chest, fronting an array of mummies that were called back from the Land of the Dead by the visible aroma of a fresh-baked cake.

"Is there any sense in saving these?" asked Holtzclaw.

"If you don't want them," said Dr. Rathbun, "then no one does."

The images were striking and finely printed. It would be a shame to let them be destroyed. Holtzclaw wondered if there was room for them at the Queen of the Mountains. But he decided that too much work would be required—taking them from the wall, carting them up the mountain, reframing them, arranging them into some custom-built display chamber—and all for an uninterested public. Not even their original owner had thought them worth saving. So Holtzclaw paused before each advertisement in turn, fixing them in his mind with a long, intentional stare, then consigned them to the wrecking crew.

Next, Holtzclaw and Dr. Rathbun investigated the tonsor's parlor. There, they found a squatter. He was reclined in a barber chair, his head leaned back into the fully recumbent shaving position, and he was snoring violently.

"It's time to go," said Dr. Rathbun, placing a hand on the man's shoulder.

He opens his eyes with a jerk. "Oh, I'm sorry, Doc. I just got sleepy. So sleepy."

Holtzclaw studied the man's face. Once a layer of dust and neglect and stubbled growth were discounted—this was the only time Holtzclaw had ever seen a dirty, hairy man leave a barber's chair—Holtzclaw recognized Clyde, the paramour of the widow Smith Patterson.

"What do you need to take with you?" asked Dr. Rathbun.

"Just my hat and my stick," said Clyde. "I am off to see the world, or rather, I have been expelled to see the world. I'd only made it as far as the tonsor's, though, before I lost my steam."

"Holtzclaw," said the doctor, "I'm certain you have some money to help refill this man's boiler. Wet his whistle for his world travels as compensation for disturbing the enjoyment of his barber's chair."

Holtzclaw's fingers found four dollars in his pocket, but he only took out two. Money was precious enough now that he begrudged funding Dr. Rathbun's reelection campaign.

"Now get on your way, Clyde," said Dr. Rathbun. "We mean to burn the place down."

Clyde got on his way, and the wave of wreckers set alight the whole block of stores.

A handsome building held Dr. Rathbun's former offices. Holtzclaw followed the doctor as he checked one last time for valuable vials. In a dark room were twelve tall vats.

"What did they hold, doctor?" asked Holtzclaw.

"Water!" said Dr. Rathbun. "The very best medicine."

"It is the cheapest, at least."

"That does not make it any less effective. And the people do need it. When I first arrived here, I thought I would have an easy time. It should be easy to be a physician to an industrious people in a salubrious mountain climate."

"Your climate is too confusing to be labeled salubrious."

"You've hit the mark, Holtzclaw. There were many bad illnesses. I saw men with twisted bones; they looked as though their torsos had been reversed on their waists. I saw children that had taken on characteristics of plants—greenish skin and an unquenchable thirst. I saw their siblings speaking only in a forest language of snorts, whistles, and grunts. Women gave birth irregularly, sometimes to babies that emerged covered in a fine powder, like coal dust or talcum. Patients came to me as geysers of yellow bile, all their phlegm and blood drained out, or else, they positively drooled phlegmatically. One poor creature exhaled clouds of phlogiston with every breath— I could not help him, and he expired in a purple mist. In the army, we had good supplies—sharp saws, carbolic acid, mercury drops. But I found that these were tools and cures for soldiers, not for Auraria. I ordered tonics from the city, but these, too, had little effect. It was medicine for city dwellers, not for poor mountain miners."

"They seem hale enough now, as a people," said Holtzclaw. "What was the solution?"

"My conclusion was that the mountain dwellers had found themselves rejected as strangers by their very environment. The new land upset their humors and essences, and thus the cure to their ills, by the theory of sympathetic vibration, must too come from the land. I read in Munde and Priessnitz and Trall about the science of hydrotherapy. They laid bare the mechanism of minerals and solutes and mixtures that had been used for centuries at healing springs. Auraria has every good and healthful type of water."

"And so you prescribe the water cure?" said Holtzclaw.

"It is the best medicine for the ills of this watery valley," said Dr. Rathbun. "Of all places on Earth, I think the waters of the Lost Creek Valley are the most potent and efficacious."

"Why haven't you announced your cure to the rest of the medical community?"

"The tourists would ruin it. They would take our cure and leave behind their poisons, dirty the waters."

"But they would leave their money, too."

"Precisely. That's precisely the problem."

Dr. Rathbun motioned that they should go, but Holtzclaw pondered. "You could have run pipes down to your office," said Holtzclaw. "Saved yourself the trouble of carting the water in such quantities from the diverse springs to refill your supply. More profit, less labor."

"Ah, we all have feet," said Dr. Rathbun, turning away. "Sometime's, a constitutional is just the thing."

The building was demolished, vats and all. The duo headed towards another block, past the squat building whose upper floors held Shadburn's offices.

"This building is ready, too," said Holtzclaw to the wrecking crew. "Everything necessary has been removed."

A ruddy-faced man began to pummel at the bricks with his maul.

Dr. Rathbun held up a hand. "You don't even want to check if Shadburn is inside?"

"I am sure he is not, and if he is, he should have the good sense to come out. This man is shaking the place apart."

"Still, I would want a look inside," said Dr. Rathbun. "For the sake of due diligence."

Before Holtzclaw could protest, Dr. Rathbun was through the doors and halfway up a staircase. He stopped at the threshold to Shadburn's workspace, hesitating to lean his head too far among the perilous towers of ephemera. "Holtzclaw, nothing has been removed. All your invoices, receipts, papers, deeds. You'll let them all go up in ashes? Even strongboxes are here." He opened one with a toe of a polished leather shoe. "Sand? Your employer kept sand in his strongboxes? There where did he keep his gold? Under the mountain?"

"There were some record-keeping errors," said Holtzclaw, shutting the lid of the strongbox with his scuffed boot heel. "I claim responsibility for not properly auditing the withdrawals."

A snickering sound issued from behind a tower of boxes and papers. There was a muffled whack, a slap of something soft over someone's head. The laughter stopped, but only for a moment before it burst forth again unbridled, now in two voices. Holtzclaw collapsed a stack of papers to reveal the intruders—Ephraim and Flossie.

"What sort of game is this?" said Holtzclaw. "This is private property!"

"We've been at our trading game," said Flossie. "You have just hoards of playing pieces here, Mr. Holtzclaw, and it's been so grand putting them in. We have a lot more to trade. Ephraim had the powerhouse, and I wanted it so bad, so I said, 'I will give you the Queen of the Mountains, but he said, 'No, you'd have to give me a thousand feet at the Amazon Branch,' and I didn't want to give up such a stretch. So, I said, 'No, I own the whole lakeshore, and that monopoly is worth much more than a powerhouse.' But I only thought I had the whole lakeshore, because Ephraim has a ticket for this little triangle, a tiny speck, and he won't give it up, even though it's worthless, but it's on the lake. I promised him the Raven Cliffs and the underground lake and the Hag's Head grotto and the ice house, but he wouldn't trade."

"Ephraim is a smart player," said Holtzclaw.

"Ephraim is a stick-in-the-mud," said Flossie. "It's not much of a game if no one makes a play."

"All right, little ones, let's go," said Dr. Rathbun. "It's past time to leave. Holtzclaw wanted to bring this place down on your heads. You can go say hello to Mama Rathbun and she'll make you some supper, and there's a big porch where you can spread out to play your game until we figure out what to do."

Ephraim and Flossie scuttled from the offices, their arms stuffed with papers. Holtzclaw wanted to protest the abduction of his property—Shadburn's property—but he was grateful, at least, that a few props for their game were sufficient reparations for trying to bury them in rubble.

From here on, Dr. Rathbun treated Holtzclaw with more distrust than usual. He insisted on peering into every room of every dwelling himself. This prolonged their investigation of the infinite Walton house to an interminable length. Holtzclaw's haunches ached from ascending fifty-two flights, which was as high as he could go before the walls became too narrow to let his shoulders through.

Every floor was empty, to a mote. Not only every artifact, even the smallest flake of rock powder and the tiniest bones in the long cow, had been removed, but also the floors had been scrubbed clean. The windows were freshly washed, inside and out. The walls were repainted.

"It's too much trouble," said Dr. Rathbun, puffing as he descended the stairs behind Holtzclaw. "To clean a building before demolishing it."

Holtzclaw agreed, and he felt a waver of hesitation before ordering the wreckers. He should invite some children to have a mud fight or paint on the walls with their fingers. Then he wouldn't be sending a pristine dwelling into the flames.

But the fire ate at the perfect building with as much greed as one filled with possessions. Fire took to the walls of the building, climbing the frame but never reaching the roof. Flames burned blue and bright; they licked and flicked with vigor. How long could the fire burn on the infinite stories of the Walton house? A week? A month? Forever?

Holtzclaw and Dr. Rathbun watched the inferno, but when they became bored, they continued their operations, investigating the rows of white houses behind the cold ash-heaps of the taverns, then the few larger homes that had once belonged to prominent families. Two more days of rising water had convinced any remaining squatters of the impermanence of their dwellings.

Holtzclaw and Dr. Rathbun arrived back at the inn formerly known as McTavish's at suppertime. It was the last building left. Holtzclaw thought it did not deserve such an honor. He wanted nothing better than to torch it as well, though it would likely stink of years of failed foreign cooking, but he and Shadburn had not yet relocated their personal effects.

"Have you packed up yet?" said Dr. Rathbun. "Is Shadburn ready?"

"Give us until morning," said Holtzclaw. "He'll take some time to dislodge. Besides, I want to keep watch on this Walton fire. During the night it will burn itself out."

"What's the danger?" said Dr. Rathbun. "Its neighbors are already ash."

CHAPTER XX

Before the stars were lit, Ms. Rathbun led Holtzclaw to inspect their pleasure boat. Rising water had come up to the construction area and touched the bottom of the boat. A struggle of gravity, weight, water, and buoyancy was underway. The water wasn't strong enough yet to lift the boat from its cradle, but soon, the balance would change, and the vessel would float first six inches, then sixty feet, above its berth.

"How will we stop it from floating away?" asked Holtzclaw.

Ms. Rathbun, barefooted, sloshed into the water towards the prow, "Come here, I'll show you."

Holtzclaw undid his boots, removed his socks, rolled up the ends of his trousers, and tucked them into awkward folds at the knee. He had taken only three steps before his clumsy tuck unfurled, and a trouser leg unrolled into the ankle-deep water. He bent over to fix it, but the other cuff came down as he worked.

Ms. Rathbun laughed. "It's only water, Holtzclaw, not poison."

Holtzclaw waded towards her. "Show me what you meant to show me," he said.

"The boat is anchored to the earth," she said, lifting out a heavy chain from where it was coiled beneath the prow. "One at the front and one at the back. There's plenty of slack to feed out to the boat at full pool, but not so much that the boat would float towards one of the banks."

"As simple as that?"

"No need for more complicated schemes. When the lake is filled, we will row out here in a launch and tow it to the dock. And never will there be anything bigger or grander on this lake than our boat."

"Well, it's quite the achievement," said Holtzclaw. He slapped his hand against the hull. It responded with a satisfying, weighty ring.

"Of course," said Ms. Rathbun. "No one will book a vacation on a pleasure boat that is only steel and engine."

"I am very close to a solution. I've laid a snare in someone's mind. Soon—maybe even tonight—the snare will be tripped."

"Do you want to tell me any more about this, Holtzclaw?" She had moved closer to him.

"It's superstition, but no. Only that if I'm right, there will be money for Shadburn and money for us."

Ms. Rathbun made a rude sound between her lips. "Shadburn! Shadburn! Shadburn! You're always thinking of Shadburn. Even when his Midas touch has fled. Even when he has shown himself to be thoroughly incompetent and useless on this project, if he was ever competent and useful on any project. You could not take any but the scraps for yourself."

"No more scraps. I'll go to the table and set my own plate."

Holtzclaw put his hand against the boat again. The structure yielded under his touch. Was it a defect in the metal, or was the boat ready to lift from its moorings?

They walked above the wide and swollen Lost Creek to the place where their paths diverged—Holtzclaw back to the the inn formerly known as McTavish's, a foot above the rising water; Ms. Rathbun to her father's splendid new house near the skeleton of the Queen of the Mountains.

Above, kinetic green lights tumbled from the purple night and into the valley. They were falling stars.

"It is beautiful, this display," he said. "Peaceful."

"Anything but," said Ms. Rathbun. "Up on the high ground, they must think they're witnessing the end of the world. They'll have broken down the chuck-luck wheel. Players will have sworn off it for good, or at least the night. At the railroad camp, men will have thrown their cards and dice and dominoes into the fire, but old hard bone does not burn. Chickens are laying eggs filled with green fire. Cows and pigs rise up onto their hind legs to dance. The usual nonsense of this place."

"Such needless panic!" said Holtzclaw. "I am glad I am here, away from it."

"You don't want to explain to the people in calm and soothing tones exactly what is happening?" said Ms. Rathbun.

"I could explain until I am blue and faint. I could tell them about the luminiferous aether and phlogiston and their interactions. How the motion of the Earth collects shattered fragments of electric fluid that are conducted through the aether, igniting as they drag against particles of smoke in the air. But that is not what they need."

"What do you suppose it is that they need?"

"They need one night of fear," said Holtzclaw. "As catharsis. Their lives have been inverted. Valley folk now live on the mountainside. Miners have put away their pans for aprons. They are permitted a time of panic and distress. Then, they will begin to accept their new circumstances."

"It's a nice enough moral, but you don't need to be the one to teach it," said Ms. Rathbun.

A large orb of electric fluid arced overhead. For a few seconds, it skimmed the surface of the river. Two green sparks, following parallel arcs, crackled and bit and snapped at each other, and then they were extinguished together in the same hollow.

Shadburn's room at McTavish's was as disordered as his office had been, before fire had filed everything into uniform cinders. He rifled through a pile of garments that had been pushed into a corner. Three of these were tossed to Holtzclaw, who folded them before putting them into a trunk. The remainder were discarded into a second pile for obvious flaws—torn sleeves, red and green stains down the front and around the collar, six missing buttons. A pair of trousers had one leg ripped away.

"I have an idea for an improvement to your hotel plans," said Holtzclaw. He recounted what he'd heard from Dr. Rathbun about hydropathy. "Already, the Queen of the Mountains is sited on two springs, one hot and one cold. We can run pipes from others on the mountainside so that the hotel can provide, on tap, all the waters necessary for health, whether for drinking or bathing. The Queen of the Mountains could not only be a stellar resort, but a first-class sanatorium, offering hydrotherapy for a wide range of ailments."

"Will vacationers want to spend their days with invalids?" said Shadburn.

"I assure you that the rich will pay even more for a cure than they will for a vacation. And you will be bettering not just your town's finances, but your visitors' health. More uplift, for everyone."

"It is a fine idea, but it will take money." Shadburn fell back into a cloth-strewn chair.

"Precisely," said Holtzclaw. "Even now I am scratching at crumbs. I am not sure that our hotel will ever open."

Shadburn sprung up and began a furious pacing. "That will never do. The lake is the lock, yes, but the hotel is the key. Keeps it shut tight."

"What do you mean?"

"Only, if there is no hotel, then who will keep up the dam, once you and I are gone?"

"We are leaving?"

"We are not immortal. Lakes should live longer than men, and I intend it to last for generations."

"It's a moot point," said Holtzclaw, folding his arms. "We don't have the money for the opening weekend. If we were wise, we would have enough capital stored to cover two seasons' worth of expenses; better, two years. Your guests don't pay their bills until the end of their stay, but before then, you have to feed and house them, as well as pay your staff. And you cannot expect the hotel to be profitable right away."

"It's true," said Shadburn, working his thumb into the cleft of his chin. His brow furrowed, as if he were considering these ideas for the first time.

"And our investor has not yet presented himself," said Holtzclaw. "From whence will our deliverance come? I am trying desperately, Shadburn, to convince one to our point of view, but I am not sure I have succeeded."

Shadburn's thumb pensively worked its way into the hard cleft of his chin as he paced to the window. Outside, the rising river had begun to overspill its banks. Fingers of water flowed between fenceposts and foundations. Smoldering ash marked the site of every former structure in Auraria, except where flames still rose from the

Walton house. The valley was in ruins. Holtzclaw had done his work well.

"There's plenty of money," said Shadburn quietly, to the window. "Positive fortunes left."

"Where? Tell me who has it. Tell me where it is."

This was not the Asheville Attitude, or the Fitzgerald Flip. Holtzclaw's urgency and frustration robbed him of his persuasive powers.

"I suppose a man like me can never run out of money," said Shadburn. "The consequences are too great."

"I want to speak in practicalities, for your own good, but you are giving me only elliptical aphorisms. I want simple answers."

"You've come to the wrong valley, then." Shadburn sighed, and his exhalation took all his wind out of him. He fell back into the chair; his limbs folded on top of themselves, in a crumpled heap. Never had Holtzclaw seen him look so small.

Once he stirred from his melodramatic collapse, Shadburn finished packing with more attention than before, perhaps eager to rid himself of his assistant. Holtzclaw continued to ply his employer with questions, but he had not been able to convert any of his elliptical phrases into realities: the name of an investor, the bank that held a strongbox. Shadburn's maudlin mood had not admitted any secrets. Behind his few words, Holtzclaw felt resignation and defeat.

Finally, Holtzclaw gave up for the night. In the morning, he would try again. It would be the most important negotiation of his career. He would confront Shadburn over a breakfast of hash browns and mushrooms, when Shadburn's happiness was at its peak.

Holtzclaw returned to his own room, extinguished his bedside candle, and climbed beneath the covers. The yellow light in the room was replaced by pulsing green flashes. The drapes dulled the glow of the falling stars.

He heard scratching at the door. At first he dismissed it as a pest—a loose mouse or other forest creature, compelled into shelter by the rising waters. The scratching became more rhythmic. There was a voice behind it, too soft to understand.

Holtzclaw fumbled with a match but could not make the candle light. He arose without illumination and put his ear to the door. The rhythmic sound continued, and now the voice was whispering his name. He opened the door only slightly, but it was wide enough for Abigail to push past into his room and close the door behind her. "You're dressed for a dinner party even when you sleep."

Holtzclaw was wearing formal pajamas—red and white striped broadcloth, with buttons that fastened down the front.

"So, you've reconsidered?" said Holtzclaw. "Are we to undertake a mining expedition?"

"Don't call it that," said Abigail. "It's an exploration, for knowledge. There is one dream that is so strange, and I don't see how it could possibly be real. In the mountain behind Raven Cliff, there is a tunnel. And I will never know if that tunnel leads where my dreams suppose it does, unless we go tonight. When this lake is filled, no one will ever see it again. It will be a part of Auraria lost forever, and I want to collect its memory."

"That's splendid, Ms. Thompson," said Holtzclaw, pulling an evening cloak over his pajamas. He was brimming with excitement. "Is it a long journey? What must I take?"

"If there is anything you need, get it quickly. You must hurry, Holtzclaw."

"Why?"

"The lake is rising! It has almost covered over the tunnel entrance. By morning, it will be filled with wild wonder fish."

This was very clever, thought Holtzclaw. She would take him to treasure, but only at the last possible moment. He could only mine it for a moment, and the transformation of poor miner to rich idler would be limited.

"Is that safe, Ms. Thompson?" he said. "What if we are trapped inside the tunnel? Drowned?" Safety was the least of Holtzclaw's concerns; he would have gone spelunking in the mouth of a bear. He was hoping that she would take him to a mine with a longer lifespan.

"Beggars can't be choosers," said Abigail. "We are going under the mountain."

Abigail had driven in a little wagon, pulled by a mule, but as she'd said, she had no digging supplies. Holtzclaw scrounged for a strongbox and found one amongst the rubble of Shadburn's offices. He wanted a second one, which Abigail could carry, but the rubble was not accommodating. Neither could he find a proper rock hammer, so instead he collected various twisted pieces of metal which would do in a pinch. Abigail rocked from foot to foot; the search would have gone faster, but she did not help him. She watched the stars that continued to fall in green streaks. At last, Holtzclaw resigned himself from preparations and climbed aboard the wagon. Abigail's mule set off with vigor.

Their path was mostly unknown to him. He had been all over the valley, but the barren slopes, the burned houses, the wrecked fenceposts, and battered work paths made the landscape new and strange. The weird light of falling stars made disconcerting shadows.

Holtzclaw tried a few meaningless pleasantries, to help the distance, but Abigail was not interested. She was fixed on their path. Holtzclaw tried to memorize their way, but he was soon disoriented. Anyway, if she was right about the rising water, he would not need to commit the way to memory. It would only even be seen by fish and mermaids.

After half an hour, Abigail stopped the cart. They were in the shadow of an immense face of rock. She coaxed the mule and wagon into a stand of broken limbs as Holtzclaw took out his mining supplies. Water lapped a few feet away. The mule, if it were thirsty, could have reached the lake by straining with its tongue.

"Where do we go from here?" asked Holtzclaw. He could not see an obvious entrance to a mine. He scanned the rock face that rose above him, but there were no wood-framed adits, iron-gated tunnels, or boarded-up passages.

Streaks of green light illuminated the cliff face rising above them. Granite had fissured and fractured. Squared-off pieces of stone jutted from the cliff or rested on the valley floor where they had fallen. A promontory emerged from halfway up the cliff and extended twenty feet into space; below, smaller cubes of stone were arrayed like a listening audience. Holtzclaw could not tell if this landscape was natural or artificial, and if it was artificial, if it was intentional or accidental. The right angles and smooth vertical faces could have been the result of rock cleavage by natural forces—granite breaks on straight internal faults—or the result of mining and blasting, or even the remains of some ancient architecture.

A spark of electric fluid floated into the valley; it touched the ground and flashed brilliantly. In the sudden light, Holtzclaw saw ten thousand black birds nesting along the ridges of the cliff. Ravens. They shuddered, stretched their wings, and settled again.

A thin waterfall tumbled through a recessed fissure in the cliff, tumbling from a buried spring. Below the falls was a triangular pool, inches away from merging with the rising lake. Its straight edges intrigued him. He hesitated, looking at the waterfall, the pool, wondering.

Then a green light flickered behind the mask of the water—a treasure light. There was a passage behind the waterfall, Holtzclaw realized; the will-o'-the-wisp crackled and pulsed its agreement.

"It's there!" he cried.

"Not so loud," said Abigail. "We all know it's there. Come on." Holtzclaw crossed the pool in three strides, the water coming past his knees, flooding into his boots. Abigail followed close behind, then overtook him. She was the first up the slick rocks on the far side and helped Holtzclaw up. The waterfall had worn the rocks into stair-like hollows. They ducked their heads and passed through the veil. The water beat against Holtzclaw's neck and back, soaking him utterly, pushing him to the ground, but he came through to the other side, to a tunnel.

The stumps of candles and the charred ends of torches were visible in the green light. They were damp, old, covered in verdigris.

"We didn't bring any light," said Holtzclaw. "We should have brought a lantern. Do we have time to go back?"

"No need, with this fellow," said Abigail. The will-o'-the-wisp bobbed obligingly. "And we can take some of these torches and candle-ends. I knew that they would be here." From an inner pocket, she withdrew several books of matches. "I'm never without fire."

When Abigail lit one of the fuel-damp torches, Holtzclaw was startled. Dark words were written into the ceiling. His eyes adjusted, and he could read familiar names. Octavia Smith. Emmett Moss. Abigail Thompson. Hiram Shadburn. Many others, known and unknown. The names had been burned onto the wall with candle smoke.

"It's not so secret, this cavern," he said.

"Oh, not this part," said Abigail. "Every child in Auraria has played here." And now Holtzclaw could add his name to the roll of discoverers. Using his pocket knife, he incised a thin H next to the other Auraria natives.

Abigail set off first, then came the will-o'-the-wisp, and Holtzclaw brought up the rear. The cavern was a warren of smooth tunnels. The entry passageway was narrow and short, like a mine passage. This opened after a hundred yards into a circular rotunda and a myriad of twisting passages, all alike. A dirt-filled pit in the center of the rotunda contained wooden boxes, trays, and tubes—equipment for refining saltpeter, yet more traces of use. Abigail continued without hesitation into a tunnel that looked just like all the others.

The trio cut left and right, turning back on themselves, following rising tunnels and descending passages. Holtzclaw did not know how far he had come below the mountain. The walls were a uniform, grey-white stone, worn smooth not by water, as he expected, but by the friction of many hands and feet.

Then they were in a progressively narrowing passage. A chasm on the floor began as a cut no higher than his ankles, but then deepened further and further, so that Holtzclaw was running in a channel up to his chest. He had to turn sideways and hold his strongbox over his head in order to pass. Abigail moved faster, urgent, playful.

"Please, Ms. Thompson, let me keep up," said Holtzclaw, gasping.

"You're not dropping dead already, are you? We're barely below the surface." Her voice was hollow, echoing back to him.

She waited for him at the end of the squeeze. The passage widened into a little domed room, filled with the debris of children's play: bits of string, fragments of bottles, fearsome warnings and club bylaws rendered in soot, tiny gold pans split in two, burst water skins.

Seeing the water skins, Holtzclaw regretted that he had not brought any himself. He was hungry, too. A sweet potato or a handful of mushrooms would be very welcome. But he pushed the hunger aside for another thought.

"Are we going to find any gold, Ms. Thompson? These tunnels look entirely too traveled. I can't imagine that the visitors would have left anything for us."

"I don't know, Holtzclaw." She continued for a hundred yards down a further tunnel, then turned around. They came back to the children's camp. "No, it's here."

"What, the treasure?" The yellow light of the torch caught glimmers in the rock.

Abigail knelt next to a flat stone.

"Under there?" said Holtzclaw. "It's too heavy for you to lift. Put down the torch. I'll give you a hand."

But Abigail got her fingers under the stone and flipped it up with a grunt. The will-o'-the-wisp shimmered in anticipation. Below the stone was a sloping tunnel, caked with dust and age. No gold, only the promise of something farther down.

Holtzclaw slid down the passage after Abigail and the green light.

On the lower level, the signs of child's play were gone, and the passages were less traveled. Still, there was evidence of use. Chunks of fallen stone had been moved aside to allow for easier travel. Holes in the wall held the burnt-out stumps of torches, which were made from river cane wrapped in ash cloth.

They snaked for another quarter of an hour, through dark passages that meandered without purpose or plan, natural or artificial. Tunnels met tunnels at regular angles and at crooked junctures. A thin current of water trickled through some of the passages, but it would not have been strong enough to have carved the entire cave. Perhaps the current had once worked here, but then had been turned to other uses.

All at once, the tunnel opened up into an immense chamber, whose ceiling was lost in inky shadows. Walls of tiny cabins, a subterranean village, divided the space. Some of his astonishment was lost to hunger, some to urgency, but most to the weariness of astonishment itself. He had witnessed so many spectacles in Auraria; this village was hardly the greatest of them.

"Have you ever been here before, Abigail?"

"No, never have. But I know it." She led their expedition into the streets that ran between the cabins. Each cabin was made of flat, stacked rocks and was roofed with wooden boards. Holtzclaw looked into several for some remnant of food—a sealed can or a piece of hard tack or jerky that would have survived well enough. His search was unrewarded. One corner of each was hollowed out into depression and lined with smaller rocks, and water bubbled up to fill the basin. The springs smelled strongly of metal, and Holtzclaw did not risk tasting it.

Staring and straining at these sights, Holtzclaw tripped over a pipe. He collected himself from the rock floor, and as he did so, he let his eyes follow the pipes in a dozen directions. It was a system of water and waste, resembling what he'd seen under Sinking Mountain. Pipes flowed to and from every cabin, collecting into branches and then a main trunk. Abigail walked on top of it, like a girl balancing on a rock wall. She held out her arms to steady herself; they wobbled exaggeratedly. Holtzclaw stayed on the solid ground and watched his footing.

The main pipe vanished into the rock at the base of a rise. Their lights illuminated the face of an enormous building, and behind that, a waterfall spattering and tumbling downwards from an unseen source. The will-o'-the-wisp signaled to them from the other side of the grand entrance.

"This is more spectacular," said Holtzclaw. "I could believe that somewhere in here, we'd find a stockpile of treasure. A rock maiden's finery, or the state jewels of an underground race of trolls."

"There's a ways to go yet, Holtzclaw, if there's anything to find."

Such a grand stone structure would make a spectacular tourist attraction, he thought. An underground hotel. Servants could be accommodated in the cabins so they would be close at hand. The chamber offered excellent acoustics for an orchestra. But would guests become weary of the stone sky? The novelty of vacationing underground would appeal for a few days, but would it last a season? And would they be comfortable swimming to their supper?

They followed the green light as it receded from the wide entrance hallway, back through a vaulted dining room, furnished with a wooden table long enough to seat two hundred, and then into the kitchens, where the soot-blacked signs of cooking fires marred the walls. Holtzclaw looked into larders and ice boxes, but there was nothing edible or bankable.

"I would think we would need to search the better rooms, if we are looking for gold," said Holtzclaw. "Perhaps there is a vault, a throne room?"

Abigail crooked her elbow to place a hand on her hips. In her other hand, she held the torch. The will-o'-the-wisp hovered beside her.

"This my expedition, Holtzclaw. We'll go where I say."

"But since we are here, we should explore..."

"Did you bring any matches? Any candles?"

"Only the strong boxes and bits of metal to dig."

"Then you're going under the mountain, unless you can see in the dark."

In a sub-basement, they passed a wheezing machine. The main trunk lines of the pipe system reappeared and terminated at a clockwork mechanism, and other pipelines, made of bright silver, made abrupt turns downward into solid stone.

A circular opening in the ceiling admitted the waterfall from above; it fell onto a worn basin, twenty feet across, into which a drain was cut. Other ends of pipes discharged here, too. A grate had been dislodged from the center of the bowl, and a rusted ladder ran inside the large waste pipe. Abigail began her descent without concern; Holtzclaw, encumbered with the strongbox, found the route much more treacherous. Halfway down, he realized that, if they were successful, the return would be even worse. He couldn't carry a fully-laden strongbox and climb.

"Abigail, how will we get the treasure back up this ladder? We should have brought a rope."

"I didn't think about it," said Abigail. "I always wake up before having to go back."

"That's the easy way out," said Holtzclaw.

The ladder ended in a downward-sloping passage that bore the water away, leaving behind damp mineral deposits that looked like mud flows. The accretions restored natural irregularities back into the artificial tunnel. The temperature had increased. Steam flowed through tunnels and tubes, again soaking any part of Holtzclaw that had dried a little since his passage through the falls. Abigail's hair hung in matted streaks across her forehead.

Hunger rumbled in Holtzclaw's stomach. He wished he'd found another of the giant peaches that the princess had given him on their first meeting. Holtzclaw tried to reassure himself—a man can live for weeks without food. But he hoped that, at the end of this journey, there was a restaurant.

In his sour mood, he bumped into Abigail, who'd stopped at a junction. The will-o'-the-wisp beckoned to a side tunnel, which sloped upwards. Abigail, though, stared down the main passage, which became a wide, straight staircase. A channel of water ran down the stairs—the mingled run-off from the hotel, the kitchens, the cabins, and innumerable springs above.

"Which way?" asked Holtzclaw.

"It has to be the stairs," she said. "Under the mountain."

"But the light has other ideas."

"I am going this way. You can trust whomever you like."

Holtzclaw followed Abigail and the path of water.

Behind them, the green light pulsed insistently. A coolness came up the stairs from below, chasing away the withering steam, and the green light was snuffed out. Abigail's torch was the only point of light; it showed only stairs leading down.

Holtzclaw counted one hundred steps, then two hundred, five hundred, a thousand. The river coursed through the channel, its sibilant rush revealing nothing about how far they had yet to go. And Abigail did not know either.

Another thousand steps passed beneath them. They stopped to rest; Abigail sat on the strongbox like a stool, and Holtzclaw sprawled on the steps. No matter how deeply they descended, they were not the first to pass here. How many thousands had made the tunnels, the village, the drainage tunnels, the stairs? How could he hope that there was any gold left for him? The first finders are the ones who are rewarded with fame and fortune. What prize goes to the very last?

But hunger, more than a fear of failure, gnawed at him; hunger that had grown out of size with his physical demands. Why hadn't he brought with him his Effervescent Brain Salts or his container of Pharaoh's Flour?

"You don't have anything to eat, Abigail, did you? A sweet potato?"

"I brought a picnic basket and a barbecued hog, of course, but Wispy and I ate them up when you weren't looking."

She rose from the strongbox, her silhouette framed in firelight. Following her, Holtzclaw put one weary foot below another. He wished that he had dried some of the mushrooms that Emmy had shown him, or that he'd filled a canteen with spiced groundhog stew, or that he'd brought a container of hash browns, dripping with fat.

It was only hundred more steps, and then the stairs ended, the tunnel turned, and they faced a wall of rich gold, colored like the yolk of an egg. Gold covered every shore of a vast underground lake.

"And there it is," said Abigail. Holtzclaw staggered forwards past here. He shook off his bewilderment, surveying the underground lake and its shoreline, trying to understand. The gold was not layered like a natural formation of ore, which would be solid and intermingled with quartz and mica. These deposits looked like the loose tailings of a mine—slag and run-off and waste, and yet, pure gold. Pipes and springs and tunnels flowed towards the lake from all directions. The lake was a low point of the valley's complicated system of natural and artificial drainage—likely, not the only such reservoir, either.

In a circle of yellow lantern light, Shadburn worked the deposit with a little hammer. He was chipping fragments of gold into an open strongbox at his feet. In the raw surface of the metal, a new light—the reflection of Abigail's torch—flickered, and Shadburn turned towards them.

"Holtzclaw? Abby? You shouldn't be here." He turned his back to the wall and held up his arms, as though he were trying to hide the wall of gold, but he could hide it no better than he could hide a mountain.

Holtzclaw came towards him. "I convinced Ms. Thompson that we needed her to ensure the success of the hotel, because you were bankrupt. But that wasn't true, was it? You never could run out of money, could you? Not when you knew about this place. Is that why we're here in Auraria? So you could go digging for gold? Finally find what's eluded you through your business ventures—a profit?"

Shadburn shook his head. "Just the opposite, Holtzclaw. I never wanted to come here again. I never wanted anyone to come here. All the flakes the wash down to this lake, all the nuggets that are carried back up—it is the delusion of this valley. Their inspiration to wasted efforts. But I decided that we needed one more investment. To be sure that we could carry on until the hotel could support itself. As you said, Holtzclaw, it could take many seasons! I didn't know you would follow me. That is so much for the worse."

"We didn't follow you. We followed Abigail's dreams," said Holtzclaw.

Shadburn peered around Holtzclaw to look at the tavern keeper. "I didn't think it was in your nature, Abby."

"Curiosity," she said. "Useless curiosity. I don't need a crumb of the gold. Seeing it is enough." She sounded disappointed.

"And how many times have you made this trip, Shadburn?" said Holtzclaw. He wasn't looking at his employer, but at the shores of gold. "How many times have you brought up a fortune without me?"

"Five. The first was an accident. I stumbled a little deeper than others. We all played in the caverns, and I wandered past all those ancient leavings, through their sewers. For a time, I believed I had done something great, but it was chance. No merit in it. An illusion of wealth."

Holtzclaw clawed some loose flakes from the deposits and shoved his gilded palm towards Shadburn's nose. "What's an illusion? This is just as good as any paper money. It's your business that's the illusion, your entire life since then. Why waste your time with unprofitable land deals? What use is there in turning some gold to less gold?"

Shadburn turned his head. "I wanted money, not gold. I meant to earn it, not just find it. Or at least, I meant for those poor miners up there to think that I had earned it. I can't let them know I just dug it up. That would make their mania so much worse. You won't tell them, will you, Holtzclaw?"

Holtzclaw did not respond. He clenched his fists; the gold dust between his palm and fingers was cold and slippery.

"These are not mineral veins," said Shadburn, his finger tracing the pipes and springs that emptied into the lake. "It's a sewer. The gold has washed up here. The moon maidens have sloughed it off, and it has flushed down through from their baths and built up in drifts in the rocks. You came past their hotel and their cottages and their pipes and pumps—or, what is left of them. You've seen the sheen on the waters after they bathe. Gold is their waste, Holtzclaw. It is the sickness that the water takes out of them, for us scavengers and night-soil men to contract in turn. Goodness knows how the moon maidens get it—it leeches into their skin from the sun or from meteors, or they catch it the same way we catch our own diseases, from bad airs or idleness or shame. Only, they've ruined their cure from overuse."

"Who's told you all this poppycock?"

"The princess," said Shadburn. "She's their Holtzclaw."

"And does she get a salary from the moon maidens," sniffed Holtzclaw, "or do they pay her in dividends and shares?"

"I would guess that they don't pay her in gold," said Shadburn.

Holtzclaw sniffed. The geology of the site was unusual, and the pipes and structures above were perplexing, but ultimately irrelevant. The story made the gold no less valuable. "I can't leave this behind, Shadburn. I'll have the railroad twins lay a narrow-gauge railroad through here. We'll have ten thousand men bring up gold by the bucketful."

"You can't," said Shadburn. "Not before the flood. The dam is closed. Soon enough, this gold will be hidden away, for as long as the lake lasts, and I mean for that to be a very long time indeed. If we don't hurry, we'll be drowned ourselves."

He was right. Holtzclaw cursed Shadburn's obsession, that should rob him of a fortune. Had Shadburn confessed his secret shame earlier, there might have been time to talk some sense into him. And Holtzclaw could have set up the wealthiest company ever seen on the continent. He would have made the great men of capitalism weep over their tiny fortunes. Holtzclaw could have sat atop a pyramid of gold, surveying the low and level world stretching out before him— his own possessions, ready for the plow.

The rising lake made all this impossible. But he could still fill his strongbox. Holtzclaw began to dig in earnest at the gold with the ill-suited tools he brought. It was slow work. Shadburn had already filled his own strongbox, but he did not offer his hammer to Holtzclaw. He watched his protege, neither helping or restraining him.

Abigail wandered the narrow lakeshore, fidgeting. Dark water quivered near her feet. Ripples washed up against her shoes. The underground lake was stirred into motion by the discharge of a thousand subterranean pipes, each flowing stronger because of the swelling river.

Every time he heard the water splashing against the rock, Holtzclaw anticipated the arrival of Princess Trahlyta. But she never appeared. With so much water pouring into her valley, perhaps she was overwhelmed.

Holtzclaw worked until his strongbox was full. Neither Abigail or Shadburn's discomfort could hurry him. He scraped a little more gold into trouser pockets and the cuffs of his coat. He put flakes under his hat brim. Only when no more gold could be crammed into his person did he let himself be led from the underground lake.

Abigail took the lead ascending the long flight of stairs. She took the lantern from Shadburn, who followed without a backwards glance, carrying his load atop his shoulder. Holtzclaw kept pace with them, but with effort; he'd packed his strongbox very full. Perhaps he had taken a little more than he needed—a few ounces less would have made little difference for his ultimate plans.

In the channel that split the stairs, water was running faster and higher. They reached the top more quickly than Holtzclaw had expected. The return trip, with each step leading closer to home, is always faster than the outward journey.

The walls of the steamy tunnels were covered in curtains of water, pouring in from cracks and fissures across the rock. Cascades tumbling from high above made the escape ladder slick and treacherous, especially with the added weight of the strongboxes. They raised the strongboxes one at a time, all three of them pulling, pushing, balancing, fighting with weight that threatened to wrench their arms from their sockets. Finally, winded and weary, they'd brought both strongboxes into the kitchen of the stone hotel.

Abigail needed no will-o'-the-wisp to take her back through the meandering streets of the cavern and its village of cabins. Overwhelmed pipes disgorged muddy soup. The brackish basins in each of the cabins ran over. Holtzclaw's arms ached and his knees complained. He wished gold were not so heavy. Why could they not have found a cache of paper money instead? A ten thousand dollar bill weighs no more than a feather. But he supposed that no process, natural or supernatural, would allow federal notes to accrete below the earth.

Rivulets ran through all the upper passages. Flotsam of childish pastimes washed into the elbows of the tunnels and broke up against the smooth rocks. At the mouth of the cave, Shadburn saw where Holtzclaw had carved his initial next to the other names written in candle smoke.

"The water will rub out the soot," said Shadburn. He sounded perturbed.

They broke out onto the surface, passing through the engorged waterfall, and stumbled across the entrance pool, which had merged with the rising river. The bright face of the moon was half-hidden behind the rim of the Raven Cliffs.

"And we couldn't go back for another load?" said Holtzclaw.

"There's no oil left in the lantern," said Abigail. She opened the fuel door and poured the contents into the river. A rainbow film shimmered across the water.

Holtzclaw removed his hat and wiped yellow dust from his brow. A few flakes of gold fell on his shoulders and half a hundred colors shone from inside the brim. He knew that he could not hold any more. Gold spilled out of him, from every pore.

When the lake covered Auraria's graveyard, the pine boxes and mahogany caskets rose up through the softened ground. The headstones had been moved to the new graveyard, but the coffins had been left behind. The dead clung to their coffins like survivors of a shipwreck. Most pitiful was little Emmy, the mushroomer, sitting on her half-rotted pine boards, toes curled away from the water. She and her kind bobbed about in the lake surface for two days until Holtzclaw was able to negotiate with a construction crew for their recovery. The coffins were tied to rowboats, pulled to shore, and re-buried in the new cemetery, overlooking Shadburn's lake. Holtzclaw paid all in gold.

Book III

When the first train crossed Lake Trahylta, the arriving tourists pressed their noses to the glass, straining for a glimpse of the pure and ancient body of water promised by legend and advertisement. Instead, they saw a prosaic brown lake, and the Queen of the Mountains, at the edge of this overgrown cow pond, was a disappointment.

Holtzclaw wondered how much money it would cost to get the tea-color out of the water, what kinds of filters and pipes he'd have to build. But before he could formulate a plan, the water solved his troubles, and for no additional charge. The tea-color came from the agitated remains of life in the valley. Soil had been swirled into solution with leaf litter. Ashes from burned homes mixed with rotten traces of bracken and branches, soggy bits of paper, and charred sand. The water broke these remnants down into the smallest possible particles, which settled and sank. Day by day, the lake waters became clearer.

Then one fine evening, a group of arriving tourists smiled as their train flew over the face of the water. The water had cleared enough to meet their expectations. Before them, the lake was pure and bright, casting a golden glow to the Queen of the Mountains. The mirror face of the lake reflected the hotel's two chief towers and all of its domes, gables, porches, and walks. Nature doubled Holtzclaw's work: one formal garden bloomed like two; the nine-hole golf course became eighteen; the manicured lawn stretched twice as far.

If the visitors took their eyes from these sights and looked downwards from the train-car windows, they could see beyond their own faces, down to the distorted lines of old roads on the lake bottom, and this was a cause for wonder.

Holtzclaw's usual perch in the Queen of the Mountains was a table in the grand lobby, near the reception desk, where the best and freshest news flowed. The first warning of any problematic local phenomena would arrive here first, and Holtzclaw could take the appropriate action should the local spirits decide to quarrel with the tourists. A certain finesse was necessary to prevent any incidents that would disrupt the air of tranquility and refinement that was meant to reign here, and Holtzclaw felt that the intermediary and conciliatory functions between the parties were his special role. He kept the books, too, as much out of pleasure as out of duty.

The lobby's ceiling rose five stories, past interior balconies that opened onto loges and mezzanines. Doors opened and closed, discharging visitors and attendants from sleeping chambers, smoking lounges, dining rooms, conservatories, and baths. A pleasant bustle was always to be found in the lobby, where overstuffed leather chairs enveloped men with newspapers and children with baubles. Here, Holtzclaw had succeeded best at capturing rhythm and order. Shined shoes, crisp creases, accurate hats, and clean gloves moved and settled and moved again. Quartets of studious-faced guests adhered to the strict rules of preference and faro. An employee in the livery of the Queen of the Mountains—gold epaulettes, white coat, a tapering, diagonal blue sash running from right hip to left shoulder—brought him a glass of claret.

"Thank you," said Holtzclaw.

"You're welcome, James," replied the employee. Holtzclaw whirled as he recognized the princess's voice, but she had already vanished as a burbling mass of arrivals flooded through the front doors. There was no sense in chasing her; she appeared as she willed, several times a day. Holtzclaw couldn't fathom her reasons, but she was not doing any harm to his guests or his staff. And unlike a singing tree or a moon maiden, her presence would not stir up any excitement. Thus, he was inclined to leave her to her game.

He turned back to his paper—a three-day-old rumor rag from Charleston. It was merely a prop. His attention was on a conversation occurring at the reception desk between Abigail and a displeased customer.

"I am sorry, Mr. Fabricatorian," said Abigail, "but there is nothing I can do."

"Hm! Why, there's plenty you can do! Look here, in the advertisements, it says, 'on the shores of a lake that looks as natural and old as the hills.' Well, that is malarky!"

"So you've said."

"There are fresh mud tracks everywhere I look. Road beds that lead plumb down into the lake. I'm out on a boat fishing; I look down, and I am floating above a cornfield. And the dam is a whopper of a thing, as plain as the nose on your face! There is too much new about the place. You should have let it sit longer in the elements if you are going to advertise 'natural and old as the hills.'"

"If you feel the advertisements are misleading, I can let you speak to the individuals who prepare our copy," said Abigail. Holtzclaw could feel her eyes burning on the back of his neck.

"What good would that do for me now, on my stay? That's right, none! What you can do is put in some older trees. Make them grow where there are just rocks now. If you are going to advertise a lake as old as the hills, your hills must look old, too! You know, vines and moss and caves and such."

"I will see if some old forest is available by catalog for overnight shipping," said Abigail.

"And the flume coming off that dam and through the gorge is a terrible eyesore. A three-man crew could pull it down in a day and give a much more sublime picture."

"There are engineering reasons why we can't do that," said Abigail. "The water has to be let out somehow, and in the absence of a river, we have a flume."

"Can't put in a forest! Can't fix a river! Pah. We are too clever, as a people, for such excuses."

Mr. Fabricatorian strode away from the reception desk, and after he was gone, Abigail sat down at Holtzclaw's table. She wore the livery of the hotel, but a silver cord looped under one arm and matching silver tassels from her epaulettes marked her as high-ranking.

"Did you write that part about 'natural and old as the hills?'" asked Abigail.

"I don't remember," said Holtzclaw. "I don't think I would have picked that turn of phrase."

"I know how we could please Mr. Fabricatorian and his friends. We could relocate the hotel to a cave. What's more natural than being surrounded by rock? Or we could place the guests' rooms in the tops of trees, connected by swinging rope bridges."

"Please don't mention it to Shadburn," said Holtzclaw. "He might think it the grandest idea he'd ever had and ask me bulldoze the hotel in favor of more rustic accommodations."

"At the least, we could consider sprinkling some more age and authenticity here and there, to improve the atmosphere."

"Fortunately, we can do that," said Holtzclaw. "It is cheap, too. The only required capital is time."

Wet thumps squelched against the glass ceiling of the lobby. Holtzclaw took an umbrella from a brass can and went outside with Abigail, onto the veranda. A rain of overripe peaches was falling. When they hit the ground or the roof of the veranda or the back of a fleeing tourist, they burst out of their skins.

"At least it isn't codfish or swamp slime," said Abigail.

"Or rocks," said Holtzclaw. "The peaches are so soft that they are unlikely to brain anyone."

A damp missile streaked at an angle beneath the veranda roof, exploding against the wooden floor into a shower of peach spray. Holtzclaw wiped flecks from his nose and brow.

A man with fragments of fruit on his hat approached Holtzclaw and jabbed a finger into his breast. "What sort of place are you operating here? If I am to be be-peached, I demand an explanation."

"Well, if you demand one, then one shall be provided," said Holtzclaw. "I can give you several, and you can choose the one that you think the best—whether most likely or most entertaining or most spectacular." Abigail laughed, and this encouraged Holtzclaw's imagination. "A shipment of old fruit was left in a railroad car, which was then blown up by an errant piece of dynamite. A cyclone stripped fruit from some forlorn native grove on the other side of the hill. A peach canning factory lost its roof in a sugar explosion. The fruit trees of the moon maidens are always above us. If they have left their orchards untended, then their old fruit would fall onto our heads in a stiff interplanetary wind."

"That's not good enough, sir," said the accuser. "I don't want to be the brunt of your little joke."

"The only explanation," said Abigail, "is that Auraria is the sort of place where peaches fall unbidden from the sky. Holtzclaw should have put that in his advertisements."

"Well, I never!" said the accuser. He stomped away across the lawn. Wet peaches splattered around him.

"Ms. Thompson, we can make something of these peaches, can't we?" said Holtzclaw. "Perhaps a kind of cobbler, or an ice cream?"

"They're perfect for homebrew," said Abigail.

Holtzclaw had copper vessels brought in from the general store in Dahlonega, express delivery. At supper, the guests were served a peach aperitif in thin, long-stemmed glasses, and there was much good-natured laughter. The confusion of the rain of peaches was converted into an amusing anecdote, capped by a party. A quartet of parlor banjo players plunked through a commemorative song. It was not great art, but it served his purpose. The guests had peaches rain upon them, and yet, they smiled.

Shadburn's quarters were on the top floor of the Queen of the Mountains, inside one of the turrets. The main room was a great circle. Panoramic windows looked out over the lawn, the lake, and the mountains. He could see all the way from the dam to Sinking Mountain.

"Come in, Holtzclaw," said Shadburn, sweeping with his hand. "I was just about to ... I don't know. I had nothing to do. I was about to sleep, I suppose."

"Well, I will give you the daily report, and you can muse over it, if you like.."

"Very fine, yes. Proceed." Shadburn lowered himself into one of the overstuffed leather club chairs. Though he'd had them custom-made, they were not the right size. He had to bend his knees in opposing directions, and that left his elbows with no comfortable place to rest. Holtzclaw chose to stay standing.

"Anything to drink, Holtzclaw? Claret?" Shadburn jumped up.

"Nothing at all. I've just come from supper."

Shadburn returned to his seat, but this time, he perched on the armrest in a half-recline. "I'm sorry, Holtzclaw. Please begin your report."

"First, I should give the good news. We have had a slight increase in inquiries for the fall season, and I believe that..."

"I heard about the peaches," said Shadburn. "That was good work. You kept the matter in check, turned it to little boon."

It was hard to be too upset when interrupted by a compliment. "I wish that I didn't have to keep matters in check. It takes a great deal of money, and I think we are missing an opportunity to attract tourists with our unique location. The tourists might enjoy a little peach rain. They might even enjoy a performance from the singing tree. The publicity would be priceless."

"Oh, that wouldn't do, Holtzclaw. I am trying to have a nice, tranquil place. A steady place. Enough to pay the bills, keep on running, make sure the dam stays looked after. Spirits have no role in that. Do you think that little princess is doing anything to threaten the dam?"

"She's busy delivering claret and telling stories. Nothing destructive. Not even a rainstorm."

"Well, that's good. But keep an eye on her. A creature like that doesn't share our interests."

"Shall I go on with the report?" said Holtzclaw.

"By all means. But jump to the best part. The most salient fact."

Holtzclaw sighed as he skipped over a page of hard-figured numbers. "That would be, I suppose, the matter of dam maintenance."

"Yes, that's essential. What's happening?"

"There's more water in the Terrible Cascade than there should be. All of it should be going through the flume."

"Do you mean, a leak?" said Shadburn. He leapt from his pose and hurried to the windows, as if he could spy the flaw from a mile away.

"It's not a leak, *per se*. More likely, there is some water following from within the dam. Springs underneath the earthworks. We could hardly have avoided building over the top of some natural fountain, here in Auraria."

"So, you think it's chance that these springs are flowing now?" said Shadburn. "You don't think that's the work of the princess?" Holtzclaw couldn't say.

"Do whatever you must to keep the dam secure," said Shadburn. "Bolster it with rocks or iron plates."

"That will cut into our reserve capital. We should have brought up another strongbox from underground."

"No matter how many strongboxes we brought up, it would have been one too few. That's the trouble. We must solve this with the capital we have." Shadburn worked his thumb into his chin. "But you have been a bit wasteful with your resources, Holtzclaw. You poured them back out in the water. You put it into that little boat out there." Shadburn waved towards the window. The metal superstructure was tied up at the shore. One and a half funnels rose from the deck, and green lights winked from the prow and stern. "What do you call it?"

"The Maiden of the Lake," said Holtzclaw.

"Queen of the Mountains, Maiden of the Lake. Mother and daughter. Not so original, Holtzclaw."

Holtzclaw crinkled the papers between his fingers. He wanted to tear them up, throw the fragments into the air.

Shadburn turned from the window. He smiled at Holtzclaw, perhaps seeing the distress in his employee's face. Shadburn's features softened. "I'm sorry, I'm in a foul mood. I spoke harshly." He walked away from the window and held out his hand to pat Holtzclaw upon the shoulder or the head. "I know how dear that creation is to you. It's a fragile little thing, like an egg. When do you open for business?"

Holtzclaw ducked the outstretched hand. "We should have launched months ago, but there is so much work yet to be done."

"I would be happy to assist you. I want to see it successful, so it can contribute to the upkeep of the lake. Perhaps you need my help to see that through. Unfinished, that boat is a bit of an eyesore on my lake."

"Unfinished or finished, the boat is mine," said Holtzclaw.

CHAPTER XXIII

A bush of wild love-apples grew on the promontory where Holtzclaw and Ms. Rathbun had built their dock. The wild love-apple, cousin to the humble domestic tomato, is poisonous, a descendant of nightshade. This single bush was unique in the Lost Creek Valley. Two perfect red globes hung near the top of the love-apple plant. Holtzclaw picked them both and placed them in his traveling satchel.

The Maiden of the Lake was tied up by sturdy ropes, as thick around as Holtzclaw's arm. It was more than necessary, he knew, but boats are expensive and ropes are cheap.

From end to end, the boat was one hundred and forty feet long, as long as the greatest of the Mississippi steamboats, and thirty feet wide. Given this area, the boat was quite light and pulled a draft of only two feet. It could navigate close to shore, and whenever the engines could be installed, it could carry its guests up even the shallowest arms of Lake Trahlyta without fear.

The hull was painted a cheerful white, set off with a red ribbon that ran from bow to stern, like a pin-stripe. Large green lights burned fore and aft; between them were smaller points of starlight for decoration. The drive-wheel at the rear was red and black and gold, with fine ironwork on the frame. Holtzclaw had opted for the less expensive single-wheel design. The double side-wheels would have been more spectacular, but the Maiden of the Lake, only a pleasure cruiser, did not need the power or speed.

The Maiden of the Lake boasted three stories, just as many as the Queen of the Mountains. The bottom deck was for the crew. There would be pleasant, if small, rooms for the cook, the captain, the helmsman, as well as a common area for the stevedores and servants to sling their hammocks at night and take their meals and leisure during the day. Executive staff—Holtzclaw, Ms. Rathbun—had rooms on the main two decks, along with the other guest cabins. Perched atop the highest story was a wheelhouse, capped with a weathervane.

From a distance, the only flaw in the Maiden of the Lake's appearance was the second funnel. One funnel was finished, capped with a decorative finial that was meant to evoke a flower, but its twin was stunted, a half-formed stem that grew from an empty engine room.

He climbed up the gangplank. Everywhere, there were costly mistakes. Since he'd last been aboard, the deck planking had been installed, but the surface had not yet been stained. Rains—of water and of peaches—had begun to eat at the boards. They were popping and swelling at the joints and would have to be replaced if the best people were to be welcomed aboard.

Entering in the main gallery, Holtzclaw saw the balconies that faced into the open interior space rising through the two upper stories of the vessel. The shells of twenty guest cabins, a dining room, and a reading parlor on the prow wrapped the three sides of a common area, which was meant for dancing, cards, and social activities. A wall of glass at the stern looked over the drive-wheel. The ceiling of the common area, too, was made from glass—or it would be, after the final installation. For now, a taut canvas served as the roof.

The upper balconies lacked their railings; they ended at unguarded drops to the floor below. Throughout the lower floor, carpet had been laid, but it was a cheap weave. Two serving counters faced each other, but the wood was a facade, an inferior amalgam of sawdust and glue.

Holtzclaw ascended the grand staircase, which connected the two stories of the common area. The stairs were finely made, an organic curve, but unfinished. The wood was raw, and the lighted golden figures he'd ordered for the bannister had not been installed. At the head of the stairs were double doors to the grand suite. These were the only worthy pieces that Holtzclaw had yet seen—slabs of shiny curly maple, inset with frosted windows of yellow glass. The doors stood ajar. Holtzclaw passed through the bare vestibule, through the bare receiving room, and knocked at the door to the bedchamber, framed in candle glow.

Ms. Rathbun wore a red silk dressing gown that formed an uninterrupted field of carmine from her throat to her wrists to the floor.

Her hair was pulled back, twirled around a chopstick. Her eyes swept him up and down. Then, understanding passed across her face, but she did not smile.

"Oh, hello there," said Ms. Rathbun. "Having a look around?"

"I came to see you," said Holtzclaw.

"Of course. How pleasant."

Holtzclaw cast an intentional look over his shoulder, back through the unfinished vestibule and towards the lobby. "There's still a lot of work to do here. It doesn't look any further along than a week ago."

"Did you come to see me, then, or have a look around?"

Holtzclaw flushed. Ms. Rathbun stepped aside, admitting him to her chamber. A shadow passed across her pale face—the door was shut.

The bedroom was furnished with familiar objects retrieved from the Grayson House. Her four-poster bed, piled high with blankets. Her dressing table and mirror. A wardrobe that barely fit below the ten-foot ceiling. Two wide bowls stood on a table. Holtzclaw placed one of the love-apples in each of the bowls. "They make a nice decoration there," said Holtzclaw.

"You'd put tomatoes in a claret bowl?" said Ms. Rathbun.

"They are love-apples, from beside the dock. Please don't cook them up thinking they're tomatoes! And you can't mean to use such bowls for claret. You don't have anything more suitable?"

Ms. Rathbun upended two tin cups from her dressing table. Brushes and pens spilled out. She placed the cups on the table, then took the love-apples from the bowls and put them on top of the tin cups.

"I think that looks better," she said. "Claret?"

Holtzclaw nodded. Ms. Rathbun filled each bowl with a measure of claret from an open bottle, then sat opposite him and studied the love-apples on their new podia.

"What are you trying to say with such a gift, Holtzclaw? They're not practical, nor are they costly. You didn't go through much trouble to get them—you practically had to climb over them to come see me."

Holtzclaw lapped at his ridiculous bowl of claret. Ms. Rathbun stared into hers, as though it were moonshine.

"This room looks comfortable," said Holtzclaw.

"By that, you mean that is doesn't look grand?" said Ms. Rathbun.

"It is the grand suite. Hadn't we ordered furniture? And artwork? There was a large format piece. Pastoral, a landscape."

"We ordered it, but it hasn't yet been received."

"It was paid for, though?" said Holtzclaw. "You presented the invoices, and I gave the money."

Ms. Rathbun wobbled her head from side to side, not committing. "I tore the bills in half. The eagle side went with the order; the pyramid sides will be delivered on receipt. Until then, they're in the strongbox."

"Here?" said Holtzclaw. "On the boat? There are safer places. The vault at the Queen of the Mountains, for instance."

"Shadburn's vault must be the least secure place that a dollar bill or piece of gold could ever land. It will be spent in two moments."

"For a good cause. To keep the dam whole. To make the hotel profitable, faster. If we don't spend, then we are all doomed."

"Do you think that, even if you charged twenty dollars a night, and another twenty for board—or a hundred and fifty—you would ever reap more that what's been sown into this valley?"

"I must believe it," said Holtzclaw. "Otherwise, it would only be prudent to stop now. Close the hotel. Break open the dam and let the waters out in an orderly way, where they will not cause any harm down river, rather than let the dam burst from wear and neglect. Save what money is left for recovery. Poor Abigail could have some to rebuild the Old Rock Falls. But Shadburn would never let that happen, though. He is dedicated to the lake, above all else. He would let every penny go first."

"Is that sound business?" said Ms. Rathbun.

Holtzclaw shook his head in the negative. "No, not at all. The most profitable business would be gold mining, but of course that is impossible now."

"Maybe that's what we should be doing," said Ms. Rathbun. "Hang all this ship work. I've read that the French have created a diving bell with powerful bellows. In this Lost Creek, in the mining days, there were dredge boats that pumped a vacuum and let men work on the river floor. Some combination of those could be used, if you could take me back to this shore of gold."

"Now you want to go gold mining?"

"I am in favor of whatever is easiest."

"Then what would we do with our half of a floating hotel?" said Holtzclaw.

"Let it sink," said Ms. Rathbun, "or let it drift into the dam and have the slow current grind it to splinters. Not put more gold into it. Why take mountains of money and wear it down into pebbles? And speaking of wearing down our mountains of money, no doubt you've noticed the flooring on the deck? Workers are coming in three days to repair it, and then that phase will be finished. They'll need their pay when they arrive."

Holtzclaw brought out a sheaf of federal notes from his satchel. He'd had the underground gold changed into paper money through visiting bankers and merchants. "This is for the insurance policies, too."

"They are paid already. I paid them first." Ms. Rathbun reached for some golden-colored speck on the floor, near her foot. Her red silk dressing gown conformed to the series of sharp lines and piercing angles of her body—leg, calf, back, shoulder, arm, neck.

"Do you know," said Holtzclaw, "I was a silk entrepreneur, at one time." He gestured towards Lizzie's sleeve, but did not quite touch it.

"Really," said Ms. Rathbun, regarding the speck between her fingers.

"Before I met Shadburn. I had a piece of land with mulberry trees. The business was set to flourish, positively flourish."

"But it didn't. "

"There were adverse, unpredictable conditions. One cannot plan for everything. Weather. Rains of peaches. Enough catastrophes can build up to ruin the best preparations, and in my youth and ignorance, I hadn't made the best preparations. Then Shadburn presented me with a better opportunity."

"I meant to ask, what does Shadburn think of the Maiden of the Lake? Is he apoplectic over it?"

"He asked if there is any good fishing from the deck. He wondered if fish would be drawn to backing and filling of the paddlewheel."

"Are they?"

"I haven't dropped a line to find out," said Holtzclaw.

"You should," said Ms. Rathbun. "He might be a better fisherman than a businessman. Perhaps that's all he wants. A place to fish."

He could have had that without any trouble, thought Holtzclaw. In Auraria, one could fish the mists of the valley and reel in catfish and stranger creatures. No lake was needed.

As he returned from the Maiden of the Lake, following the winding shore, he mused over his next move. The dam needed constant attention, and that required money. And their only source for it was the hotel itself. He needed to accelerate the profitability of the Queen of the Mountains, for all of their sakes. And that would take strategy, spectacle, and money.

The first idea that struck him was simplicity itself. The Queen of the Mountains needed a water-born mascot. Other mountain hotels—the Seelbach, the Finley, the Aaron, which advertised in the same publications—did not have the same range of luxuries as the Queen of the Mountains. They had not been built on top of a mountain of gold. But they did have, in their neighboring bodies of water, curious attractions that excited the imagination of their guests: lake monsters. The Seelbach hosted Slippery, a charming creature with a rotund body and a thin head perched at the end of a long neck. The Finley had Finny, who in every way was Slippery's twin, save that its colors echoed its master's livery. The Aaron Hotel had a creature of a different sort—it was long, sleek, and silvery, and when it made leaps from the water, it unfurled a set of gossamer wings. This creature went by the name Airy or Aary, depending on the wit of the copy writer.

Guests peered over the sides of the steam launches into Lake Trahlyta, looking for a monster, but they only saw vague shadows cast by catfish. Holtzclaw thought they should order their own totemic creature. It would attraction attention.

"It's only pieces of art they have," said Shadburn, when Holtzclaw explained his idea. "No real monsters, of course. Commission an illustrator instead."

"Our fantastic valley should go one better. We have the money for a real beast, a real wonder. Nothing less would be suitable. Get some freshwater whale, a giant squid, something respectable and tangible."

"A water monster does not reinforce the dam," said Shadburn.

"Nothing will reinforce the dam forever," said Holtzclaw. "Only a successful hotel could do that. It will take in the tourists' money and put it into the earth."

Holtzclaw wrote away for a mail-order catalog of aquatic creatures and ordered a suitable one. But he could not wait on his hands for it to be delivered.

CHAPTER XXIV

The Queen of the Mountains encouraged among its guests a habit to take constitutionals and perambulations after meals. Many visitors confined themselves to the treadmill, which was the term for the loop of verandas that girdled the hotel. But for guests that wanted a more scenic walk, the Queen of the Mountains provided many groomed trails.

The most popular path wandered through a shady bower, then followed a trickling creek for a half mile, inclining slightly. The creek tumbled over a cliff, and the path looped behind the falls, before continuing up a short run of stairs. Some people stopped here, judging the waterfall pretty enough; they might have continued had there been an elevator. Those who climbed the stairs followed the path for a quarter-mile until it ended at a spring flanked by two structures. The first was a pavilion under which guests could obtain mineral water, mixed drinks, and salted snacks. The second was a cairn of white stones.

Holtzclaw liked to take the walk twice per day, once upon rising and once after dinner, to aid with digestion, but after ordering the lake creature, he had missed two constitutionals in a row because of a sudden crisis. A muddy rain of stones had fallen down the back of the dam, and Holtzclaw had had to supervise a crew to shore up the earthworks. Because they were working forty feet above the ground, harnessed and tethered, they demanded hazard pay. Holtzclaw wished he could plumb the innards of the dam, but exploratory diggings would only exacerbate the decline.

Without his constitutionals, his creativity and digestion were suffering. And the good functioning of both was essential, if he was to lead the hotel to a rapid success. On this occasion, he made a point of a leisurely late afternoon stroll, to see if some great advertising campaign would spring from the land.

Princess Trahlyta, in hotel livery, sat at the spring, running a toe through the water. She was about to begin telling a story, and a crowd of children pressed near her. Holtzclaw did not know why she took the time to tell tales for the tourists. Perhaps she felt compelled by a sense of rural hospitality. After all, her name was enfolded with the advertising materials. Perhaps she was bored, with so many of her springs and rivers plugged up. Her own employers hadn't been seen in the valley.

Holtzclaw only half-listened to her retelling. She changed the story each time to suit the audience, but the essence of the tale remained the same. She told that this spring had once been the home of a beautiful maiden, the Queen of the Mountains, after whom the hotel took its name. She bathed herself daily in the waters of the spring, and they keep her eternally young, eternally fresh, eternally happy. She saw many ages of the world from within the waters of her spring. Mountains grew from pebbles to mighty peaks to pebbles again. Mighty creatures that lumbered across the land eroded into the tiny animals we know today. The Queen of the Mountains watched as the cold turned the water, drop-by-drop, into a sheet of ice, and then watched as the sun undid that work with ease.

Then a warrior and his party came over the mountains. They were surprised by their enemies, and the warrior was mortally wounded. His comrades left him beside a river to die, as was their custom. Blood rose from his wounds like a fine red thread, twisted into knots by the current. His blood sacrifice opened the bowery to the queen's spring, which had been hidden from the eyes of birds and fish and men and mountains. The spring waters knitted his flesh back together. The flowing stream laved away bruises and straightened broken bones. It smoothed the wear and worry from his face and plucked the gray hairs from his head.

The warrior lifted his head and saw the beautiful, young maiden. She swam through the shimmering waves, her long slender arms and long slender legs parting the water. He believed that she had healed him out of love. But the Queen of the Mountains, did not love any man or woman. They were like pebbles to her, like mountains, like fish or birds. The Queen of the Mountains loved water, which was eternal, and loved rivers, which flowed forever. She had not healed the warrior. This was the power of the spring and its minerals.

But the warrior wanted to take the maiden back to his people to be his bride. He bound her hands and feet, because she frothed and crashed like an angry rain. He took her up on his back and carried her away from the spring.

They traveled for an hour, and the maiden wept. They traveled for a day, and she stopped. When the warrior set her down, he saw that her face was lined with wrinkles. He thought it was from weeping. They traveled for another day. The maiden grew thin and frail. Her hair was streaked with gray; white moss grew on her hands and feet. On the third day, her breathing was raspy and shallow, a hollow whisper of age and death, and the warrior found that he was carrying an old woman. The Queen of the Mountains, had aged with every mile she had traveled away from her spring and her valley.

The warrior turned back. He could not take an aged, dying woman home to be his bride. He came back into the valley while the Queen of the Mountains still breathed, but he could not find the spring. The bowers had closed again. He pleaded with the maiden to open the way so that she could be restored, but she did not hear him or she refused to obey.

The warrior remembered how the bowers had opened for him before, when he was mortally wounded, and he drew his dagger to strike a blow to himself, knowing it would not be fatal, but his hand hesitated at the apex of its rise, and he saw that the maiden was already dead.

So he laid her to rest beside another spring that he found. It was not her eternal, healing spring, but it would remind her of it well enough that she would sleep soundly in the earth. He buried her beside the spring and set up a marker of white stone.

"Do you mean, that one?" said a child, pointing to the cairn beside the walled spring. The princess—the storyteller—nodded.

The monument to the Queen of the Mountains was easy to find and frequently visited. It was near a hunting path that became a route for fur traders, then a road for emigrants passing through the mountains, then a passage for carriages and stagecoaches carrying miners and chests of gold. Travelers stopped to water their horses and themselves at the spring, and they saw the cairn of white stones. They found other white stones and placed them on the cairn. Whether this was a gesture of respect or a way to participate in a popular fashion was known only to the traveler.

"Do we make a wish when we add a white stone?" said a man.

"If you like," said the princess. "But it won't come true, unless you wish for the right thing, for certainties. Rain, or a flood."

"I'm going to wish for a mountain of gold!" said a boy with a raccoon-skin cap.

"That's a waste of a wish," said the princess, and the boy began to cry.

"Did you have to put this place at such a height from the hotel?" asked a young, fat man, wiping away a thick layer of sweat with a handkerchief he withdrew from his pocket. "You could at least get it off these stairs. How I hate stairs! Wasn't the grave supposed to be convenient to the road?"

Holtzclaw knew that they could have put the monument anywhere they liked. It was not really a grave. The white stones were chipped fragments of marble, left over from the bathroom in Shadburn's suite. Shadburn had conceived of the idea of a gravesite as a walking destination and *memento mori*. Holtzclaw had wanted to place it above the waterfall, thinking that the combination of sights—the grave, the waterfall, the spring—would make a more attractive whole. Princess Trahlyta had concocted the backstory on her own, and in her telling and retelling made the canonical version. But she had engrained certain flaws that undermined the whole. The bit about the road was one of them; also, why would the bower open for a mortally wounded warrior, a stranger, but not open for its similarly dying mistress?

But the princess never listened to Holtzclaw's recommended emendations. She persisted in her errors; they had already been worked deeply into the legend of the cairn.

Holtzclaw's mind turned around the tale, searching it for inspiration. Could he write up the story in a book? Send it to the bookshops in the city, drum up interest in the hotel with this light and romantic tale? Never any money in books, he decided. And the literary treatment would only make the flaws in the princess's tale more easy to spot.

Ah, but he could invent a holiday! What better way to commemorate the wounded warrior, the dying princess, and the pile of discarded bathroom marble that marked their time together? He could put on a banquet. The Day of the Evening Star—that was as nice a title as any. Romantic enough, and yet impenetrable and vague. He would have the banquet in two weeks; a deadline inspires the best work. That was precious little time for advertisements and announcements. He'd have clubs in Milledgeville and Charleston distribute fliers, rather than waiting for notices in monthly magazines. The urgency and suddenness of the affair might even prove attractive to the clientele that considers themselves wealthy enough to be carefree. They could come for the Day of the Evening Star, leave their money, and be off by Pullman car to the next fabulous celebration.

Holtzclaw came back from his constitutional vivified and hungry. It was not yet time for the formal supper seating, so he decided to take his meal at the hotel's other dining room, a replica of the Old Rock Falls. A high corridor directed guests towards the main dining room, but those that cast a glance to the right, down a short passage, saw an impressive two-story facade that had been constructed for the New Rock Falls, complete with a wide indoor veranda.

Guests who continued inside found themselves in a truncated version of the Old Rock Falls. The New Rock Falls had no second story, despite the appearance of the facade, but guests were not bothered. The worn pine floor had been salvaged from the Old Rock Falls and relaid into this space. Certain load-bearing pillars, though, had interfered with the layout, and clever carpentry was needed to cover up replacement boards.

Holtzclaw entered the dim space. The wall lamps, formerly fueled by oil, had been wired for electricity. For those that remembered the old dining area, the new light in the room was difficult to accept. It was too bright, too clean, too steady. Guests who had seen only the electrified New Rock Falls complained that the lighting was too yellow, too dirty, too flickering. They wondered if country folk could be expected to dine in such meager conditions.

The walls were covered with the daguerreotypes and lithographs salvaged from the Old Rock Falls. Two were missing; the layout of the photographs was unbalanced without them.

Holtzclaw sat at a table beneath one of the gaps, covering the emptiness with his head. Not much could be done about the other gap. The piano in the corner plinked out a ragtime rendition of an old fiddle tune.

A guest in a purple cravat leaned over to him. "It's a nice player piano, eh? I always think that's such a marvel. Springs and gears that manage to make something that sounds so human."

"It's not a player piano," said Holtzclaw, "It's Mr. Bad Thing. He's a ghost, I think, or some other spirit."

The man in the cravat sniffed, incredulous, his tone shifting. "Well, that's a different matter. His timing is irregular—his sixteenth notes sometimes have a dot to them, and I have heard several duff notes in his scalar runs. This Mr. Bad Thing should take lessons. His style wouldn't be tolerated in the sorriest Charleston rum houses."

"Isn't it a little remarkable that Mr. Bad Thing plays the piano from beyond the grave?"

"Not in the least, even if it is true. He's no better than an amateur. Why should he get recognition above his talent merely because he is an evolute ghost?"

Hulen, the headless plat-eye, occupied his stool. Abigail had promised that he could return to his familiar haunt, on the condition that his murderous head-snatching cease. Holtzclaw, suspicious at first, had been convinced when he'd witnessed Hulen's joy at being reunited with his old stool and mug. A test parade of wax heads were paraded in front of him; Hulen only laughed and called for another round, for which he'd paid in silver coins from a never-ending supply in his pocket. Hulen proved to be quite popular among the youngest of the visitors. Even now, three youngsters stumbled around the dining room, their heads pulled down below their sweaters or their collars re-buttoned above their eyebrows, and chased their siblings.

"Don't get ahead of yourself! Aha!" said Hulen from his stool. "You don't want to get brained! Aha! Keep an eye out! Aha!"

The guardian of these youngsters drained a glass of wine and gathered her charges, a little put out by Hulen. No one who made such obvious and silly puns could be trusted around children, and the transparent trick of his wardrobe reflected poorly on the establishment, which should have thought more highly of its patrons.

Holtzclaw's sweet potato stew was brought out by Abigail herself. "Ms. Thompson, why are you running bowls and stirring stews? Don't the kitchen staff need your supervision ahead of the supper service? And aren't there new arrivals coming in on the 5:30 train?"

"I have to do this cooking myself. Anyone else would make a mess of it. They'd burn the sweet potatoes, or give Hulen buttermilk instead of white lightning! I've spent a lifetime getting these rituals right."

Holtzclaw smiled. "Ah, the sweet potatoes! How are they received?"

"The guests throw up their hands and plead for mercy! And it's only the puree and the coffee that have sweet potatoes in them. I could give them what I used to serve at the Old Rock Falls at the height of the season. Sweet potato chips cooked in sweet potato oil, a salad of sweet potato shoots, a baked sweet potato, and a bed stuffed with sweet potato vines. Do they want an authentic experience or not?"

"They want their idea of an authentic experience," said Holtzclaw.

"I suppose that's why they complain that there are too few windows opening to the outside. Why would an authentic mountain boarding house, like the New Rock Falls, not have larger windows, to enjoy the views over the water and breezes coming ashore? A man in a top hat asked me why the New Rock Falls didn't have swinging half-doors and more ranch hands, gunfighters, and the like? I told him they had killed each other off. It was my little joke to serve toast with sheep-fruit marmalade in the formal dining room. The best people all praised it. They thought it was quince, or lingenberries, or some other imported wonder. When I told them it was a local fruit, some women said that they were gardeners and wanted to see the shrub. So I led them out to a grove, up the hill. All that weeping and screaming on the vine when we plucked some fresh sheep-fruits. They were horrified!"

"There is no food that one can eat without guilt," said Holtzclaw. "Except, perhaps, for mushrooms."

♣

After supper, Holtzclaw walked the veranda. He was waiting on new arrivals that were supposed to come by the evening train, but a rock slide had blocked the tracks. The carriages he'd sent for them had not yet returned. To distract himself from baseless speculation, he opened a newspaper and tried to read it beneath the glow of the electric lights. He had barely made it past the ads for the rival hotels when someone cleared her throat and placed the tip of her parasol on the top of Holtzclaw's newspaper, pulling it down.

Across the fold, Holtzclaw saw three older women. The central figure was dressed in royal purple; her lieutenants, in lavender. All three wore matching, broad-rimmed yellow hats with a green ribbon. On the ribbon a badge with the letters BWCS.

"Walk with us, Mr. Holtzclaw," said the leader.

Holtzclaw stood as commanded. He and the leader went out in front, with the lieutenants a half-step behind. They descended a staircase and then turned four abreast onto the long, continuous series of verandas, porches, and covered walkways that formed the treadmill of the hotel. Guests coming in the opposite direction— already at fault for walking counterclockwise on an odd-numbered date—were chased into side passages, down stairs, or into alcoves.

"Mr. Holtzclaw, you are no doubt aware of our operations," said the leader.

"I must plead ignorance, ma'am," said Holtzclaw, "and please take that only as a sign of my lack of knowledge, and not as a slight against your organization."

"See, such a polite man," said the right-hand lieutenant.

"That is why we must ask him," said the left-hand lieutenant.

"Yes, we will ask him, after introductions," said the leader. "We are the ruling council and chief players in the Billing, Wooing, and

Cooing Society." The three women held out their hands and vibrated them up-and-down in a flutter, like wings on a tiny bird.

"I am Almeda, the Reader of Mysteries," said the leader. "This is Vera, the Tender of the Entwined Rose and Briar. This is Luella, the Poetess of the Stirring Heart. We offer healing to the lovesick and wholeness to the heartbroken. We are the active agents in this resort of the passions. Consider us healers. Kindred spirits."

They all briefly halted to make reciprocal bows and curtseys, then they picked up their stride again. A small child, ringed in ribbons, sheltered himself behind a column.

"If you'll forgive the impertinence," said Holtzclaw. "We did not intend for our hotel to be a place of passions. It's a health spa."

"Of course, that is what you will say," said Almeda, the Reader of Mysteries. "Who would advertise that his hotel is a place where marriages may be made, contracts brokered, partnerships forged? It would sound too mercenary, too boiled in profits. But it is the real reason any of these good people are here. They need us; your employer needs us. Now tell me, Mr. Holtzclaw, are you a confirmed bachelor?"

"That question, Ms. Almeda..."

"In deferences to our rank, the appropriate form of address is 'Your Graciousness,'" said Almeda.

"As I was saying, even overlooking the indelicacy of that question, I would not be able to answer it. I'm a bachelor, yes, but by confirmed, you mean..."

"I mean," said Almeda, "are you confirmed to live out your life as a bachelor because of the peculiar arrangement of your heart and your proclivities, or do you see your bachelorhood, as we do, as a broken state, in need of remedy by marriage?"

"Then I am not a confirmed bachelor," said Holtzclaw. "But I hardly see why that would matter. Did you have some business to discuss? Are there problems with your rooms? What is it that I can do for you?"

"It is not what you may do for us, but what we may do for you," said Almeda. "We have two primary roles here at the Queen of the Mountains, as set forth in our founding documents. The first role is the instruction of dance etiquette, and in this we have made great strides. The lines of the quadrille are much more crisp than at the beginning of the season, and we find that far fewer ladies are offering their hands on the turn with their pinky fingers held aloft, in the Scottish fashion. The second role, and in this we take more pleasure, is in the arrangement of introductions between eligible parties. We have decided that you, Mr. Holtzclaw, will be taken under the wing of the Billing, Wooing, and Cooing Society. We will find you a suitable match."

Almeda, Vera, and Luella again flapped their hands, as though soaring on a breeze.

The eccentricities of these particular visitors were becoming more difficult for Holtzclaw to tolerate.

"Well, that is a very kind offer," said Holtzclaw, "but I must decline. I have work to do."

"Nowhere in the project is there opportunity for your disagreement," said Almeda. "Your cooperation is appreciated but not mandatory. Some of our most enjoyable challenges and noted successes have been over the objections of the players."

"Do you remember the Marquis and the pork princess?" said Luella.

"Of course we remember," said Vera. "How could we forget such a savory reception banquet?"

"I said it for him," said Luella, jabbing a thumb towards Holtzclaw. "Because he did not see how bitterly they fought their fate, until that fateful ham shank brought them together."

"Then it is agreed," said Almeda. "At least, by all parties that have a say in the matter. Now, we will be making a series of introductions for you. The first will be to a Ms. Abigail Thompson, whom, as you may be aware, holds a position of some authority at this hotel, and who, besides, has an estate of her own, obtained by the sale of her property to a land developer and his assistant."

"I have worked very closely with Ms. Thompson for months," said Holtzclaw. "I consider her an ally in our work here."

"Yes, but you have not been introduced," said Almeda.

"Perhaps that word does not mean what I think it means," said Holtzclaw.

"You need not be concerned with it," said Almeda. "All will be orchestrated. Now, the second introduction we have planned is to Ms. Elizabeth Rathbun. She is heir to a medical practice here, and her father is a local politician—the mayor, I believe. On a social rank, this match is more favorable. She has a respectable personal capital, as well, according to our sources. She is owner of a floating hotel called the Maiden of the Lake."

"I know Ms. Rathbun quite well, too," said Holtzclaw. "I'm her partner, in her boat project."

The foursome had come to a temporary halt at one of the mineral water stations. An employee ladled mineral water into silver cups for Holtzclaw and the women. They drained the contents while walking and returned their cups to next station on the treadmill.

"Yes, you may know her," said Almeda, "but again, you have not been introduced."

"I fail to see the value in your introductions, if you are only presenting me to people with whom I'm already familiar."

"Mr. Holtzclaw! How can you be familiar, without having been introduced?" said Almeda. Her lieutenants blushed so deeply that the color of their faces clashed with their clothing.

"Not in an improper sense, of course," said Holtzclaw. "Until not so long ago, this valley was a less refined place. One could not rely upon the Billing, Wooing and Cooing Society..."

The women performed their ritual. They took pride in the delicacy of the winglike motions. Only their fingertips quavered. No bird could ever hope to soar on such minute movements.

"...upon such societies to perform the social niceties needed for conducting commerce," continued Holtzclaw.

"Then we will look to your recent guests," said Almeda, Reader of Mysteries. "Eligible parties that have not yet been tainted by familiarity without an introduction. Ladies?"

Vera, the Tender of the Entwined Rose and Briar, placed a pair of reading spectacles on her nose and withdrew papers from her portfolio. Holtzclaw had never seen a portfolio shaped like a parasol before; it was an ingenious and socially acceptable solution. The paper that Vera consulted was labeled with a case file number and bore BWCS letterhead.

"Emmagreen S.," said Vera. "An Old World firebrand. She is, and I mean this in the most complimentary and delicate way, a capricious and demanding person, prone to fits of rage if her will is not obeyed. She arrived a fortnight ago and has changed suites five times."

"Oh yes," said Holtzclaw. "Her."

Vera noted this on her paper. "Emmagreen S. also has poisonous blood," she continued. "Not poisonous to her, naturally—I think it makes her immune to most of the infirmities that afflict the human race. But it is harmful to those who touch her—which would only be necessary after the courtship has been completed, and thus, of little concern to us."

"My apologies, but I have a categorical aversion to poisonous people," said Holtzclaw.

"There is another candidate," said Almeda.

Now Luella withdrew her file. These women carried with them a great deal of paper, Holtzclaw realized. "A wisp of an Oriental aristocrat. Her name is unpronounceable, which complicates introductions. Our intelligence indicates that she will be arriving by train in six days. Her fortune was made in some quintessentially Oriental fashion—tea export, or the manufacture of antiquities, or some such."

"If I may interrupt, Poetess of the Stirring Heart," said Almeda, the Reader of Mysteries, "I received updated information this morning that suggests she is an...artist. A painter and sculptor of some talent."

"As a supplement to her business fortunes?" asked Vera. "Because we have not disqualified ladies who play with watercolors between luncheon and tea."

"No, as her sole support. There is no export business. She eats by her art."

Luella folded the information paper and tore it twice. She deposited the shreds in the hands of a passing hotel employee.

"There are more suitable candidates, Holtzclaw," said Almeda. "Never fear. Why, just last evening, we caught sight of a splendid creature. Very beautiful. A charming laugh. Her bones suggest she may be royalty, though we are not sure from where. The chin is not right for the European rulers; it could mean she's descended from one of the South Seas kingdoms. She is proving to be somewhat difficult to talk to, as she keeps fleeing from where she is bathing when we approach."

"She had a rabbit face," said Vera. "Pointy ears. Coal-black eyes."

"It is our imperfections that make us charming," said Almeda.

By the time Holtzclaw rid himself of the meddlesome women, worked his figures, gathered the latest on the dam repairs, and tried to deliver his daily report to Shadburn, who was already asleep, it was midnight. The lobby desk was unstaffed. A small party played faro at a round table; they talked in low voices, as though afraid of disturbing their slumbering compatriots.

Holtzclaw did not retire to his room but took the steam elevator to a lower floor. The corridor leading to the baths was tiled on all sides with an irregular green and white pattern. Iron gates barred the entrance to changing rooms; Holtzclaw unlocked them. A row of wooden stalls provided a place for guests to doff their formal clothing and put on the bathing costumes provided by the Queen of the Mountains. For men: a one-piece garment that stretched from just above the knee to the shoulder, featuring a blue diagonal stripe. For women: a similar garment that had an optional wrap around the waist to provide modesty towards the ankle but still—and here was the delicate matter—expose a measure of skin to the action of the mineral waters. If the swimming attire were too conservative, then the waters could not be absorbed effectively.

The bathing chamber was dark; Holtzclaw threw the switch. Lights activated in series, down the long chamber. As they warmed up and glowed brighter, their buzzing came into harmony. Holtzclaw had ordered all the bulbs together, and when any burned out, he replaced them all as a set. Bulbs made together all hum in the same key;

bulbs mixed and matched from different lots were apt to be sharp or flat. The healing action of the water would be upset by any dis-harmony. At least, this is what Dr. Rathbun had advised. It was on his recommendation that the Queen of the Mountains provided ew-ers of mineral water on every flat surface and that employees pulled wheeled barrels over the croquet field. Likewise by Dr. Rathbun's advice, mineral water was not provided at mealtimes. Then, it was alcohol, especially whiskey, to aid digestion, and for children, pickle brine.

It was not enough to only drink the waters, said Dr. Rathbun, though that was an essential part. Bathing, too, must be performed at appropriate times and in appropriate ways, for optimal health, and in correct combination with the patient's needs and other mineral waters consumed. Mineral water could be classified into eight vari-eties: saline, sulfur, white sulfur, chalybeate, epsom, lythia, plyant, and freestone. The Queen of the Mountains had sources of each flowing to its baths, pumped from locations all over the valley, but not every source was pure. For instance, the cold waters from Moss's spring were rich in epsoms but also held a measure of white sulfur. Patients who needed to consume epsom rarely needed white sulfur, which could cause unwanted imbalances. Thus, they were advised to bathe in chalybeate waters to draw out the excess sulfur. Bathing, in such cases, was not itself therapeutic, but an antidote to side effects of the actual cure.

Dr. Rathbun diagnosed Holtzclaw's recurring pain as a common condition to new residents of the valley. The debris of the Lost Creek Valley—its peculiar collection of sediments, minerals, fogs, humidi-ties, and ghosts—collected in the turns of the intestine. Holtzclaw protested that he was not a resident, merely a long-term visitor, but Dr. Rathbun told him that his bowels evidently disagreed. Dr. Rath-bun prescribed alternating consumption of saline water, to break up the internal mass, and plyant waters, to charge the intestines with the necessary solvents to prevent further accretions. This was fol-lowed by bathing in a heated sulfur water, which awakened the ingested ingredients by temperature and smell, for precisely fifteen minutes. Then, a cold cascade of freestone water was to be applied instantaneously to rinse away sulfur residue and halt the heating action, so Holtzclaw's gut would not become over-cooked.

The bathing hall provided eight long pools, large enough for twenty people at once and deep enough for even the tallest bather to submerge himself fully. These were supplemented by two dozen overhead basins, for greater variety in topical application. Water was delivered into these basins by either heated or refrigerated pipes. The bather stood directly underneath the basin and pulled a handle to release the entire contents over himself at once.

Holtzclaw found the taste of the saline water very unpleasant, and Dr. Rathbun had given him license to mix it with a stabilizing substance. Holtzclaw measured a spoonful of Pharaoh's Flour into a cup that he then filled with saline water from a tap. He drank the whole in one draught, then entered the steaming sulfur bath. He had to lower himself carefully, by degrees, letting himself adjust to each new level.

As the water rose above his navel and his stomach, Holtzclaw winced. The pain became sharper, then after a moment he felt it widen, growing less acute as it spread. Then the pain was gone—or nearly gone. Holtzclaw could still feel a faint stripe of discomfort in the usual place. It was a ghost that had not yet been washed away.

A soft splashing disturbed him from his restorative thoughts.

"Come in on the pipes?" he said, addressing the presence of the princess. He did not scamper to shelter; his bathing suit was modest enough.

"No, by the power of my feet," she said. They were swirling the waters of the lythia bath, next to the sulfur one.

"I'm surprised to see you here," said Holtzclaw. "These aren't your kind of springs."

The princess walked the perimeter of the bathing hall. She looked into drains and and pipes. She sniffed the waters. "You have made the best of it," she said. "They are like tiny underground lakes."

Holtzclaw turned around so he could watch her; he propped himself against the rim of the bath on his elbows. "Tell me plainly: are we enemies, princess? Are you trying to destroy the dam?"

Trahlyta said nothing. She finished her patrol, then sat at the edge of the sulphur bath, beside Holtzclaw. Again he found himself debating from a position of weakness. He strained his neck to look up at the small, seated princess.

"Why do you want this dam, James? What purpose does it serve for you?"

"To rid this valley of gold. Hide it away."

"Then we are not enemies." She stirred the water with her feet. For the first time, Holtzclaw noticed that she had only four toes on each.

"I mean, those are Shadburn's reasons," he said. "I gave you his reasons. I have my own. You've seen my work. The Maiden of the Lake."

"There's no such creature, James."

"I assure you, there is. Soon enough, she'll launch with her first guests. She will sail the narrow ocean of her world."

"And you've always wanted to be the master of a hotel, have you? Captain a steamship that putters around a lake? Why work for dreams that are not your own?"

The princess rose from beside the sulphur bath before Holtzclaw could respond; he did not know what to say. She walked to each other basin in turn. Her soft feet padded against the tile. She lifted a handful of water from each, then let it fall back into the basin. She pulled the handle on an overhead water basin—by the steam and smell, a heated epsom bath. A cascade tumbled before her, then ran off through a complex network of pipes and into the lake.

"They will do," said the princess. "The usual baths for my employers are presently unavailable. They are flooded with water or tourists. And yet, they need to get clean."

"Why do you have employers at all? Why aren't you free to do as you please?"

"The natural and supernatural worlds grow into each other. You must remember, you middle mortals are all very short-lived. A decade, a century—these are very brief moments of time for terrapins and Trahlytas. Mountains and ghosts live for eons. They becomes friends."

She picked up the tin of Pharaoh's Flour from where it rested beside Holtzclaw's cup and smiled as she saw Amenhotep's laughing face on the label.

"I like him," said the princess. "His laugh rings like rain."

"How do you know what his laugh sounds like?" said Holtzclaw, climbing out of the hot sulfur bath. His prescribed time had passed.

"We are old acquaintances," said the princess.

"But he's as tied to the desert as you are to the springs of this valley."

"It's not so simple as that," said the princess. "We can all visit the moon. We have an exposition there, once every age or so. We build a palace of crystal, and the moon maidens wiggle their noses, and it is a grand time. But cold, so cold. Golden starlight sticks to your skin, and you want a vacation—someplace warm, for a swim."

"Are there moon men, too, to complement the maidens?" Holtzclaw asked. "Where do they go on their holidays?"

"They go on hunting parties with the pharaoh Amenhotep III. He leads them across plains of sand so white and blameless that they feel they are walking on clouds. The moon men find strength in his laugh and smiling eyes. But his friendship is only mercenary. He is an employee, James, like you and me."

A panic interrupted the afternoon tea hour, echoing through all the stories of the Queen of the Mountains like a thunderclap. A pink-bonneted woman, sitting before cucumber sandwiches, had had a green snake crawl over her shoes. She emitted a long, high-pitched wail that drew every ear, then burst into guttural noises, like she was drowning in her own tears.

Flying leaps upset tables and chairs. China fell and shattered. The streak of green flashed across the dining room and vanished below the baseboard. This disappearance did not bring relief. Now, the snake was inside the arteries of the Queen of the Mountains. Its vile green head could pop out anywhere—from below a pillow, from the spigot on the washbasin. Huddled masses evacuated to the lawn. What was the terrible creature doing to the food, the water, the alcohol? How would its oozes and essences affect the springs? Would supper be delayed; would the menu be changed?

Abigail banged at the baseboard with the end of a broom. Holtzclaw fetched her a crowbar to remove the wood paneling. They failed to find the intruder. The Sky Pilot was called to assist. Holtzclaw made sure to parade him past the huddled masses, who gave a heartened cheer. The Sky Pilot was laden with tools and weapons: a bow and stuffed quiver, a long rifle, an unsheathed bush knife. Little boys and girls, their faces screwed up in courage, broke away from the body and joined the Sky Pilot as his irregulars.

"A green snake is nothing to worry about," said the Sky Pilot, and his irregulars nodded their assent. He stalked along a long corridor, stopping every ten feet. "What you need to worry about are the hoop snakes. They put their tails in their mouths and then they roll down the hill towards you, and they'll clobber you so good!"

All the irregulars agreed that this snake was far worse than a green snake.

"That's nothing compared to the coachwhip snake, though," said the Sky Pilot, opening each drawer in a high boy. "The coachwhip snake is long and black, just like a carriage driver's crop. If the coachwhip snake comes for you, it'll put its tail down your throat so that you can't scream, and then it thrashes you with its body, like you're a disobedient horse."

The irregulars shivered and squealed with fear and excitement; they rummaged through the linens in the laundry but found no sign of the green snake.

"There are snakes that have very powerful venom. They have poisons that make you swell up. One of those snakes bit on my walking stick, and it swelled up to the size of tree. I sold it for railroad ties, and they made a mile of track from my walking stick. But then the rains came, and all the poison got washed out, and the railroad ties shrank until they were toothpicks. I got to sell the toothpicks, though."

Abigail smiled over this story; the irregulars were fascinated.

"There are stronger venoms, too. A snake bit on a watermelon, and when the watermelon broke open, it caused such a flood that the valley has never seen, before or since. It was such a gush of water. This lake is a puddle compared to that watermelon flood. The top of Sinking Mountain was gone under the pink juice. I would have been washed away, but I grabbed on to a black seed, which was as big as a house, and I set up a campfire and a cabin there."

"We all had to ride on seeds for weeks," said Abigail, "and if we wanted to visit our neighbors, we had to swim. We all got covered in sticky juice and some of us got carried away by ants."

"The only good thing," said the Sky Pilot, "was that the valley smelled like August for two whole years."

The irregulars drank from the ewers of mineral water, pretending that it was a potent antidote. They administered rituals and poultices to each other. The Sky Pilot turned out comforters and duvets. Pillows were cast aside. He upended a fainting couch and used his knife to slice open a feather bed.

"The worst snake of them all, though," said the Sky Pilot, "is the trance snake. Because it doesn't matter how brave or strong you are— it will fascinate you to helplessness and tickle you to death. To meet one is to die."

This made the irregulars pause. How would they deal with such a threat? Such a creature was not just. It took no notice of merit or talent; might and courage were futile. Death was only luck then. They shook with distress; their balance had been upset.

The Sky Pilot's face broke into a wide smile, and he stretched his broad, powerful arms out to his distressed adherents. They curled up close to him, to his smell and his wisdom and his weapons, and they knew that there was no such thing as a trance snake. He had only been testing them. Their fear and doubt had brought them through.

"Now, since we can't find that green snake, who in any case is not at all dangerous," said the Sky Pilot, "what should we do?"

"We'll take the hotel apart!" said one of the irregulars.

"Burn it with fire!"

"Set the dynamite!"

"Freeze the walls and smash them with a hammer!"

"Turn on all the taps and flood it out!"

"Electricity!"

"Falling stars!"

"All very good ideas," said the Sky Pilot. "So good that we must try them all. But we can't! There are people that live here. See, Abigail lives here. She's a nice enough fellow. We can't blow up her house. Holtzclaw, too. We can't wash his house down into the valley."

The irregulars nodded. This made very good sense to them.

"So what we will do," said the Sky Pilot, "is send out a second green snake, who in any case is not at all dangerous. The second snake must be just like the first one, the same kind and the same age and the same temper."

"Then where ever the first one went, the second one will go, too," said one of the irregulars.

"They'll fight!" said another.

"When they fight, they'll try to eat the other one up!"

"Who will win?" said the Sky Pilot.

"They are both alike, both will win and both will lose."

"At the same time, too!"

"Each one will start to eat the other, and then they'll eat each other up, at just the same time!"

"Gulp, and both are gone!"

"No more snake!"

"No more snake," agreed the Sky Pilot. He took from his belt a brown burlap sack; he untied the top and withdrew a green snake, about ten inches long. The snake tasted the air with its pink tongue and looked up sleepily at the assembled irregulars.

The Sky Pilot lowered his hand; the snake flashed away, a green streak, and vanished through a narrow fissure beside a water pipe. The irregulars burst into cheers.

CHAPTER XXV

Thus passed the two weeks that preceded the Day of the Evening Star, the holiday that commemorated nothing but an invented story. Despite the short lead time, the bookings at the hotel had increased in anticipation of the event. The banquet would cost far more than these additional bookings would bring in, but no matter. It was imperative that this nascent holiday succeed on its debut, or the first tourists, returning disappointed, would ensure that the hotel never lived to celebrate the day's anniversary.

A special train arrived with refrigerated cars, disgorging ingredients into waiting pots and pans. Holtzclaw watched a troop of employees unfurl tablecloths in the dining room. A passing air current caught one end of a silver-spangled cloth, tugging it from the hands of its handlers. The middle of the cloth shot upward to the ceiling, and the cloth danced and played far out of reach.

"Now Mr. Bad Thing, don't you have some piano to play?" said Cannie. "Leave us alone to get our work done."

The air began to come out of the tablecloth, and it descended slowly. Cannie grabbed the corner of it, and the tablecloth sprang to life again. It lifted Cannie off the ground; her toes skittered across tabletops.

"Abigail! Abigail!" called Cannie, clinging to the hem of the tablecloth.

Abigail appeared from the employees' passage. "This is why you can't get that melody in 'Summer Afternoons,'" she scolded. "You're always messing with the tablecloths instead of practicing. Get back to the piano, if you ever hope to get any better. Or do you want me to hire somebody new?"

The tablecloth deflated. Cannie tumbled to the tabletop; the cloth, inanimate, fluttered over her.

"It's been this way all day, Holtzclaw," said Abigail.

He followed her down the elevated employees' passage into the kitchen outbuilding, where she issued orders to a team of white-aproned cooks. Copious helpings of paprika went into one pot; some sort of sea creature into the other. Holtzclaw was unable to count the number of tentacles per creature; they knotted together in a mass within the broth. A giant oven like a mouth consumed dough and expelled crusty bread. A lean boy stood knee-deep in feathers that he had stripped from game birds; the carcasses were stacked beside him like cordwood.

Abigail turned to a small stove that held a single, large pan. Inside were flakes of color—green, yellow, and orange.

"Ms. Thompson, what's this one?"

"Wild ramps, scrambled with eggs, and a sweet potato hash."

"It's not enough for a banquet portion."

"The New Rock Falls will be open," she said. "For any that have an appetite for its sort of food."

"Do you think anyone will come?" said Holtzclaw.

"The regulars would like to be fed."

From across the kitchen came a sharp snap and a yelp of pain. A cook did battle with the largest lobster that Holtzclaw had ever seen. It was four feet from head to tail, dark brown with pink spots. The cook held a colander in front of his face and had a long meat fork in the other hand. He lunged for the lobster, but the lobster blocked deftly, then executed a perfect riposte.

"It's only an old and ornery creature, and it wants compassion," said Abigail. She gathered the creature in her arms. It looked up at her with its dark points that were its eyes. Its claws waved in the air but did not snap. Abigail drew it closer to her chest. Then she put a knife between its eyes and pressed until the shell cracked. A yellow goo oozed from the wound, and the lobster was still. She handed it back to the cook.

"The way you were holding it," said Holtzclaw, "I thought you were going to spare its life. Release it into the lake."

"You can't put a saltwater lobster into a freshwater lake," she said, "no matter how much mineral water you give it. Better to let its ghost flow freely away."

A tall pot filled with water at a rolling boil began to rock back and forth, and peeled potatoes began to spring and leap from within.

Each potato had a horrible face, with red eyes tilted inwards and leering row of teeth.

One potato leapt from the pot and landed on Holtzclaw. It set into his tie with its starchy fangs. Instinctually, Holtzclaw struck at the attacker and smashed it against his chest. Now, he was covered with particles of scalding potato. His wails were cut short by a second assault. Other potatoes were springing higher and higher from the water. Abigail found a cutting board and slammed it over the pot.

"Holtzclaw!" said Abigail. "Be useful for once and hold this down."

Holtzclaw pressed his weight against the cutting board as Abigail ran to the larder and returned with a tin of Pharaoh's Flour. It was still sealed. She put her fingernails under the lip and pulled; the seal pulled up with a sucking sound, and Holtzclaw caught a whiff of a desert breeze. The laughing face of Amenhotep winked at him—it was so much more pleasant than the grinning leers of the potatoes.

Abigail lifted a corner of the cutting board and tipped in a draught of Pharaoh's Flour. Instantly the pot stopped rocking. The grinning mouths were gone. Inside were only peeled potatoes, boiling facelessly.

"All day, Holtzclaw," said Abigail. "All day."

Holtzclaw sat across the table from Shadburn, who occupied the central seat at the head table. To Shadburn's right and left, following the custom of alternate seating by gender, were women. On one side was a railroad baroness, whose husband was on a late evening hunt with the Sky Pilot. On his other side was an actual baroness. Her title continued to be inherited even though the barony from which it derived had fallen into the sea during an earthquake four hundred years ago.

Holtzclaw, too, was flanked by women, or at least the idea of them. The chair to Holtzclaw's left supported a frail form clad in a black dress. She was the owner and operator of a Carolina corundum mine.

The chair to Holtzclaw's right should have been occupied by Lizzie Rathbun. He needed no introductions from the Billing, Wooing, and Cooing Society when he asked her a week ago for the pleasure of her company. She had assented then, but when Holtzclaw came to collect her, she gave her excuses. She said that a small party, like the one Holtzclaw had put together for this Evening Star trifle, demanded the same level of preparation and charm from Ms. Rathbun as a spectacular ball. She felt that, in this case, her investment would not be adequately rewarded. For a more spectacular event, she would be sure to appear in fine style.

Her rebuff wounded him, and he could not conceal his ill humor while he sat at the banquet table. He looked across her empty chair at an ovine man, a politician. He had tight white curls in his hair, and he bent low to consume salad by pressing it between his fat lips. The eighth seat, between the actual baroness and the corundum mine owner, was held by a wealthy newspaper magnate, who had risen from humble beginnings—owning only the five newspapers he'd inherited from his father—to control a printing empire of more than two dozen publications. Shadburn, with a certain pride, noted that Auraria's *Miner's Record and Spy in the West* was not a part of that empire.

Holtzclaw had changed from his potato-smeared suit and tie into evening clothes—tails and white gloves. All the men were attired similarly, even Shadburn. A tailor and advisor had spent all afternoon with him, selecting everything from shoe polish to hair cream to cufflinks.

A waiter brought a magnum bottle of claret to Shadburn's side. He presented the label to Shadburn, who studied it for several moments. Holtzclaw was sure that Shadburn was just counting to five in his head. It was uncorked and a small portion poured for Shadburn, per ritual.

"Very good," said Shadburn. "An excellent year."

The employee poured the bottle around the table—a glass each for the railroad baroness, the actual baroness, the corundum miner, the ovine man, Shadburn, Holtzclaw, and the newspaper magnate.

Holtzclaw knew the claret was corked before it touched his lips. The odor was unmistakable. But the baronesses had already downed several mouthfuls; Shadburn was halfway through his glass; the ovine man gargled his beverage between his mutton chops. Holtzclaw set his glass down.

"Is something the matter, Mr. Holtzclaw?" asked the actual baroness.

"Not at all, Your Ladyship. Simply no taste for it this evening, I'm afraid."

"No taste for it?" said Shadburn. "I didn't think it was possible. Drink up! It's excellent for the constitution, just as good as the mineral waters, if consumed in proper proportions. Isn't that right, Holtzclaw?"

Holtzclaw choked through a sip, which was enough to satisfy the curiosity of the table.

The many-armed epergne, holding an assortment of olives, tranchets of celery, an India relish, and burgherkins, was cleared away. In its place was laid a plate containing a filet of baked red snapper *au gratin*, served with steamed rice. Every grain had arrived by steam power—Auraria offered only sweet potatoes. Shadburn ate with unusual restraint, taking only as much as the baronesses. Holtzclaw left half his portion. The fish tasted too much like the miles it had traveled.

Next was presented a roasted lamb and mint sauce, accompanied by boiled potatoes and creamed okra. The creamed okra was a noxious slime, despite Abigail's best efforts. Holtzclaw could not bring himself to eat the boiled potatoes; he saw faces in them. He turned the plate so that the line of lamb bones would serve as a defensive palisade should the potatoes decide to rise up again. Shadburn and the baronesses and the ovine man ate with gusto, but the corundum miner picked at her food.

"Is everything all right, Ms. Chambers?" asked Holtzclaw. She nodded, but she, too, had turned her potatoes away.

Next came the lobster. It could not provide enough flesh for all the hungry diners, so Abigail had stretched it into a consommé. Holtzclaw avoided the broth and nibbled instead on pieces of mountain trout that were served on a tray of mixed smoked seafood.

A platter of cold meats passed from hand to hand—veal, beef, bologna, duck, and something pickled that had lost all taste but brine. This was followed by a chicken salad. The greens were still cold from their voyage in a refrigerated car.

Dessert arrived. Gooseberry pie, compote of pineapple, preserved ginger, and steamed plum pudding with a hard sauce. Holtzclaw had hoped for peaches, but evidently, they had all gone into the homebrew.

When all had been cleared away, the party received coffee and tea cakes. The square confections, no bigger than a thumbnail, were covered in white icing and topped with a blueberry.

"It was a splendid meal, Mr. Shadburn," said the actual baroness, lifting her glass and voice, "and in fine company. We have commemorated the Day of the Fallen Star splendidly, and with food as elegant as you would see at Saratoga." A general sound of approval circled the table. "I must say, Mr. Shadburn, that given your upbringing, I supposed that you would be a rather rustic figure."

"What Her Ladyship means is, we had heard you were rich," said the railroad baroness, "but you didn't seem rich."

"We thought you were only a codfish aristocrat," said the actual baroness.

"Then you put out a banquet such as this," continued the railroad baroness, "and your cufflinks are splendid, and one cannot doubt that you are a gentleman."

Shadburn smiled. "I have a very comfortable living, and I am pleased to share that comfort with you, my guests, and with the town where I was raised."

"I suppose it would be easy enough to be rich here," said the corundum miner. "There were gold mines here, weren't there?"

The baronesses lifted their eyes in wonder at the very word: gold. Even the ovine man was stirred to an emotional reaction—he put down his tea cake in mid-bite.

"It was, in fact, very difficult to be rich," said Shadburn. "The story of gold here is complicated, and that is why we are trying to expunge that reputation. We don't put it on our advertisements."

"Why ever not?" said the actual baroness. "You see how a man's eyes glitter at the very mention."

"It's an era of the valley's history that has passed," said Shadburn. "But you must consider this money talk impolite."

"Not in the least," said the railroad baroness. "On the contrary, I find it the most pleasing and fascinating of subjects.

"Were there any big strikes?" said the actual baroness. "Great fortunes? Did some serf find a nugget the size of a potato and buy an estate? Did a stranger leave a heap of gold dust to repay some kindness? Oh! Was anyone murdered?"

"What a question, Your Ladyship!" said the railroad baroness. "Of course people were murdered. Where there is gold, blood runs through the streets like rainwater! You should have asked, 'How many people were murdered, and which murders are still talked about in the saloons?'"

The actual baroness continued. "I heard that in the California rush, a man blew up his own brother with black powder as he slept, for fear that he would divulge the secret of a mine they'd found together. Did any of that happen here?"

"I know of none," said Shadburn.

"Pity," said the actual baroness. She swirled the coffee in her cup sullenly, then poured in more cream and sugar, until the contents of her cup resembled dirty snow. She quaffed it in gulps, leaving a line of cream on her upper lip.

"How about double-dealings?" said the railroad baroness. "Shady sales? A man who tunneled under his neighbor's claim and mined away all the good minerals, undetected? Bawdy houses? Rough saloons? Gunslingers and their women? Betrayals? Explosions?"

"There's little to tell," said Shadburn. "There is only disappointment, jealousy, and waste."

The actual baroness crossed her arms, "Were you cheated out of a land claim, Mr. Shadburn? Tricked into buying a salted mine? How did the gold business disappoint you?"

"I have made my money in land development," said Shadburn. Holtzclaw thought that, if gold and money were two separate things, then this statement was not a lie. "I have always been in land development, which is an enterprise that rewards hard work, determination, pluck, and talent."

"No, it's sitting on land and hoping the railroad comes through," said the corundum miner.

"You are describing land speculation, ma'am. Land development is a systematic process, a science, the goal of which is to call a higher and better use from the earth. Take, for example, this hotel. Would you credit, ladies and gentlemen, that this dining hall sits on land that was once a farmer's field? What did Moss grow here, Holtzclaw?"

"Ice," said Holtzclaw, thinking of the cold winds blowing from the neglected spring house door. "Under the ice, sweet potatoes, I think."

"See?" said Shadburn. "A pasture of frozen sweet potatoes has become a formal dining room."

"To what end, Mr. Shadburn?" said the corundum miner.

"Why, to so many ends that I could not list them all! For the edification and uplift of the people of the valley—to show them with money what money can bring. To give them a better employment than to scratch in the dirt for some shiny metal that they may never find."

"Now we have wandered away from money into less interesting topics," said the railroad baroness. "Altruism—what's more tiresome than harping on all the good you've done? Let's talk of something else. What is next for the Queen of the Mountains?"

Shadburn looked to Holtzclaw. "We have a season's worth of holidays and banquets, don't we?"

"You should have a gala," said the railroad baroness. "That is the pinnacle of the social calendar."

"Oh, a gala!" said the actual baroness. "That would be so grand. A party like this is the perfect practice exercise, but you are capable of much more. Have an orchestra; let us dance the figures. Set it for the end of the season. I have the perfect dress for it."

"I will summon my circles," said the railroad baroness. "They will all come, if I can promise a great enough spectacle. There are parties every day, you see, but galas promise more wonder."

"What do you think, Holtzclaw?" said Shadburn. "Could we arrange such an event, if our baronesses request it? What could stop us?"

The table cloth billowed at the far end of a table. Holtzclaw startled, but it was only the passing breeze of a debutant, made by the sweep of her spangled gown and the vacuum of her male companions standing for her.

"Nothing, Shadburn," he said. "Nothing at all."

It was not long before Holtzclaw's meager meal at the banquet had been worn away, and his stomach grumbled. He left his tabulations, put on his shoes, and descended from his room to the kitchen. Before he reached it, he saw that the lights in the New Rock Falls were still aglow.

Shadburn sat at a table, bent over a heap of food. Mr. Bad Thing plinked out a popular melody from one of the follies.

"Ms. Thompson saved a plate for me," said Shadburn.

"Does she have any more?"

"There's more here than I can finish, Holtzclaw. Find yourself a fork."

Holtzclaw retrieved one, then checked under the counter for claret. There was a bottle of a serviceable maker and year. Shadburn shook his head, declining a glass. Holtzclaw took a pull from the neck of the bottle.

"Ramps and eggs and bacon," he said, tucking in to Shadburn's plate. "You didn't ask Abigail for hash browns with wild mushrooms?"

"I didn't want to be a bother, Holtzclaw. The ramps were already prepared. They are quite good, aren't they? We should have them at this gala."

"I think they might be too pungent for our rarefied clientele."

"They eat cheeses that would stir the dead."

"Yes, but they have a tradition of eating such foods, and for them, ramps would be a novelty."

"Hmm," mused Shadburn.

"You cut a fairly convincing character this evening," said Holtzclaw, "with your cufflinks and your air of charity and wealth."

"It's a strain, Holtzclaw. It isn't the sort of work that agrees with me, nor the sort of food." Holtzclaw saw the weariness in Shadburn's posture. His shoulders slumped over his hash browns. His awkward frame, too tall for the furniture, was not at ease. Shadburn was uncomfortable even in his own creation.

"Do you think you can last through a gala, then?" said Holtzclaw. "There are other options for attracting attention, getting tourists. We could style the Queen of the Mountains as the premier place to find a suitable spouse, for yourself or for your undesirable children. There are lonely hearts, even among the rich. Or, we could open a gold mine. Not a real one; as you've said, that's impossible. We could bury some flakes, here and there, and little nuggets, too, and the tourists might think it a lark."

Shadburn pushed away his plate, even though there were morsels left. He had lost his appetite. "I think, of those options, a gala sounds best. A grand one, a spectacular one. It is what those baronesses want; it's their will that should guide us, since they are our guests. And it would seem the easiest for us to realize. It would take only money."

Holtzclaw brought out a pen and paper. "Who should be the entertainment?"

Shadburn held up a hand. "Tomorrow, Holtzclaw. For now, let this codfish aristocrat eat in peace."

CHAPTER XXVI

At daybreak, Cannie intercepted Holtzclaw in the hallway and laid at his feet a new crisis. The door to the refrigerated storeroom had been left opened overnight. Holtzclaw followed her to the kitchen. As he entered, he was blasted with a blizzard wind. Fires were blown out. Lobster broth became an unappetizing sorbet. Chilled salads turned into ice shards.

Abigail was wearing a heavy overcoat and had a length of cloth wrapped over her face. She had rigged together an oil lamp—a forbidden device—with an extra hand bellows, which boosted the flame and gave it a short range. The instrument was pathetically inadequate to this task, but it could have been used for *crème brûlée* and soup *au gratin*.

"Your flamethrower isn't going to melt this," said Holtzclaw, turning his face from the wind. Icicles dangled from his eyebrows.

"It may get me as far as the refrigerator motor," said Abigail, "to disable it."

"Can we cut the power farther up the line?"

"Not unless you want to put the whole hotel into darkness," said Abigail. "I think Shadburn's wrath would fall upon us both."

"Then you must go," said Holtzclaw. "For the greater good."

Abigail vanished into a whiteout of snow. Tongues of flame were visible through the driving curtain of flakes, but then they, too, were gone.

Holtzclaw and Cannie and the other anxious employees retreated to a sheltered camp in the corridor, where they could still peek out across the frozen wasteland. For many minutes, they waited. Holtzclaw shivered and paced. Icicles danged from the eaves of their shelter. Cannie rubbed her hands, trying to work some life back into them. If they were thus afflicted here, what was Abigail facing?

"She should have reached the motor by now," said Holtzclaw. "I have to go after her."

Cannie restrained him. "She doesn't need rescue," she said.

A groan and a high whine filled the kitchen. The walls trembled. There was sputtering, coughing, and then a gnarled death rattle of metal on metal. The wind ceased and the weather improved. Snow settled down in drifts between the stoves and along the pantry shelves.

"See, I told you," said Cannie.

Holtzclaw ventured towards the storeroom. His boots slipped along the stone floor, which was thick with ice. He skittered towards a table arrayed with paring knifes but arrested himself by clinging to a counter stacked with flash-frozen vegetables. Walking and skating, he arrived at the ice house door, which was frozen open.

Abigail stood over her slaughtered foe. A spanner emerged from the mechanism of the refrigerator motor. Springs and gears hung loose and lifeless. Pipes were twisted, burst, and splayed from its innards.

"You killed it," said Holtzclaw.

"It was life or death," said Abigail. "The hunter or the beast."

Without a refrigerator motor to stand against it, the Georgia summer began its assault on the kitchen. Hardly an hour had passed before the thickly-layered frost had melted. The salad greens withered, and consommés could not be chilled. A replacement motor was on order, but if there weren't ice cubes in the baronesses' whiskey glasses by the evening, Holtzclaw feared a riot.

He rode out to the Terrible Cascade, ready to pay handsomely for the Sky Pilot's assistance. But the Sky Pilot did not ask any more than his ordinary rates. He promised regular deliveries of clear, perfect cubes to the hotel's ice house until the motor could be replaced, and he offered straw and blankets to help preserve the salad greens and sorbets. It was a very agreeable resolution. Holtzclaw would have been suspicious of the dealing had he been negotiating with anyone other than the Sky Pilot, who throughout their fraught acquaintance had always been guileless and plain-spoken.

As Holtzclaw was returning from the Sky Pilot's cabin in the shadow of the dam, he met a party that was departing from their visit with the Great and Harmless and Invincible Terrapin Under the Mountain, and they harangued Holtzclaw with complaints.

"It looks like a leather puppet," they said. "You can see the seams and stitches. What is it, six people inside a mechanical turk?"

"I assure you, there is no trick," said Holtzclaw. "It is an honest terrapin."

The guests spilled out a mess of dissatisfaction and complaints. All the terrapin's stories were about the old days, with no regard for the modern audience. Also, it was a liar. The raven is not black because it stole fire and escaped through a hole in a tree—it's black because it tried to steal grapes from a chimney. The terrapin's stories did not even have an internal consistency: first it said the river valley was carved by a Great Serpent; then, it said by tears of a weeping mountain and that the mountain is still weeping today; then, by some sort of footrace, and the paws of animals great and small beat the valley into a high road. Sometimes the terrapin began a story with promise, but then spoiled it with details. It told about beautiful women that descend from the moon to bathe in the water of the valley, but then the terrapin said that these women have long ears and little rabbit noses and eyes that are solid black, with no whites, no color. How can a women be beautiful if she does not have eyes of cloudless blue or gemlike green? That terrapin had no gift for storytelling, and charging such prices for a ticket was highway robbery.

"The fundamental problem with your show," said one of the guests, "is that your star is just a big terrapin. You can see a big terrapin anytime. All you have to do is get very close to a small terrapin. What's the difference?"

"So, if the spectacle featured, let's say, the Great and Harmless and Invincible Giraffe Under the Mountain, but it told the same stories, you would be happier about that?"

"Giraffes are already big."

"But they don't live in caves under the Georgia mountains," said Holtzclaw, "and that would be novel, at least."

The guests were ambivalent. Novelty was not their primary concern. "Forget the animal. Let's have something with more spectacle. A real show!"

"The Great and Harmless and Invincible Terrapin does sing," said Holtzclaw. "Did it not play a melody for you from its shell? Perhaps the Song of Gladness, or the Rondo of History, or the Melody to Sever the Water from the Sky?"

"It should play show tunes instead," said one of the guests.

"It should play accompaniment for a singer," said another.

"A famous singer!"

"Dasha Pavlovski!"

Pavlovski was an Old World sensation who, for the last ten years, had made an unceasing tour of national and provincial capitals. His warm tenor caressed his favored themes: purity, eternal love, the blossoming of a flower, sad partings, warm returns. His green eyes pierced through layers of fashionable clothing and stirred the hearts of women who had never permitted themselves to feel so much as a flutter of romance.

"If you have Dasha Pavlovski, then you don't need a boring, old terrapin at all," said the guests. "Or a giraffe."

There were squeals of excitement—not only from the women, but also the men. They knew that they would be the likely beneficiaries of any passions Dasha might stir.

"If you are going to have Dasha Pavlovski," said one of the guests, "then you should build him a different theatre, or have him sing in the ballroom. It is much too far to go all the way down those cliffside stairs into that valley and into that cave. A pox on that. Our legs and feet are tired before we even sit down to enjoy a show. Why didn't you have an elevator put in instead?"

A peculiar train stood at the depot. Instead of passengers and mail, it carried fish, and among them, Holtzclaw's lake creature. Four of the cars, aquariums on wheels, held schools of black bass, which Shadburn had ordered to provide stock for fishermen. As each tank was lowered into the lake, the bass scattered in a flurry of frantic fins that dissipated into barely felt ripples.

The fifth car contained the lake creature, and Holtzclaw was chagrined to find that the lithograph from the catalog was not a good likeness. The catalog showed a smiling beast, pleasantly plump. It was supposed to be some sort of Carpathian trout, specially raised for its temperament, a triumph of selective breeding. But the creature that arrived was thin and lithe—at least twenty feet long, if all its coils were unwound. The head resembled an alligator's, with a snub snout, prominent nostrils, bulging yellow eyes. Its teeth did not fit neatly inside its jaws; they snaggled upwards and downwards. Some of its scales were marred with a whitish growth. In other places, the creature had thick tufts of black hair. Its locomotive appendages were short and tipped with bony claws, simultaneously evoking legs and fins, as though it could not decide how it wants to propel itself through life.

The creature paused from its angry thrashings to press its underbelly against the glass facing Holtzclaw and the assembled crowd. Yellow slime began to leak from a passageway below its ventral fins. Holtzclaw realized it was defecating. This operation completed, the creature returned to its struggles. The joints of the glass made a sandy grinding that sounded weak, weakening.

"Well, are you going to set it loose?" said Shadburn.

"I can't put that creature into our lake," said Holtzclaw. "It doesn't belong here."

"It doesn't belong anywhere," said Shadburn.

"What do you want me to do with it? Return it to sender?"

"What would that accomplish?" said Shadburn. "We'd be out transportation costs, with not even a monster to show for it. You could take it to a taxidermist and we could mount it above the entranceway."

"I don't want to look at it every day," said Holtzclaw.

"Then do whatever you like, Holtzclaw."

The creature opened its mouth. Two black tongues slithered across the glass. The crowd drew back. A child began to cry.

Holtzclaw went to Sampson's chuck wagon at closing time. He placed a folded note on the counter, above the hollow where payment was to be left, and matched it with a cube of polished gold. He turned his back, waited, and turned again to find that the note and the gold were gone. Sampson had taken the catering commission.

The next afternoon, Abigail had her staff set up the outdoor tables and retrieved the roasted creature from Sampson's fire pit.

Two days later, the guests returned from their afternoon recreations and naps to find that tank was gone. In its place, there was a spread of food laid out on tables on the lawn. Checkered blankets were spread out over the verdant hillside that stretched between the hotel and the lake. The tables were loaded with festival foods—buttered corn, potato salad, water rolls, lobster claws. The star delicacy was a filet of white meat.

It was no secret that the hideous creature had provided the picnic. Men and women laughed that they had never eaten such a thing in their life, and they were not apt to forget it. Children squealed and played and begged for a second helping of the sweet flesh.

Many guests came up to Shadburn, tucking into his third plate, and pressed his hand. It was a triumph, they declared. They thanked him for the splendid hospitality—they hadn't eaten such food even in the best palaces of Europe.

"We should order another one," said Shadburn, during a pause in the adulations. "Let's see the Seelbach and the Finley claim that they have barbecued their monsters."

"I'm not sure how to put that into our advertising copy," said Holtzclaw. "'Hideous aquatic abominations roasted for your culinary pleasure.'"

"That's fine," said Shadburn. "Why not that?"

Holtzclaw would have passed up his bath but for a sharp jolt of pain that leapt through his midsection. Weary though he was, he decided he could not forgo his treatment.

He descended in the elevator into the basement of the hotel, changed into a swimming costume, and was about to open the door into the bathing hall, but he stopped. From behind the door came splashes and patterings of feet and the glow of green light.

Holtzclaw turned the handle and winced as the sound of the lock mechanism echoed against the tile.

An attendant regiment of will-o'-the-wisps illuminated the bathing hall. One stood at each end of each mineral pool. The orbits of their lesser lights kept a regular time.

Moon maidens, nine by Holtzclaw's count, reposed in and around the mineral baths. As they cavorted, they dove below the water, leaving just their rabbit-like ears visible above the waterline. They let the gentle current of the springs carry them from one end of a pool to the other. They chased each other like children, running on the slippery tile but never losing their footing. They laid themselves down and drew curious hands through the water, as one might feel fabric or fur—the moon maidens had three long fingers and a thumb on each hand, tapering from the wrist to pointed nails. Their skin glistened with gold, coming from their pores. Gold floated on the surface of the water, reflecting the glow of the will-o'-the-wisps.

Princess Trahlyta traveled among the moon maidens, executing chores. She reprimanded a flagging will-o'-the-wisp whose orbiting lights fell out of rhythm. She fetched a towel for a moon maiden who rose from the epsom bath. The moon maiden's damp ears drooped forward, becoming tangled with her long, silver hair. Across her midriff was written an alien anatomy—the muscles and sinews did not knit together in a human way.

Another moon maiden emerged from the water and crossed to the reservoirs of mineral water that were mounted on the wall. She sniffed at the tank, sniffed at the drain, sniffed at the descending chain. She wrapped two of her fingers around the handle and pulled. A cascade of water fell upon her back—the hot water sizzled and spit against the maiden's skin, sending up clouds of steam. Gold flakes swirled into the drain pipes.

Holtzclaw remembered himself. These creatures were in his baths; they were his guests.

He tried to close the door gently and slink away, but he fumbled the handle. The door wailed in its frame; metal raked against tile and stone. The moon maidens whirled towards the noise. All of their black, iris-less eyes were upon him. Holtzclaw realized he had left them no route of escape. How would they flee if there were no paths leading into the woods, no clear routes up the mountain and into the sky? If trapped, would they fight? Would they fix Holtzclaw with paralyzing stares? Would he fall into a stupor and awaken in some starlit clearing, miles away?

Instead, the moon maidens popped like soap bubbles. Their solid forms shimmered, iridescent, then vanished into droplets. All of them vanished in the space of two seconds, and then their will-o'-the-wisps were extinguished, too. Holtzclaw was left alone, in darkness.

He fumbled for the switch to turn on the electric lights. The bulbs snapped on, one-by-one, and buzzed overhead. In the sickly, flickering light, the gold residue that had stuck to the drains and grout was green and unappealing. It would have to be cleaned up before the first guests came for the morning baths. In the best case, the green slime would reflect poorly on the cleanliness and hygiene of the pools; in the worst case, someone would recognize the slime as a form of unsettled gold, and there would be a flurry of interest. Pans and shovels and drills would be brought into the bathing hall. People would dig up the lawn with whatever they could find—the ends of brooms, old shoes, candlesticks, lamp stands.

Holtzclaw unlocked a supply closet, looking for a brush and rag. The princess grabbed a bucket from beside him.

"I thought you'd vanish with the moon maidens," said Holtzclaw.

"I can't," said the princess. "Too much work to be done, and it isn't right to leave all the clean-up for you."

"I'm grateful for the help."

"It's a simple chore, if it's only a little gold, in a little place," said Trahlyta. "I've done much harder work. I've negotiated with oreads that want higher mountains and whispering shadows that want darker valleys. I've reprimanded the tentacled deep-dwellers who can never keep appointments for maintenance work that needs to be done on the pumps and pipes. I've tried to please the great and harmless and invincible creatures that want new lodgings. I've made channels for flood waters and kept the lakes in their borders."

"Why would a princess do such chores? Do they at least pay you well?" Holtzclaw filled his own pail with water from a mineral water spigot.

"They pay me nothing," said Trahlyta. "Only lesser beings need rules and rewards. The catfish sweep the riverbeds because I give them peaches from my orchard. The rain falls because I promise it release."

The work went quickly for two collaborators. At the princess's suggestion, they used the chalybeate waters, which provided superior scouring power. The greenish gold foamed up when the water was applied, and a rag wiped the white residue away with little effort. Soon, any conspicuous traces of the moon maidens' auric tailings were gone.

"But there's a lot more gone through the pipes," said the princess. "It's swirled down into the lake and it has ended up in great drifts. We can clean up here all we like, but there will still be gold in the water."

"Sounds like quite a mess."

"It's a thousand years of work, James. A rainstorm couldn't get rid of it all, and a rainstorm is all that I can do."

"Then we've done you a favor, putting a lake over the gold."

"You've only swept the mess under the rug," she said. "But yes, you have done me a favor, which I intend to repay."

Holtzclaw picked up one of the towels that had fallen when the moon maidens vanished. The towel was not the monogrammed ter-rycloth variety provided by the hotel; instead, it was very thin, made of a sheer cobalt-blue silk, and it glistened with moisture and tiny colors of gold.

The princess took the towel from his hand. "They're delicate, James."

"I know how to handle silk," said Holtzclaw. "My first business was a silkworm concern."

"It's spun moonlight," said Trahlyta, "or woven ice, or some such."

"No," said Holtzclaw, catching a corner. "It's silk. See the wicking on the fibers? The change in the sheen when it's turned in the light? It is perfect silk, and with a magnifying glass, I could even tell you from what province it came, if it is foreign or domestic."

"Let's assume foreign," said the princess. "Moon silk from moon silkworms."

But Holtzclaw was certain that there was nothing remarkable about their towels. They were ordinary silk. He winced as a spasm of pain pulsed in its usual place. He remembered why he'd come to the baths in the first place. "How long does it take," he asked the princess, "to become adjusted to Auraria? Or was your change so long ago that you don't remember?"

"If you exchange your blood for mineral water, Holtzclaw, your life becomes entwined with the valley. You'll be landlord to ghosts."

"They are, at least, interesting guests."

The bathing hall was silent, save for the faraway hiss of pumps and pipes. Holtzclaw wished for the soft splashing of the moon maidens, the susurration of their silver hair through the water. He wished for their footsteps across the tile and for their voiceless laughter when the ice-cold water poured down on them. He turned, expecting that the princess would have vanished silently, as was her wont. But she still stood beside of the mineral bath, contemplating the electric lights.

CHAPTER XXVII

E mmett, the apothecary, mounted a stage that he had built onto the rear of a mule-drawn cart, which was parked at the base of the lawn, along Trahlyta Boulevard. From here, he declaimed his cure in a sonorous voice punctuated by chords strummed on a fretless banjo. His white suit was gleaming and spotless in the midmorning sun. He had already attracted a crowd; Holtzclaw stood at the edge of the assembled mass.

"Step right up, step up, please don't be shy, you'll want the best view, the very best view, for what promises to be a sellout wonder. Those of you hanging near the back may not get a chance to buy—the happy folks up front will snap up all I have!"

Emmett took a deep breath.

"Professor W's Pleasant Potation and Universal Panacea Wine Draught! It's a mouthful, but if we put into its name all the wonders and works, every healing herb and efficacious effervescence that the good Professor W puts into his elixir, we'd be here half the afternoon just to say it once!

"Professor W's Pleasant Potation and Universal Panacea Wine Draught! It goes down cool and smooth, but warms your belly from within! A pleasing drink served warm with honey or over ice in a mint julep glass. Yes, every season is a fine one for this drink.

"Drink Professor W's Pleasant Potation and Universal Panacea Wine Draught at breakfast time, to oil the mechanism of your body and lubricate it to run its best! Pour it at night to still the thrumming activity of the day and replace the buzzing whine of gears with the hum of nightingales.

"Professor W's Pleasant Potation and Universal Panacea Wine Draught is known to medical science to benefit the sufferers of diphtheria, scrofula, explosive dysentery, suspended rickets, mountaineer's bends, Elder's tremblers, catarrh, athlete's-catarrh, meretricious vapors, chronic and acute bubo, Picket worms, ice mites, accreted detritus, and any other disease or disorder that gnaws at the human condition. Yes, one draught treats them all—even the ones we don't know about yet! How many diseases will never be discovered thanks to Professor W's powerful creation?

"Professor W's Pleasant Potation and Universal Panacea Wine Draught treats all female complaints, and does so better than Andrew's Cold Sarsaparilla Tea—pour that swill out the window! Professor W's Pleasant Potation and Universal Panacea Wine Draught treats male complaints better than General Tamlin's Gunpowder Thunderbolt and Strawberry Cordial—feed that useless powder to your dogs!

"Professor W's Pleasant Potation and Universal Panacea Wine Draught has a thousand uses in the marriage bed—but you already know that, clever girl!

"Now, folks here at this hotel think that they have a monopoly on cures. But what have they got? Water! Some of it smells bad. Some of it is hot; some is cold. But it's all water! See, there's Mr. Holtzclaw right now. Jimmy, it's nothing but water, is it? Your silence, sir, is deafening. Professor W's Pleasant Potation and Universal Panacea Wine Draught is an actual medicine! There are chemicals, ingredients, natural herbs, formulated cordials, and extracted essences. For the easing of your pains and the curing of your infirmities, which will you choose? A glass of water, or a potent potable?

"Professor W's Pleasant Potation and Universal Panacea Wine Draught has thirty scruples of anvil shavings to every bottle, and we activate it with a grain each of silver, gold, and lithium. What for? Why, metal magnetism! You'll gain a harmonic vibration with all the metals of the world. Know how many coins you have in your pocket without counting! Never lose an earring again! Feel which pips on the dice are heaviest—which ones want to come up in the next roll! Find a mineral spring in your own garden, and stop paying Jimmy Holtzclaw here his outrageous prices.

"And did you know that Professor W's Pleasant Potation and Universal Panacea Wine Draught will heighten your sense of smell? Food tastes better; the musk of men and the perfumes of women are more beguiling. Gold, too—gold has a smell. It is a pungent spice that comes up from the wet earth and can be smelled miles and miles away. And after a regular course of treatment with Professor W's

Pleasant Potation and Universal Panacea Wine Draught, when it has filled your body and sweetened your blood, you too can follow your nose. Your only care in life will be sharing with your fellows the benefits that you have enjoyed—long life, good taste, and prosperity—thanks to Professor W's Pleasant Potation and Universal Panacea Wine Draught. It is your elixir of full potential, your portal to a new and better life. Who will buy, and who will be left behind, a sub-human on this new, wonder-filled world?"

Emmett strummed the banjo—it was close enough to being in tune—and lit into a rough rendition of the medicine show standard "I Heard the Voice of a Pork-chop." All the while, his assistants, dusty-faced boys, collected money by the fistful and handed out bottles of Professor W's Pleasant Potation and Universal Panacea Wine Draught. The elaborate, lithographed label folded out into a length of paper as long as a man's arm, where the whole of Emmett's speech was printed, word-for-word.

Emmett reached the end of his song, then threw his banjo up into the air; it twirled twice before he caught it and strummed the final, resolving chord. The crowd clapped approvingly. Emmett stepped off the platform and reached for a bottle of his draught.

Holtzclaw threaded through the crowd and addressed himself to Emmett. "Do you think we could have a brief word?"

"Why sure, Jimmy!" Emmett patted him on the back. "Let's head over there for a minute." They were ten steps towards the indicated spot when Emmett turned back over his shoulder and cried, "Jimmy Holtzclaw wants to silence me! What can he be afraid of? That no one will need to buy his bath tickets? That no one will need to stay at his pricey hotel?"

The crowd pressed closer to the vending wagon, eager to rid themselves of dollar bills. More cases of Professor W's Pleasant Potation and Universal Panacea Wine Draught were unloaded from the wagon. Money flew everywhere, and Holtzclaw's innards rumbled with anger.

"Now, Jimmy," said Emmett, when they were out of earshot of the crowd. "What can I do for you?"

"You can stop sullying my name in your pitch."

"You can't take it personally; it's just business," said Emmett. "You're a good patsy when I'm up on the wagon, so stuffy and fussy. We're still friends, Jimmy!"

"Then at least stop peddling your dangerous wares to these people, some of whom are already ill."

"There's nothing dangerous about it. It's Pharaoh's Flour, Effervescent Brain Salts, and plenty of alcohol—a mash of whatever's just out of season. A scruple of this, some grains of that. I stir it up in Mrs. McTavish's bathtub, water it down with some of your spring water. There's nothing dangerous about any of that."

"If not in the ingredients, there is danger in your sales pitch," said Holtzclaw. "You promise the moon, but what do you deliver?"

"These people are betting a dollar that somewhere in here is an aid for their infirmities. Maybe there is, after all. And if nothing comes of it, well, at least there is a lot of liquor in every bottle."

"You can't sell a panacea in one bottle!" said Holtzclaw, throwing his hat to the dirt.

"Oh, can't you? Then what's this lake?" said Emmett. "Solve our gold fever and our livelihoods! New neighbors and new things to buy! Some pumpkins! We don't need your help to turn out all right. Look at those people, throwing their money at me. All they want is a song-and-dance, a little liquor, and a fancy label."

Holtzclaw was still seething when his stormed into the New Rock Falls, looking for supper or succor. He had been insulted, but insults had rolled off him before. More infuriating was that Emmett's business was more profitable than his own, and with so little effort.

Inside of the New Rock Falls, all was dark and still. The piano was silent; Hulen the plat-eye was abroad. Holtzclaw's anger felt too hot for this dim, cool place. A single bulb illuminated two bowls that were already waiting on a table. Shadburn hovered over his own, picking out the mushrooms and eating them first.

"They are best enjoyed alone," said Shadburn. "They have a complicated flavor; it isn't right to bury it with too many other tastes, you see."

Holtzclaw would have preferred to eat by himself, letting his sour thoughts run out, but propriety did not permit it. He joined Shadburn at his table and tucked in to a bowl of sweet potato stew. There was restorative, heartening power in Abigail's recipe—perhaps it could be mixed with a little liquor and poured into bottles with a fancy label: Ms. Thompson's Local Restorative. It sounded simpler than pleasure boats and moon maidens.

Holtzclaw told Shadburn about Emmett's universal panacea. "Do you think that we can force him to stop his medicine show? He's on our land; we can move him off."

"If you trim the weed in one place, he will sprout in another."

"He's not our only weed," said Holtzclaw. "The golf course is drowning in them. The gardeners cannot tame the grass. Scrub pines sprout overnight on the fairway. Ivy gets into the sand traps."

"It's a ridiculous sport," said Shadburn, "and we don't have the weather for it. If you were fishing instead of playing golf, at the end of the day, you'd have a fish or two for supper. What do you have after an afternoon of golf? Fewer golf balls."

"So, should I let the land go fallow?" said Holtzclaw. "Or try to turn it to some higher and better use?"

"Why not put in a sawmill?" said Johnston or Carter, emerging from the shadows at the far side of the restaurant.

"Or a tannery?" said the other, pulling himself into the light.

"This is a private establishment, gentlemen," said Shadburn, upstarting. "If you want to speak with me or my associate, you may make an appointment."

"You have a poor history of keeping to your promises," said Johnston or Carter.

"So, we'd prefer to talk now." said the other. "Settle matters, as they stand."

"You promised us industry."

"You promised us busy trains three times per day."

"And we have a growing hotel," said Shadburn. "A great gala planned that will stuff your trains with money-laden people."

"Yet there are hills of virgin timber," said Johnston or Carter.

"Many furred creatures that scamper below them," said the other.

"So why will you not build a sawmill?"

"Or a tannery?"

"None of those things need a lake," said Shadburn. "Any money we put in to them would not reinforce the dam. Thus, they have only secondary value, and we have not cared to trouble ourselves with them."

"That is nonsense," said Johnston or Carter.

"You've broken your word to us."

"We may be forced to take legal recourse."

"Unless recompense is offered."

The railroad twins paused.

"There is gold, of course," said Johnston or Carter.

"Gold is the best industry of them all," said the other.

"If we had mineral rights to certain places, we could overlook the matter of broken promises."

"There would be more than enough to repay our patience and expenses."

"So, it is not about sawmills or tanneries, then," said Holtzclaw.

"Where there is gold, all other pursuits become unimportant," said Johnston or Carter.

"Even sawmills and tanneries," said the other.

"Even railroads. Even hotels and mineral springs."

"Gold is the best industry of them all."

"You see, Holtzclaw?" said Shadburn. "You see how gold has destroyed these people. They could have been sharp businessmen, but their lust for gold has distracted them, blinded their business sense. They'll trust a man's promises—build him a railroad, even—while knowing nothing of his character or his motives, and they will not even insist on a contract. And for all of their work, what have they gotten?"

"A tidy profit on the dam," said Johnston or Carter.

"Paid in gold."

"That's a paltry sum," said Shadburn. "They could have done so much better, couldn't they, Holtzclaw? I tried to turn them towards honest work—I tried to improve them just like the rest of this town.

But they have sold it all for eight colors of gold. A macule floating upon my wonderful work."

Johnston or Carter donned their hats in perfect synchronization. In the great sea of silence that had formed between Holtzclaw and Shadburn, their departure made only a ripple.

Two bowls of sweet potato stew cooled on the table; spoons lay idle. Holtzclaw studied each floating morsel in the stew. Finally, he scooped up a spoonful and swallowed. What use was there to storm and rage, in crashing against the bulwark of his circumstances? His fortunes were inseparable from the dam, the lake, the Queen of the Mountains, the Maiden of the Lake. They would all flourish or flounder together.

Holtzclaw reached the end of his bowl without looking up, and he saw that Shadburn, too, had finished; he leaned back in his chair and emitted a satisfied belch.

"Do you think that they'll sue?" Holtzclaw asked Shadburn at last.

"It would be foolish. What would they seize?"

"Money, land, the hotel..."

"All impermanent things. They hardly even count as possessions. You can't carry them with you, and thus, they fall out of your possession. Besides, they cannot seize what no one owns."

Holtzclaw was trying to clear his head with a brisk walk on the treadmill, but he was intercepted by an old woman. She had been looking for him all day, she said. She wept against Holtzclaw's shoulder. He extended both arms to their full length, then bent them at the elbow, forming the loosest shape that could still be called a comforting embrace.

"It is just so horrible, Mr. Holtzclaw. I have been cruelly, cruelly defrauded. I am ruined! Positively ruined!"

"Mrs. Piscene, if you can compose yourself, you can tell me your story. I will get us some coffee."

"Tea," said Mrs. Piscene, who then emitted another wet sob into Holtzclaw's collarbone.

Holtzclaw fetched a tea service from the kitchen. He had hoped to return with Abigail as well and press her into service comforting Mrs. Piscene, but she was not to be found. Mrs. Piscene's tears still leaked from her eyes at a constant rate. She stood, moving to accept another embrace, but Holtzclaw waved her back into her seat.

"Now, you'll tell me what has happened," said Holtzclaw. "Please."

"Well, I had such a strange dream," said Mrs. Piscene. "There was a river, and brown fish swam in it. One was very ugly—he had whiskers. He came right up to me, up out of the water, and put his head on a flat rock just in front of me, and he spit up gold!"

"That is a strange dream," said Holtzclaw, "but, I gather, not particularly unusual in the valley."

"That is not what Mr. Barren said," said Mrs. Piscene. "I went to his booth up in the hollow."

The camp, which had been established to house the dam and railroad workers, still flourished in Asbestos Hollow. While one could play faro for pennies at the Queen of the Mountains, the Asbestos Hollow camp offered bigger stakes, and when a guest tired of mineral water and whiskey, he or she could buy more potent potables.

Mr. Barren had listened to the dream that Mrs. Piscene recounted, asking her to close her eyes and replay it across the stage of her eyelids.

"He asked about markings on the stone," she said. "Scooped depressions that looked unnatural, a pair of lines or fissures, approximately parallel. I'd seen the very thing! Mr. Barren became excited. We went a mile from the workers' camp, to the shores of a river—a creek really."

"Did he rob you there, by the river?" said Holtzclaw. "Did he make threats against you?"

"The opposite," said Mrs. Piscene. "We searched for half an hour, and then Mr. Barren pointed to a large, flat rock. It wasn't quite the place I had seen in my dream, but we lifted that rock, and there was a cache of treasure! A very small one, yes, but real gold. There were five coins, two plain rings, a little bag of dust—a hundred dollars' worth. Mr. Barren was no less astounded than I, or so he acted.

He offered to split the treasure equally between the genius and the guide, neither of whom would have succeeded without the other."

"I put the treasure into a corner of my Saratoga trunk. That night, I had another dream. I went deep into the earth along a set of stairs. Miles and miles I walked, so hungry and thirsty. Then, when I felt that I would faint, the stairs ended at a wall of gold at the shore of an underground lake."

Holtzclaw shifted in his chair. "You have no family roots here, do you? Were your parents mountain stock? Did they pass this way in their emigration?"

"No, we are from New Jersey," said Mrs. Piscene. "I took the dream to Mr. Barren. He knew of a cave that matched in some details. Its entrance was a sharp decline, at the angle of a staircase, and natural rocks that were stacked and broken, like stairs. He had explored only so far; a rock fall blocked the passage. To clear it would take money and manpower."

"And this is when he took your money," said Holtzclaw. "You gave him an investment, and then he absconded with it."

"Oh no, not at all! I gave him money, yes. I put in the treasure that I had found with him, and half of what I'd brought, besides—that's five hundred dollars. The next day he already had a find. He and his brother and two other men were digging. They pushed through the wall of rock, where they found a man's finger bones! There were traps and trip wires, thin reed mats stacked over spiked pits. He could not take me there. It was too dangerous. But they had found something."

Mrs. Piscene's voice had dropped very low. Holtzclaw found himself leaning forward, straining to hear, as though he were enthralled. "Mr. Barren opened a battered chest and showed me a thousand-dollar cache! All worked gold. Coins, rings, bracelets. I could choose which half I liked. I offered to let him keep the whole as a future investment, but he said that it was unneeded. He and his workers had enough supplies for the moment."

"This is very curious," said Holtzclaw. "Mr. Barren hasn't robbed you of anything yet. Instead, he's returned your whole investment now, by my calculations."

"So you see why I trusted him," said Mrs. Piscene. "I could hardly carry all that he had given me. I put the treasure in my trunk, with the rest of my money, all together.

"The third night, another dream. But this was a nightmare. I was being carried away in a flood, buffeted against rocks and under waves, barely able to breathe. Around me were many creatures—silver women, pale and lean, with long ears and rabbit faces. I ran to see Mr. Barren.

"He told me that he was glad that I had come; I must have seen in my mind's eye that there had been a terrible accident. His brother had been caught by a trap inside that treasure tunnel. A heavy stone loosed by tripwire smashed every bone in his hand. I felt complicit in that man's suffering. My dream portended the revenge of the deep ghosts. The trap was only their first sign, but my dream revealed the final fate of all who had sullied themselves with the stolen treasure. I asked him how I could save us. I only wanted to do what was right, whatever that was, and save us all. He told me that all the money that had been taken from the tunnel must be returned. The corruption would have spread to other money I had. This money could be cleansed and returned. But I must bring every coin, even the ones in my purse, even the ones sewn into the hem of my dress, because if any of it was not brought to be cleaned, the deep ghosts would not be appeased. I ran to the hotel and returned with the whole of my money in a sack. I gave it over to him willingly and waited with anxiety as Mr. Barren performed the cleansing."

"That was a mistake," said Holtzclaw.

"I know that now," she said, "but in the fear and guilt of the moment, I was bewildered! He told me that I had done the right and noble thing. His rituals were successful and the corruption was dissipating. Already his brother was starting to recover. He returned the sack with my money to me, and it felt just as heavy as before. I was told not to open the sack for three full days, to let the energies ferment and the doom to evaporate, or some nonsense. I agreed, of course, but away from Mr. Barren's tent, my mind began to operate more clearly. With the promise of treasure behind them, his words were suspicious. I waited one day then opened the sack. What should I find?"

"That, at last, you had been robbed," said Holtzclaw.

"Yes, at long last!" said Mrs. Piscene. "Inside that bag was just scrap and junk. So that is how I come before you in my destitute condition. I was too credulous, too eager, too compassionate. Mr. Barren bought my trust with two deliveries of treasure; he calculated his scheme to ruin me utterly. I was greedy, I will admit, but he was greedier."

"You want us to pursue this Mr. Barren?" said Holtzclaw. "He is gone, of course; he fled the moment that he delivered to you that sack worthless of possessions."

"Then there is no recourse for me," said Mrs. Piscene. "A poor, penniless woman. How shall I pay my expenses at your hotel? What will become of me?"

"The forgiveness of your debt to the hotel is within my power," said Holtzclaw. "You'll receive no bill from us, for lodging or board. You cannot very well return either to us, nor could we repossess them."

"That is very kind of you, Mr. Holtzclaw. And for travel? How shall I make it home, without the kindness of strangers?"

"I can give you some money," said Holtzclaw. "A little charity, from my own pocket."

"If it's enough for a second-class sleeping ticket," said Mrs. Piscene, "then I'll be most grateful. Those hard benches in the third-class car are so hard on an old woman's back."

She looked up at him, her eyes shining, and held out her hand.

"It was a fantastically complicated scheme," said Holtzclaw to Ms. Rathbun, aboard the Maiden of the Lake.

"You're proud of what you've done then," said Ms. Rathbun. "Of your charity."

"Yes, I suppose."

"It was no sacrifice for you. The money you gave her was from your underground find, yes? It was not earned money."

"There is no difference, is there?" said Holtzclaw.

"Oh, there is no difference in how money is earned, but there is a difference in how it is spent. And you, Holtzclaw, have wasted it."

"Charity is never a waste. Uplift can never be a waste."

"You've never heard the name Piscene? It's a fishing concern out of the Northeast. It has a thousand boats plying the waves. Its nets sweep the ocean clean."

"Coincidence," said Holtzclaw.

"That woman is the owner. She was here to take a rare piece of leisure. The society papers reported on it, because the woman is not known to spend a cent that she does not mean to, especially for a pleasure trip. There was a rumor she was here for some important business deal."

"How would such a savvy businesswoman fall for the tricks of a common charlatan like this Mr. Barren?"

"She wouldn't. She would be much more likely to apply those same tricks to elude a hotel bill. The Charleston Chomp, the Cincinnati Slip-off, the Asheville Attitude, the Fitzgerald Flip. The rich are the most skillful at keeping their money."

Holtzclaw raised a finger in protest, then let it fall. In retrospect, he saw how easily he'd been deceived. Mrs. Piscene had used up every trick, and only to get out of a hotel bill. It was such a small thing to a rich person like her, and yet it was a hammer blow to Holtzclaw, a hammer blow against the dam.

"I'm sorry, Holtzclaw," said Ms. Rathbun. "Maybe you'll consider this instructive. Another precious lesson."

"That's the whole of my life," said Holtzclaw. "Mistakes and failures and lessons."

"But there are galas, too," said Ms. Rathbun, cheerfully. "Tell me about the one that you're hosting at the Queen of the Mountains. I've seen the posters."

"Please, forget it for the moment. That is an unrelated matter, at an entirely different hotel. The Maiden of the Lake needs our attention. We must set a plan..."

"That's no way to talk, if you are hoping to have a spectacle! Are you expecting a good crowd to come in from Milledgeville? Have you sent invitations to your seasonal guests?"

"I have to send invitations to the guests that are already here?"

"Oh yes, they demand it. Who will be the entertainment?"

"I am exchanging letters with the impresario for Dasha Pavlovski. But let's put it aside, because compared to our joint enterprise here on this boat, and all the gold we've invested in it..."

"Dasha Pavlovski!" said Ms. Rathbun. "Why, that's quite the coup, if you succeed."

"I had half-decided to give up on him and get some local entertainment instead. You can see Dasha anywhere."

"Oh no, you must strive for Dasha. He only appears at the best venues. They did not even get him at Saratoga. What will you do for refreshments?"

"We'll have bottle after bottle of wines," said Holtzclaw. "I have booked a train car full of them. Some rare and ancient clarets, too. I'll set some aside for us. Since it is a special occasion, there will be moonshine, too. But let's get back to the Maiden..."

"No one will be interested in such a rural drink," said Ms. Rathbun.

"I mean, the shimmering bowls that knock a grown man flat with his dreams. A unique experience, to be sure."

"I know."

"Then what would you serve instead?"

"Mint juleps," said Ms. Rathbun.

"In all my time here in the valley," said Holtzclaw. "I have never been offered a mint julep."

"Well, we shouldn't want to continue the disappointment. And it is a costume ball, yes? What will you wear?"

"How about a paired costume, for the two of us?"

"Not the front and rear ends of a horse," said Ms. Rathbun.

"How about lord and lady? Shepherd and shepherdess? Knight and damsel? Pharaoh and..."

"I think I shall be Queen of the Mountains," said Ms. Rathbun. "Do you think anyone else will pretend to that title? I have a splendid dress in mind."

"And I would be the King of the Mountains?"

"Why yes, if you would like to think so. I would not object at all."

Ms. Rathbun tilted her head. Candlelight caught her profile, and her beautiful face was framed in fire. Then she stood up, with her hands clasped before her. Holtzclaw stood, too, involuntarily, a social reflex. It was the end of their meeting, and Holtzclaw bade her goodnight with two kisses, in the air, to each side of her ears, and she returned them in the same ethereal medium.

And then, he was outside of her chamber, and she was within, and nothing had progressed, nothing had been solved. Her able command of the Asheville Attitude had compelled him to leave unsatisfied. The splendid doors were shut fast behind him.

As Holtzclaw was walking down the gangplank, heavy with regrets over what he should have said to his partner, one of the hotel's steam launches raced past, turning the calm lake into a foaming sea. Its paddlewheel threw a high tail of water into the air behind it. Holtzclaw heard happy laughter—a man's and a woman's, intertwined. When the boat passed, Holtzclaw was courageous enough to whisper a few naughty words toward the fading vessel, but they were lost in the engine noise and the spray.

Then the steam launch exploded.

A high-pitched whine preceded the main burst, then a tremendous force burst in every direction in an instant. A percussive wave rocked the Maiden of the Lake. Holtzclaw ran back aboard and lowered the ship's runabout, a white craft that was meant mainly as a decoration. But it was seaworthy; within a minute, he was on the oars, pulling with full strength towards the disaster.

Twisted shards of metal and splinters of wood bobbed on the waves; among them, a man and a woman climbed over each other, trying to stay afloat. Holtzclaw held out an oar and pulled the two grasping survivors to the runabout. He retrieved the man first, then the woman. To land her and her sodden skirts, Holtzclaw had to grab her beneath the armpits. Were it not an emergency, it would have been indecorous.

"Was there anyone else? Any others with you?" said Holtzclaw to the dazed pair.

"No, just the two of us," said the man.

"Out for an evening stroll, just a stroll," said the woman.

"We'll get you back to the hotel," said Holtzclaw. "You're very lucky. It's a wonder the flesh wasn't scalded from your bones. Why were you going flat out?"

"We had to go fast," said the man, "to keep up with the green light."

"Such a lovely evening," said the woman, "and such a lovely light."

Holtzclaw rowed towards the lights of the hotel, where a crowd had gathered at the lakeshore. No other launch had come up to meet him—they didn't expect survivors. When the crowd saw the two rescued guests, dazed and damp but largely unharmed, they gave a smattering of halfhearted applause and dispersed. But the Billing, Wooing, and Cooing Society members were ashen and aghast, as though they'd seen two corpses. They saw the reputations of one of their finest matches in ruins.

"So the two of you were out, alone, in that boat?" said Almeda, the Reader of Mysteries, of the Billing, Wooing, and Cooing Society.

"There was a green light," said the man. "Isn't that enough of a chaperone?"

"Not at all," said Vera, the Tender of the Entwined Rose and Briar.

"Not at all," said Luella, the Poetess of the Stirring Heart.

"We rescind our approval," said Almeda. The three yellow-hatted women made gestures with their hands like a bird flying away. "The birds of happiness will coo no more for you."

The Billing, Wooing, and Cooing Society fluttered away. The rescued couple, leaning on each other, hobbled back towards the hotel. Holtzclaw stood alone, rubbing his aching shoulders. One by one, the electric lights ringing the lawn were ignited. Each one, as it burst into brilliance, erased a constellation from the evening sky.

CHAPTER XXVIII

Holtzclaw walked arm-in-arm with a beautiful woman in a dress of midnight blue, spangled with silver stars. They took a turn around the treadmill—not the walkway of the Queen of the Mountains, but a wide path on the upper deck of the Maiden of the Lake. A soft rain began to fall, and the laughing pair ducked inside. They were at the top of the grand staircase, overlooking the humming atrium. Men in fur and women in silk opened their purses to spill rivers of gold. Cascades of gold dust fell from cracks in the glass-domed ceiling. The air was hazy with metal. Holtzclaw turned towards his lovely companion, and she turned to him. Her rabbit face broke into a smile; her nose wiggled joyfully. She placed a four-fingered hand on his cheek; her slender, narrow fingers were cold on his skin.

The walls shook with the sound of an explosion. The boat rocked, tossed by a sudden wave. In an instant, the world reversed. Gilding and furniture splintered to pieces. Glassware vanished into a hail of icy fragments. Nothing that Holtzclaw had bought and paid for was left intact.

Holtzclaw's companion tumbled forward; he caught her in his arms. Her silver hair was sticky with shimmering black fluid. Water roared. The current was pulling them down.

Holtzclaw could not shake this dream when he awoke. It persisted at the corner of his mind, even after he drank a glass of claret and a full pitcher of mineral water. He thought of a bath, but he was not sure which waters were prescribed for nightmares. So, Holtzclaw drew on an overcoat and set out for a midnight constitutional.

He found himself on top of the dam, which was farther than he had intended to walk. To the north, the lake stretched for miles; to the south, there was a steep drop to the Sky Pilot's cabin and the craggy emptiness of the dry Terrible Cascade. Water bubbled through the spillway and down the flume, crossing the line between these contrasting environments. From a single spot, he could contemplate the quiet stillness of the lake; then, needing only to turn his head, he could revel in the sense of smallness that only deep drops and great distances can provide.

But this was as much comfort as the dam could give him. The earth was damp under his feet. Somewhere below were winces of strain. The railroad twins had all but confessed to shoddy work, and Holtzclaw did not know enough about dam construction to catch their deception before now. To keep their artificial lake locked inside its borders for more than another few seasons, he and Shadburn would have to build another dam right on top of the old one. And that would take a mountain of money.

"A pleasant night?" The princess peered from over the top of the flume, resting her arms on its wooden side. She was standing in the water flowing to the powerhouse, unperturbed by the strong current.

"Unpleasant dreams," he said. "Indigestion, I think." He leaned against the dry side of the flume. The wooden supports sagged under his weight, and he backed away.

"Many times," said the princess, "bad dreams are blamed on indigestion when they're the work of revengeful fish ghosts."

"Why, I have saved the lives of many fish," said Holtzclaw. "Shadburn and I have given them a beautiful, safe place in which to cavort and breed."

"It isn't their lives or their deaths that they are revenging," said the princess. "Life and death are common and natural to them. Do you know how many fish are in this lake? Two million and eight! Now it is two million and six, because two small fry have been swallowed by a hungry predator. Now it is two million and thirty two, because catfish eggs are awakening."

"Then why do the fish want revenge?"

"Their ghosts are not free to float to the sea. That is where they dissolve. That is where all the dead go, because that is where all water is meant to be. Water has a cycle, but the dead cannot follow it. They stay in the ocean and are worked into particles. All the minerals of the earth go, too. Every grain of gold will one day be held in suspension in seawater—or should be—and the sea snails will be the richest creatures of them all."

"So, the fish ghosts torment me with nightmares so that I will set them free?" said Holtzclaw.

"No," said the princess. "They torment you because they have nothing better to do."

"At least, they aren't attacking the dam. It has enough enemies, natural and unnatural."

"Oh, they are doing that, too. They have no love for the dam. The wild wonder fish carry it away one mouthful at a time."

"You said we weren't enemies!" Holtzclaw wanted to stamp his feet, to punctuate his indignation, but he stopped himself. His petulance might weaken the dam.

"We have a common goal. To see the land scoured clean of gold. We disagree on methods, but my way is better."

"What is your way, princess?"

"To open the mountain and let the waters out."

"And then what will happen to the Queen of the Mountains? The Maiden of the Lake?"

"We will come through just fine," she said.

Her pronouncements were rarely soothing to his peace of mind.

Holtzclaw took a high, circuitous route back to the hotel. He was still working through the lingering effects of indigestion and fish ghosts. The road was reminiscent of the Lost Creek Valley in the days before the lake. Desire paths, worn by ranging tourists searching for shortcuts, weaved between old trees, and the sound of running water filled the air. Creeks dropped through stones, rills passed over the road, springs gushed from openings in the mountain. The moon shone between the branches and showered Holtzclaw's way with silver light. From somewhere below, in a hollow carved by a branch of the river, came the sound of joyful laughter.

He was near one of the places where he'd seen the moon maidens at play. The site hadn't been drowned by the lake. Holtzclaw found the rough staircase that led from the path down to the short stone wall at the water's edge. A cold breeze blew back against him, the breath of the valley across the face of the water. The laughter continued from upstream. Holtzclaw hunkered down, carefully following the inner edge of the wall, towards the rocks in the bend.

When he came close enough to make out the figures that gamboled over the rocks, he realized that he had made a terrible mistake. Instead of moon maidens, he saw young people from the hotel: heirs and heiresses, prodigals, dandies, scions, and society artistes. Their cries and giggles turned into the barnyard braying of animals.

Holtzclaw turned to creep away along the path he'd taken, but he slipped on wet leaves, flailed, and tumbled into mud. His graceless fall caused a commotion. The tourists rushed to investigate.

"It's that mopey fellow!" said one of the young men. "Always hanging around, talking like a book. What's his name? Handclaw, right? Or Wholecloth?"

"Out for a peek, are we?" said another.

"Wanted to catch some youngsters at their game?" called one of the women.

"Raspberries, raspberries!" All the bathers made rude noises with their lips, then panted with paroxysms of laughter.

"Say, you're not here to spy for those dusty women in the yellow hats, are you? What do they call themselves? The Cooing and Booing Society?"

"Billing and Cooing Society! Like birds."

The youngsters danced around, each making an idiosyncratic impression of a bird: flapping arms like wings, jutting their necks back and forward, hopping from one foot to the other.

"Caw-caw! Ku-ku! Ka-ka-ka-chu!"

"That's not what they do," said Holtzclaw. "It's not even a good impression. But I don't mean to defend them; I'm no ally of theirs."

"Well, say whatever you want to them," said one of the women. "Doesn't matter in the least to me." She curled around the outstretched arm of an eligible bachelor in a striped bathing suit—one of the hotel's standard issue, far off hotel grounds.

"Why are you even here, Holdcow?"

"It's just ... I thought you were someone else."

"Oh, so we're not good enough? You wanted to peek at someone else? Wanted a better view than what you got?"

"That is not it," said Holtzclaw, "that is not it at all."

"You think we should leave?" said one of the young men. "You've got no right to tell us to leave. It's going to take a lot more than some sad word to make us go. No one's trespassing."

"If you're going to tell us it's not right, or not decent," said one of the women, "then you can just eat a fig."

"I don't mean to spy on anyone," said Holtzclaw, "or chase anyone away. You can stay. I had just wondered, when I heard you..."

One of the youngsters dashed out of the calf-high water and clambered onshore. "Brr! Sure got cold!" Others followed him, clustering for warmth.

"A powerful frost just then!"

"Like ice is coming down the river."

The trees hissed with a sudden breeze that stung at damp hands and feet and faces. "Mr. Wholecloth, you brought some frosty winds with you."

The youngsters scurried back along the shoreline path, leaving Holtzclaw shivering and alone. Flakes of gold curled at the edge of the water.

At first, Mother Fresh-Roasted only had a wooden tray from which she sold interesting rocks to children: staurolite, also called a fairy cross; flat worry stones, with a depression made in them for the friction of concerned thumbs; arrow heads and petrified wood.

Then she bought a pushcart and expanded her selection to include devices and remedies for helping young girls dream of their future husbands. One popular set included a red wax candle and a polished metal bowl. The bowl was filled with mineral water, then the candle was lit, and after it had burned for some time with the girl's thoughts fixed upon her future mate, the candle was tipped above the bowl, wax fell into the water, and the cooled, abstract shape was interpreted as a clue to the future mate's profession. An additional guidebook helped to decipher these shapes, because not all of them resolved into well-known implements. Some were ancient forms, some purely symbolic, and a very few were outright unlucky. An adaptation was available for boys who wanted a hint as to how they would die, with most symbols pointing to violent misadventure.

On the strength of these sales, Mother Fresh-Roasted had opened open a sprawling emporium, to which Holtzclaw traveled to ask for her guidance. Her store consisted of three buildings connected by breezeways. Enormous porches provided ample rocking chairs where customers could enjoy a refreshing glass of Professor W's Pleasant Potation and Universal Panacea Wine Draught or a bottle of Dr. Pep. Children and adults gorged themselves on sticky-sweet confections: maple fudge, sugar crystals, whirly twists, and poppy rocks.

Holtzclaw envied Mother Fresh-Roasted. Her products were local—the glowing honey from her fire-bees, ice cream egg sundaes laid by snowball hens, daguerreotypes of tourists posing with her pet deer, from whose back grew a peach in full fruit. And Holtzclaw was certain that she had fewer problems with baronesses than he did. She needed no agents or partners, and her establishment was always humming with conversations and coins.

He looked for Mother Fresh-Roasted among the penny whistles, tins of stewed tomatoes, and corn-husk brooms. He paused in front of a rack of gold-prospecting supplies. A girl was trying to reach a tin pan on a high shelf. A pair of boys selected a full kit: picks, shovels, pans, leather pouches to hold collected flakes, and printed instructions.

Holtzclaw put a hand on each of the boys' shoulders. "Little friends, I can assure you that your search will be fruitless. The geology of the land, after the installation of the lake, and the peculiar mechanism by which gold builds up in this valley, precludes any big strikes."

The boys looked at each other in bewilderment.

"All I'm saying is, it's a waste of time," said Holtzclaw. "Save your money, or buy candy which you can resell to the people crowded around the spring houses."

"That's boring," said one of the boys.

"It's a much more sound plan for a profitable business," said Holtzclaw, "and a much better way to spend an afternoon."

The boys took no heed of him; they scurried away to make their purchases.

Holtzclaw found Mother Fresh-Roasted at last in the produce section of her store, which had large wooden bins holding corn, beans, nuts, mushrooms, ramps, and sweet potatoes. In one bushel were just-picked sheep-fruit; they made soft bleating noises, as though in their sleep.

"Sweet potatoes!" said Holtzclaw. "You think you can sell sweet potatoes? We cannot give them away at the hotel."

Mother Fresh-Roasted picked one up. "Then you must be doing something wrong. Why wouldn't someone want a sweet potato like this?" It was a collection of several potatoes that had grown together. From a certain angle, it looked like a person, with a body, two stumpy legs, and two arms, one considerably longer than the other. Mother Fresh-Roasted held it like a doll, rocked it in her arms, and the sweet potato wiggled its limbs and cooed. "What did you need, Holtzclaw? I'm very, very busy, you see. The snowball hens are running a fever, and unless I give them ice cubes to sit on, their ice cream chicks will just be puddles of milk."

"We are planning a gala, you see, at the hotel. No expense spared."

"That's no way to run a profitable business."

"It's our only chance at it. We must plan something spectacular, something that will draw a great crowd from far away. You seem to have a knack for such things."

"How about a quartet of self-playing instruments?" Mother Fresh-Roasted pointed to a throng of listeners crowded around a stage. Two auto-banjos, an auto-dulcimer, and an auto-autoharp broke into a lively rendition of "Leather Britches." Some of the listeners, still in their traveling finery, linked arms and swung in rough, failed approximations of square-dance forms.

"Mechanical?" asked Holtzclaw. "Clockwork?"

"Mechanical!" said Mother Fresh-Roasted. "Of course not, Holtzclaw! This isn't a factory. This is Auraria. We run on spirits, not steam."

"Spirits can play the banjo and the dulcimer and the autoharp?"

"They can be taught. And anyone can play the autoharp."

"Well, they are pleasant enough and crowd-pleasing. Let's have them. What else?"

Holtzclaw placed his order for poppy rocks, which he had seen at the Grayson House. He ordered moon pies, to be baked fresh the night before the gala, glowing with luminous fire honey. He requested a dozen spools of thread that would wind themselves around the ankles of true lovers, causing them to trip into each others' arms.

"I thought you'd want an elegant gala, with waltzes and lobsters," said Mother Fresh-Roasted.

"Waltzes! Lobsters! They are universal. I want a spectacle that only Auraria could make," said Holtzclaw. "The gala-goers will carry the name of the Queen of the Mountains to every club and chowhouse in Milledgeville, and we'll have a full booking for the very next week and every week thereafter. Where else could they go to see such wonders?"

"You can be certain of a spectacle," said Mother Fresh-Roasted.

"That leaves only Dasha Pavlovski. We are trying to have him for the chief entertainment, and I imagine that his handlers will have special requirements. When I'm told what they are..."

"Dasha Pavlovski? Never heard of him. Not grand, not strange. You need to talk to a friend of mine, the singing tree. Oh, but the singing tree puts on a grand show! Unique in the world!"

"If he's a tree, then how does he get on stage? Do we have to dig him up and repot him for each number?"

"He doesn't need to have his roots down all the time," said Mother Fresh-Roasted. "He gets up on his root tips and he can skitter wherever he would like. He knows all the old favorites: 'Possum on a Rail,' 'Squirrel Heads and Gravy,' 'Let the Mermaids Flirt With Me.'"

"It's just that the guests, you see, have their hearts set on a big star, like Dasha Pavlovski."

"The Singing Tree is a big star! When I was a girl, I liked no one better. I saw his branches waving in the moonshine bowl. Then one night, I went to hear him sing, and there were wisteria vines, in purple bloom, creeping all over him. Oh, I was heartbroken! But it was for the best. They are good together, the tree and the vine."

"If Dasha Pavlovski is booked, then we'll ask this tree friend of yours."

"You will have to ask him soon; his schedule fills up. Just this afternoon, he's playing two weddings and a wake."

Abigail and Holtzclaw sat at a table in the New Rock Falls. Through the windows that opened back into the hotel, Holtzclaw could see a dozen people loitering on the front stoop. The feedings at the main hotel were running slowly, a consequence of a complicated tableside flambé that was being extinguished by inexplicable cold winds. Holtzclaw had called Abigail away for a planning session, and the dining room troubles had grown in her absence.

Meanwhile, the New Rock Falls, which had plenty of open tables, had no paying customers, but a full complement of spirits. Abigail ladled up bowls of stew and filled cups with a hot drink derived from roasted sweet potatoes, all while trying to formulate a menu.

Holtzclaw read off what they'd selected so far. "Groundhog, lobster tails, oysters on the half-shell, squirrel brains, fresh-squeezed caviar, wild coney and wild venison, scalloped potatoes and sweet potatoes. If it grows here, put in on a plate; if it has to be shipped in refrigerated cars from across the country, put in on a plate. I want ramps so pungent that the paint comes off the wall. And honey like liquid gold."

"And Shadburn is agreeable to all of this?"

"He practically insists," said Holtzclaw, "as long as it benefits the hotel, and thus the brings in money that we can put into the dam. And I can think of no greater benefit, no bigger spectacle, than to invite all the local spirits and have them mingle with the most splendid elements we can find from outside the valley. I think that these tourists need to see a little of the real Auraria, with all of its eccentricities. They need to appreciate the sweet potato, as it is prepared here."

Abigail smiled. "And to top it off?"

"The *pièce de résistance*? Another barbecued sea monster, I think. And a complex cake with as many tiers as possible. Cover it in flowers. Have you picked a costume yet?"

"Won't I be wearing hotel livery, as part of the serving class?"

"Oh, no," said Holtzclaw. "Senior staff will be our guests, and no one is more senior than you. You are expected to attend and enjoy, in all your finery. If you need a stipend towards your wardrobe, it is available."

"Not necessary. But if I am not in the kitchen, it will just fall apart. Grinning faces will get into the potatoes again. We'll have a blizzard from the refrigerator."

"It's true," said Holtzclaw, "but necessary. It will be a talking point."

"Mr. Bad Thing will kick up a wind beneath the tablecloths. Ladies will be abashed."

"I forgot about him!" said Holtzclaw. "A thousand pardons. He is most welcome. Where shall I deliver his invitation? Is 'Mr. Bad Thing' his full title, or is he an esquire?"

♣

Only the Billing, Wooing, and Cooing Society was busier than Holtzclaw in the days leading up to the gala. They sought to ensure that no one of worth would attend the gala without proper accompaniment. Among their recent victories was the matching of a cross-eyed scion of a peppermint concern to an obese belle-dame of a New England dynasty. No less remarkable and thrilling was the merger of two great houses that had, until recently, been set in a frosty war of words against another. Reconciliation was made in the betrothal of a blonde-haired, blue-eyed son to a blonde-haired, blue-eyed daughter. Their union was commemorated with the signing of favorable railroad tariffs through the middle states.

An official dance card for the gala had been created in the shape of a fan. The obverse showed a picture of the Queen of the Mountains, bedecked in summer evening splendor, with the moon rising behind her; the reverse had twenty slots, where the lady could record her companion for twenty dances—three waltzes, four quadrilles, two square dances, a contra dance, an Old Country Stomp, a mazurka, a molasses boiling promenade, two serenades, a polka, two mixers, two lancers, and a big set. The Billing, Wooing, and Cooing Society members hosted instructional opportunities for the formal dances. The rural ones, Holtzclaw promised, could be learned on site. He knew this was a lie: a contra dance is no less intricate than a mazurka, and the patterns of molasses boiling were distinguishable from a complete chaos only because its able dancers never collided.

Holtzclaw brought a dance card to Ms. Rathbun aboard the Maiden of the Lake. In her presence and by her leave, he put his name in every slot, for every dance. That was as official as any contract.

He was hastening back from this personal journey when he was intercepted by the Billing, Wooing, and Cooing Society. They caught him by the elbows and turned him onto the treadmill.

"Walk with us, Holtzclaw," said Almeda, the Reader of Mysteries.

"I have so much work to do," he said. But the women would not hear of it. They boxed him in with the sweep of their dresses.

"Dearest Holtzclaw," said Almeda, the Reader of Mysteries, "we have selected a gala partner for you. She is a duchess, from one of those bellicose countries that shrink after every war in which they entangle themselves. Anemic, consumptive, shy and inelegant, but rich as they come, and an ideal match for someone like you who is ambitious, comfortable, but can't seem to get ahead financially. The simplest path for you, Holtzclaw, would be to marry into wealth. Here is your chance. She has been a difficult case, and you have been a difficult case, and we think that it is a splendid solution."

"Two special projects solved," said Vera, the Tender of the Entwined Rose and Briar.

"Yup" said Luella, the Poetess of the Stirring Heart.

"Ladies," said Holtzclaw, "I appreciate your help, and I am sure this sickly duchess is both as rich and delightful as you say. But I have already placed my name with a lady for her dance card, exclusively. I will be accompanying Ms. Elizabeth Rathbun to the gala."

The faces of the Billing, Wooing, and Cooing Society members flushed purple.

"You have done this outside of our assistance," said Almeda "Thus, we cannot endorse your match."

"It's of no concern to me whether you endorse it or not," said Holtzclaw.

"Oh, it will be. It will be of concern," said Almeda, "if you do not escort our duchess to the gala."

"Grave, deep, utmost concern," said Vera.

"Big concern," said Luella.

"If the duchess is sickly, wouldn't she rather spend the gala evening taking a treatment in the baths?" said Holtzclaw.

"The baths," said Almeda, "are where people spend their idle hours between galas. Even the anemic and consumptive want to attend galas. They are the harvest time, where all that has been sown through social effort will be reaped."

"Must I be the one accompany her?"

"If not you, then someone," said Almeda. "Else her offended nation might go to war against someone, maybe against your valley. Do you want to be invaded?"

"There is little risk of that, I think," said Holtzclaw.

"There every risk that you will lose our alliance and our friendship," said Almeda. "The Billing, Wooing, and Cooing Society"—obligatory flapping gesture—"is a powerful force, Holtzclaw, and it can be with you or against you. So, if you choose to defy our match, then you must find a replacement escort for the duchess, if you want our good will."

"I don't want honorary membership in your society," said Holtzclaw, "and I don't think I need your good will. After the gala, I am certain that I will no longer need you."

"Ah, but you do, Holtzclaw," said Almeda. "Your guests are not here for your mineral waters and your fresh mountain air and your vague notions of healthfulness. They sound nice enough in your advertisements, but they are irrelevant. Even fine foods and fine clarets have a lesser role—they are necessary, but ancillary. Your guests are here to make business deals and marriage matches. They are searching, Holtzclaw, for a good marriage for an aging daughter or an incorrigible son. A corundum miner may meet a steel baroness, and social graces will broker a business deal. It is sound business, but the soundest part is to keep us, your most skilled practitioners, happy. What does Saratoga have that you do not? You have a dozen different springs; Saratoga has one. You have a shimmering lake; Saratoga has a muddy field. But whose rooms go for a higher rate? Saratoga's, because the matches are more profitable. The people are better, Holtzclaw. But you could have their success, Holtzclaw. Your resort could be even greater. A good word from us, a well-brokered match whose fame flows back into the society circles, is worth a dozen hot springs and a thousand sunrises over the lake. Now that we are clear on the structures of power, with whom will this poor duchess be attending the gala? Will you break your engagement with this Rathbun woman?"

The Billing, Wooing, and Cooing Society, on their second lap of the treadmill, came to a sudden halt as a figure barred their way.

"Oh, hello, princess!" said Holtzclaw to his rescuer. "I am very glad to see you. Yes, introductions. To the members of the Billing, Wooing, and Cooing Society"—the three women flapped their hands—"may I present Princess Trahlyta, Queen of the Mountains."

"Enchanted," said the princess, dipping at her knees in the perfect imitation of a curtsy.

"I have known very few barefoot princesses," said Almeda. "Exactly where is your kingdom?"

"These springs," she said. "The valley. An hour upriver; the same downriver. And thousands of miles beneath my feet."

"How can we help you, princess?" asked Holtzclaw.

"I've come, as always, to help you, James," said the princess. "I overheard you talking about the sad consumptive duchess, and I wanted to propose an eligible match for her. He's a royal acquaintance of mine. We've held court together many times."

"He is a guest here?" said Almeda, arching an eye. "One that has escaped our notice?"

"No, a resident of the valley," said the princess. She ducked into an alcove and led out by the hand a tall, slender man. He wore a green day suit of a satin-like fabric, accented by gold cufflinks. His hair was cut very short, in the huntsman's style. He held a handkerchief in front of his face so that Holtzclaw could not see if he was bearded or smooth-shaved.

"This is Prince Rano," said the princess. "You'll forgive him, please, for the handkerchief. He has a hay fever."

Prince Rano executed a crisp, deep bow, despite the handicap of having to keep the handkerchief in front of his face. He then raised a finger to excuse himself, then dashed away a dozen feet before loudly—and somewhat exaggeratedly, thought Holtzclaw—blowing his nose.

"A prince, you say?" said Almeda.

"Of a long and ancient line," said the princess.

"One of those Old World ones, then? There are so many that it's hard to keep track."

"He is a better creature than his origins suggest," said the princess. "I have know him for many years—purely in state and functionary roles—and he has always carried himself with a spring in his step."

"What can you say of his character?" said Almeda.

"Chiefly, he is a sociable creature," said the princess. "He loves to make music in the evenings and take healthful swims. He stretches his legs in the out-of-doors. He is a connoisseur of all foods, native and exotic, though there are some winged things he likes better than others. He has friends and relations throughout the world, and he is quick and eager to travel. I think he would be an excellent match for your sad, rich duchess."

"Are there any others that can vouch for his character besides Your Majesty?"

"I would be happy to duplicate all the praises that Princess Trahlyta has heaped upon Prince Rano," said Abigail, who stepped out from a doorway. Her hair was dusted through with Pharaoh's Flour; it coated her hands and made them ashy.

"There are two motions," said Vera.

"One more is needed, by the law," said Luella.

"And you, Holtzclaw?" said Almeda. "What do you think? Is this Prince Rano an eligible match?"

"Oh yes," said Holtzclaw, who had never met Prince Rano before in his life. "I can only sing his virtues. We are not well acquainted, but in our short but firm friendship, I have seen his worth. He is so quick-witted that when he plays at cards, he always wins, if he wants to, but he is wise and gracious enough to know that sometimes, he should let others win instead. I think a match with him would be a credit to your society."

"And a credit to your hotel?" asked Almeda.

"We will write it above the door in ten-foot letters."

"If the match is successful, you should put the faces of Prince Rano and the duchess in cartouches at the corner of our next advertisements, encircled by gold bands. It would be the best money ever spent. It would ensure the fame of your hotel for a generation. To have placed such a one as the consumptive duchess with a suitable match—what a coupe!"

"Coo-coo!" said Vera.

"Coo-coo-coo!" said Luella.

For the next few nights, at dinner, the unfolding story of the legendary match was passed around every table. The consumptive duchess, so weak in body but powerful in name, did deign to be introduced. The Billing, Wooing, and Cooing Society, supporting the consumptive duchess under her arms, met Prince Rano in the shadows beside the fireplace. The half-light concealed his face, but firelight twinkled in his large black eyes, and all were charmed.

Prince Rano and the consumptive duchess took their dinner together at a large round table; the other seats were filled out by their many chaperones. The prince had a toothache. His mouth was wrapped with gauze; his voice was an odd croak. But he talked of many subjects that interested the consumptive duchess, whose own voice was a reedy wheeze. The prince had spent many moon-filled nights paddling the river, singing his ballads and love songs. He had seen mighty cataracts and thickets of trees; he had been through swamps and dry creeks. Once he had wintered in a hollow log, shivering though the season and subsisting on what he could catch.

Prince Rano and the consumptive duchess walked through grassy meadows decorated with wild flowers. Their chaperones were just a step behind. The prince's hay fever still bothered him. His face was always screwed up as though to sneeze.

In the evening, Prince Rano and the consumptive duchess sat in a chaise lounge on one of the upper porches and looked over the lake, where fireflies drew complex signs to their allies and enemies. The consumptive duchess put her hand to the prince's cheek, to look into his eyes, but Prince Rano bashfully turned away. The Billing, Wooing and Cooing Society made much of this show of virtue and decorum. Rumors abounded that the prince was soon to propose. The Billing, Wooing, and Cooing Society gathered their accolades. Already, applications were being posted for their next matrimonial project.

One evening, after these events had become the talk of the hotel, Holtzclaw was in the midst of writing one last plea to Dasha Pavlovski's handlers; the words, though, would not come. Holtzclaw had ceased believing in them; he was considering the possibility of hiring a more spectacular local entertainer. There was a knock at the door of his little chamber. Abigail and Trahlyta stood outside, snickering like schoolgirls.

"Tonight's the night, Holtzclaw!" said Abigail. "The duchess, the prince, the bird women—they'll all get what's coming to them. You have to come see."

Trahlyta smiled as broadly as Holtzclaw had ever seen.

Prince Rano and the consumptive duchess were taking a moonlit carriage ride around the lake; the Billing, Wooing, and Cooing Society members followed in a second vehicle, at just enough of a distance to grant the couple their privacy, and yet near enough to see and approve every move.

The driver of the first coach had been told to stop at the top of the dam. Trahlyta and Abigail, with Holtzclaw in tow, hid behind the far side of the flume.

The prince and his beloved descended from the carriage. She pressed her hand to her chest; the prince gazed romantically into the vast emptiness of the Terrible Cascade. Starlight reflected in a single tear that slid down his cheek, but all the rest was lost in the night. He dropped to his haunches, took the hands of the duchess, and felt for his pocket. The Billing, Wooing, and Cooing Society plunged into raptures, holding their breath as they anticipated the splendid climax. Abigail and Trahlyta stopped their mouths with their palms.

But then, a dragonfly flashed past the prince's eyes nose. Prince Rano could not suppress his instinct. He whirled towards the morsel, tongue loosened. A moonbeam fell across his face, which was wide with happiness—the prince was a frog! Now, after just a glimpse, it was all so clear—the black bulbous eyes, the rounded snout and lipless mouth.

The consumptive duchess stepped backwards in surprise, and the throat of the frog-prince swelled up from consternation and chagrin. He fled into the lake with a flying leap, his green suit becoming slick amphibian skin.

The Billing, Wooing, and Cooing Society reached towards the consumptive duchess to draw her into their absorbing bosom, but the duchess stopped their hands. She shook free of her bonnet and her boots and leapt after the prince, into the lake. Despite her terrestrial frailty, she was an excellent swimmer, and she frog-kicked towards the green and lanky open arms of her prince. They swam in the moonlight, and powerful strokes took them farther, farther from their chaperones, farther into the waters, farther into the night.

The women in the Billing, Wooing, and Cooing Society fell, like upended dominoes, into each others arms. Employees loaded them into the baggage compartment of the carriage.

Abigail and Trahlyta linked arms and promenaded and then did molasses turns and cartwheels, over and under, time and time again, until they were giddy and nauseous. Tears streamed from their eyes.

"It was a mean-spirited trick," said Holtzclaw to them, as their glee subsided. "You should not have plucked the consumptive duchess so cruelly."

"Do you think we meant to trick anyone but those horrible bird-women?" said the Abigail.

"There is no better creature for the poor duchess than a playful frog-prince," said Trahlyta. "She'll want to stay here forever, and there will be only joy between them."

"Well, I think we've made some eternal foes of the Billing, Wooing and Cooing Society," said Holtzclaw.

"The birds," said the princess, "have always been our enemies."

A s invitations were received and supplies for the gala began to accumulate in the Queen of the Mountain's storerooms—and her treasury commensurately to dwindle—frog-duchess miscegenation was only the first of many wonderful signs. The sulfur springs poured orange juice, and the cold springs blew out blizzards. A parade of spectral forms harvested glowing mushrooms from crevices in the hallways. Sweet potatoes, though boiled and split open and filled with butter and brown sugar, arose from diners' plates and marched in military rows. Sheep-fruit roamed over the croquet lawn and ate the blades of grass down to nubs. The earth disgorged shiny yellow rocks, which were snatched up by eager capitalists of every sort; however, when they were inspected by the children that had bought kits and guidebooks from Mother Fresh-Roasted, the rocks proved to be wet clumps of mud, laced with mica.

The reaction to all these events among the guests was unbridled enthusiasm. As portents for the upcoming gala, they were hugely effective. The artifice was first-rate; the tricks were so convincing that they seemed supernatural. Holtzclaw received much unmerited acclaim. Whenever peaches tumbled from the sky to explode in a shower of juice, or whenever a rumbling from a fissure sounded like a snoring beast stirring in its sleep, the guests quivered with anticipation. They debated costumes, tried new hairstyles, and made engagements. They spent an extra hour in the baths, to fortify their constitutions for anticipated debauchery and social graces, for twenty dances in a row, for marriages and matches. To Holtzclaw, this was a great encouragement. He felt that his preparations were on the right track, and the guests were accepting them in the proper spirit.

Word spread of the fantastic artifice, and booking increased. The Queen of the Mountains was fully engaged for the week of the gala, every room occupied. Their gala would welcome the largest possible crowd. All railroad cars into the valley were heaped to capacity with people and things; Johnston and Carter could not have failed to see the profit in such an event.

Holtzclaw was supervising the installation of new shelves in the cold areas of kitchen, which were needed to store up a quantity of ice cream chicks for the gala. A sleepy Shadburn found him there.

"It's a perfect chaos, Holtzclaw," said Shadburn, scratching his head under his hat. "All of this loudness and nonsense. Is this all for the gala?"

"I've thrown the doors open. Invitations have been sent to every evolute ghost with a mailing address."

"Well, if that's what you think best. It's just so exhausting." Shadburn sighed. "As long as there's a lake, then I've done my part. I'm not needed here."

Holtzclaw did not say anything; he did not disagree with Shadburn.

"You and Ms. Thompson have everything well in hand," continued Shadburn. "I had thought that I would try something else, another project."

"Perhaps, in a few seasons, you'd have the capital to start something, if all goes well at the gala."

"A few seasons! That's such a long time away. Too many wearisome banquets between now and then. Maybe I will borrow something from the vault right now."

"You won't find a crumb, Shadburn. All of the money has been sown back into the earth, in anticipation of a great harvest. It has either gone into the dam or into the gala. "

"Oh," said Shadburn. He rubbed his cheeks with the heels of his hands, working away drowsiness. "Well that's very good, very good. I suppose that it wouldn't do it go fetch any more gold from down below, either. Couldn't do it anyway—there's a lake in the way. But perhaps I could collect a few dollars and make a start with some of these ice cream chicks. Where do they come from?"

"They hatch from snowballs that Mother Fresh-Roasted's frozen hens lay," said Holtzclaw.

"Would she sell a few of these, do you think? A franchise opportunity? What do you think the return on that would be, Holtzclaw, if we were to take it out to, say, Charleston or Augusta? Or Milledgeville? Wouldn't the people there think it just the top of fashion?"

"I wouldn't know," said Holtzclaw. "The hens probably wouldn't be happy, out of the valley."

His employer nodded. "Well, I'll think it over." Shadburn picked up two ice cream chicks from underneath—one chocolate, one strawberry. He cupped them in his hands and began to leave the cold storage room, but then turned back.

"Just to be sure—you didn't invite those foreign women to the gala, did you? The moon maidens?"

"They didn't invite us to their valley," said Holtzclaw.

On the eve of the gala, green lights drew the hotel guests and staff onto the lawn, around the kitchen. The lights orbited the building latitudinally, at irregular speeds and intervals. A bright flash from one of the orbiting green spots illuminated the awed faces.

"It's going to be quite the party, isn't it, Mr. Holtzclaw?" said one of the guests, elbowing Holtzclaw in the ribs chummily.

Holtzclaw excused himself to look for Abigail. She was organizing a brigade of employees near one of the spring houses.

"What is this, Ms. Thompson?"

"I think you know, Holtzclaw," she said.

"It could be an electrical discharge. A short in the refrigeration system or the flood lights."

"But it isn't," said Abigail. Holtzclaw nodded his head.

The green lights pulsed faster, and their brown cousins dimmed. The orbits grew larger, and Holtzclaw shuddered to see green lights spreading down the elevated corridor that connected the kitchen to the main structure of the hotel.

"If there is a fire, we will have to destroy the passageway," said Holtzclaw. "We can't let the flames spread to the hotel, not on the night before the gala. Should we get the explosives?"

Following the best building practices, the kitchen was set a little distance away from the main hotel, but it was connected to the whole by a two-story covered walkway, to provide the wait staff with an enclosed passage by which to deliver hot food to the dining room. The walkway was supported on just three arches, and at each of their keystones, there were panels to which small explosive charges could be set. In case a fire should break out in the kitchen and threaten to run out of control, the linking passageway could be destroyed quickly and cleanly, and the fire would never spread to the dining room or ballroom or guest quarters. It was the height of prudence to have enough dynamite on hand at all times.

A mournful keening began to rise from the mountainside, building in pitch and volume. The air smelled like smoke; children sniffled. A few fat raindrops fell and then, as if the sky changed her mind, a hot wind blew instead. All at once, the will-o'-the-wisps popped, like bubbles, and in their place, a low purple fire clung to the kitchen building. It roved in ectoplasmic tongues over the wood and brick and stone.

"That's it," said Holtzclaw. "We need to blow up the passage. Cut off the kitchen for loss and save the rest of the hotel."

Holtzclaw ran to the storeroom, unlocked the cherrywood box that contained the dynamite, and placed several charges into the hands of trained employees. The team approached the kitchen passage, but Abigail held up her hand to stop them.

"What, you want to try to put it out?" said Holtzclaw. "There's no time."

Abigail walked towards the kitchen building, now consumed in purple flame, and up the front steps. "Toasty, but not too hot," she said. "Just right for a cookout. Our friends, the will-o'-the-wisps, are only doing their part for the evening's entertainment. They have been bored lately. Nowhere to go, no one to lead."

She lead a few employees into the kitchen and brought out fixings for an impromptu roast. Children cooked sausages on the end of green twigs. The purple fire seemed content to crisp the edges of the treats. Holtzclaw kept an eye on the passage, to see if the flame would spread, but the flame obediently stayed confined to the kitchen building.

"It's a whale of trick," said one of the guests, again throwing an elbow towards Holtzclaw.

"No trick," he said. His hands were still clammy from the gravity of the decision he'd made, even if it had not needed to be carried out.

"I've pulled the same stunt at my own boarding house, when the guests could do with a bit of a shakeup," said another guest, joining their friendly circle, his mouth rimmed with grease. "You run the show the same way a carnival fire-eater does: it's a simple trick of converting animal fluids to vapor and thus preventing the chemical fluids from mixing with the solids."

"Quintessentially," said the first guest.

"We'd set it off with fireworks, though," said the second. "It's the sesame on the bun, Holtzclaw. Too bad you don't have fireworks, though."

"You have that dynamite," said a third guest, as the friendly circle swelled to a parliament. "What were you going to do with that?"

"You already brought it out from its wrappings. Where did you mean to set it off?"

"Say, you didn't actually mean to explode part of your hotel?"

"The fire isn't real, is it? It's only a lark, yes?"

"My trunk! My antique Saratoga trunk!"

So to prove that the hotel had never been in danger and that the dynamite was only for their entertainment, Holtzclaw was forced to sacrifice a disused spring house. The purple fire burning on the kitchen building subsided and died as more heads turned towards the main event. Dynamite—enough to bring down the kitchen passageway and thus enough to obliterate a spring house—was packed into the earth, within and around the little building. Holtzclaw let a sugared-up youngster light the fuse. Dust and dirt was scattered in a fine, even mist across all those assembled.

When the smoke cleared, a geyser of icy water rose from the crater, and a new creek started to trickle down the slopes. Guests lit cigars and called it the most stupendous trick they'd ever seen—a far sight better than that ordinary purple fire, and something that could only come to a crescendo on the morrow, at the gala.

"I think this will be the most successful party I've ever thrown," said Holtzclaw.

"Without a doubt, the most memorable," said Abigail, shaking cinders from her hair.

CHAPTER XXXI

On the day of the gala, while cooks loaded loaf after loaf into the ever-hungry oven, and employees set the tables, and drapers hung the cloths, and the carpenters laid the stage, and banjos and dulcimers tuned themselves, and animate spools made sure their threads were tangle-free, Holtzclaw slipped away to collect Ms. Rathbun. He put on his costume for the gala, which he thought would be a more gallant way to meet her. No one else was in costume yet; Holtzclaw felt, briefly, special.

When he climbed aboard, he did not take any love-apples with him, though the bush was drooping with fruit. The over-plump red globes strained at their skin; one had burst into a mess of juice. Holtzclaw kicked it into the lake before the other love-apples started to complain.

The Maiden of the Lake still only had one and a half funnels. The covering to the common area was clouded over with moisture, inside and out. A fuzzy verdancy bloomed in the corners of the dining room. But all of this mattered less, now. There would be time enough for all of these little concerns, because the Queen of the Mountains was at full capacity, and the gala would win over even the most bleak hearts to the unique charms of Auraria. After the Queen of the Mountains was flush with tourists' cash, and the dam made rock-solid, there would be an infinite time for Holtzclaw and Ms. Rathbun to complete their project and make it perfect in every detail.

Lizzie Rathbun reposed at the top of the grand staircase, waiting for him. She wore a yellow summer dress and a wide-brimmed hat. Beside her was an overstuffed canvas sack.

"It's time, Lizzie!" called Holtzclaw. "You're not in your costume!" He gestured with exaggerated hands at her modest clothing and at his elaborate dress.

"Holtzclaw, you look a fool," said Ms. Rathbun. "What are you wearing?"

"It's a fancy dress gala," said Holtzclaw. "Everyone will look a fool."

"Yes, but there are costumes that highlight foolishness and costumes that highlight elegance. One can be a princess or a queen or other regal figure, or one can be a clown or a ... whatever you are."

"I'm a pharaoh. One of the oldest and noblest monarchs."

"They wore bedsheets and head dresses?"

"It was the best I could manage," said Holtzclaw. "I rather like it."

"You didn't have to wear it here," said Ms. Rathbun.

"Well, what is your costume? Is it in your bag? Let me get it for you."

Ms. Rathbun hefted the bag over her shoulder and angled her body away from Holtzclaw. "I can manage. I won't wear my costume between here and the hotel. It's too delicate. I'll want a few minutes to sort myself when we get back to land. Besides, I don't want to be the first partygoer to arrive in the empty room. There's no fashion in it."

"There's a dressing room ready for you," said Holtzclaw. "You can choose your moment to make your arrival. It is all as you would like."

"I am not used to such cheer out of you," said Ms. Rathbun. "It's wearisome."

"I have no reason to be sad." Holtzclaw beamed as broadly as the Pharaoh Amenhotep III on the box of Pharaoh's Flour.

As Ms. Rathbun descended the gangway, slumping under the weight of the bag she carried, she lost her footing. Holtzclaw arrested her fall, indecorously and instinctively grabbing at her waist hemline, but that only served to put him in jeopardy as well. The heavy bag swung backwards like a pendulum and pulled the pair back onto the plank. They skittered onto land, their feet failing and stumbling beneath them, and then came to rest in the branches of the love-apple bush.

"You see why I didn't want to put on my dress too early?" said Ms. Rathbun, extracting herself from a precarious prisons of limbs and over-ripe fruit.

"You've traded in your legs for a fish tail," said Holtzclaw.

Ms. Rathbun heaved her cargo onto her back and set off down the path. Holtzclaw hurried to keep up with her but kept throwing backward glances towards their empty ship.

"She'll be all right, unattended?" said Holtzclaw.

"If it sinks, it's insured," said Ms. Rathbun.

"Yes, but insurance would not pay if we just abandoned her without a captain or crew. It's negligent."

"Then we'll say that you went down with the ship, Holtzclaw."

Holtzclaw was among the first gala-goers to arrive in the ballroom, and the automatic instruments struck up a jaunty swing. Behind him came a parade of costumes: Swiss girls and Scottish lassies, shepherds and highlanders, fishermen and brides, Ceres, Apollo, sailors, the Spirit of Young America, bumpkins, and enough Morning Stars and Evening Stars to white out the firmament. Holtzclaw's Pharaoh costume was well-received, but no one recognized the source—the box of Pharaoh's Flour. Holtzclaw had tried to make his costume a perfect copy, down to the fold of the loincloth and the pharaoh's laughing eyes.

The members of the Billing, Wooing, and Cooing Society, who had donned formal wings and plumed crests, were most distressed. They lamented that they had not issued more strict guidelines regarding costumes. Too many rich guests were dressed rustically, as squaws and maids and miners; too many of the Auraria natives were princes, viziers, and courtiers. Dress was meant to distinguish the higher strata of society from the lower, but the gala threw the whole ordered nature into disarray.

A quadrille was completed with acceptable, if not flawless, timing. Fire-bees on strings orbited a bowl of punch, their green tail lights blinking in rhythm with the opening strains of a mazurka. Three men and a woman, dressed as descending ranks of spades, from ace through knave, were overtaken by rivals dressed as hearts, in a game of human-sized faro. A turkey wearing a man's hat strutted into the center of the dance floor and partnered with a woman who resembled a hatchet, provisioned with a gleaming blade.

When Lizzie Rathbun entered the hall as the Queen of the Mountains, Holtzclaw's pharaonic heart flooded. She was arrayed in gold, the only suitable attire for her chosen theme. Her hat was a series of interlocking rings, polished to a high shine. Her golden hair tumbled below shoulders in cascades. The dress was a marvel of workmanship, with fine silk interwoven with threads of real gold, so that it flashed as she turned. Holtzclaw caught her hand; she danced a turn with him, then spun away. She entered into the whirl of the waltz, leaving Holtzclaw behind.

Her every footfall landed on a precise beat as she greeted barons and baronesses in demotic French. She bowed to pashas and princes, dripped disdain onto the squaws and maids and miners. A mass of admirers filled the space around her with flesh and noise. She held a champagne flute along her forearm. Effervescent bubbles tickled at her skin, and her laughter rang like money above the plunk of the automatic banjos.

At last, Holtzclaw was able to approach her near the concessions table, where the current of people gathered into eddies in front of the sweetest treats.

"Hello, Lizzie!" he said, with as much brightness as he could muster. "You are a charm, my dear. A perfect, rich delight."

"Oh, thank you, Holtzclaw. What is it that I can do for you?"

Holtzclaw leaned closer to her. Perhaps she hadn't heard him; perhaps she'd misunderstood.

"Well, I had hope to have a dance. Or, rather, all the dances. We are here together."

"That is rather presumptuous, Holtzclaw, I'm flattered, but we haven't even been properly introduced."

"Introduced? What about the Maiden of the Lake!"

"That is one sort of partnership, not another."

"There was an understanding between us," said Holtzclaw. "I invited you."

"You invited all these people. By name."

"But I invited you especially, and you accepted."

Ms. Rathbun laughed. "That was before I knew that you had created such a sparkling atmosphere here. A real spectacle. Why, you can't expect me to honor such hasty commitments, when there is finally some high society here. You've brought the life of the old capital into Auraria. Too bad it's only a one-night engagement." Between them emerged the round face of a great pasha, grinning from underneath an eggplant-colored turnip.

"But, your dance card," protested Holtzclaw. "Look at your dance card. You let me sign my name for each of the dances. The quadrille, the molasses boiling..."

"That's paperwork. It's meaningless."

Her hand was caught by the silk-gloved paw of the pasha. She let herself be spun away into the sweep of the crowd. In the whirl of faces, Holtzclaw saw that the pasha was Bogan, the old miner, who had frequented the Grayson House. Ms. Rathbun had forgotten her own regulars. To see her dancing with a poor miner rather than a rich idler was only a very, very small comfort to Holtzclaw's wounded pride.

But Holtzclaw could not let this disappointment sully the whole event. No, his was only one twisted heart, and not even the richest or most worthwhile here. To let himself be defeated by a single wave of Lizzie Rathbun's hand was pure foolishness. In fact, it was better for the hotel that she was free to dance with as many of the tourists as possible. They would all stay for the season, hoping for a match with this comely Maiden of the Lake.

Shadburn clapped a hand on Holtzclaw's back, in silent camaraderie. He was dressed in his sharpest suit, trying to look like an oil man or marquis. But the suit had become ill-fitting over the months, and Shadburn now resembled the worst sort of codfish aristocrat. His pant legs were too short. His cufflinks were tarnished, which proved that they weren't gold, as Holtzclaw had once thought. Shadburn couldn't fasten the jacket around his middle, on account of hash browns and mushrooms. Holtzclaw followed Shadburn towards the buffet table, where feasting forks tore chunks from a barbecued sea monster that had been baked under a mountain of salt. Its clouded eyes pleaded with those who braved looking their dinner in the face. The many-tiered cake was already half consumed, and the remainder was at risk of falling over, supported only by certain load-bearing buttresses of icing. A spring of sugar syrup started at the summit of the cake, became a running river brûlée, then tumbled into a lake of caramel on the lowest tier. A deposit of ice cream oozed slowly into fields of red velvet cake. A layer of bittersweet chocolate morsels and smashed cocoa biscuits was studded—or spoiled—by frequent deposits of golden raisins. The whole confection rested upon a polished mirror, so the confusion and splendor of the cake was doubled, as in water. Only Pharaoh's Flour could have accomplished such culinary wonders. Holtzclaw winked at the cake, pleased with what was wrought. He moved to take a piece for himself, but a farmer and his milk-cow barred his path. They persisted so long in slack-jawed astonishment that Holtzclaw gave up on getting a slice. He didn't need to taste the cake to know that it was splendid. The tourists would believe only their tongues.

A oriental dowager empress turned away from the table, having eaten her fill. Holtzclaw blinked several times before he understood that beneath the heavy makeup and layers of luxuriant silk was the widow Smith Patterson. Behind her, carrying her carmine parasol, was a new paramour, dressed in short pants; he was the inheritor of a vegetable canning enterprise, a strapping young fellow that the Billing, Wooing, and Cooing Society had been sorry to lose. The widow Smith Patterson, holding her weighty headpiece in place, bowed to a plump hen—Mother Fresh-Roasted's costume was an immense coat of feathers. She withdrew egg-shaped confections from a hidden pocket to give to children.

Animated spools unwound their threads, catching gala-goers and knotting them together in complicated lines. When the automatic orchestra, accompanying a living fiddle player, struck up a melody for a molasses boiling dance, the threads were pulled tight, and the complex dance was executed precisely along the guide wires. Holtzclaw found himself pulled into the whirl of the dance, and then he was face-to-face with Ms. Rathbun. She beamed at him; perhaps, in her happiness, she'd forgotten the hurt that she'd dealt him. Under her eyes, she'd rubbed a powder of gold, and her cheeks were flushed the color of love-apples. He tried to summon the right words, to show that he was wounded but proud; a bit of cutting sarcasm would have been excellent. But his mind was filled with the squall of the fiddle and the rhythm of feet on the ballroom floor, and he could not make even the faintest meaningful grunt.

The automatic banjos skipped when Princess Trahlyta entered the ballroom, and the color drained from Lizzie Rathbun's face. The princess's dress was the trump to Ms. Rathbun's, whose claim was at once recognized as pale pretension. Princess Trahlyta's dress shared the same excellent cut and ideal proportions, the same geometric wonder of a hat made in interlocking rings of gold, but rather than being simply adorned with golden thread, it was pure gold, worked so fine and thin that it draped like silk and shimmered as she walked. She was the color of an egg yolk, of a sunrise. Her skirts billowed into a mountain of pure wealth. Green lights surrounded her and pulsed with urgency and glee, following the electricity of her movement.

Ms. Rathbun pressed her lips so tightly together that her mouth disappeared into the tension of her face. Kicking her feet, she broke the threads that guided her feet and stormed from the ballroom. Only Holtzclaw remarked her departure; the rest of the gala-goers, native and tourist, did not seem to notice.

The ballroom floor was upheaved by a jet of steam breaking from under the mountain and a cold spring of water that shattered a corner of the stage. Thirsty ball-goers caught the spring water in their hands—they said that the water tasted like wine. So many liquors were flowing out from the hotel that the waters could not help but absorb that flavor. Children wavered, exhausted, among deposits of poppy rocks and honeybun confections. Dancers fell into the laps of sofas, feet reversed over their heads. Three curious consumers were knocked senseless by three bright bowls of moonshine. White lightning shivered and cracked overhead, exploding electric lightbulbs and loosing the fire-bees that had been trapped inside. A rain of tiny ice crystals started to fall, a result of atmospheric tumult in the high ceiling of the ballroom. An immense silk tablecloth unfurled itself above the ball-goers and was buoyed aloft by breezes from turning skirts.

Abigail arrived at last, and she was a matchstick set alight. Her red curls were aflame; literal tongues of fire were rising from her hair. She'd persuaded some old fire spirit to nest, for an evening, on the crown of her head, though no doubt certain tourists thought it was only a simple trick of converting animal fluids to vapor and thus preventing the chemical fluids from mixing with the solids. Where ever she went, the crowd cleared before her, astounded. She knelt to permit marshmallows to be roasted above her curls. The rain of ice crystals melted above her; she was a bright streak of red and life.

Hulen, the headless plat-eye, lumbered across the dance floor. A dozen children shrieked with delight, clinging to his legs. Around him was a cluster of admirers who had all dressed up as their favorite resident eccentric; it was an easy costume to make, and yet effective. If Abigail's costume was the most spectacular, then Hulen's natural form was the most beloved.

The band had stopped playing; they were looking towards Holtzclaw. The hour had come for him to introduce the special guest, the evening's crowning entertainment. He clambered on stage. The babble of conversation flowed around him, passing from tourist to native to spirit and around again. There were yelps of surprise, discomfort, and happiness. The pyrotechnics of Abigail's hair thrilled the crowd; the storms in the upper atmosphere of the ballroom soaked and chilled them; Hulen's headlessness made them laugh. Yes, they were ready. They could meet the guest of honor.

"Ladies and gentlemen, people of Auraria, esteemed guests from Milledgeville, Charleston, Chattanooga! Welcome to my gala!" He threw his arms in the air. Some people turned to listen; others were too enraptured by local wonders. That was all right, even better. "Ladies and gentlemen, some of you have been in the finest concert halls in the world. You have seen performers with great talent, long histories, and classical repertoire, who have performed before kings and queens. But you have never seen such a one as this, who has performed for moon maidens! I myself was skeptical of this performer; I was skeptical of the whole valley. But I have been here a year now, and I have set down roots, and I believe there are unique charms. Spirits and pursuits that will call you back, season after season. And the Queen of the Mountains will be here to welcome you."

"Get on with it, Handcow!" said someone from the back of the ballroom, his voice cutting through the noise of conversation.

"I will! I am! I wish to present to you a performer that most of you have never met..."

"Not Dasha Pavlovski?" called a stable boy near the stage. His paramour, a fabulously rich scullery maid, clutched at the stable boy's arms. Her eyes welled with tears.

"You can hear Dasha Pavlovski in any palace from London to Lisbon!" said Holtzclaw, swelling with pride. "But only here at the Queen of the Mountains, may you witness a spectacle like no other! A sensation for the eyes, the ears, the heart, and the mind that will leave you breathless and thoughtful and eager to return again and again for encores for yet another of the Old Songs. Without further ado, I introduce to you, ladies and gentlemen—Auraria's native star, our own singing tree!"

Holtzclaw burst into a frenzy of applause, which was not echoed by the audience. Perhaps the crowd hadn't heard him clearly. But they could not fail to remark upon the coming wonder. A tree leaned its branches from the wings into view of the audience, and a rustle ran through its leaves. Its roots skittered across the stage gracefully as it pulled itself up to the spotlight. The branches dipped low to the ground in an imitation of a bow.

The sound that the tree produced was like the call of birds, or more precisely, the gurgling noises of drowning turkeys on the hillside. Then it shuddered, pardoned itself for the inauspicious start, which it blamed on the misty and chaotic atmosphere of the ballroom, and lit into "Fly Around My Pretty Little Miss" in a rich baritone voice. It was not one of the old songs; Holtzclaw had thought a jaunty folk lyric might be a more tempered introduction.

The tourists had seen many remarkable phenomena at the Queen of the Mountains. And yet, all of these happenings could have been artifice. The purple fire that burned over the kitchen the previous night could have been a chemical trick. Strange rains of peaches and fish could have been dropped from hot air balloons or shot out of cannons. The flying tablecloths, dancing in the air, could have been controlled by wires. The automatic instruments and roving spools could be clever clockwork automata. Even the Great and Harmless and Invincible Terrapin could have been a sham—it was large enough to host a team of puppeteers.

But those who tried to find the artifice in the singing tree were challenged by the thinness of its limbs, the grace of its swaying movements, the skittering of its roots, and the way its leaves shuddered in perfect anticipation of every swelling note. It had the purity of a living, musical creature. It was simple, guileless, beautiful, and beyond this sublunary world.

"Burn it with fire!" called an enraged baroness from beneath shepherdess trappings. Other blood-filled shouts joined with her battle cry. A wet thud hit the stage; a love-apple burst into juice. Table legs were broken into torches, lit from candelabras and sparking electric lights. Contrary calls to peace and quiet were overruled—Abigail and her allies could not quell the tourists' rising rage. The tree uprooted itself and fled for the door, swaying to avoid missiles and embers.

"Wait, please!" said Holtzclaw, lifting up his hands.

It had been too much, too soon. The tourists, addled by moonshine and claret, their brains already spinning from the mazurka and molasses boiling, were now called upon to believe in something truly supernatural. They had endured a molasses boiling dance and a barbecued lake monster and automatic banjos and all the other tricks for the sake of novelty. But they could not forsake their beloved Dasha Pavlovski for the strangeness of a singing tree.

CHAPTER XXXII

When the riot of tourists, in pursuit of the singing tree, exploded into the night air, their hot ire was instantly cooled by a wind blowing from Lake Trahlyta. In the ice-rimed water splashed a thousand silver figures. The orb of moon hanging in the sky was dull and ashen; the moon's light had relocated, temporarily, to the face of the lake. A congress of moon maidens had come to bathe in the mingled mineral waters. The hum of their language and songs, at a distance, merged into a faint buzz, no louder than a hive of firebees or the hum of electric lights.

The singing tree took advantage of its pursuers' confusion. Throwing root over root, it reached the edge of the forest and was lost among the limbs.

"Was this your spectacle?" said Abigail, her enflamed hair sputtering and dying in the cold night. "You hardly needed a singing tree to set it off."

"I think that I did," said Holtzclaw. "I mean, I wasn't trying to set anything off."

Tomatoes and torches were dropped to the ground. The tourists shielded their eyes against the glow of the lake. They rubbed their hands and blew into their palms, against the cold. Moonlight enveloped the Maiden of the Lake. The completed funnel and its stunted sibling trembled as the moon maidens crashed against its hull. The boat was a dark macule against the silver mirror of the lake. Holtzclaw looked for Ms. Rathbun, to judge her by her reaction to these events, but she wasn't to be found among the gawking crowds. Her golden dress should have been visible from across the mountainside, but he could not see her.

Some of the gala-goers trickled down the lawn, towards the waters. At the head of the expedition were the members of the Billing, Wooing, and Cooing Society. There were enough maidens to make married men of a generation, if only the maidens could be lured to land.

Holtzclaw wrung his hands. What would happen, if the tourists met with the moon maidens? The singing tree had provoked a riot, and the moon maidens could provoke much worse. A gold-hunting frenzy. A mass hysteria of disbelief. Or worst of all—the Billing, Wooing, and Cooing Society could succeed at snagging some of the moon maidens into fashionable marriages. Ten thousand moon maidens would be carried from their beloved valley and healing springs. If every city had its moon maidens, oozing gold into any waiting hand, who would remember Auraria? Who would remember the Queen of the Mountains?

A disheveled figure pushed through the mess of guests towards Holtzclaw; the figure assailed him with loose, ineffective fists. Holtzclaw grabbed the man by his shoulders and shook him, to give him some sense. The man raised his head, and Holtzclaw recognized the face of his employer. His face was prickled with whiskers and stained with distress.

"Holtzclaw, I said there could be no moon maidens," said Shadburn. He hurled his shoe—its mate had been lost—towards the moon maidens, but it fell far short of its target. It landed near Almeda, the Reader of Mysteries. Shadburn slumped onto the lawn.

"Ms. Thompson, please," said Holtzclaw. "Take care of him. I can't. I can't do it anymore."

Abigail took Shadburn by the hand and lifted him up to his feet. He looked up at her with wet eyes. "We'll get you cleaned up and settled down, Hiram," said Abigail, as they stumbled back towards the Queen of the Mountains, leaning on each other. "We'll get you something to eat."

Princess Trahlyta was standing next to Holtzclaw. Her golden dress had been replaced with her traditional blue homespun garment. "I told them not to come," she said, "but they were excited to hear the singing tree. They wanted to try this tremendous bath that you built."

"They are pests," said Holtzclaw. "Beautiful, lunar pests."

"They think they can show up where ever they wish. Bathe where ever they wish, as often as they wish, and that there will be no lingering effects. They don't know how much work I must do to clean up after them, so that the water will be clean the next time. Now they are spoiling my work. The cold will stop the workings of the deep, scouring currents. It will dull the appetites of the wild wonder fish. And my scouring brush will not work as I mean it to."

"And their freezing and splashing will weaken the dam," said Holtzclaw.

"Yes, weaken it too soon."

"I can scare them away," said Holtzclaw. "A loud noise will shoo them. A stick of dynamite."

She shook her head. "A stick of dynamite is such a little thing, James."

"What can you offer instead? A thunderclap? An earthquake? A volcanic spew? Could you arrange any of these?"

"Not a one. My great roar is yet to come. I suppose it will have to be dynamite. Would the moon maidens hear it all the way up the fingers of the lake?"

"If it is placed right," said Holtzclaw.

"Then go, Pharaoh!" said the princess. "For our common goals."

Holtzclaw dashed to the storeroom, all the while fumbling with his keyring—needlessly, it turned out. The door to the storeroom was unlocked, as was the cherrywood box that held the dynamite. Inside, there were only two sticks left. Did they really use so much to blow up the spring house the night before? He paused just long enough to swallow a draught of Effervescent Brain Salts, to quiet the complaints of his knees, and hurried on.

When he came over a line of boulders, he saw the fractured and scarred rock that marked the former site of the Hag's Head. A few months of weather had begun to heal the wounded hollow that Holtzclaw had carved with the hydrocannon. Moss grew over the northern faces of boulders. Scrubby laurel rooted in the muddy tailings. A spring of wild ramps emerged among gravel.

The orbiting lights of a will-o'-the-wisp filled the hard cleft that had been the Hag's chin, which the hydrocannon had turned into a solid-rock resonator. As he crept closer to the treasure light, he saw Emmy, the mushroom girl, scratching at the ground, just where

Holtzclaw had meant to place the explosives. Green lights whizzed around her head, over her hands, and through her hair.

"I'm looking for a truffle," said Emmy. "They are the best mushrooms."

"Do you think there's one here?" said Holtzclaw.

"It's what the green light showed me," said Emmy.

"Then let's look," said Holtzclaw. He scooped up dirt with his nails and let Emmy crib through the loose soil. The will-o'-the-wisp pulsed brightly, but Holtzclaw had other concerns. Now, the hole was deep enough for the dynamite. Emmy looked at him, her eyes welling with tears.

"This isn't the place for a truffle," said Holtzclaw. "They grow under trees, not under rocks."

"I know," said Emmy. "I thought this one was different. What are you planting?"

"Nothing that will grow," said Holtzclaw.

He took Emmy's hand and led her from the hollow. The will-o'-the-wisp blinked seven times—three long bursts, two short, two long. It was pleading with him in its complicated pattern language.

He let Emmy strike the cord, and then he scooped her up and ran. The princess was ahead of them, somewhere. She bent back the branches so that they could fly.

The earth turned over on itself and shook off its long sleep. The explosion thundered through the valley, magnified by the natural amphitheater in the rock. Emmy wailed; she clapped her hands over her head, and Holtzclaw pressed her close against him for safety and reassurance.

The echoing roar of the dynamite lessened with each reverberation, and in half a minute, it had faded to a whisper. Holtzclaw set Emmy down on her own feet. Together, they walked to a rocky outcrop that had a view over the lake.

The moon maidens were gone. Above, the moon stuttered like a lightbulb coming alive, brightening to its customary silvery glow. On the surface of the lake, gold colors shimmered like stars. Sparks were still falling from the sky. Some embers were more powerful than others; when they fell to earth, they sounded like metal clattering on stone.

Holtzclaw caught something before it rolled away. It was a gold coin. He picked up another from a puddle. On its obverse was the image of a bumblebee. There had been a cache under the Hag's Head, just where the will-o'-the-wisp promised, and Holtzclaw had blown it up into the sky.

Emmy pulled at Holtzclaw's hand. Sleep tugged at the corners of her eyelids. She wanted him to take her home, to her gravestone. She didn't care to search for coins, and neither did he.

The lawn around the hotel was deserted, and the corridors and halls held only the bored shadows of liveried staff. Dan slept beneath a pile of napkins. Cannie piloted a broom across the empty dance floor. Ephraim and Flossie gathered candy wrappers, ends of tickets, shreds of dance cards, and discarded handkerchiefs—they bickered over their value before discarding them in waste bins. Moss rinsed out glasses; Bogan wrung out rags. Arma and Gertie swept, collected, and sifted. Mountains of food turned brown and tepid. Abigail, a thin wisp of smoke smoldering from her hair, stacked automatic banjos to the side of the stage, where they still plucked the notes to "Sourwood Mountain." Enormous tablecloths rolled themselves away.

"Where are our guests?" asked Holtzclaw. "Not in bed, are they?" It was too much to hope.

"They've gone for gold," said Abigail. "They've taken every soup bowl, every spoon. When the tourists realized what was floating across the water and falling from the sky, there was a pandemonium, to make the singing tree riot seem like a child's tantrum. Expensive clothes were ruined. The explosion didn't phase them, nor did a thousand rabbit-faced women popping like bubbles. None of that mattered. One poor lady had her hair pulled off; it would have hurt her more if it weren't a wig, but still, she had stuck it to her head with glue. Now, there are rich people running all over the hillside, thinking that they'll strike it richer."

"What about the staff? You're all still here. Aren't the Auraria natives supposed to be treasure-mad?"

"We know that you can't expect to dig up anything, at night, with a spoon, with such a crowd stirring up the waters. The colors are too few and scattered. There's no money in working anything before it's settled. We've lived in this valley for a very long time; we have some sense."

Holtzclaw waited and watched from the veranda, looking over the lake and the spots of lamplight that flickered over the mountainside like fireflies. Many were clustered at the dam; they must have reasoned that coins and colors would be carried to the earthworks by the current.

At some late hour, a cold rain started to fall in fat, heavy drops. The turn in the weather did not dampen the seekers' desires. Only weariness turned them back, in proportion to their passion. Through the night, a thin stream of dispirited tourists returned to the hotel. Swiss girls and Scottish lassies were sweaty and mud-stained. Highlanders, fishermen, clowns, and bumpkins were torn and sagging. Shepherds and shepherdesses were soaked to the skin. Nearly all were empty-handed, and those who had found a coin or a few flakes were saddened that they had not found more. They kept their bowls and spoons, and in the morning, Abigail could serve only toast, for want of cutlery.

CHAPTER XXXIII

All the next day, the rain fell. The treadmill was abandoned and the mineral baths were empty. Emmett's stage wagon was stained with spilled drops of that sensory-enhancing remedy, Professor W's Pleasant Potation and Universal Wine Draught. Shattered bottles littered the ground. The Asbestos Hollow camp was sparsely populated, too. Many of its dwellers had been hired as guides to search out treasure caches and interpret dreams of fortunes.

Out on the dam, there was a buzz of activity, despite the cold, constant rain. The tourists had raffled off land claims by lottery. Three dozen smallholders dug with spoons and ladles that they had stolen from the kitchen. They scooped sand into china bowls and the crowns of fine silk hats, trying to pan out nuggets; their poor technique, though, left them with nothing.

The actual baroness and the steel baroness ran a more organized effort. They had set up their gold mining cooperative beside the spillway and flume. Under their orders, a work brigade composed of eligible sons and daughters had already taken down the breakwater beams from the dam's face, and now they were carting away the protective stones from the dam's facing so they could reach the rich mud beneath.

"Get off!" cried Holtzclaw. "All of you!"

"What, what?" said the actual baroness. The hem of her dress was caked in mud. "You can't mean that your dam is so flimsy that it cannot stand up to a few gold hunters?"

Holtzclaw demurred, not willing to confess his fear. "You've no right to dig here. It's private property."

"We've paid for full use of the resort facilities," said the railroad baroness.

"That privilege does not extend to undermining important structural features." Holtzclaw broke up the work brigade and expelled all the diggers, even the baronesses, waving them away with his hat as though shooing flies. But when he returned after dinner, they were back in greater numbers. His protests had only convinced them that something must be hidden inside the earthworks. Water swirled into scars, widening them.

The Billing, Wooing, and Cooing Society did not participate in the mining activities. The rain hurt their bones, they said. Instead, they occupied a lonely table in the lobby, playing faro under inconsistent misconceptions about the rules. Holtzclaw hurried past them, but they rose and barred his way.

"Walk with us, Holtzclaw," said Almeda, the Reader of Mysteries.

"Not on the treadmill," said Vera, the Tender of the Entwined Rose and Briar.

"We've worn it out," said Luella, the Poetess of the Stirring Heart.

"I have to see to urgent matters," said Holtzclaw. Alarmed employees had reported that the far side of the dam showed peculiar upwelling of damp earth.

"We are more urgent," said Almeda. They steered him by his elbows, out into the weather. Holtzclaw, captive to the Billing, Wooing, and Cooing Society, followed the path to the white cairn. The woods rang with rushing water; the waterfall roared, churning with mud. The pavilion beside the white cairn was empty. No other guests took their constitutionals, and no employees were on hand to offer mineral waters in fine silver cups.

"It's not much of a resort, Holtzclaw," said Almeda, the Reader of Mysteries, "if everyone is wasting their time at work, not leisure."

"Perhaps they consider treasure-hunting more enjoyable than match-making."

"That's rubbish," said Almeda. "Your guests are a poor sort of people if they are led astray so easily. We are bored, Holtzclaw. And boredom breeds restlessness, which breeds indigestion, which breeds bad dreams."

"Too many bad dreams," said Vera.

"Can't sleep," said Luella.

"I have it on good authority," said Holtzclaw, "that many nightmares attributed to indigestion are really the work of revengeful fish ghosts."

The three yellow-hatted women made gestures with their hands like a bird flying away. "The birds of happiness will coo no more for you."

"The birds have always been our enemies," said Holtzclaw.

On the third day of rain, the pipes burst in the basement of the Queen of the Mountains. All the waters in all the baths—saline, sulfur, white sulfur, chalybeate, epsom, lythia, plyant, freestone—overflowed their basins and mingled together in a single pool.

Nothing could be done to unmix them, so Holtzclaw took his bath anyway. He swam from one end of the long bathing hall to the other, passing above the old paths and patterns of the baths. The stairs, grates, and basins below his feet reminded him of the roads and foundations one could still glimpse through the clear waters of Lake Trahlyta.

He heard someone clear her throat. "What is it, princess?" said Holtzclaw, not turning.

"No princesses here," said Abigail. She stood on the highest step of the entryway, above the level of the rising water.

Holtzclaw floundered for solid ground, finding none.

"Are you practicing your frog-kicks for the flood?" said Abigail. "Not out trying to save the dam?"

The peculiar upwellings that Holtzclaw surveyed yesterday had been caused by springs that flowed inside of the dam's structure. The rains made these springs—made all the springs of the valley—run with new strength, and thus, their discharge had come to the dam surface. There was precious little that he could do to fight these flows.

"We're trying to bake bread upstairs, in the kitchen," said Abigail. "The bread won't rise. The air is too wet. We'll have nothing for breakfast."

"I'll have some bread brought in by train. Some spoons, too. More than we need, because they are apt to disappear after every meal, if our guests keep wanting to dig."

"The tracks are washed out," said Abigail. "We've just heard. That's what I came to tell you. A freshet destroyed them at the Hag's Head, just where you were blasting on the night of the gala. You've made enemies of the railroad twins, and they won't make repairs. Too much muck, too few profits. We were never so trapped in the old days, Holtzclaw. We always had sweet potatoes. But you blew up our spring house."

Holtzclaw could rebuild the spring house, but it would be no comfort to her. He had no way to fill it.

On the fourth day of the rain, Holtzclaw spent too much time in the New Rock Falls with the tailings of his dinner—half a turnip, a few stewed ramps, a can of pineapple. It was the best that he could find as the supplies dwindled. He checked the sideboards, but there was no claret, nor white lightning, nor moonshine.

His latest survey of the dam had been dispiriting. The springs inside, continuing to flow, had carved out hollows that revealed much greater troubles in the core of the dam. It was evident now that the railroad twins had used very poor clay in their construction, and they had not layered it with enough rocks to stop it from oozing downwards. Cracks had occurred during the curing process. Holtzclaw blamed himself for not questioning their methods, but perhaps no earthworks could have withstood internal erosion from so many springs.

Repairs, for the moment, were impossible. The tremendous quantities of necessary supplies could not be brought over the rain-gutted roads from Dahlonega, and even if, by some good grace, the railroad tracks could be returned to use, Holtzclaw had no money to pay for workers. It had all gone into the gala—he and Shadburn had catered their undoing.

To distract him from fruitless worry, he studied the daguerreotypes on the walls. The people and places they showed were familiar. He'd crawled over the valley, buying every rock and hollow, and he'd come to know them well. A young Abigail, her hair in tiny curls, perched on the porch railing at the Old Rocks Falls. Just beside her was a young man with familiar shoulders—Hulen, the plat-eye. His eyes were soft, and he had a beard. Shadburn, as a boy, wore a miner's pan on his head and held up a finger covered in gold dust. He saw Ephraim and Flossie with a woman, perhaps their mother, standing in front of a law office that read "Deeds Notarized." Walton rode atop an abnormally long cow. A skinny chap in a dapper hat played the piano at the Old Rock Falls. Picnickers ate beneath the Hag's Head or on flat rocks in the middle of the Sugar Shoals. Edgar and Eleanor Strikland held hands. The princess watched a line of girls and boys toss their lines into the Lost Creek. Even she looked a little younger; her hair had fewer traces of silver.

Even if the lake were drained, these lost people and places would not be restored. Time and tides had done their damage. Mountains and valleys and dams cannot keep out all the forces of the world, and the dead and headless can never be made whole again.

On the fifth day of rain, a wrenching, keening song arose from the Terrible Cascade. Holtzclaw raced out to the dam at once, worried that someone had sounded an alarm. The gorge face of the dam was damp and soft.

But the song was not being played by any who watched the dam. It came from the cave of the Great and Harmless and Invincible Terrapin.

Holtzclaw ran down the wooden stairway that had been built to the cave. His feet threatened to glide out from under him at every step; Holtzclaw clung to the handrail and felt in more peril than when the Sky Pilot had lowered him down, suspended on a rope.

"Little morsel, I am angry!" said the Great and Harmless and Invincible Terrapin, shouting out to Holtzclaw when he saw him enter his cave.

Ten guests, their dancing clothes stained brown with five days of digging in the rain, picked up stones in their puckered hands and tossed them at the fleshy parts of the terrapin. When the assailants struck a blow to some tender spot, the Great and Harmless and

Invincible Terrapin let out a sharp note of pain from his internal instrument; though invincible, he could still be wounded.

"Little morsels, why do you do this?" said the Great and Harmless and Invincible Terrapin.

"We want to see if you're really invincible," said one of the guests.

"Why?" said Holtzclaw.

"It's something to do," said a guest. "It's a challenge. If we did kill him, it's no loss. He isn't much use to anyone. He's run out of stories, and the ones he tells over and over are boring."

"I have many more stories," said the Great and Harmless and Invincible Terrapin, "but I do not wish to tell them. It is too wet and yet too dry, and my leathery skin does not bear it well."

"See, that's boring," said one of the guests. "He's boring us."

"But he is harmless," said Holtzclaw.

"Then he won't fight back," said one of the guests.

"But he is invincible," said Holtzclaw.

"Then he won't mind that we're trying to kill him," said one of the guests.

"I just don't understand," said Holtzclaw. "He is harmless, so there is no call to kill him; he is invincible, so you cannot kill him. You are only annoying him."

"Then we'll drive him away, and we'll take all the gold he's guarding. He has to be guarding some treasure, yes?"

"He's blocking a cave," said another. "A treasure tunnel, or a grave made of jewelry, or appreciated stocks and bonds, or Old Masters."

"If I were a rich man," said one of the guests, "I would hide my fortune behind a giant terrapin, because who would think to look there?"

"He is guarding ice," said the Sky Pilot, panting. He had heard the Great and Harmless and Invincible Turtle's keening song; he had raced from high on the mountain to the aid of his friend.

"Ice?" said one of the guests. "Ice comes out of an ice box."

"That is not the right sort of ice," said the Sky Pilot.

The guests laughed. "Who can tell the difference? Who cares?" They had already thrown most of the large rocks to be found in the cave, so they hurled handfuls of pebbles, river stones, and gravel, both at the terrapin and the Sky Pilot.

The Sky Pilot drew his knife.

"No, little friend, let them be," said the Great and Harmless and Invincible Terrapin.

"Must you be defenseless, even if you are harmless and invincible?" said the Sky Pilot.

The Great and Harmless and Invincible Terrapin swung his head. "If I were no longer Harmless, then I would not be Great or Invincible, and all the Old Songs would be silenced. And yet, I cannot stay here, if these little morsels persist with their violence. Their stones may chip my shell, and then the Old Songs would play out of tune. No, I must depart. I will withdraw from this valley, and the mountains that sit on my back will fall in on themselves, and the earth will shudder and shake and settle."

"You can't go," said the Sky Pilot. "I will kill these people who threaten you. I will kill six of them with a single shot of my bow, and the last two I will truss up like hams, as a lesson."

"But there will always be more, little friend," said the Great and Harmless and Invincible Terrapin.

"Then I'll pull up their rails and wash out their roads. I'll burst their dam. I'll plug up all their springs and wash all the gold down to the sea, so that all the speculators and developers will have no call to disturb us."

"You cannot do this, and I cannot let you do this. You are small and mortal, and I am great and invincible. But you may come with me, little friend, and we will let this valley be as it wishes to be, and we will be unchanged. I have been here too long, among the little morsels."

"Where will we go?" asked the Sky Pilot.

"Down," said the Great and Harmless and Invincible Terrapin. "Down where all the great and invincible creatures sleep. There is fire there, and ice, and fields of flowers, too—so many flowers, you would have thought the world could not hold them all. It is like the old times, down in the deep. Take no possessions with you, little friend, if you wish to come; you need none of these artifacts of the mortal world."

The Sky Pilot sloughed off his equipment—bow, quiver, gun, and pack. The tip of his knife broke when it fell to the cavern floor. He flung his hat back towards Holtzclaw. The Sky Pilot pulled himself up onto the shell and climbed to the top; he curled into a hollow just behind the turtle's neck.

The Great and Harmless and Invincible Terrapin blew a deafening chorus of the Song of Parting, then rose up on his claws and stepped backwards, into the deep. The little morsels scattered in terror. The mountains of the valley suspired and sank, and the dam wept fat tears down its barren, lonely, beaten face.

Shadburn ran towards Holtzclaw, who stood outside of the terrapin's cave, watching the dam shudder as the notes of the Song of Parting reverberated through the earth. "Tell me, Holtzclaw, what you are doing so that this dam does not fail me." Shadburn put both his hands on top of Holtzclaw's shoulders. "We can't let this lake be emptied, not with so many rich idlers scouring the mountainsides. It is so much worse than before. They will find the horrible gold from the moon maidens. They'll know where it came from, where I came from."

"The whole core of the dam is sodden," said Holtzclaw. "The railroad twins did not use good clay, and they didn't pack it well or leave it enough time to cure. We paid them for a dam, and they gave us a bath plug. "

"They are treasonous, perfidious scoundrels," said Shadburn. "Deal breakers. Base humans with hidden motives. Unfit to bear the title of businessmen."

"They can't bear all the fault. We put the structure on top of running springs—though it could hardly be avoided in this valley—so the dam is washing away from the inside, too."

"And we can't open the floodgates?" said Shadburn.

"They're permanently sealed," said Holtzclaw. "The railroad twins said it was necessary, given the weight of the water and the size of the lake."

"A lie, I'm sure. They left out the floodgates to save some money—my money, given in good faith—for their own pockets. Worse, you believed them! What sort of nonsense is that, a dam that cannot be emptied?" Shadburn picked up a pebble and hurled it towards the great and harmless and vulnerable dam. The stone glanced off the water-streaked face of the dam, and a new rivulet started to flow from the bruise.

"Do whatever you can," said Shadburn. "Pack on more mud. Bring in stone, bricks, and tree stumps. Tear down the hotel and dump the rubble down into the canyon, if it will help. Scrap your pleasure boat that is bobbing senselessly upon on the lake. It will do you no good if there is no lake on which it can float."

"If the water keeps rising," said Holtzclaw, "then no reinforcement will save the dam."

"Then you must ask the rain to stop."

Holtzclaw wandered for a day, looking for the princess. She had never answered his beck and call; she'd just appeared, as she willed, near watery places. With the lake rising quickly, the rains crashing down, there was no place left that was more wet or watery than any other. The whole valley was one rushing river, one churning lake. Holtzclaw looked across the churning surface of the lake, choked with runoff and debris. Across the water, the Queen of the Mountains shone with a few feeble electric lights. The Maiden of the Lake rocked in the current; it looked gray and dingy, already worn and old and yet never opened. In the distance, the railroad bridge, abandoned, was buffeted by a sudden freshet bursting from the mountains above.

Trahlyta was not in the baths of the Queen of the Mountains. She was not attending the white cairn, telling legends to visitors. She was not at the Sugar Shoals or the Five Forks Creek, which was an angry cataract. Holtzclaw was soaked to his core; mud caked his trousers to the knees. Only the crown of his head, sheltered by his fine Auraria hat, was still dry.

He saw a small, familiar sign post: "water" and an arrow. He laughed; the sign could have pointed in all directions and been just as truthful. But the sign once again guided him in his need.

Holtzclaw followed the side path. Old chestnuts loomed overhead, dripping icicles. Tree trunks were rimed on the windward side with ice, layered like verdant moss. The frosted path widened into a clearing. In the middle of her rock-lined spring, Trahlyta reclined on her island.

"Hello, James. Lovely weather, isn't it?" she said, without a trace of irony. She radiated delight.

"The weather is causing me trouble, princess. The lake is rising."

"Oh, it's not trouble," said Trahlyta. "It was necessary."

"To do what?"

"To stir up the deep currents. To impel the wild wonder fish to dig."

"Why wait until now? Why not wash the dam away months ago?"

"Because, James, you were so excited about your gala. And I thought it might be instructive for everyone, but especially you."

"So, you won't stop the rain, then?" said Holtzclaw.

"It's the simplest act in the world," said the princess. "But it won't save the dam. Enough raindrops have fallen on the mountainsides; they will run off the stone summits and down through the channels of the earth, come out springs again, and they will all make their way into the lake."

"And then?"

The princess made a popping sound against the side of her cheek, like a cork being pulled from a bottle of claret.

"But I've worked so hard," said Holtzclaw. "For silkworms, for Shadburn, and with so little to show. And if this dam bursts, and the lake rushes out, then I will have nothing."

"Then you have been do the wrong work," said the princess.

"What about the people who live downstream? Won't the dam flood their lands? Won't there be a great disaster, like at Johnstown?"

"Not at all. Below us, the land is wide and flat. There will only be some muddy fields."

"How can you be sure? Have you ever left this valley to see for yourself? How do you know what the waters do in someone else's domain?"

"I've met the Queen of the Lowlands at our conferences," said the princess. "She's blonde and heavyset, with wide footsteps—a hearty eater. You might like her. Now James, you trust me, don't you?"

Holtzclaw searched himself and was surprised to admit that he did.

"Then I will stop the rains for you," said the princess, "and you will destroy the dam for me."

CHAPTER XXXIV

In the early morning hours of what was to be the sixth day of rain, Holtzclaw kept vigil from the dark veranda of the Queen of the Mountains. Next to him was a bottle of rare and ancient claret. His ears, so used to the rhythmic patterns of the droplets falling on the roof and earth, immediately noticed when the noise of the rain changed. The tempo slowed, and droplets fell in uneven accents and syncopations. And then, there was no rain.

Lamplights awoke within the hotel. From inside came muffled cheers.

Still, all around him was the sound of water. Creeks and rills ran high; springs gushed up from beneath the golf course and bath pavilions; burst pipes churned forth streams of mineral waters; droplets shook loose from leaves when breezes rolled off the mountaintops.

Shadburn emerged from the hotel with his fishing rod and reel slung over his shoulder, like a soldier's gun on parade. He held up a small silver pail. Writhing pink worms peeked over the rim; one, boosted by the teeming mass of life beneath it, escaped over the edge. Holtzclaw watched it squirm between the boards of the veranda to a wet, happy freedom.

"Oh, Holtzclaw, still awake, eh?" he said. "You should get some sleep, now the weather's settled down. Or do you want to come fishing? They'll be biting better than ever. They're always hungry after the rains end."

Holtzclaw politely declined. He stayed on the veranda of the Queen of the Mountains, alone in the early morning stillness, to watch the sunrise. When the sun broke above the top of Sinking Mountain, there was a green flash—so brief and subtle that, had Holtzclaw not been staring at the mountain, he would have missed it. The stars slipped from their places in the dawn light, quivering and falling as if they were fat with dew.

His rumination was interrupted by two explosions. Twin rockets shot up from the dam, overpowering the morning twilight. Their trails glowed an angry red—they were distress signals, launched from the Maiden of the Lake.

Holtzclaw flew to the dam. He slid on mud slides and tumbled over fallen limbs, but he picked himself up, time and again, and finally reached the scene of the disaster. The Maiden of the Lake was lodged against the entrance to the spillway. The powerful current, still coursing down from the mountainsides and into the lake, held the boat in its precarious place, where it blocked the flow of water into the spillway. The flume that led from the top of the dam was dry.

A wave crashed into the Maiden of the Lake, rocking the one and a half funnels. Holtzclaw heard splintering wood and twisting metal. The current was trying to force the pleasure boat down the flume, while at the same time, the rising lake pool threatened to topple the boat over the face of the dam. The lake, already high, seemed to be rising before his eyes.

Lizzie Rathbun stood on the rear deck, watching out for someone. Holtzclaw ran onto the top of the dam, his feet squelching in the soft earth. He approached the boat through the dry flume and and clambered aboard. Ms. Rathbun met him.

"The boat slipped its mooring and drifted here," said Ms. Rathbun. "And we have no engine to free ourselves." Holtzclaw admired her neutral tone. He did not share her calm.

"This is not an accident, is it?" said Holtzclaw. "The ropes were too thick to come undone or to break. It's sabotage. Do you know who's responsible? The moon maidens? The princess? Shadburn? The railroad twins?"

Ms. Rathbun rolled her eyes. "I haven't any idea, Holtzclaw. Really, I don't."

"Then there's only one solution," said Holtzclaw. "Scuttle the ship. We have to clear the spillway if the dam and lake are to survive. If the water starts coming over the top of the dam, there's nothing we can do to stop it. The dam will burst."

"I knew that you'd choose loyalty to your employer's business over your own."

"Either we sacrifice the boat, or both are lost," he said. It was not loyalty, but logic. "First, we'll get you off the ship. Then, I'll go back up to the hotel. I hope there's a piece or two of dynamite left. I'll put a charge below the waterline, on the opposite side from the spillway. We'll hope that it's powerful enough to open a gap in the hull that will let the boat sink in time, but not so powerful that it will damage the flume any further."

"Oh, there's no need to go back up to the hotel," said Ms. Rathbun. "There are explosives here. If you need them, take them. But I can't condone it. I must register my protestations, at least formally."

"Can't you see the danger? The boat is a loss in any case now. If the flume isn't cleared, then the boat will be destroyed when the dam bursts—it will be dashed to pieces on the canyon walls as the lake goes roaring down the Terrible Cascade."

"Still, I protest," said Ms. Rathbun. Yet she led him back to her suite, at the head of the grand staircase. Two deeply crimson love-apples were the only remaining decoration—all the other furniture had been removed. Ms. Rathbun opened a wooden crate to reveal two sticks of dynamite, a length of fuse cord, a blasting cap, and even a flint for sparking.

"It's only prudent," said Ms. Rathbun, in response to Holtzclaw's questioning expression.

They went to the lower deck, the servants' level, and Ms. Rathbun pointed to certain welded seam. "Now, if I were you, I'd put the dynamite right here. It's a weak spot, I'm sure. While you get prepared, I will work up some tears and warm up my screams. And you must haul me off the boat by my hair. I will wail and cry and scream and plead, but you will be deaf to all my distresses."

"Why is all this necessary?"

"Because, Holtzclaw, of the insurance claims. For natural disaster, floods, acts of weather, the policies pay very little. Several pay nothing." Ms. Rathbun's voice welled up with tears; her voice cracked, then she decided it was the wrong timbre. "But if you, dear Holtzclaw, sink it for your own reasons: out of malice, or the need to preserve your employer's property, or jealousy, or spurned romance or the desire to crush your competition by any means—and all of these are very plausible motives, Holtzclaw—well, that is an action-able injury, with a guilty party to pursue, and I am entitled to much greater compensation from the insurance claims."

"Don't you mean, 'we are entitled?'" said Holtzclaw. "This is my ship, too. If I set the charge, then there's no recourse. It's destruction of my own property."

"There's not a paper with your name on it," said Ms. Rathbun. "On all the receipts for furniture and fixtures and painting, for the work that was done here—there's only Elizabeth Rathbun. You were worried about your employer's reaction, so you kept your name out of it. Not that Shadburn cared in the least."

Holtzclaw stifled a small chuckle, but he could not stop a smile from escaping. "It's too complicated by half," he said. It was not the Charleston Chomp, the Cincinnati Slip-off, the Asheville Attitude, or the Fitzgerald Flip. Her trick did not deserve its own name. "If crime was in the cards, you could have just clubbed me over the head and taken my gold months ago."

"I would rather wait for the money to come to me."

Holtzclaw considered refusing to play his part; he could leave Ms. Rathbun on the boat, retreat up the hill, and watch the lake build up behind the clogged spillway. But she had trapped him—for the lake to survive, the boat had to be destroyed.

Holtzclaw set the charge in the place Ms. Rathbun had indicated and spooled out the blasting cord. He did not pull Ms. Rathbun by the hair—she decided that would be too far out-of-character for Holtzclaw, but she did summon convincing tears.

Chattering gawkers crowded the shores of the lake; they cheered and hollered as Holtzclaw and Ms. Rathbun emerged from the twisted, straining boat. They witnessed Holtzclaw striking the spark as Ms. Rathbun implored him to stop. Then Ms. Rathbun stuck her fingers in her ears.

The shock of the explosion made Holtzclaw stumble. He turned back towards the sawdust and spray. The spillway was choked with debris; the flume was a smoking wreck. Its iron supports gave way; rivets and pylons and buttresses tore from the cliff wall with sharp sounds, like choleric voices of birds. The battered and weary dam sagged several more feet, carved out by the stresses of the explosion. It was a mortal blow.

"We only set off one charge!" said Holtzclaw. "It was enough to punch a hole in the hull, not destroy the ship."

"Well, there was a good deal more than one charge on the boat," said Ms. Rathbun into Holtzclaw's ear. He could barely hear her over the ringing of the explosion. "I cleaned out your storehouse at the gala. I couldn't chance that some number-twiddler—some Holtzclaw—would try to deny my claims. How can the bills of sale be refuted, if the furniture and coats of paint and fine silks in all the guest rooms have been washed across a thousand lowland acres?"

Then she fled, forcing tears, along the crumbling summit of the dam and into the waiting arms of mud-stained society women.

If the dam had been whole and strong, then even fifty sticks of dynamite would not have been enough to ruin it. Men and women cannot make mountains, but a dam is as near as they can come; it is geological and immense, an artificial wonder. But Holtzclaw's dam had been poorly built, frequently assaulted, eroded from without and within. Rich tourists had dug from the top, and wild wonder fish had nibbled from the bottom. Lake Trahlyta was high, and its waters were eager to continue to the sea.

Holtzclaw stood transfixed as water poured over the blasted depression and down the far face of the dam. The cut deepened, like a knife pressed into yielding flesh. The spectators on the lakeshore wailed and cheered and drank and sang. Abigail and Shadburn flailed their arms at Holtzclaw. He saw them, but he didn't move.

Princess Trahlyta stood on top of the blade of water, pacing back and forth. "You knew the lake couldn't stay, James," she said. "It started to fail from the day the floodgates were closed. It lasted only as long as I meant it to last. I have opened the mountains, and I will let the water out."

Holtzclaw ran, and Princess Trahlyta became a great wave. A torrent crashed over the dam, tearing chunks of earth away, splitting the earthworks through the middle. All the force of the lake was released at once. The Terrible Cascade quenched its thirst; its waterfalls drank again from the waters of the valley. Shimmering ghosts of vengeful fish flowed out toward the sea.

CHAPTER XXXV

Riders poured off the mountains and into the lowlands, minutes ahead of the flood waters. But instead of inspiring people to seeker higher ground, the alarms drew them to the shores of the river below the Terrible Cascade. Families packed umbrellas and picnic baskets for the spectacle. Entrepreneurs brought watercolors and charcoal pencils to illustrate the astounding scene, hoping to sell their drawings to newspapers yearning for sensation.

The crowds waited, but there was no crashing wall of water. The river bubbled above its banks then spread far across the level bottomland. It was a disappointing scene—less dramatic than what had transpired on the dam itself. The flood waters got into the dusty roads and loamy farm soil, making swathes of mud. Cart wheels got stuck. Best dresses, which spectators had worn on the chance that they would be drowned in the floods and that those who recovered their bodies would appreciate their sartorial elegance, were stained at the hems.

Auraria's reputation as a gold-mining place was not forgotten, and some of the spectators swore that the spreading waters had a golden sheen to them. A few people brought washtubs or frying pans and tried to pan some of the water that dampened their feet, but in the lowlands, gold panning was not a common skill. The panners caught only bits of mica and shiny shards of iron and steel and minute yolk-colored flecks that could only be discerned by the sharpest-eyed children among them.

The only report of treasure was highly suspect. A small boy had been chasing rabbits when the ankle-deep water came rolling through to tickle his toes. He returned home bearing on his back a gasping catfish larger than himself. The boy's mother, filleting the fish for supper, cut into its belly. Inside were a hundred dollars of gold dust and six coins, decorated with pictures of bumblebees, terrapins, and chestnut trees.

❧

In an hour, Lake Trahlyta drained completely. Most of the crowd had dispersed long before then. After the novelty had worn off, watching the water run out of the lake was no more enthralling than watching a bathtub drain.

The waters left behind a sodden mess in the valley: black oozing mud, half-rotten stumps, gasping aquatic life, and the old forms of existence before the lake. All of these combined to form a powerful odor. The guests of the Queen of the Mountains waved their hands in front of their noses and called for sweet smells. Even a rag soaked in the sulfur waters, they said, was preferable to what came up from the lake. Five days of rain had not been enough to force gold seekers off the mountainside, but a whiff of the valley's new aroma sent them fleeing.

In front of the Queen of the Mountains, a line of carriages stood waiting for Saratoga trunks and their human companions. Those who could not get a cab left on horseback or on mules or stuffed into wagons behind their possessions. Barons and baronesses trudged behind wheelbarrows that held a season's worth of clothes.

Townsfolk trickled back into the valley, exploring what had been revealed. Under all the half-decomposed muck of leaves and limbs, they could follow the familiar desire trails: paths of courting, bootlegging, and ginsenging. From old cornfields, root cellars, barns, and porches, they gathered bass and mussels. Charred foundations harbored pink-flanked salmon and cherry-red crawfish; freshwater shrimp bobbed in glass bottles. From the entrance to an abandoned mine, brook and rainbow trout spilled forth. Inside the Cobalt Springs Lake swam a trio of catfish, circling each other and struggling for room. An enormous catfish had expired on the town square. The townsfolk tipped it into the Lost Creek, reduced to its historic dimensions. It followed its old mazy motion along the valley floor, past the foundations of old Auraria, and then between the divided halves of the dam and down the Terrible Cascade, through the soggy lowlands and out to the ocean far beyond.

In the aftermath of the dam's bursting, Holtzclaw could not find Shadburn. He was not in his quarters at the top of the hotel, nor in the New Rock Falls. There, the only spirits were Mr. Bad Thing and Hulen, the headless plat-eye. The former was packing barware into a straw-lined crate; the latter took pictures down from the wall.

Holtzclaw walked the perimeter of the lake, searching Shadburn's known fishing spots. He found his way to the artificial promontory and the boat dock from which the Maiden of the Lake had begun its ill-fated last cruise. The love-apple bush there looked desiccated; the fullness of its fruit was past, and drying orbs hung from the branches, quivering and complaining. Amazingly, the dock still stood, despite the forces of the evacuating lake. It jutted precariously into empty space; eighty feet below, a rill tumbled towards the main branch of the Lost Creek. Holtzclaw walked out to the end, testing the sturdiness of the structure.

The valley, for once, was clear of mist. He scanned the entire valley from this high perch, looking from the dam, to the blasted site of the Hag's Head, to the top of Sinking Mountain, to the Cobalt Springs Lake, to the clearing where the Queen of the Mountains stood. Tiny specks of people spread out over the oozing mud; another line of specks followed the roads away.

"Don't fall, James," said the princess, from behind Holtzclaw.

"I don't intend to," he said.

"It's just that, you've fallen many times. Muddy cart tracks. Wet rocks. Bowled over in an explosion. You even fell into that love-apple bush. You're like a foal that has not worked out the mechanics of its feet."

Holtzclaw teetered back towards the land. Trahlyta caught his hand, and he felt a vast relief.

"Are you looking for your employer?" said the princess.

"He's somewhat less luminous and therefore more difficult to spot than yours, princess."

"Shadburn's gone back to the Raven Cliffs, to the moon maidens' old resort."

Holtzclaw sighed. "I'd thought as much. I don't know how to get there. I don't suppose you'd take me back to the lake of gold, eh?"

"If you like," said Trahlyta.

"Must I cover my head? Close my eyes? Ride in darkness to keep the secret?"

"Not at all. You can draw a map if you like, leave sign posts."

"Shadburn went through so much trouble, all to hide it away."

"He needn't have worried. It is a very different place now."

"I'll need light sources, provisions, equipment, food, water. Last time, I was caught unaware by the difficult voyage."

The princess waved her hand, dismissing his preparations. "Last time, you took the difficult way."

They walked together, slowly, over the land. She led him around a rock that resembled a long, slender animal; then they wandered over a ridge line, made of muck, that was being erased by a cheerful spring. From her footsteps sprang small, cobalt-blue flowers. Holtzclaw stepped carefully so as not to crush the fresh and fragile blooms.

Sooner than he anticipated, they were at the cliffs. The eyes of many ravens were upon him. There was a single caw, unintelligible, but the other thousands were silent. Holtzclaw and the princess slipped into darkness, a pale white light illuminating their path. They traveled through impossibly narrow cracks. Tunnels led to tunnels. Holtzclaw saw signs and symbols: a stylized lizard, hieroglyphics, a lifelike charcoal drawing of a four-fingered hand. If these were secret tunnels, they were still well-traveled.

Then they came to the great domed cavern with its pipes and cottages. A waterfall traced an arc from the high ceiling to the large stone structure that crowned the cave. Green lights gleamed from every window. And on seeing it again, Holtzclaw was astounded. The roofline of the building, the wide verandas with overhanging eaves for shade, though there was no sun underground, and even the long staircase up to the grand entrance—all were familiar. This building was the twin of the Queen of the Mountains. Shadburn had designed his hotel, consciously or unconscious, as an homage to this underground place. Holtzclaw wondered if there was an older, nobler original—a palace made of lunar marble or cast in pure silver or gold.

"Why did the moon maidens abandon this place?" said Holtzclaw.

"Taste and fashion changed," said the princess. "Rumors and memories clung to the walls. The birds, too, caused trouble. When the Raven King made his pact with the chickadees, there was a great deal of squawking before the territories were settled. But the most profound reason, I suppose, was an uncharitable spirit that arose among the holiday-goers. The moon maidens, even the sickest, didn't want to be near others who were sick. How foolish! Their condition isn't even catching—at least, not in a casual way. Those who weren't here for the cure, who were here for congresses or leisure, demanded that the sick be put out of the hotel, into these cabins. It's fortunate that your hotel never reached that point, James. It would have made you sick in your heart."

The tumbling waterfall ceased for a moment, and Holtzclaw and the princess went through an archway that was revealed behind it. They followed a spiral staircase, which descended much more directly than the wide, shallow flight that Holtzclaw and Abigail had traveled during his earlier visit. Still, he grunted and puffed from the exertion.

"You could have put in an elevator," said Holtzclaw. "If you were expecting this many visitors."

"It's only mortal legs that protest over stairs," said the princess.

Holtzclaw took a dose of Effervescent Brain Salts from the bottle in his coat pocket. The princess took it from him and poured a measure of the salts into her own mouth. Her eyes bulged in surprise, as though cold water had been splashed in her face.

Before the salts could even charge his extremities, Holtzclaw and Trahlyta reached the underground lake, though it was almost unrecognizable. All signs of gold were gone. Instead, the lake lapped quietly inside a glistening white chamber made of marble and quartz. Square columns, which had been buried in runoff before, supported vaults in the ceiling. All the rock was polished smooth, but the angles were imprecise—the polishing had been done by flowing water.

"Isn't it so much more pleasant?" said Trahlyta. "The flood carried all the waste to sea. The pressure of the lake above us broke up the jam and swirled the gold into suspension. And when the dam burst, the quick emptying cleaned this chamber to a high polish."

Holtzclaw ran his hand over one of the columns. It felt as smooth as silk.

"You aren't disappointed, are you?" said the princess.

"Disappointed? No, I don't believe that I am."

"You've saved me a millennium of work, James. That isn't much time for pharaohs and princesses—we are patient—but mortals, like our employers, are more demanding. "

"So, my dam and my lake were turned into a scouring brush?"

"Shadburn's lake and dam," she corrected. "Yes, and a very good one, too. It's cleaned not only this reservoir, but a dozen others, and every rivulet and vein in between. "

Holtzclaw walked towards the lakeshore and lifted some of the water in his cupped palms. It had no color, no smell, no taste. He turned back towards the princess, but she was gone.

In her place, gazing into darkness, was Shadburn. He was sitting on the clean marble floor, cross-legged, leaning his back against a strongbox, tossing some shimmering object up and down in one hand. A bright lantern glowed behind him, turning his bald head into a burning lightbulb. Shadburn did not stir from his thoughts until Holtzclaw put a hand on his shoulder.

"Oh, hello, hello!" said Shadburn. "Some pumpkins! What a show, eh?" He threw the shiny object that he'd been juggling out into the lake. It skipped twice, then sank.

"A spectacular success," said Holtzclaw. "Just what you wanted."

"I suppose it is, Holtzclaw. Yes, a success. Every evidence, washed away, and even more thoroughly than I'd planned. A total, permanent success. And we didn't need a hotel at all, did we? A lake and a dam were enough. How did I let you convince me that we needed a hotel?"

Holtzclaw kept a diplomatic silence.

Shadburn smiled. "There's not a crumb left in the Queen of the Mountains either. Just enough for two third-class tickets back to Milledgeville. We'll have to be more careful with money, in the future. It's simply splendid." He stood, hooked his thumbs under his suspenders, and gave them a jaunty snap. "Say, Holtzclaw, you aren't hungry, are you? I'm famished."

He opened the lid of the strongbox. Inside was a picnic of two peaches, a pint of mushrooms, and a sheep-fruit. The only cutlery was a rock hammer.

"I forgot to take it out," said Shadburn.

Of all the many loose ends he and Shadburn were leaving, the cairn troubled Holtzclaw the most. Future by-passers would take it for a meaningful monument and give it undue reverence. A wandering traveler would think something profound and wonderful had happened there. Someone might try grave-robbing, and he might be unlucky enough to find something—a cache of coins, a spool of thread, a stairwell.

Holtzclaw picked up some of the smaller stones from the cairn and tossed them out into the woods. The larger ones he carried away and dropped haphazardly. He buried some stones under handfuls of dirt, and others he wedged beneath young trees, hoping that roots would envelope them.

"They say it's bad luck to take the stones away," said Abigail. She'd followed him up the path, or perhaps she'd only been passing by chance.

"We said it was bad luck. We invented that," said Holtzclaw. He stood back from the scene and tried to judge if it looked natural enough. "Well, what do you think?"

Abigail scanned from side to side and shook her head in the negative. "It started out as a snare for the tourists, but now it might as well be a natural feature, like the Hag's Head or the Terrible Cascade. In twenty years, no one will be able to tell the difference."

"What will you do now, Ms. Thompson? There's no hotel to run anymore."

"Of course, there is. I'll put back the Old Rock Falls. The floors and daguerreotypes are salvageable. I'll build it right where it used to be."

"Back to the way it was, then? It will be like we were never here."

"Not quite. I haven't dreamed about gold since the dam break."

"And I don't suppose you will ever again."

"Whatever will we do with ourselves?" said Abigail. "Bogan and Moss and all the rest?"

"You'll be pioneers, settling a new land."

"Nothing's ever new," said Abigail. She picked up a white rock—a chipped piece of leftover marble made poignant by a fairy tale—and folded it into Holtzclaw's hand. "A souvenir."

CHAPTER XXXVI

The roads out of the valley were very bad, rutted by rain and by the hoards who had fled ahead of them. Shadburn slept. His head smacked against the wooden panels of the carriage whenever a wheel dropped into a depression, but he wasn't disturbed from his rest. Holtzclaw stayed awake. He contemplated his fingernails and his future.

In Dahlonega, Holtzclaw and Shadburn boarded a train, which they changed in Gainesville, reversing the journey they had made a year ago. As the steam locomotive came to a stop in Milledgeville, smoke brushed the window panes. Holtzclaw remembered that this was home. He had a dwelling here, filled with many things—books, ledgers, clothes, hats, gloves. He'd forgotten about his possessions; it had been so long since he possessed them.

"Shadburn, I need a holiday," he said to his employer.

"You've just spent a year at a mountain resort. Where else could you go?"

"Nowhere," said Holtzclaw. "I mean, I'll stay here. Milledgeville. I need a reacquaintance with my life."

"There's too much to do. We must research our next opportunity. And there are bound to be some consequences arising from the last one. A little paperwork. A few legal questions."

"I'll defer those matters to you," said Holtzclaw. "You seemed bored there, at the end."

"Very well. But make your time useful! I want you back, refreshed and ready to work, as soon as you are able."

Holtzclaw opened the door to his dwelling. A stale aroma reached him; it was his own scent, but he had not remembered it. All his possessions were untouched, exactly as he had abandoned them when he'd left for Auraria on short notice. Holtzclaw took beloved books from his cobwebbed shelves and ran his eyes over the pages.

The words existed in some nebulous state—not new, exactly, but not familiar, either.

Next to the books, he placed some artifacts of his travels: the small, white rock from the cairn of the Queen of the Mountains; a pouch that held the eight colors of gold he had panned out of the Amazon Branch under Ms. Rathbun's supervision; a bottle of Effervescent Brain Salts; an empty tin of Pharaoh's Flour. He consulted with a dozen apothecaries, but they could not restock his supplies. Some goods could not be bought in the old capital.

Sleep escaped him in his old, unfamiliar bed.

By day, he wandered the streets, an unending constitutional. The brown bricks were stained by too many fingerprints. The round dome of the old capitol, glided in a thin layer gold leaf, was dull. It was only mineral gold, lifted from some hard-rock vein.

Holtzclaw took his meals in a new restaurant every night. Nothing pleased his palate. One night, he ate a lobster tail that tasted as though it had very little fight in it. Another night, he ate boiled potatoes in a slop-house—the potatoes had never grinned back at anyone, and they were lifeless, too, on his tongue. Mushrooms tasted as though they had been desiccated by salt winds. Spring onions sprinkled on meats looked like blades of grass—their flavors unremarkable. Even when the clarets were excellent, the water tasted empty. Pain returned to his bowels. He asked for barbecued sea monster or squirrel's head stew—waiters sneered.

He went to the produce market and bought five large sweet potatoes, each the size of his head. The recipe promised a light and fluffy soufflé, but Holtzclaw, for his efforts, was rewarded with a charred mistake. He ate it anyway, to dispose of the failure in the most thorough way possible.

Two weeks passed, then a month. Milledgeville remained strange to him. One evening, Holtzclaw's after-supper perambulation took him along the edge of the state house square, down a flagstone path that was the treadmill for Milledgeville's fashionable set. A sudden sight made his heart leap from its low state. A woman in a glittering gold dress caught the yellow sunset. She was illuminated, flood-lit. The Queen of the Mountains had descended to the Wire-grass.

Many people saw her, but she saw Holtzclaw. She approached him, a beam of sunlight made visible by the dusty street, and as she did, Holtzclaw was disappointed that she was not the Queen of the Mountains, but only the paler pretender.

"Hello, my dear Holtzclaw," she said. "What a pleasant surprise. What are you doing in Milledgeville?"

"Hello, Lizzie," said Holtzclaw. "My employer has his offices here."

"Still under the thumb of Mr. Shadburn?"

"Presently, I'm on vacation."

"How lovely. Then you will have time to join me for coffee."

Ms. Rathbun piloted Holtzclaw to Milledgeville's most prestigious coffee house. The *maître d'* placed them in front of the window on the merits of Ms. Rathbun's glittering self. The crisp, white linens crackled as the waiter placed cups and saucers and plates of edibles on the table. He poured coffee, black and oozing, from a silver ewer.

Ms. Rathbun consumed a cucumber sandwich from between her fingers and nattered incessantly. Holtzclaw swirled his beverage but did not drink.

"So the insurance companies were reluctant, you see, because of the size of the claim," she said. "But all the paperwork was in perfect order. It was only right, given the truth of the matter: you exploded my boat, Holtzclaw, and this violent act happened before the dam break. A hundred witnesses saw it. Thus, the companies had no choice but to pay. Those were the terms of the contract, in black and white." Ms. Rathbun drew her face up in concern. "They haven't pursued you, have they, my dear Holtzclaw?" She put one hand against her chest and the other on Holtzclaw's elbow.

"I haven't heard a word," said Holtzclaw, "but I've been on leave. Perhaps they've bankrupted Shadburn. It wouldn't take much to finish him off."

"Well, I am glad that my adventure has not been ruinous to you," said Ms. Rathbun. "I would've felt, how do you say, remorseful. After all that you've done for me." Her hand remained on Holtzclaw's elbow.

"So, you've settled here? In Milledgeville?" said Holtzclaw.

"Oh yes, very nicely settled. I have a pleasant apartment, furnished with silk. There is a gala every night, with only the finest European dances. No molasses boiling reels or other rural nonsense. There is always splendid food. Creatures have been shuttled across the continent for our culinary pleasure."

"We had all that at the Queen of the Mountains, too," said Holtzclaw.

"Your kitchen staff didn't know how to prepare it. Here, all the food is generally more delicious. The coffee is divine. Clarets, too! We used to have claret in Auraria, do you remember? What swill. It's only the vinegar that they ship to the provinces. I've seen Dasha Pavlovski twice. The tickets are fabulously expensive because there is such demand. But it's a trifle. The women are all wonderfully coiffed. They are like fine-plumed birds."

"You've taken to the place well, and the place has taken you," said Holtzclaw.

"Yes, a very good match," said Ms. Rathbun. She looked from side-to-side, consulting the surrounding tables for anyone she knew, then leaned in close to Holtzclaw's ear. "But sometimes, it feels small. Unable to contain me. There are lovely people, to be sure, but provincial, still. I wonder how I would get along in New York or Paris or Venice. I suppose I would take to those just as quickly. I wonder what food they serve at their galas. How poor the clarets of Milledgeville would seem."

"What's stopping you from going?"

"The opinions of others. Some of the society women think it's inappropriate that I have no escort, no helpmeet. I tell them that I have all that I need—by that, I mean money, which can be exchanged at favorable rates for anything else that I desire. But they want that I should be billed, wooed, and cooed."

Holtzclaw shuddered.

"My society friends say they will take me to Saratoga for the season. They are un-optimistic, though. They say it is a bad time for a good match. Too many people! Some are refugees from your hotel, Holtzclaw. My society friends say that the Queen of the Mountains, in its short time, made many successful matches. A consumptive duchess met her heart's desire—a prince, no less! Ah, but it's all moot. There's no lake, so there's no hotel, so there's no matchmaking. Now, I'll have to go to Saratoga. It's all so much work! I don't fancy being dragged all the way to the northern provinces, especially when there is a suitable match right here."

The hairs on Holtzclaw's neck stood up.

"It would not be much of an effort for you, Holtzclaw. You would still be generally free. You are a codfish aristocrat, but we'd give you a plume of feathers and no one would know. Your only duty would be to make an appearance at galas and dinner parties. You enjoy those well enough, don't you? Please don't think there would be any special emotional attachments required. We'd begin here in Milledgeville at first, and then we'd go abroad, where ever we like. When we settle, I could set you up in a little business, if you like. A silkworm concern? A little guest house? You could bottle your own claret."

Holtzclaw swirled the coffee in his cup. It looked like the drying mud in the Lost Creek Valley.

Holtzclaw met with Shadburn at an eatery near the capitol. The cook was a transplanted mountain man who fled when the gold mines faltered. He served a passable version of hash browns, which Shadburn tucked into with more gusto than Holtzclaw.

"It's been a pest of a time without you," said Shadburn. "Have you cleansed yourself of what was bothering you?"

Holtzclaw demurred on the question.

"Well, I have been through some wild legal machinations," continued Shadburn. "I have been answering claims from insurance companies. They represented your boat—or rather, not your boat, but Ms. Rathbun's boat. They had already paid out an enormous sum to Ms. Rathbun and wanted compensation because an agent in my employ had caused the loss."

"I am sorry for that," said Holtzclaw. "I can offer explanations, but not excuses."

"No apologies necessary! It has all panned out well. None of the law suits could land a blow. I had no deeds! I had not filed any claims. I was no more an owner of that hotel than any other man or woman, foreign or domestic. Legal agents went looking for certain key legal documents—property deeds, warrants, and claims. And do you know who had them? Ephraim and Flossie, who traded them for other pieces of paper in their complicated game. These two had no assets other than the papers themselves. The courts seized the deeds and then liquidated them at auction. Who would want land still caked with mud, without any mineral resources, unimproved? No one, but its former owners! They bought the land back for only a fraction of what we paid them."

"How was it all so orderly?" asked Holtzclaw.

"Dr. Rathbun, while a civic authority trusted by the courts to administer the land auction, is also a kind and wise man," said Shadburn, "with goals not too distant from my own. Not every piece of property was restored identically. Some former inhabitants took land on the opposite side of the valley, where the light suited them better. Some reassembled properties that had been split in family and factional conflicts in generations long forgotten. Some former owners didn't want to come back to Auraria at all. This was their prerogative, of course. They earned their independence."

"How have they earned it? By suffering through our schemes? You should have just put gold coins into bushel baskets and left them at the doorsteps of your friends and relations. I would have hand-delivered them, if the sweat itself were somehow important."

"That would have solved nothing. Dissolved nothing."

"I cannot help but think that you are redefining your terms of success after the fact. You've shot a rifle, then drawn the bullseye around it."

"So have many other capitalists."

"It's remarkable, Shadburn," said Holtzclaw. "A savvier business-man would have failed utterly and been sued seven ways to Saratoga."

"My lack of acumen is my greatest strength," said Shadburn. "The only trouble is that Ephraim and Flossie were terribly put out by the loss of their game pieces."

"You can't please everyone," said Holtzclaw.

"Oh, but how I tried."

"Did the railroad twins, Johnson or Carter, join in the proceedings at all?"

"I told you, Holtzclaw, that they had no legal claims. No contract. And even if they thought that they could make a case, they wouldn't want to answer for the shoddy job they did on the dam. They could have opened themselves to liability from the insurance companies."

"What about the hotel? Did the plaintiffs claim that as well?"

"It will be torn down for scrap. The wood and stone and brick will be of use to anyone who wants to put up a farmhouse or dry goods store. Ms. Thompson has extracted the New Rock Falls and is putting it back on its historic foundations. The New Old Rock Falls, or just the Rock Falls, if the adjectives cancel out."

"Then it's all wrapped up in a neat little package," said Holtzclaw.

"Well, it's the best I could do, at any rate," said Shadburn. "The work there is finished, or my part is, anyway. If I kept tugging at threads, I would be apt to unravel something. I am useless if I am not being industrious. Now, on to future matters. I think we will try our hand at silkworms. There was an article recently in *Harper's*. They are a specialty of yours, if I remember. We'll make an honest try of it; we'll start with just the capital in our pockets. It'll be a piece of redemption."

Holtzclaw emitted a profound sigh. "I can't, Shadburn."

Shadburn frowned. "Well, it doesn't have to be silkworms. We could make some islands off the Gold Coast, near Savannah. We just push rocks into the ocean until—poof!—there is an island. The hydrocannon would make short work of it. Hardly any cost to it. There are many people—honest and industrious but not pedigreed, my fellow members of the codfish aristocracy—who would like a seaside house. But the authorities at Jekyll and Cumberland won't let them build next to the baronesses. Would that suit you any better?"

Holtzclaw shook his head in the negative. He felt like he should make some oration, but he couldn't find words. He relished this rare speechlessness as a sign of genuine emotion.

"Oh, I've got a present for you," said Shadburn. He pulled from his pocket a wadded piece of paper. He unfurled it and pointed to notarized signatures and a gold seal. "It's the one deed I did keep. I thought you might enjoy it, as a bonus payment for a job well done."

The deed described a parcel of land at the head of the valley, encompassing fifty acres of forest land, mineral and access rights to the tunnels of an abandoned mining operation found beneath Sinking Mountain, and, most characteristically, an artificial body of water, cobalt-blue in color.

"I've never owned a lake," said Holtzclaw.

"It's more of a pond," said Shadburn. "Not big enough for a boat. But you could build a little cabin there if you ever need another vacation."

"Let me buy it from you," said Holtzclaw.

"I don't want your gold, old friend."

CHAPTER XXXVII

Morning, always late to come to the Lost Creek Valley, was further delayed by the tailings of a rainstorm. Blue mist flowed into the hollows, forming the ghost of the lake. Breaking the fog was a dogtrot cabin, ringed by a wide porch. Holtzclaw worked on the front stoop, cleaning up from the previous evening. An automatic banjo had gone out of tune; Holtzclaw twisted the pegs until the banjo was again strumming itself in a major key. The singing tree, splayed across the cabin steps, slept off the heavy dram of sugar water it had imbibed last night. Holtzclaw nudged its trunk. The singing tree rustled its branches, which could not help but emit an amiable melody, then rose, bowed, and returned to the woods, throwing root over root. Not all nights were so rambunctious, but from time to time, Holtzclaw and his guests enjoyed great festivities.

At first, Holtzclaw had had a hard time in the valley. For months, he worked under Emmy, the mushroomer. She showed him how to hunt up ginseng, which Holtzclaw sold to itinerant medicine men. The city apothecaries wanted the invigorating herb for a new line of carbonated cures. The flood of the lake had sown new goodness into the soil; the ginseng came up strong and vigorous.

With his savings, Holtzclaw invested in a partnership with Sampson, the unseen master chef. Holtzclaw built for him a respectable establishment but did not smooth over Sampson's notable eccentricities. They became part of the legend of the place, and its fame spread beyond the valley. Turkey drovers and tourists ate at long benches with miners and farmers and shopkeepers. An article in the Milledgeville paper awakened substantial interest, and Holtzclaw had to open a second location, so that all eaters could be accommodated. He had still never met Sampson; Holtzclaw deposited his share of the revenues into a shallow hole behind the kitchen.

The springs in all their varieties—saline, sulfur, white sulfur, chalybeate, epsom, lythia, plyant, and freestone—ran clear and pure from a hundred sources. Holtzclaw's palate, trained by years of claret, found subtle distinctions among all the different waters.

Some of the more pungent may have had healing powers, but these he ignored, not wanting to compete with the patent medicines. Instead, Holtzclaw bottled the four varieties he found most delicious. Each bottle had its own full-color label, lithographed in batches by a printer in Gainesville. Specialty stores in Milledgeville took regular delivery; the water mixed well with a variety of fine spirits.

At last he had enough capital to outfit a hotel of his own. At the edge of the Cobalt Springs Lake, he built a cabin, which was his home, office, and kitchen. The front stoop hosted fiddle songs and molasses boiling dances and, four times a year, gala events under the stars, where natives and tourists dressed in their finest and danced the country quadrille. The guest quarters for the hotel were located under the mountain, in the passages of the Sinking Mountain mine. The temperature and humidity in the tunnels were ideal for those suffering from rheumatism and consumption. For other visitors, the novelty of sleeping in an old gold mine was attractive enough.

When the human guests were asleep, the moon maidens ran soundlessly through the deep tunnels, their silver hair glistening, and then, bursting to the surface, they fell like moonbeams into the cobalt-blue lake.

Holtzclaw finished the cleaning on the front-stoop and slipped back into the cabin, carefully, so as not to wake Abigail. She was just beginning to stir in their bed. He located his fishing rod in the twilight of the room and left before she awoke. He peeked in on Hulen and Hiram, their five-year-old twins, who had the same fiery curls as their mother, to make sure that they were still sleeping peacefully.

The sun hadn't yet risen over Sinking Mountain; Holtzclaw navigated the roads by familiarity. He stopped for a drink at a cold spring, which he'd named the Sweet Potato Pool. It ran for only ten feet before it joined with the more substantial Hulen Creek. From the creek bed, Holtzclaw scooped a handful of black sand. He dropped this into the crown of his hat and worked the pan. The hat showed six colors of gold, which worried him. He rinsed the colors away.

He stopped at a rocky knob, clear of trees, that afforded a view of the valley. Holtzclaw was not so limber and sure-footed that he risked dangling his feet over open space, but he went close enough to the edge to cast his line into the mist. Auraria was invisible beneath him. The sky and the lake of mist were the same smoky blue, mirrors of each other, but he could not say which was a reflection of the other.

The babbling of a spring became clear behind him.

"Hello, princess," said Holtzclaw. "It's been a long time."

"Has it?" she said. "Time is so difficult to remember. You look puckered and wrinkly, James. Like you've been bathing for too long. And what happened to your hair?"

"It has retired, but I haven't."

"Have you caught any fish?" she said.

"I've never figured out the secret," said Holtzclaw. "Perhaps all the mist-dwellers swam out to the sea."

The princess dug in the earth with her bare, four-toed foot.

"I've seen colors of gold in the rivers again," he said. "For two decades there were none."

"Someday we'll need another flood," she said.

"When?"

"Oh, not for many, many years. You'll be long dead, little mortal, unless you become great or harmless or invincible."

"That's a relief," said Holtzclaw. "I'll sit on my gravestone and let others do the work."

"No," said the princess, "you won't."

Rain fell on the bushes of purple sheep-fruit, on ginseng and mushrooms and ramps, on chestnuts and on the singing tree, going home. Water ran from a thousand springs. Creeks, rivulets, and cascades took up their voices. The valley was an instrument playing the Old Songs.

Holtzclaw cast his fishing pole. Across the lake of mist, he could see the bit of land that he had made, a piece of new earth in a very old world. He had meant to take down the rotten wooden dock, but the promontory was overgrown with love-apples. Just at the end of the dock was a green light, nearly extinguished by the morning sun rising over the mountains. Holtzclaw lifted his hand in greeting, and the will-o'-the-wisp signaled back, with promise and thrill, in its own complex pattern language.

A NOTE ON SOURCES

Several elements of Shadburn's story are based on the Lake Toxaway Hotel, an ambitious North Carolina project that required construction of what was, at the time, one of the largest dams and artificial lakes in the United States. While the hotel became popular, the industry promised by the Lake Toxaway Company to the Southern Railroad never developed. When the dam at Lake Toxaway burst in 1916, the hotel fell into ruin. The dam has since been rebuilt, and the area is now a posh mountain retreat for wealthy people retreating from Atlanta. Huge resort hotels are no longer in fashion, but the lake is ringed by fantastically expensive guest houses. (See Jan Plemmons' *Ticket to Toxaway*.)

Tallulah Gorge, in the northeastern corner of Georgia, was home to a series of waterfalls alternately called sublime and terrible. The town of Tallulah Falls was a popular resort through the 1890's. When the Tallulah River was dammed in 1913, the greatest individual beneficiary was a German immigrant named Augustus Andrae. He had attempted to raise silkworms in Georgia, but after his failure, went to work at one of the Tallulah Falls resorts. He bought properties above the flood line and made a fortune selling lots for summer homes after the dam was built and the lake reached full pool.

Georgia claims to be the site of the United States first gold rush (though an eighteenth century fever in North Carolina came first). The center of earliest mining activity in the Georgia mountains was the town of Auraria, a few miles southwest of its rival town, Dahlonega. At its peak, Auraria was home to a thousand people; it had twenty stores, fifteen law offices, a hundred homes, and confectionary shop. It published its own newspaper, *The Miner's Record and Spy in the West*. Auraria was passed up as the county seat, not for lack of vigor, but because of land ownership issues, and thus Dahlonega survives today. Auraria is now only a historical marker, a few houses, the fallen ruins of a boarding house, and the collapsing structure of a general store. Occasionally, one will see a few bored teenagers standing in the river; they're holding a beer can in one hand and a gold pan in the other. See Merton Coulter's *Auraria: The Story of a Georgia Gold-Mining Town* for more background.

Georgia's Vogel State Park is the site of Lake Trahlyta, an artificial pleasure pond that is emptied by a picturesque waterfall.

North of Dahlonega is Porter Springs, a parcel of land that is now thick forest but was once the site of a luxury hotel advertised as the Queen of the Mountains. It was known for its exceptional local cuisine and rigorous application of mineral waters, as well as the fact that the connections separating its buildings were rigged with explosives, in case of fire.

Nearby is a cairn of white stones, which was a popular destination for those taking a vacation at the Queen of the Mountains. It was just far enough from the hotel for a respectable post-luncheon constitutional. The cairn is more often seen nowadays, but less often visited. It sits on a traffic island at the intersection of US 19 and SR 60, which both bend awkwardly to avoid the stone pile. A historical marker identifies the pile as Trahlyta's Grave, though the legend recorded there conflicts with my story in several key ways. According to archaeologists and historians, it's unlikely that the cairn marks a burial site—it's only a souvenir from an earlier era of tourism.

ABOUT THE AUTHOR

Tim Westover is an award-winning writer in Esperanto. His 2009 short story collection of speculative fiction, *Marvirinstrato*, was short-listed for Esperanto Book of the Year. *Auraria* is his first English-language novel. He lives in suburban Atlanta.

Learn more about this book at:

www.QWPublishers.com

Connect with the author at:

www.TimWestover.com